MARIGOLDS IN BOXES

REBEKAH SPIVEY

LEGENDARY
Publishing

ISBN (Hardcover): 978-1-955342-97-1
ISBN (Paperback): 978-1-955342-96-4

Published by Holon Publishing
A community of Legendary Leaders, Sages, Authors, and Creators.
www.Holon.co

HOLON
PUBLISHING

For Casey the bravest person I know. Thank you for always having my back.

For Women Writing for (a) Change Bloomington and its members who have nurtured, inspired, and supported my journey to become a writer every step of the way.

BLURBS

Rebekah Spivey is a wonderful humorist. In Marigolds in Boxes, she draws her readers into a quirky, hilarious small-town world, filled with nostalgia, unique characters, and twisting plotlines. Her wry sense of humor and keen observation skills will keep you intrigued and laughing out loud the whole way through. Marigolds in Boxes is a fun ride - perfect as a summer read, or anytime you need an escape.

—*Kim Evans, author of What I Gave to the Fire*

———

I'm excited to announce my novel will be published this spring 2024.

I'd like to thank Jeremy Gotwals at Holon Publishing for his invaluable guidance and advice to help me complete this years-long project I'm here today to tell you a little about what's happening in my book.

I've created a mostly fictitious small Indiana town, Chanceville.

If you grew up in a small town, live in one now, or know someone from a small town, I think you'll recognize the characters and quirkiness that small town life can bring.

My hope is that you'll discern the underlying theme of love. That we love each other, not in spite of our flaws, but because of them.

That although we may not always agree, but we are there for each other when a need might arise.

Feud. Churches.

That's where our story begins.

There are mysteries, loves, losses, bad love advice to name just a bit of what you'll be reading about.

That's it for now. Stay tuned for more!

—*Rebekah Spivey, author of Marigolds in Boxes*

PUBLISHER'S INTRO

On a rainy spring evening in a bustling coffee bar, I had a call with a new friend that I felt I had known for a lifetime.

I was relieved.
Every bone in my body knew I had found the fit we were looking for.

We had just signed a major author.
The kind of author that popstars bring as their hot date to the Grammys.
You know who they are...

This author didn't need one of our good editors.
This author author didn't even need one of our great editors.
We had plenty of both.

This author needed an editor who was more than great.
Great editors are friends that you want to keep around for as long as you can.
At least until your book is published.

But Rebekah Spivey isn't just a great editor.
She's a friend you want to have long after your book is published.
A friend you want to keep forever.

Rebekah Spivey is Legendary.

As I finished my bourbon iced coffee, I thought about the future.
I didn't just have a good feeling about Rebekah.
I hoped from that moment that she would become a fixture of my business.

And from that moment, she became more than that.
She became an integral part of something much bigger.
And a friend for life.

When people ask me if I have business partners, Rebekah comes to mind.
She isn't my business partner in the usual way that you think of business partners.
At the time of writing this, she doesn't own shares in Holon Publishing.

She likely should, however.

Without Rebekah, our company would not be the same.
Through rain, wind, and snow. Through deserts, trials, and war.
Through a global pandemic, arduous troubles, and beyond,

Rebekah has weathered countless storms with us.
She stayed on the ship at times when others would not.
She was there for me in the hardest and bleakest of times.

You could argue that in some ways, our company not only survived, but is now thriving, because of her.

If for no other reason than this:

When times were at their hardest, and I contemplated throwing in the towel on the publishing business, Rebekah was there. With love and encouragement, she reminded me of my purpose.

She reminded me that I didn't choose this business—the business of helping legendary people share their stories with the world. She reminded me that this business, like Rebekah, had chosen me.

Rebekah has played a role in almost all of our greatest projects at Holon Publishing.
Hundreds of authors have written better books because of her.
Legendary authors, who have lead legendary lives, and have published legendary books with our company.

Now that she's helped countless authors become Legendary, we have the esteemed honor of bringing you Rebekah's debut novel, *Marigolds in Boxes*.

To say that this book, like Rebekah, is very near and dear to my heart, would be an understatement.

The book you now hold in your hands represents a new era.

A new era for the author, as well as our company.

It is my wish that this book will bring you abundant laughter, inspiration, and perhaps even a few tears.

May your life become more Legendary and meaningful as a result of having read this book.

And please,

PUBLISHER'S INTRO

Share this book with at least ten of your friends.

You can thank me later.

Jeremy Gotwals
Founder & Publisher
Holon Publishing

ACKNOWLEDGMENTS

I have so many people to thank, and I'll do my best not to leave anyone out. I grew up in Connersville, Indiana which inspired me to write about Small Town, U.S.A. I created Chanceville, Indiana as way to write about that experience with much gratitude for the material during the first 19 years of my life it provided. When I think of material I have to thank my family for the endless supply of stories to write about with love, laughter, and understanding.

I have so much gratitude for Beth Lodge-Rigal who founded our chapter of Women Writing for (a) Change Bloomington and its members who have nurtured, inspired, and supported my journey to become a writer every step of the way.

I love to write in coffee shops. There have been many over the many years I have spent writing *Marigolds in Boxes*. I started at the long gone Bakehouse East. I moved on to Katie Mysliwiec Slavin and the crew at Needmore Coffee and Farm Stop of Bloomington. Thanks to those establishments for offering their spaces that nurtured my creativity.

I want to give a heartfelt thank you to my dear friend, Rachael Norton who came up with the idea to give me a cash donation to help support getting *Marigolds in Boxes* published. Rachael told another dear friend, Susan Failey, who heard some of the very first drafts of the book. Susan immediately jumped on board and they both gave me a more than generous donation that paid for David Orr's design of the book cover.

Special thanks to my talented cousin, Diana Fricke for the professional quality and quite flattering photos she took of me for my book cover and website. I couldn't have been more pleased with the results.

I hesitate to name individuals because I would never want to leave out someone. I will do my best to acknowledge my gratitude for the support I have been given for all of my writing. My writing sisters who I count as my valued friends and kindred spirits. I'm especially grateful for my son, Casey Snedegar.

Rebekah Spivey
April 2024

Visit the Author Website

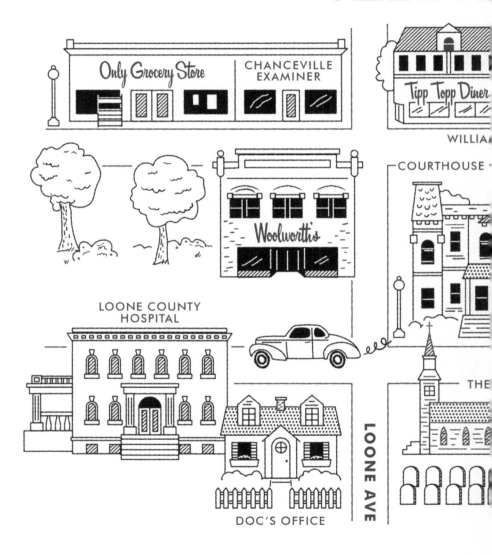

Only Grocery Store

CHANCEVILLE
EXAMINER

Tipp Topp Diner

WILLIA

COURTHOUSE

Woolworth's

LOONE COUNTY
HOSPITAL

THE

LOONE AVE

DOC'S OFFICE

NT LOCATIONS IN

LLE, IN

LOONE COUNTY LIBRARY

SHERIFF

LOVELY LOCKS

MARIGOLD ST

HEM & HAUL

STEELE'S

THE BLIND POODLE SISTERS

MAIN AVE

HIGH HORSE HARRY

HES

MAIN ST

CHANCE ST

HENDRIX FUNERAL PARLOR AND WAX MUSEUM

INTRODUCTION

The founder of Chanceville, Indiana, Arnold Chance, had planted only marigolds in his window boxes since the town was incorporated in 1845. Legend has it he liked the no-nonsense colors of those flowers. The tradition continued long after Arnold died in 1908. His flower boxes got a fresh coat of plain tan paint on every year's last day of March. The citizens of Chanceville, Indiana, could set their calendars by this. So many people admired the cheeriness of the gold petals with their russet tips that they began planting marigolds in their flower boxes. And that's how Chanceville became known as the "Home of Marigolds in Boxes." Once in a while, a few people would get a wild hair and decide to branch out and plant begonias or petunias. Then they would tire of the stubborn marigold planters driving by and shouting, "What's the matter, marigolds not good enough for ya?" That harassment would drive them right back to planting marigolds the following year.

For the most part, the citizens of Chanceville lived in peace until 1950 five years after World War II had ended in 1945. That is where our story begins. This does not mean all was as sunny as the brightly colored marigolds in boxes dotted all over town. As you will discover, even the smallest towns can have their dark underbellies. There are silly feuds, secret agendas, and even murders that may come to light as our story unfolds.

1

FEUD

Ned Cochran and Tarsal Henley had known each other for years. They sat on the church board together until the feud started over who qualifies to be buried in the church graveyard. They stayed on good terms because Ned mostly ignored Tarsal's prickliness. Most days, he could handle it.

It all started when they began building the church that would sit in the center of the block on the south side of the town square. World War II had ended five years prior, in April of 1945, and Ned was discharged from the U.S. Navy at the war's end. The church where Tarsal and Scapula Henley had been married was burned down four years after their 1946 wedding when a candle caught the dry Christmas tree in the church hall on fire.

The congregation had long been contributing to a building fund. With the insurance payout, they had more than enough money to build a fine new church. Ned and Tarsal had the skills to head up the building committee, so once the board voted to release the funds for the new building, the two men headed to Woodington's Lumber store with their blueprints to set up the order for the materials that would become their new place of worship.

On the way to get supplies, they stopped at the Tipp Topp Diner for a hearty breakfast of scrambled eggs and Sid Topp's famous venison sausage, washed down with strong black coffee. They were excited about the project and couldn't wait to get started. Tarsal made his living as a builder, and Ned, who still lived on his family farm, made his living as an electrician. Ned's cousin Ted Henley, a church elder, was a plumber, so they covered the big three expenses. With the free labor of other church members, they could afford to buy high-quality materials and build a beautiful church.

Tarsal and Ned were sitting at the crowded counter at the Tipp Topp when Reverend Trout Finn came in. Ned and Tarsal flanked Hubert Patterson, who was finishing his coffee, and gave up his seat to the reverend as he shuffled out the door, forgetting, as usual, to pay his check. The minister squeezed in between Ned and Tarsal as the red vinyl-topped counter stool groaned in protest under the weight of him.

"Did you hear about the Widow Collins?" asked Reverend Finn as he eyed the cake display.

"Nope," said Tarsal through a mouth full of eggs.

"What about her?" asked Ned.

"Well, she went over to... yeah, the number one, three eggs over easy, coffee and orange juice, a short stack of pancakes, two venison sausage patties, toast, and a side order of bacon, Sid," said the reverend. "Anyway, she went over to Summerville to care for her sister, who'd been feeling poorly. She stepped on the cat's tail, causing the poor creature to screech so loud it scared the living daylights out of the Widow Collins. Literally. Her bad ticker just stopped."

"Say, Sid, I'll have a slab of that chocolate cake to hold me over until my breakfast is ready," said the reverend. Tarsal and Ned slid looks at each other behind the reverend's back, taking in the expanse of his substantial backside.

"They read her will yesterday," he said as he dug his fork into the huge slice of cake. "It's the darnedest thing. She wants her poodle Foo Foo's ashes buried with her in the family plot in the church graveyard."

Tarsal was taking a big gulp of coffee and sputtered it all over himself and the countertop. "Why would she want to do a dang fool thing like that?" he said as he dabbed the countertop with this napkin.

"Foo Foo was her companion for twelve years, and she always said he gave her more attention than that husband of hers, Joe Collins, ever did. She was looking forward to spending eternity in heaven with Foo Foo," said the reverend. Ned tried not to look his way when the reverend talked because his tiny corn peg teeth were smeared with chocolate cake and icing.

"I think that's nice," said Ned. "I wonder how she feels about spending eternity with her late husband, Joe."

"That's nice? That dog's not going to heaven. It's a dog, D.O.G. It doesn't have a soul. It's an animal." Tarsal tried to keep his voice down, but he was getting worked up. He lived in a black-and-white world. Keep things simple was his motto. In his mind, there were no gray areas. Ned was the opposite; he loved the idea that he would be reunited with the collies that his family had raised since he was a boy, especially Bess, who was eleven years old and had failing kidneys. To Ned, being surrounded by God's creatures was one of the rewards of heaven.

"You're not going to let this sacrilege happen, are you, Reverend Finn?" Tarsal eyed the reverend suspiciously.

"Sacrilege?" asked the reverend through the last mouthful of cake. He scraped the plate with his fork, not wanting to miss one crumb. One lonely piece of cake was left in the display case, and he was seriously considering asking Sid to wrap it up to take with him. It would hit the spot later when he was writing the Sunday sermon in his office.

"Reverend Trout Finn! Don't you think it's a sacrilege?" Tarsal wasn't going to let it go. After all, he had his reputation as the town know it all to maintain.

"I guess I never really thought about it. I'm not sure it really matters all that much. The Widow Collins was a faithful member of our church her whole life and contributed quite handsomely to the building fund. I think it's a matter of respect to honor her last wishes," said the reverend as Sid refilled their coffee cups.

"I think it's horse hockey. And I don't want some unholy ashes in our graveyard," said Tarsal through his clenched jaw.

"I don't think it's your decision alone. The church board will have to make that decision if you're going to protest it," Ned said, thinking someone had better be the voice of reason.

He could see Tarsal was building up a head of steam about this, and he didn't want him to blow up here in Gossip Central. Reverend Finn groaned when Tarsal mentioned bringing the board into it.

Tarsal and Ned had to move their plates and cups over to make room as Sid served up the reverend's order. All the reverend wanted to do was eat his breakfast in peace. He wished he had never mentioned it and put the ashes in the coffin with the Widow Collins. Only problem with that plan was Hal Hendrix, owner of Hendrix Funeral Parlor and Wax Museum, would be handling the arrangements, so you couldn't get anything past him. And he wasn't sure how Hal felt about animals and heaven.

And that's how The Feud began. That following Monday night at the temporary church board meeting place in the back room of Mother Mary's Pool Hall, the first item on the agenda was the Widow Collins' request. The ten members were evenly divided, and no one would budge. Tarsal led the crusade to keep Foo Foo's ashes out of the church graveyard.

"It's against all I believe in. That graveyard is hallowed ground. Why, we have soldiers in there who lost their lives for us. I don't think they'd be honored to lie next to some soulless mutt."

Ned shook his head, "Now you're just jumping to conclusions, Tarsal Henley. You don't know what those soldiers believed. Some of them might have had K-9 dogs in the service. Dogs who saved their lives, they might have wanted the same thing as Widow Collins."

"And you're making up stories to prove your ridiculous point, Ned. Just because you were in the navy doesn't make you an expert," said Tarsal, pointing his finger at Ned.

"Well, Tarsal, you saw exactly zero action from your dad's farm when you got a deferment to stay home to run it and take care of your mother and sister after your dad passed away, which I understand. I really do. Just don't make assumptions," Ned shot back.

Reverend Finn and the other board members shifted uncomfortably in their chairs; this was getting too personal. They'd better do something fast before these two called each other unpatriotic sons-a-guns and came to blows.

Their pastor suggested, not too optimistically, that they take another vote. Of course, the results were the same: five for and five against. The reverend was the eleventh member on the board and only voted in case of a tie. They all looked at him, waiting for him to clear this up once and for all.

"I'm going to abstain. Either way, my vote will split the church in two. I can't risk that. You need to work this out amongst yourselves," he popped two antacids in his mouth, trying to calm the fire of the ever-present and totally puzzling heartburn that had plagued him lately. Upon hearing this, every member leaned back in their chairs, crossed their arms in unison, and sat in silence.

"You don't have the luxury of waiting each other out. The Widow Collins' funeral is the day after tomorrow," said Reverend Finn.

"The bottom line is, I'm not changing my mind, and I'm not building a church with the likes of you, Ned Cochran."

"What's that supposed to mean?" Ned asked.

"You'll find out. And that's all I've got to say on the matter for now," said Tarsal as he stormed out the door. Later that night, he called Ned and told him to meet him at the church lot in the morning at 8:00 sharp.

The next morning, Ned arrived right on time at the empty church lot where Tarsal was talking to Frank Stenner, the county engineer. Frank was setting up the transit.

"What's going on, Tarsal?"

"Stand back, Ned. We're dividing up this lot," shouted Tarsal, waving his arms about.

For a few heartbeats, Ned stood there with his mouth wide open, unable to process what he had just heard. As Tarsal's words sunk in, Ned could feel his blood pressure rise. "You can't do that. What authority do you have?"

Tarsal had turned his back on Ned, who grabbed him by the shoulder and spun him around.

"Tarsal, have you lost your mind?"

Whether or not Tarsal had lost his mind was irrelevant. Ned thought he was just plain nuts, and ignorant, and selfish, and judgmental. It was a never-ending list that would grow as the years passed. Ned Cochran was tired of the battle and simply wanted a church again.

Tarsal had summoned the rest of the church board and the Reverend Finn. When they were all assembled, with no hope of settling the graveyard with animals argument in their lifetimes, they took a vote. They unanimously agreed to build two churches on the same lot.

That's how there came to be two churches built back to back on the same lot south of the town square of Chanceville. The lot was split down the middle, with the old graveyard staying on Tarsal's side. The new graveyard would be on Ned's side and allow pet burials. The first person to be buried on Ned's side was the Widow Collins, along with Foo Foo's ashes. The second person who needed burying was the Reverend Finn, who choked on a Vienna sausage while sitting on a park bench watching the new constructions. God works in mysterious ways. Many of the residents of Chanceville believed He turned that sausage sideways in the reverend's throat to save him the painful task of deciding which church to pastor, or his greatest fear might come to pass that neither new church would want him.

The reverend's death did not signal the end of painful decisions. He had to be buried, but where? Which graveyard? The church board had split the vote evenly when Tarsal coerced the board to build two new churches on the lot. They held an emergency special session at Mother Mary's Pool Hall. Ned said he was sure Reverend Finn would want to be buried in the new graveyard because he didn't have a problem with the Widow Collins being buried with Foo Foo's ashes. She would be buried in the already established graveyard that was on the site of Ned's church as it was known for the time being. And Tarsal said it was only fitting that the reverend be buried in the old graveyard because Tarsal's search committee had brought him here five years ago.

"So what, Tarsal? Everyone here knows he thought animals could be buried with their humans," said Ned, trying to stay calm without much luck.

"Prove it, Ned," said Tarsal as he sat back with a smug look on his pug-nosed face. He was prepared to stay there all night if it took that long to settle this. He never cared much for the reverend after they brought him here, and it didn't matter much to him where he was buried. But he was not about to let Ned Cochran win any argument if he could help it.

"I can't prove it. But I know who can settle this. I just got word before I came over here that the reverend's sister, Alpaca Finn, is on her way here from Minnesota. She'll arrive tomorrow on the noon train. As next of kin, she can make the decision. I think it's time to call this meeting adjourned," said Ned over his shoulder as he walked out the door.

2

THE ARRIVAL OF ALPACA FINN

Alpaca had several hours to think about her brother's life and what had led him to the ministry. She wasn't ready to think about her own reasons for being eager to relocate to a tiny Indiana town.

Her brother, Trout Finn, left Saints of the Lakes, Minnesota, as soon as he graduated from high school in 1928. Although their parents had not been particularly religious and only attended church sporadically, Trout told her he decided to attend seminary training and hoped he would be protected by God against bullies. "Maybe God would protect me. Everyone else I know has let me down, might as well give the Lord a try," he said.

He was a fat baby and would continue to be fat until the day he died. Alpaca was older by a year and was as lean as Trout was fat, a fact that their parents managed to mention every single day, stopping short of accusing him of stealing food out of her mouth. She was never interested in food, too busy reading every book she could get her hands on. Her idea of heaven was to work in the town library. He told her once that his idea of heaven was calorie-free food and lots of it.

She and her brother were never close, mostly due to the wedge their parents had driven between them. Trout always came out on the losing end of their comparisons of the siblings, whether it be weight, academic achievement, or popularity. She found a diary that he left behind when he went to seminary. In it, he wrote about school being a nightmare. How he was teased mercilessly about his weight, his clumsiness, and his poor eyesight, which resulted in the wearing of thick-lensed glasses. She remembered he was mostly called Whale Finn and Four-Eyes, with cartoons of glasses-wearing whales showing up on school bulletin boards. No wonder he couldn't get out of town fast enough. Alpaca felt sorry enough for her brother that she tore those cruel drawings down as soon as she saw them, mainly because she didn't like how they reflected on her, having a ridiculous brother like Trout.

Alpaca sensed she was admired, if not exactly popular. She was purposely aloof and cultivated a classy look. She graduated at the top of her class. With her dark beauty, she stood out like a fish on a tractor in the Norwegian agrarian/fishing settlement of Saints of the prettily situated on Lake Honkatutu. She enjoyed her status in the community and had no desires beyond finding a handyman who would build a pedestal and set her right on top of it and working in the county library, breathing the rarified air of knowledge, romance, and adventure.

When Finn left home for seminary school, it was almost as if he had never existed. No one seemed to miss him or even ask her or her parents how he was doing. About a year after Trout left, he had to return home for the double funeral of his parents, who had died when their car slid off the road one icy night and went through the ice on Lake Honkatutu. Trout had been so thoroughly forgotten that Alpaca overheard some town folk at the service ask him how he knew Mr. and Mrs. Finn.

She realized his humiliation was complete when, at the reading of the will, the attorney announced that Alpaca would inherit the house and what little savings their parents had. Their reasoning was that as a pastor, he would always have a home and a living provided. Their daughter's future was not quite so certain as she had not managed to acquire a husband. Their Grandmother Chagrin, Mrs. Finn's mother, was the one with the fortune in the family. Alpaca was named her executor, but her brother had not been told of the particulars of the contents of her will. Grandmother Chagrin had serious heart problems. Who knew how long she would last?

It appeared to Alpaca that Trout tried his best to stay on her good side. She was never mean to him, merely indifferent, which probably hurt almost as much. After he returned to seminary school, he began his letter-writing campaign to his sister. She guessed that he hoped if he stayed in touch with newsy letters about the people and places he was familiar with and how hard it was to make ends meet on a pastor's meager salary, she would look on him favorably when the time came to divide up Grandmother Chagrin's money pot. Neither knew that their grandmother had changed her will the year before she died and was leaving all of her money to the local animal shelter.

Alpaca was mostly uninterested and slightly puzzled by these missives. She couldn't imagine why her brother thought she was interested in him or people she would never meet or places she would never go. All of her travel was accomplished through books. She did not keep the letters, but she had a mind like a steel trap. When Trout's untimely demise sent her to Chanceville, Indiana, she was able to mine the details he had written about that small town and its denizens to her advantage and the astonishment of said denizens.

She packed those old memories away as the train approached the Chanceville depot while she checked her makeup in her compact mirror.

3
ALPACA MAKES AN ENTRANCE
AND THEN SOME

Ned and Tarsal were at the station the next day, waiting for the noon train to pull in. They weren't putting their differences aside. Neither one trusted the other to be alone with Miss Finn and not attempt to sway her decision of where to bury her brother. They didn't know what the reverend's sister looked like, but she wouldn't be hard to spot if she resembled her rotund brother. The train steamed into the station right on time. There weren't a lot of passengers getting off the train that came down from Chicago, but Ned and Tarsal didn't see anyone who looked much like Reverend Finn.

Someone tapped Ned on the shoulder, and when he turned around and saw who it was, he let out a little "oh" before he could stop himself. There stood a tall woman who was as thin as the reverend was corpulent.

She began pumping his hand with a death grip, saying, "Ned Cochran, I presume," before they could even offer their condolences.

"I'd recognize that sickly, pale, freckled face anywhere. My dearly departed brother mentioned you so often." Turning to Tarsal, she began pumping his hand.

"And you must be Tarsal with that black oily hair and pug nose."

Tarsal and Ned looked at each other, flabbergasted.

"Well, come along now. Don't dawdle; we've got things to do. There are my trunks over there," Alpaca said as she pointed to four large steamer trunks suitable in size for an ocean crossing and summer in Europe.

The two men looked at each other, and Tarsal muttered, "Good Lord, it looks like she's settling in 'til the end of time." Ned coughed, trying not to laugh.

They could tell by looking there was no way they could lift those trunks, but they gave it a valiant try. Ned felt something start to pop in his back and let go right quickly. He went into the depot and asked Charlie Towne, the station master if they could borrow his four-wheel flat cart. Charlie said sure and came out to help them load the trunks.

"Now be careful how you set them down, gentlemen," Alpaca instructed them. "I've got my good china in there."

By this time, all three men were huffing and puffing.

"Why on earth did you bring your own china?" Tarsal wheezed.

"I know the ladies of the church will expect me to hold formal teas, and Dear Brother mentioned quite frequently how, um, frugal you parishioners are. I wasn't sure if you would have a proper tea service suitable for my needs."

Neither Ned nor Tarsal could think of a civil reply, so they removed their hats, wiped their foreheads with their handkerchiefs, put them back on, and thanked Charlie for his help. Then they started pushing that cart up the slight grade to the parsonage, with Alpaca fussing at them the whole way.

When they finally arrived at the parsonage, Nate and Tarsal were dismayed as they surveyed the steep front steps until they remembered that the reverend always entered from the back porch that had a ramp to make it easier for him to get his portly self into the house. They went around to the alley and the back of the house. After much grunting, groaning, and backsliding, they got the trunks into the kitchen.

They reminded Miss Finn of the church board meeting that evening in Mother Mary's Pool Hall at 7:00.

"Very well, gentlemen. I'll take it from here. I'll put everything away. You can come by to fetch me for the meeting and store the trunks in the garage," Alpaca told them.

They agreed to call for her at 6:30 to put the trunks away and that Ned should return the cart to Charlie since it was on his way home. And that was the last time Tarsal and Ned agreed on anything.

Alpaca spent the afternoon cleaning, putting her things away, and tisk-tisking at the slovenliness of her late brother. Everything was covered with a not-so-thin layer of greasy dust from the fuel oil furnace in the basement. On the bathroom sink sat a dish with a bar of soupy soap floating in it. The sink was coated with hair, and she had to hold her breath when she scrubbed the toilet. The bathtub wasn't too dirty; she suspected that was due to the fact that her brother's large frame wouldn't easily fit into the deep, quite narrow tub.

She pulled off her bright yellow rubber gloves when she finished that nasty cleaning job. She took off her smock, items she had rightly surmised she would need, washed up in the now sparkling bathroom, and went into the kitchen to see if the food situation was as hopeless as the rest of the house. Luckily, some caring person (Gardenia Cochran) had left a roasted chicken, a plate of sliced tomatoes, a carton of small curd cottage cheese, and a dish of fresh strawberries in the reasonably clean icebox. The good Samaritan must have given the icebox a quick clean also. It was good enough for today.

The food suited Alpaca just fine. Light and healthy, that's how she liked to eat. She made herself a cup of tea using a fine Darjeeling loose tea and a favorite porcelain cup and saucer she had brought. Alpaca always used two saucers, a smaller one on top of a slightly larger one. She believed in neatness and not taking a chance of dribbling tea on clean tablecloths. She had quickly disposed of the red and white checkered oilcloth tablecloth on her brother's kitchen table. And spread one of her everyday linen tablecloths to cover the scratched table top that belonged to the parsonage.

After she had finished her meal, she cleaned the Formica surfaces in the kitchen, washed up the dishes, and went upstairs to change the bed and put on clean sheets that she brought with her, quickly disposing of her brother's sheets in the burn barrel. After she got settled, she would dispose of all of her brother's clothes in the same manner. Then Alpaca took the broom outside to make the front porch habitable. She also brought a bucket of hot, soapy water and her yellow rubber gloves to clean the old wicker porch furniture. Once that task was complete and the furniture had dried, she sat down on the wicker chair that looked the sturdiest, one her brother probably never sat in, with its narrow seat. She started thinking about the timing of her brother's death and how that got her out of Saints of the Lakes just before things got ugly. There were few eligible bachelors in her hometown, and the ones who were single were substandard, in her opinion. Alpaca was forty-one and tired of supporting herself and being the village's old maid or, to some minds, a fallen woman.

Chanceville was slightly larger than Saints of the Lake, and she hoped there was more marriage material here. She would have to be clever with how she went about getting a man this time. She knew from experience it's not a good idea to get the women of your hometown all riled up against you. They tend to get a little territorial when it comes to their menfolk. Alpaca also knew from experience that she had a certain allure to men.

As she had that thought, a man came strolling down the sidewalk. He saw Alpaca sitting on the porch, stopped, took off his straw fedora, and bowed low at the waist.

"Hello, dear lady. You must be the late reverend's handsome sister. I'm Johnny Perkins," he said in a soft Irish brogue.

"Good day to you, Mr. Perkins," she said.

"I'm so very sorry for your recent loss. A lovely lady such as you should never, ever have a hint of sorrow to trouble her fine brow," said Mr. Perkins as he arranged his face into its most sincere visage.

Despite herself, Alpaca blushed, thinking Johnny Perkins must have kissed the Blarney Stone before he left Ireland.

Alpaca thanked him just as sincerely as he returned his hat to his head and told her he hoped to see her very soon under happier circumstances. Interesting man, she thought to herself and, if she remembered correctly from her brother's letters, Mr. Perkins was a widower. Yes, very interesting.

About the time Johnny Perkins was disappearing down the street, along came Harold Freeman whistling songbird calls. He stopped mid-warble when he looked up and saw Miss Finn framed by the white high back wicker chair on the reverend's porch.

"And who might you be?" Harold asked in his usual blunt manner.

"I might be Alpaca Finn. And who might you be?" she asked in her likewise blunt manner.

"I might be Harold Freeman. Oh, you're the late reverend's sister. I heard you were coming into town, didn't know it was today. But I guess you didn't have the luxury of time. Reverend Finn isn't getting any fresher."

She blinked and tried to be upset with his crudeness. Still, Alpaca, being her ever-practical self, couldn't argue with Harold's logic.

"I'm so sorry. That was rude," he told her.

"No apology necessary. You are quite right, and when I have an unpleasant task to take care of, I like to get it done as quickly as possible. I have some difficult decisions to make in the days ahead," Alpaca said.

"Well, ma'am, if I can be of service at all, please don't hesitate to ask. I live on the next block in the yellow house with the big front porch. You'll see my tabby, Kissy, lounging on the front porch railing most afternoons," he told her.

"That's kind of you, Mr. Freeman. Everyone is being so thoughtful. It makes my burden lighter," Alpaca responded.

Harold bid her good day and made his way down the sidewalk toward his house, whistling all the way.

Alpaca leaned back in her chair and thought about the two gentlemen whose acquaintance she had just made. She was trying to remember if Brother, as she called him, had mentioned Harold

Freeman in his missives, but nothing came to mind. He certainly seemed like a lovely man and, hopefully, single. He didn't mention a wife. Yes, this could all work out just fine. There are two possible candidates on her first day here. Maybe, for once in his life, Brother had done something useful.

Of course, she would miss him. Well, probably not if she were to be totally honest, but these new circumstances following his death might be the ticket to her future. Some might consider her an old maid, but she had desires and needs like every other sentient being on this good earth. After this ridiculous business of her brother's burial site was settled, she would see about a job at the local library. Yes, she was ready for a fresh start, and this could be it.

She had asked Ned and Tarsal to point out Hendrix Funeral Home and Wax Museum on their way to the parsonage. It was nearby, so she walked over there after resting on the porch a bit to make the unusual arrangements for her brother's burial.

4
ALPACA MAKES A DECISION

All heads turned as Alpaca entered the back room of Mother Mary's with Ned and Tarsal trailing behind. Like those two gentlemen, everyone else on the board expected a female version of Reverend Finn, short and quite round. However, Alpaca was the exact opposite of her blond, blue-eyed brother. She was almost six feet tall, with her dark hair pulled back in a severe bun at the nape of her neck; her full lips served to soften the harshness of her hairstyle and the penetrating stare of her black eyes. She was quite a striking figure.

Everyone to a man automatically stood up and nervously smoothed his hair, if he had any. All appeared to stand at attention. That was the kind of respect Alpaca demanded without ever uttering a word. Of course, every board member was a man because, after all, it was 1950, and women had their place, which was not on a church board overtly making essential decisions and running things.

Alpaca knew her place, and that place was wherever she decided would be most advantageous to her needs.

With a slight nod to Tarsal, Alpaca indicated she was ready to be seated. He pulled out her chair for her. Ned loved that Alpaca could command bossy Tarsal with a slight nod of her head. After she was seated, Ned and Tarsal took their places at the table as everyone sat on the edges of their seats, avidly awaiting the words Alpaca would speak to settle, at least part, their current situation.

"Gentlemen, thank you for promptly convening after my arrival today. I don't believe in wasting time. And I am confident that Dear Brother would not want his untimely demise to add further conflict to your dilemma. I was afforded ample time to think while on my train journey from Minnesota to your lovely state, and I have made a decision that I believe will be satisfactory to both factions.

I know from personal conversations with my late brother that he wished to be buried here and not back in our hometown, Saints of the Lakes, of which he had no particularly fond memories. (That was putting it mildly.) "I paid a call on Mr. Hendrix at the funeral parlor this afternoon, where he allowed me to spend a little time alone with my brother's body, which was good because I hadn't seen him in years. Although he did send pictures of himself occasionally. Mr. Hendrix. advised me that due to Dear Brother's rather large, um, girth, a suitable casket might come at an extra expense even with the discount that Hal, er, Mr. Hendrix, would apply in light of his fondness for the reverend. I am a woman of limited means but do not want to accept charity. The reverend's funeral is not the church's expense, and he could only afford an extremely modest burial policy," she said as she watched each board member squirm in his seat. Alpaca attempted to be as diplomatic as possible, but tactfulness was not where she comfortably lived.

"I've come to the practical conclusion that he should be cremated, an affordable expense covered by his policy, the ashes divided evenly and given to each faction to bury in your respective graveyards."

"But—"

"Keep quiet, Tarsal," said Ned.

Alpaca cleared her throat and continued, "Hal, Mr. Hendrix, tells me he can complete the preparations in time for a small reception here at Mother Mary's on Saturday morning if that's agreeable with everyone. Mr. Cochran and Mr. Henley will each be given a container with half the remains of my brother, and each group can conduct their own graveside rite."

Ned saw that Tarsal was about to object, so he quickly said, "It's a sensible solution. There's been enough squabbling, which is this good lady's decision to make. With that settled, let's address the matter of Miss Finn's accommodations. She has mentioned to Tarsal and me that she would like to make Chanceville her home. I make a motion to allow her to remain in the parsonage until the board can dispose of it and divide the proceeds. There is no mortgage, and Miss Finn has agreed to pay the light and water bills."

"Maybe you'd just like to buy it yourself, Miss Finn, at a reasonable price, of course," said Tarsal. All heads turned toward Alpaca.

"Thank you so much for your kind offer. But the house is in a rather sad state, and I cannot afford the cost of repairs and a mortgage. I'm still trying to sell my home in Saints of the Lakes. This will give me time to find an inexpensive apartment or a room in a boarding house. My needs are specific but quite simple."

Nine hands shot straight toward heaven to approve the motion to allow Miss Finn to stay in the parsonage until it sold. Ned looked at Tarsal, who was examining his cuticles.

"We have a majority, so we don't need Tarsal Henley's vote. Motion approved. Let's go home," said Ned.

Ned and Tarsal bumped into each other, trying to approach Alpaca. "I guess we'll both walk you home," said Tarsal as they escorted her out the door.

The rest of the board members shuffled out, wishing this hadn't been a church board meeting because a cold beer at Mother Mary's bar sounded real good about now.

The following Saturday morning dawned clear on the town of Chanceville. By 10:00, it was bright, white-hot. Alpaca was hoping the services would be short and sweet. Oh, of course, her late brother, the basically unlamented Reverend Trout Finn, deserved a decent burial, well, burials, actually, but one also had to be practical. Simple graveside rites, then on to Mother Mary's for cool lemonade and finger sandwiches made by the ladies of the church would do just fine. This would also give her the opportunity to invite the ladies to tea next week.

She hoped the church women would think that fighting over dogs going to heaven was too ridiculous to acknowledge so she wouldn't have to hold two separate teas, doubling the work and expense. She wanted to get established in Chanceville society, such as it may be, and then acquire a husband if all went according to the plan.

Each half of Reverend Trout Finn was laid to rest in the already established graveyard and the ground that would become the new graveyard with what could be diplomatically termed quiet respect. An outside observer might have interpreted it as a "let's get it over with" attitude. Nevertheless, the duty was completed. The hot, sweaty, and about-to-turn cranky bifurcated congregation trooped into the back room of Mother Mary's Pool Hall for some of Oblivia Young's watered-down version of lemonade. At least the drink was cold. The ladies of the church had spared quite a bit of expense. They made finger sandwiches with cucumbers and tomatoes from their very own gardens. After all, it wasn't Godly to be ostentatious. If the Reverend Finn had been watching from his perch in heaven, he would have thought it was slim pickings, indeed.

Now that everyone was cooled down and their appetites were somewhat sated, Alpaca decided it was time to put her plan into action. She couldn't just move into town and go after the men folk. No. She had to sidle up to it, make it look like it was one of the church ladies' ideas. Alpaca went into the Ladies' powder room. Then made sure her face was adjusted into proper Grieving Sister demeanor before approaching Oblivia, whom she had heard from her brother was the self-appointed leader of polite society in Chanceville.

Oblivia did her best to keep a pleasant aura about herself, but she was losing that battle with her long face and pinched nose. She always looked like she had detected a foul odor in the air.

"Hello, my dear," she said to Alpaca as she pressed her thin lips into a smile. Sadly, it always came out as a grimace. "I'm Oblivia Young. Despite the unfortunate circumstances, I'd like to officially welcome you to our town. Were you close to your brother?"

Alpaca's first thought was it would be hard to get close to someone with such a large circumference as her brother had. But from what Alpaca had briefly observed of Oblivia, she detected not one ounce of humor in her matronly body, so she decided to go for a diplomatically balanced answer.

"We were very close as children (bald-faced lie), but when Dear Brother received the call to the ministry and went off to seminary school, we naturally drifted apart (bald-faced truth). Don't misunderstand; his death was a horrible shock (mostly to himself, she thought), but one must go on, mustn't one?" said Alpaca.

"Oh, my goodness, yes. The Good Lord knows I've had my trials and tribulations with my husband, Henry and my son, Chester. But one does learn to cope," said Oblivia, as she fanned herself with a fan on a stick that looked like it had been rescued from the church long before the fire, keeping with the divided congregation's frugal reputation.

Alpaca put on what she hoped would be her sincere face, touched Oblivia's arm lightly, and said, "Since I'm going to be a member of this community, I would like to hold the occasional afternoon tea. Do you think you could help me with the guest list? I'd like to be able to invite both congregations and have just one tea. Do you think that would be possible?"

"What a marvelous idea," said Oblivia, nearly chirping. "Yes, I think it would be quite possible for both groups to meet peaceably." Oblivia leaned closer to Alpaca, her heavily applied Avon perfume, To a Wild Rose, causing Alpaca's eyes to burn and tear up.

"Confidentially, it's mostly that loud-mouthed Tarsal Henley who created this kerfuffle. We women don't really care about that silly feud all that much. I would certainly be more than happy to help you. I'll get to work on a guest list this afternoon. You just let me know the date, and we'll send out the handwritten invitations together. Now, don't you cry, my dear. Your brother is in a better place," she whispered, totally missing the cause of Alpaca's tears.

Alpaca smiled her Mona Lisa smile as she had chosen the perfect pawn in Oblivia Young.

5
THE GREAT TEA PARTY SCHEME

True to her word, Oblivia met with Alpaca the next day, and they worked out a guest list for an afternoon tea to be held at 3:30 a week from Thursday. The ladies who received their invitations were nearly hysterical with anticipation. On the invitation list, in addition to Oblivia Young, were Trachea Carmichael, Old Doc Trueblood's nurse; Sara "Sugar Pants" Peterson, disgruntled housewife; Miss Mayrose Mayhern, retired schoolteacher (who would never attend); Sadie Stenner, piano teacher and wife of county engineer Frank Stenner, whose late sister, Doris, had been married to Johnny Perkins; Fern Oldhat, owner of the Lovely Locks Beauty Salon and cousin to Harold Freeman, whom Alpaca had already met and quite liked the looks of; Geraldine Nurse, head librarian at the Loone County Public Library; Celia Matthews, married to James Matthews, the brother of bachelor Milton Matthews.

Alpaca had met Milton when she was in Steele's Hardware to buy bug spray to get rid of the spiders that had made themselves at home on the front porch of the parsonage. With this guest list, Alpaca was optimistic that this tea would mark an auspicious beginning for her grand scheme.

None of these ladies had any notion of what society life was like in Saints of the Lakes , Minnesota. But they all wanted to impress Miss Alpaca Finn, and if there were strings attached to this invitation, the ladies were prepared to be yanked. After what seemed like an interminable amount of time, the much-anticipated day was upon them.

The ladies arrived promptly at 3:30, perfumed, powdered, and dressed in their Sunday finery. Those who could afford it bought new frocks. Those who could not tried to breathe new life into their old dresses with new matching sets of costume jewelry purchased at the Woolworths.

Most of these ladies had been to the parsonage while Reverend Finn lived there. They had seen first-hand that housekeeping was not a priority of his. They were curious to see what Alpaca had done to make the place habitable. If she had not done anything (which they doubted), they would be drinking tea from greasy chipped cups and sitting on dusty chairs, but as they entered, they saw all was sparkling. Alpaca had worked miracles with the place. The ladies could even see out of the windows that had been so dirty they kept prying eyes from seeing inside as they casually strolled past the parsonage when the late reverend was the occupant.

Alpaca ushered them into the dining room, where the table was laid with candelabra and fresh flowers, all on a starched and ironed ecru linen cutwork tablecloth. Alpaca was more of a nibbler than an eater but tried to be mindful that her guests probably had heartier appetites, so the table was beautifully laid with see-through thin slices of shaved roast beef made into sandwiches, the requisite watercress and cucumber sandwiches, all cut into geometrically perfect triangles, celery sticks stuffed with creamy peanut butter, various and sundry pickles and olives, and radish rosettes.

For dessert, there was a homemade white-layer cake. The silver cake stand she inherited from Grandmother Finn sat in its rightful place at the head of the table, reflecting the snapping candle flames. Her china was pure bone-white porcelain with no frivolous flowers cluttering up the swirled pattern at the base of the delicate cups and the edges of the sandwich plates; those were inherited from Grandmother Chagrin on her mother's side.

She was glad she had refused Brother's request when he asked to take those things to the parsonage when he moved to Chanceville. She knew he would never entertain and would be so lazy that when his everyday dishes were dirty, he would use the good china for his meals. She shuddered to think what state they would have ended up in. Broken mostly, she guessed.

When the women were ushered into the dining room, they oohed and aahed out loud, ostensibly at the fine table but also at Alpaca, who was dressed in a champagne-colored linen dress that provided a pale palette for her obsidian eyes and shining black hair. She wore a matching set of jet earrings and necklace, which caught the candlelight and sparked off her eyes. Her makeup was so expertly applied that the ladies weren't sure she was wearing any; there was just a hint of color on her cheeks and lips. Every lady in that room silently decided they were long overdue for a makeover; maybe they could get Alpaca to advise them.

Alpaca asked Oblivia if she would help with the tea service, and each guest secretly despised her for receiving that glorious honor. Oh yes, this tea party would be an excellent topic for gossip at the Lovely Locks. The ladies retired to the front parlor, where they balanced plates precariously on their knees and nervously made small talk while trying not to slurp their tea.

Alpaca was the epitome of discretion, asking only the right questions to bring them out of their shyness without seeming to pry. She found out many of the things she was interested in knowing, mainly the status of several men she thought The Tea Ladies (that's how she thought of them now) might have connections to. She did her best to show equal interest in the female relatives of The Tea Ladies so as not to raise suspicion or jealousy among them at this stage of the game. She already knew what her next step would be.

Before they knew what hit them, Frank and Sadie Stenner had

arranged for their brother-in-law, Johnny Perkins, and Alpaca Finn to have dinner at their house. Johnny had gallantly offered to pick Alpaca up and drive her to the Stenners. When they arrived, Frank and Sadie had the impression that things weren't getting off to a good start. Alpaca was tight-lipped throughout the meal, starting with the wedge salad, moving on to the Salisbury steak, mashed potatoes, and green beans, and finishing with a fruit cocktail and angel food cake. Johnny was a different story. He chatted all the way through the meal. Unfortunately, every sentence started with "Doris always said, or Doris liked." This happened in spite of the dagger looks that Frank and Sadie were shooting his way. Finally, after what seemed like an excruciatingly long two hours, Alpaca thanked the Stenners and said that after that lovely meal, it was such a nice night. She felt like walking home.

On her walk home, she decided she might as well scratch Johnny Perkins off her list.

Alpaca was at the Lovely Locks Beauty Salon for her bi-weekly shampoo/set a few days later. The shop was abuzz shortly after Alpaca had arrived; Fern Oldhat popped in with the exciting news that her cousin, Harold Freeman, whom everyone thought was a confirmed bachelor, had just become engaged to a lady he had met over in Liberty at his square-dancing class. Harold became the second man to be scratched off Alpaca's list. Oh, well. He was shorter than she was, anyway. Maybe she'd stop by Steele's Hardware and see if Milton Matthews was still qualified for her list. Better yet, he was definitely taller than she was.

6

MILTON DISCOVERS MAYROSE

After she retired from thirty-eight years of teaching first grade, Miss Mayrose Mayhern went to tea every Thursday morning at ten o'clock at the White Jasmine Tearoom. In the months leading up to her retirement, Mayrose had thought more and more about the quiet congeniality of the tearoom. She loved teaching first grade, but the children seemed to take more energy from her these last few years than she could renew overnight.

Mrs. Little, who owned the tearoom, soon realized that Mayrose ran her life with military-like precision. Every Thursday morning, Mayrose arrived promptly at ten, not a minute before or after, always dressed quite tastefully. Her attire consisted of a two-piece wool or linen suit, depending on the season. Her jewelry consisted of a single strand of pearls with matching earrings, stockings with arrow straight seams to compliment her two-inch pumps, a tasteful hat, and, of course, because it is 1950, matching gloves.

Mayrose did not bring a book or a newspaper to read to the tearoom as many of the male customers did. Nor did she like sitting by the big bay window where she could observe passersby. She so enjoyed the ritual of the tea service that she did not want any distractions. And besides, Mayrose believed it was rude to read in restaurants. Reading was for libraries.

When the weather allowed, she walked the six blocks from her home to the tearoom downtown on the square. If the weather was inclement or the forecast changed, she drove her 1945 five-year-old mint-condition Chevrolet sedan to the tearoom. She was proud she could drive.

Mayrose's mother, Margaret, had never learned to drive, so Mayrose drove her wherever she needed to go after her father, Michael, died. He had never encouraged that activity for women. His public opinion was that he enjoyed taking his wife and daughter places. Still, his private opinion was that particular skill would give women a little too much power and freedom. Mayrose wanted to be independent, and on this specific point, she insisted that her father teach her to drive. He reluctantly agreed, finding it hard to deny his beloved daughter and only child of anything she felt strongly about. She was a good daughter and student. He had no actual argument that would stand up against the logic of the ever-practical Mayrose.

It was a freshly washed April morning when Mr. Milton Matthews first laid eyes on Mayrose. He looked up from his paper when he heard the bell tinkle over the tearoom door. She wore an oat-colored linen suit with a powder blue blouse and matching powder blue hat with two ivory silk rosebuds wrapped in a small amount of netting on the brim. Her low-heeled pumps were the same oat color as her suit. She carried a handbag that matched her pumps. Her hat was perched firmly atop her carefully coiffed silver-blond hair. Now, Mr. Matthews, being a man, did not notice these exact details, but he certainly appreciated the overall picture. He stared unabashedly as Miss Mayhern said good morning to Mrs. Little and nodded at several other customers on her way to a table in an alcove near the back.

Mr. Matthews, a retired high school history teacher, was new to Chanceville. His brother and sister-in-law had retired there from Richmond, Indiana because of the excellent golf course, and they persuaded Milton to retire there, also. He liked Chanceville, the golf course, and the company of James and Celia. Still, he soon discovered that he was not totally ready for retirement. He took a part-time job at Steele's Hardware just to be able to interact with people a few days a week.

He had never married and was used to living alone, but he didn't want to spend all his time alone. He loved talking to people and had a knack for teasing their stories out of them. Milton had the habit of jotting down notes and stuffing them in his pockets. Someday, he would organize his jumble of notes and write a book filled with the rich stories people had shared with him. He had shoebox after shoebox stuffed with notes. The boxes were stacked to the ceiling in the closet of his den. He planned to stop by Williams Brothers Stationery Store and Haberdashery soon and take a look at their typewriters.

On his days off, he enjoyed the hominess of the tearoom and the cheery clink of porcelain cups and saucers coming together. Some days, he liked to sit in the back and read his daily paper or work on the crossword puzzle. Other days, he sat by the window and watched people as they walked by and went about their daily lives.

Milton could make up stories about people without ever talking to them. He believed that what people let you see on the surface most often had little to do with who they really were. That's why the lady he later found out from Mrs. Little was Miss Mayhern so intrigued him. She was quite particular about how she presented herself to the world. He could see that at first glance. Milton would pop into the tearoom whenever it struck his fancy. So, it took him a while to realize she was always there on Thursdays at ten o'clock. As he began observing Mayrose regularly, he would sometimes jot down notes on the backs of old receipts or slightly used napkins; other times, Milton would wait until he got home to write down his observations. He noted that Mayrose always took a seat at the same table in the back.

Good to know he thought.

7
MILTON MAKES NOTES

The following Thursday, when Milton saw Miss Mayhern at the Jasmine Tearoom, he noted how she always managed to pull her chair out without making that scraping sound against the big black and white tiles of the tearoom floor. She then set her handbag directly in front of her on the far side of the little round table, always with the muted gold clasp facing her. As soon as Mayrose sat down, she removed her gloves. She started by pulling up on the left-hand pinkie finger and progressing along that hand until finishing with the thumb and pulling the glove entirely off. She then held that glove in her left hand and proceeded in the exact same manner to remove her right glove. Mayrose then fit both gloves together, finger matching finger, thumb matching thumb, laid them in her lap, smoothed them out the bottom to top precisely three times, and then carefully draped them across the top of her handbag, with the cuffs facing her. She wore a dainty garnet ring set in rose gold on the ring finger of her right hand. It had been her Grandmother Mayhern's, and she treasured it. As soon as her gloves were removed, she adjusted this ring so the garnet was set squarely in the center of her finger.

By this time, Mrs. Little was coming over to take her order, even though Mayrose always ordered the same thing. Mrs. Little took her order with the doomed hope that someday, some bright and shining day, Miss Mayrose Mayhern would order Something Different, something other than a pot of Earl Grey tea, no lemon, milk, no sugar, and a bran muffin, no raisins.

After the tea service was brought to the table, Mayrose would always rearrange things to her liking. The teapot was on her upper right, with the handle and the spout on a parallel line with her handbag, teacup, and saucer on her left, and a dessert plate with muffin to the right of the teacup. Once everything was squared away to her liking (sometimes these things were only moved a quarter of an inch), she would place the tea strainer on her teacup and pour her tea. She added a small amount of milk, stirred the tea carefully, and took a tiny sip. Then she alternated sips of tea with delicate bites of muffin, wiping her mouth at the corners after each bite of muffin with the pale pink linen napkin. This routine never varied. No matter how many times Milton observed this ritual, he never once saw any variation. He even started counting the bites she took to finish the muffin. It was always twenty, and for the life of him, he could not figure out how she managed that.

One Thursday morning in May, just as the tulips were fading and the peonies were opening up to their full beauty, Milton arrived at the tearoom a little before ten and greeted Mrs. Little.

"Good morning, dear lady."

"Good morning, Milton. Isn't it a lovely day?"

"Not as lovely as you, Sweet Pea."

"Oh, go on with you, you big old teddy bear."

"Fine, how about a bear hug then?"

"Just go to your table and drink your tea."

She smiled and shook her head as she watched him take a seat at a table in the back next to the table where Mayrose always sat. Just as soon as he sat down, Mayrose came in the door. As she neared her table, Milton stood, bowed, and said, "Good morning."

Mayrose stopped in her tracks, looked at Milton, nodded primly, and sat down with her back to him. He picked up his paper and rather noisily folded it so he could work on the crossword puzzle. He noticed that if he rattled the paper quite loudly, Miss Mayhern's shoulders scrunched slightly, which made him chuckle softly to himself, resulting in more shoulder hunching. Milton finished his tea and decided to sit on a park bench and finish his crossword puzzle. He might make a few more notes of his observations of Miss Mayhern's tea ritual. It was too lovely a day to sit inside and breathe walled-in air. He passed Mayrose without acknowledging her, deciding he'd pestered her enough for one day.

Mayrose watched as that annoying man, whoever he was, left the tearoom. Good riddance to him and his rattling paper, she thought to herself. Still, there was something familiar about him, something solid and comforting from a long-ago memory. When he first started coming into the tearoom, she had noticed his interactions with Mrs. Little and the patrons of the White Jasmine. People seemed to be drawn to the warmth of his company, like the comfort of a soft old sweater.

She learned from his sister-in-law, Celia Matthews that Mr. Matthews wasn't born in Chanceville like Mayrose was and probably was just here for that massive waste of time, golf. She couldn't imagine why anyone would want to drag a heavy bag of clubs around all afternoon, hitting and following a tiny white ball. Maybe it was for the reward of a drink in the clubhouse at the end of the round, but she didn't believe in drinking either, so her disapproval was complete. That Annoying Man was probably a drinker, which could explain why he was so everlastingly cheerful.

Mayrose mentally washed her hands of Milton Matthews for now.

8

MILTON MATTHEWS LAYS AN EGG, AND ALPACA FINN GOES FISHING

Miss Mayhern hadn't given another thought to that man until she entered the tearoom the following Thursday and saw him sitting at "her" table. Her already straight backbone stiffened even straighter. What was Mrs. Little thinking, giving this stranger her table? Mayrose decided she wouldn't give him the satisfaction of reacting as Mrs. Little escorted her to a table to the right of the alcove.

She took a chair that allowed her to turn her back to Milton, which annoyed her because now she was looking at the kitchen passthrough where the food orders were served instead of the soothing décor of the tearoom. As she gave her order to Mrs. Little through clenched teeth, she thought about not ordering the bran muffin, shortening her time in the tearoom. Still, she would not play his ridiculous game. She would not change her routine, not one iota.

As Mrs. Little passed by Milton on her way back to the front counter, she shot him a look. He raised his eyebrows and hunched his shoulders as if to say, what did I do? She had warned him not to take that table, but he insisted, saying it would be a funny little joke and he would give it up when she came in. Mrs. Little tried to tell Milton that, as far as she could determine, Mayrose Mayhern had no noticeable sense of humor. And if he thought he could trick Mayrose into paying attention to him, he was about three bricks shy of a chimney.

Milton realized Mrs. Little was right. He went over to where Mayrose was seated with the intent of apologizing to her and assuring her he would never play that trick on her again. But she was mid-ritual and would not be interrupted. Mayrose soon discovered that Milton could be just as determined as she was. He stood there, motionless, patient, while she drank her tea and finished her muffin in exactly twenty bites. She wiped each corner of her mouth, folded her napkin in a perfect triangle, laid it beside her teacup, and looked up at him, her eyes bright blue flint, challenging his ability to say something sincere that would make his breach of etiquette all right with her. If Miss Mayhern were prone to the vernacular, she would think, "fat chance." Milton walked away, realizing this was a battle he would not be winning, not today, at any rate. He said good day to her and left.

When Milton left the tearoom, he did not notice the smartly dressed figure of Alpaca Finn following him around the corner. He was on his way to Williams Brothers Stationery Store and Haberdashery to look at their latest selection of typewriters.

He was also searching for a new pen, always in search of the perfect pen. A few weeks ago, he bought the new Eversharp Skyline and found it less than ideal. It wrote in fits and starts and could have been more dependable. Milton was lost in a pen display when he heard someone clear their throat several times. He finally looked up, and there stood Alpaca on the other side of the display counter. He nodded and went back to looking at all of the lovely pens.

Alpaca was never one who could suffer being ignored. She came around to Milton's side of the display and lightly touched his arm. Milton took a step back.

Alpaca quickly removed her gloved hand from his arm. "I'm Miss Alpaca Finn, sister of the late Reverend Trout Finn. Your sister-in-law, Celia, pointed you out to me one day when we were in Steele's Hardware. You were busy, so I told Celia I could meet you another time.

It's good to meet someone else new to Chanceville," said Alpaca. She was 5' 11 ½" and enjoyed being able to actually look up into someone's eyes. Milton's were a warm brown. She imagined that the corners of his eyes crinkled when he smiled.

"Um, nice to meet you, too," Milton finally managed to mumble as he returned to looking at pens. He wasn't seeing anything new that caught his fancy (in more ways than one) and was ready to move on to the typewriter displays.

"Excuse me," he said as he tried to move past Alpaca, but she was playing defense and blocked the aisle.

Seventy-five-year-old Mr. Williams the Younger came over and asked Alpaca if he could help her with something. He knew Milton could find his way around the store.

"No, thank you," said Alpaca. "I was looking for a specific brand of notecards that I don't believe you carry," Alpaca sniffed.

"If you just tell me the company's name, I'm sure we could order them for you," said Mr. Williams.

"Is that the time?" Alpaca said, looking at her watch. "I need to talk to Mr. Matthews for just a minute and then be on my way to an appointment. Could you please excuse us?"

Mr. Williams the Younger stroked his pencil-thin mustache, nodded, and walked away. He hadn't worked with the public since he was a boy without learning to read people. He knew when he was being dismissed. Even at his advanced age, it stung a little to be rejected by such an attractive lady.

Alpaca, resisting a sigh, looked up at Milton and tried gazing deeply into his eyes. Still, he was looking at something over her shoulder. She started to lay her hand on his arm again and thought better of it.

"Excuse me, Miss Trout, it was nice meeting you, but I would really like to go over and look at the typewriters."

"It's Miss Finn," she said, trying to keep the annoyance out of her voice. "Are you a writer? That's very exciting," she said before he could answer.

At this point, Milton only saw her as an obstacle and wanted her to move. As he had demonstrated earlier in the tearoom, he was usually a man of great patience. Still, her presence was starting to wear thin. He bobbed to his left, and she shifted to her right. He bobbed to his right, and she shifted to her left. He was thinking of picking her up and moving her when she finally came to the point.

"I was wondering if you would like to come to my house for dinner one evening soon," she asked.

"I'm afraid I'm busy that night," said Milton, thinking of pivoting like a quarterback and doing an end around the pen display.

"I didn't say WHICH night."

"Oh," Milton said softly. "It's just that I'm working on a big project and won't be available for quite some time. I do appreciate the invite, though."

The bell over the door tinkled, and Alpaca was distracted just long enough for Milton to make a beeline for the typewriters. Alpaca followed him, told him she wished him luck with his project, and left it at that.

"Uh, huh," Milton said, clearly distracted by the beautiful new Underwoods and Remingtons.

Alpaca exited the store, but she was not close to exiting Mr. Milton Matthews's life. Oh, no, not by a long shot.

9
MILTON GETS A NEW BABY

Milton liked the Underwood Noiseless model's looks. Still, he also liked the friendly clacking of the typewriter keys when he got on a roll with his story writing. It sounded like progress to him. The Remington Deluxe was more his style, sleek and low to the ground. Mr. Williams quickly produced a sheet of paper for practice when Milton asked if he could take her for a spin. Milton only had to type one sentence to know the Remington Deluxe was his new baby. He left the shop whistling, excited to get home with his brand-new typewriter and a ream of off-white bond paper to hold his words.

When Milton turned the corner and passed the White Jasmine Tearoom, he couldn't help but look in the window to see if Mayrose Mayhern was still there. Instead, he saw Llama Trout, or whatever her name was. Strange lady, he thought. And that was Milton's last thought about Alpaca Finn for quite some time.

Alpaca saw Milton walk by and thought she perceived his step quicken a bit when he saw her sitting in the tearoom. Her list of eligible bachelors was quickly dwindling. Several candidates whom she thought had potential turned out to be real duds, but Milton, to her mind, still had great potential.

She had to figure out the key to getting his attention. She would start by making his sister-in-law Celia her new best friend, but first, she had more urgent business to take care of. She needed to find a job. The money Darrell Davis had given her before she left Saints of the Woods would soon run out. She probably shouldn't have taken the money, but Darrell felt guilty about her reputation being ruined when his wife and then the other ladies in town found out he had been sneaking around with her.

10

ALPACA LANDS A JOB

Geraldine Nurse loved her job at the Loone County Library, but she had worked there for twenty-five years, and every day was starting to feel the same as the next. The only new thing in her life was Alpaca Finn's tea parties. Geraldine enjoyed a good mystery, and her innate curiosity told her that the late Reverend Finn's sister was up to something. It kept her coming back. She'd known the other ladies most of her life, and none of them ever had anything new to say at Alpaca's little soirees. It was always the same old gossip, but the tea and pastries were excellent, and she enjoyed staying quiet and watching Alpaca work the room.

At last week's tea party, Trachea Carmichael, Old Doc Trueblood's nurse, had to help Doc with an emergency, so she didn't make it to the tea party, which made her fair game. Everyone hoped she didn't bring her usual dried-out baked beans to next week's annual town picnic on the 4th of July. They knew it couldn't be washed down with the oh-so-sour, watery lemonade made by Oblivia Young. It tasted like she used one shriveled old lemon for the whole pitcher and salt instead of sugar, which nobody had mentioned since Oblivia never missed Alpaca's teas.

Geraldine also never missed a tea party because she didn't want to be the target of their barbs. She believed people who held public or community jobs would be unwise to gossip about the town folk, so she never joined in. It was entertaining enough to watch Alpaca do her thing.

"Celia, what is Milton's favorite pie?" asked Alpaca.

Celia looked puzzled but answered, "I believe it's gooseberry. Why do you ask?"

"I heard that Sunday is his birthday, and I thought I would bring his favorite pie to the picnic."

"Sounds good," mumbled Celia. She wanted to get back to the gossip.

Alpaca then turned her attention to Geraldine Nurse. Here it comes, thought Geraldine.

Alpaca had been buttering her up ever since the first tea party. As time passed, Geraldine could see that nearly all of Alpaca's line of questioning had something to do with the menfolk of Chanceville. Geraldine couldn't figure out why Alpaca was so nice to her. She had no brother, dad, or uncle. Her son, Nathan Nurse, who would join Doc Trueblood's practice when he finished his residency, was way too young for Alpaca. At least she only seems to be interested in gentlemen her age.

"Geraldine, what a lovely dress you're wearing today. Is that new?" asked Alpaca as she topped off Geraldine's tea and offered a delicate porcelain saucer filled with tiny lemon wedges.

"Thanks, Alpaca. It's not new. I wear it quite frequently," said Geraldine as she took a lemon wedge, thinking, "Get to the point, Alpaca." She knew Alpaca never missed a detail and that her frequent wearing of that dress would be discussed if she ever missed a tea party.

"Well, it always looks fresh and pretty on you, dear," said Alpaca as she set the saucer back on the tea cart. "Not like that threadbare cotton print, Annie Pat wears to every function she attends. You'd think her wages at the Shop-A-Lot would allow her to afford a new dress once in a while."

Geraldine wasn't going to bite on that one. She knew that Annie Pat had a brother who couldn't keep a job, and helping to feed his children was where most of Annie Pat's money went. She certainly wasn't one to talk behind people's backs, even if it was to defend someone. Geraldine wanted to avoid getting caught in Alpaca's gossip snare. Annie Pat was a good friend of Geraldine's, and what she did with her money was no one else's business. Geraldine sat back, folded her arms, and waited for Alpaca's next move. She didn't have to wait long.

Alpaca looked around the room, and it seemed everyone was happily engaged in conversation and enjoying their tea and ladyfingers. She delicately cleared her throat, "How are things at the library, my dear?"

On the surface, this seemed like a casual question. Still, there was nothing casual about Alpaca, and Geraldine immediately felt its weight.

"Quiet as ever," said Geraldine.

"I certainly hope you're not working too hard, my dear," said Alpaca, clearly missing the tiny joke.

Geraldine's patience was starting to wear thin. She had just about had all of the "my dears" she could stand for one day, and besides, there was no way she was this woman's dear.

"No, but I will be getting ready for the annual book fair soon. It's a lot of work." And as soon as she said it, she knew that she had just given Alpaca her in. It was all she could do to keep from wincing.

"As you know, I plan on making my home in Chanceville and will only be able to remain in the church parsonage until they sell it. I need to find a job as soon as possible to afford to move because my house in Saints of the Lakes still hasn't sold. I began working in our library in Saints of the Lakes straight out of high school, working my way up as assistant to the head librarian, who would prefer to die on the job rather than retire. I have quite a bit of experience. I would love to come to work for you if you think I could be of service," she added, looking demurely down at her well-manicured nails.

Geraldine took a few minutes to mull this over. Her most recent assistant, MerryLynn Tarmack, had recently decided that the library was way too quiet for her and had gotten a job as a waitress at Tony's 24-Hour Mechanic and Roadhouse. Geraldine needed help. She needed someone organized, which seemed to be one of Alpaca's strong suits. Once, when Geraldine had taken some of the tea things into the kitchen, she noticed that Alpaca's spices were in alphabetical order in their rack. Little white labels were taped to all the cupboards' doors as if hordes of people were coming through the parsonage who didn't have time to hunt for what they needed. Still, it was a form of cataloging, a good skill for a library worker. But what cinched the deal was her distrust of Alpaca's motive. She offered her a part-time job on the spot. And because each lady had one ear tuned to all peripheral conversations, all heads turned when they heard that. Alpaca looked triumphant.

Geraldine thought it would be a smart idea to keep an eye on Alpaca on behalf of the good people of Chanceville.

11

THE BLIND POODLE SISTERS

Everyone in Chanceville knew The Blind Poodle Sisters, Annette and Babbette. They didn't pay much attention to their eccentricities. Still, Alpaca Finn was fascinated with them when they came into the Lovely Locks Beauty Salon when she was there for her biweekly shampoo/set. They came in all cheery and laughing, honking the bicycle horns attached to their white canes and announcing loudly that the Blind Poodle Sisters had arrived as if people didn't recognize them.

Annette's dress was made of a print of giant sunflowers, and Babbette's was of gigantic roses. They wore multiple strands of bright plastic beads and oversized hoop earrings. The twin's legs were bare and quite hairy.

Their big brown eyes, longish noses, and curly blond hair made them look quite similar to the canine whose name they bore. Alpaca, who never missed a detail, noticed a little blond fuzz above each of their upper lips. Lindy put Alpaca under the dryer. She and Misty Mae quickly went to work on Annette and Babbette, respectively. The sisters simultaneously crooked their index fingers, beckoning Misty Mae and Lindy to bend down as they whispered in their hairdressers' ears. Alpaca was sure she was missing out on some juicy gossip, which her own canine-like hearing would undoubtedly have been able to pick up if not for the noisy hair dryer she was sitting under.

The sisters' hair just needed a quick trim. They had gone on their merry way, arm-in-arm, by the time Alpaca got out from under the dryer.

It was an absolute scorcher that day. The twins were wearing, to Alpaca's mind, extremely skimpy sundresses. Much too risqué for ladies who appeared to be in their mid-forties.

"Um, Lindy, who were those two women, and who on earth dresses them?" asked Alpaca.

"That's the Blind Poodle Sisters," said Lindy. "They've been blind since they were ten and can still remember how they loved bright colors. They have their maid, Poppy Smith, buy the loudest, most garish clothes and accessories she can find. They like to make a statement."

"They certainly do that," said Alpaca. "They actually have a maid?"

"Oh, yes. Their daddy, Muddy Poodle, actually named Melvin, was the richest man in Chanceville. He owned Poodle's Pie Factory and Poodle's Five and Dime. Their mama believed twins were unlucky. She ran away with a handsome traveling preacher right after the twins were born. Muddy never remarried, so Annette and Babbette were his only children. Daddy left them a bundle. I guess he's been gone 'bout six years now. They live in that big brick mansion on the corner of Main Avenue and Main Street, across the street from where they're building the new churches," said Lindy. "You know, the house with the twin poodle statues on the front porch."

"I could hardly miss it. Those statues are pink!" said Alpaca, shaking her head.

Lindy poked Alpaca in the back of the head with her rattail comb and told her to hold still.

"Every time I walk by there, it looks like there's a party going on," Alpaca added.

"Muddy Poodle wasn't in the family mausoleum a day before the twins made Poppy paint those statues," Lindy explained. "He would have had a fit. He sent all the way to Paris, France, for those statues. He kept a tight rein on his daughters, what with them being blind and all, always worrying hisself silly over those girls. They didn't waste any time kickin' up their heels after Muddy passed."

"I noticed they were bare-legged and, um, not exactly well groomed in the leg and underarm department," said Alpaca.

"Oh, they like to be au natural, if you know what I mean," said Lindy, winking.

"You mean, they don't wear undergar—?"

"According to Poppy, not a stitch!" said Lindy.

The Blind Poodle Sisters walked arm in arm down the street talking about how bored they were and hoping something exciting would come into their lives soon.

12

ALPACA HEARS IT THROUGH THE GRAPEVINE

Alpaca Finn heard through the Chanceville Grapevine, which had been alive and well as long as Chanceville has been Chanceville, that Milton Matthews was in the Loone County Hospital. The only thing she could find out was he had had minor surgery. The hospital was near the parsonage, so Alpaca decided to walk over there and pay him a visit. She could not pass up a chance to insert herself into eligible bachelors' lives. This would be her opportunity to show him she was a caring person. It had not escaped her that he would be a captive audience.

She took exceptional care with her appearance that day; she chose a dark purple suit and a creamy white blouse to accentuate her dark eyes and hair. After observing Miss Mayrose Mayhern always wearing gloves, she had taken to wearing gloves, and Milton seemed intrigued by the plain (to her mind) spinster. Fortunately, she had been to the Lovely Locks the day before and had those pesky gray hairs touched up. Her only jewelry was a modest gold watch given to her by an admirer before she left Saints of the Lakes.

It was a lovely autumn day, just right for a short walk. She wouldn't have succumbed to sweating even if it had been a scorcher.

Alpaca never let anyone see her sweat. She stopped at the hospital's information desk and found out that Milton was in room 211. She made a quick stop in the ladies' room to check her makeup and hair, which was pulled back into such a tight French twist that there was no way it could have moved. When she was satisfied with what she saw in the mirror, Alpaca made her way to Milton's room, reminding herself she should quit thinking of him as Milton, lest that slip out. For now, it was Mr. Matthews.

She tapped lightly on his door and walked on in. He was asleep. She sat down quietly and waited, taking this opportunity to give him a thorough look over, liking what she saw. His white hair glowed in the sun that was shining through the window. She remembered his warm brown eyes from their encounter in the stationery store. His hands looked soft and uncalloused. Alpaca was still sitting there when Nurse Jackson came in to check his vitals. They were both surprised to see each other.

"Oh, I didn't know Mr. Matthews had company," said the nurse. At the Tipp Topp the other day, she had heard that Miss Finn was on a mission to find a husband and was immediately suspicious of the visitor's motives.

"Mr. Matthews is a dear friend. I felt it my duty to call on him to find out how he is faring," replied Alpaca.

"Of course," said Nurse Jackson, not believing a word of it.

Milton woke up when Nurse Jackson put the blood pressure cuff on him. He smiled at her and closed his eyes again. He'd had an emergency appendectomy in the early hours of that morning and was still pretty groggy.

"You have a visitor, Mr. Matthews," said the nurse.

"Must be my brother or sister-in-law," said Milton before he looked over and saw Alpaca sitting there dressed to kill, so to speak.

"Why are you here, Miss Trout?" asked Milton, trying to make sense of this through the fog of pain medication.

"It's Miss Finn, Mr. Matthews. Of course, it's not unexpected for you to be a little fuzzy after what you've been through," said Alpaca, going on a fishing expedition.

"What have I been through?" asked Milton, not taking the bait.

Nurse Jackson smiled, thinking Miss Finn had met her match.

"Well, you know, your illness," said Alpaca, casting out once again.

"Oh, that," said Milton as he closed his eyes.

Alpaca thought she detected a sly smile. This wasn't going to be easy. That's okay, she thought; I like a challenge.

Nurse Jackson finished recording Milton's vitals and told him everything looked good.

"I'll be back later to check on you," she told Milton. "Please don't stay too long. Mr. Matthews needs his rest with what he's been through." She couldn't resist adding. "Just press your call button if the pain gets too bad."

"Make it soon," he mumbled and gave her a wink before closing his eyes again.

Alpaca cleared her throat and stood up. Milton opened his eyes in anticipation that this woman might be leaving. Instead, she laid a book on his hospital tray table.

"I brought you this book, The Fascinating History of Chanceville, Indiana. I have one myself, and I did find it fascinating," she told Milton.

"That's very kind of you, but there's no need to bring me a gift," said Milton.

"It's my pleasure. I'm sure, after what you've been through, you'll need something to distract you until you're able to return home," Alpaca said, continuing to cast. She had plans to nurse him back to health once he was released from the hospital.

Somehow, through the haze (probably self-preservation kicking in), Milton managed to beat her to the punch.

"I'll be going to James and Celia's once I'm released. I'll enjoy sharing this book with them," he said.

This statement had the effect of simultaneously bursting her bubble of caring for him and making her gift totally impersonal. Despite that, she sat back down.

He was about to tell her he was tired and wanted to sleep when Maxine Crabtree, notorious hospital volunteer, came in with her cart of magazines and candy supplied by the Hospital Volunteer Fund. Milton let out an inadvertent groan. Hadn't he been tortured enough today? He had heard all about Mrs. Crabtree at the Tipp Top Diner.

"GOOD AFTERNOON, Mr. Matthews," said Mrs. Crabtree, who was quite deaf and apparently thought everyone else was too.

Milton merely nodded, futilely trying not to engage her.

"Is there something on the cart you'd like?" she asked.

To get rid of her quickly, Milton pointed to a golf magazine.

"Of course," she said. "As soon as we pray for your speedy recovery."

"That won't be necessary," he said.

"Of course, it is. Only the Lord can heal. Only He can give me permission to give you this magazine," she said.

"Then I guess the Lord doesn't want me to have this magazine because I don't want to be prayed over or preyed upon," he said, looking at Alpaca, who shifted uncomfortably in her chair.

At that, Mrs. Crabtree whirled her cart around, running over Alpaca's highly polished black leather pump, mumbling something about heathens and their concubines.

"I'm very tired and in some pain," said Milton as he rang for the nurse. "I think it's time for you to go."

"Of course," she said. "I'll be back tomorrow to check on you."

"That's not necessary at all. My brother and sister-in-law are keeping a close eye on me. Thank you.

Even though she knew she was being dismissed, Alpaca walked over to Milton's bed and tried to pat his hand, which he immediately withdrew. She left without a word.

"Take a look at this inscription, Nurse Jackson," said Milton as he handed her the book Alpaca had brought him.

"To Dear Mr. Matthews, I look forward to discussing this

fascinating book with you for many happy hours. All the best, Alpaca," Nurse Jackson read out loud. "Looks like you have an admirer."

"Oh, please, haven't I suffered enough today?" said Milton, shaking his head.

"Yes, you have. But I have a feeling this won't be the last you see of Miss Finn. It's time for another pain shot. And I'll make sure you get an extra serving of chocolate pudding for dessert to help soothe your jangled nerves," she said, winking at Milton.

13
THE MANY THORNS IN SARA "SUGAR PANTS" PETERSON'S SIDE

Sara "Sugar Pants" Peterson had decided to become a volunteer at the Loone County Hospital. She hoped seeing people who were really sick might take her mind off the hot flashes and moodiness that had been plaguing her lately. She had been working there a month now and wasn't sure if she could tolerate Mrs. Crabtree much longer. She always seemed to be there no matter what day Sara volunteered. How often did the woman have to be told she didn't want to pray with her before they started their shifts? Sara believed in God but was not one to waste His time on the little things. Sara knew she had been short-tempered lately. She had been especially prickly since last week when she was washing her bedroom windows in the vain hope she could cheer herself up with a sparkly clear view of their lovely backyard.

Her husband, Tim, had called her Sugar Pants since they were first married. She had always thought it was sweet and special, only for her, until that day. She saw him in the backyard standing at the fence; she leaned out the window to ask him if he was ready to come in for lunch when she saw him talking to their neighbor Althea Goodnight. She heard him say," Your rose garden is outdoing itself this year, Sugar Pants."

She didn't wait to hear Althea's reply but gently eased the window, sat on the bed, and cried hot tears. Lately, she cried at the least little things, but this didn't seem little; it seemed big, too big for her to accept, too big for her to let go of. Maybe she would smother him in his sleep one night and bury him under those precious roses he admired so much, with the added benefit of laying the blame at Althea's feet. My God. What was wrong with her? Talk about overreacting. But thinking about the plan made her feel better. It gave her something to focus on besides the humdrumness of window washing and lunch making.

She guessed she was going through the change. She was about the same age as her mother was when she went through it. The constant complaints she remembers hearing when her mother and her friends got together for coffee every morning made her want to smother herself with a pillow rather than go through this crazy-making phase of life.

The next day at the hospital, Sara managed to extricate herself from Mrs. Crabtree. She spent a pleasant afternoon chatting with patients and their families while handing out magazines and candy. At the end of her shift, Sara was getting her purse out of her locker when she saw Mrs. Crabtree barreling down the hall, the old cart's wheels protesting squeakily at its breakneck speed. Mrs. Crabtree's face was so red that her pink circles of rouge disappeared into the redness of her face. She was huffing and puffing so much that Sara feared the old gal might faint.

"What is wrong, Mrs. Crabtree? Are you all right?" asked Sara.

"Water. I need water," gasped Mrs. Crabtree as she leaned on the cart. Sara went to the water cooler and returned with a Dixie cup of water. She helped hold it for Mrs. Crabtree, whose hands were shaking mightily.

'There, that's better. Thank you, my dear," said Mrs. Crabtree.

"Do you need to see a doctor?" asked Sara.

"Oh, no! I just had a run-in with that newcomer Milton Matthews and the creature visiting him," answered Mrs. Crabtree.

"What on earth happened?" asked Sara, curious despite herself. It was about that time Nurse Jackson and a nurse's aide named RaeAnn came over to see what all the commotion was about.

"He was just plain rude. Imagine not letting me pray for him," said Mrs. Crabtree. The other three stifled laughs, not daring to look at each other. "And the late Reverend Finn's sister was there visiting. It looked like she had had her claws sharpened at the Lovely Locks Salon and was ready to sink them into Mr. Matthews. Even though he's a heathen, I feel sorry for him if he falls into her web."

"Let's get out of here," Sara mouthed to Nurse Jackson and RaeAnn. They nodded and scattered as quickly as they could. They knew from experience they didn't want to get caught up in Mrs. Crabtree's drama.

Faster than you could say, "Let us pray," news of the "hospital incident" had spread all over Chanceville.

Coffee and gossip was a favorite combo of the patrons at the Tipp Topp. Luckily the supply of both appeared to be endless. They wouldn't have to wait long for something new to chew on .

14
ALPACA STRIKES OUT AT THE JASMINE TEAROOM

Alpaca had been working as Geraldine Nurse's assistant at the Loone County Public Library for almost a month when she reported for work the next morning after the infamous "hospital incident." She took one look at the little smirk on Geraldine's face and knew she had already heard about what happened at the hospital with Mr. Matthews. She had seen that smirk before on the faces of some of the ladies in Saints of the Lakes when they found out she was leaving town.

The fact that everyone in Chanceville probably knew what she was up to wasn't going to make her mission any easier, but she would not be deterred. She had fled once. Never again.

Alpaca worked five days a week with Thursday mornings off. She had specifically requested this schedule, and Geraldine knew this wasn't a random request. Alpaca always had a plan.

On a Thursday morning about a month after she had visited Milton in the hospital, Alpaca strode into the White Jasmine Tearoom. She wore an understated gray suit with a tailored white blouse, matching gloves, and a gray velvet bow headband perched in front of her tightly wound French twist. She wore three-inch heels; Alpaca enjoyed accentuating her height when it worked to her advantage. Small pearl earrings and a watch were her only accessories. As soon as Mrs. Little saw Alpaca Finn make her entrance into the tearoom, she knew the day was about to get a good deal more interesting.

"Good morning, Miss Finn," said Mrs. Little. "I'll show you to a table." She enjoyed giving her customers the personal touch.

"That won't be necessary," replied Alpaca as she scanned the room for the table that would best suit her purposes. She chose the bay window in the front, where she could see onto the street to her right and the rest of the tearoom to her left. That was fine with Mrs. Little. The tearoom wasn't too busy yet and wouldn't put too much of a burden on Janey, her part-time waitress. Besides, Mrs. Little was more than a lot curious about why Miss Finn chose that particular table.

Mayrose Mayhern arrived promptly at ten o'clock, as was her custom. She was barely inside the door when Alpaca Finn swooped down on her.

"Good morning, my dear. I'm Miss Alpaca Finn, as you probably know. It's so lovely to see you. Please join me at my table. I'd love to have tea with you and get to know you better since I'm now a permanent resident of Chanceville. I'm hoping to get you to attend one of my afternoon teas as you have yet to do."

It was about this time that Milton Matthews arrived, his first time in the tearoom since his surgery. After quickly assessing the situation, he stood with Mrs. Little behind the counter to watch the unfurling of Alpaca's plan and the resistance with which it would surely be met.

Miss Mayrose Mayhern, dressed in her soft pink linen spring suit, took precisely two steps back and looked Miss Alpaca Finn all the way up and then all the way down at an excruciatingly slow pace.

"No, thank you, Miss Finn," she said. "I always prefer taking my tea alone." Her words were like icy swords cutting Alpaca to the quick.

Alpaca and everyone else in the tearoom stood there as if frozen, except for Mayrose, who stepped briskly to her usual table in the back. If you had been a keen observer of Miss Mayhern over the years, you would know that what passed for a smile was a microscopic upturn of the corners of her mouth. She couldn't abide pushy people, and as far as she was concerned, the equally obnoxious Mr. Matthews & Miss Finn were a matched pair.

Still stunned, Mrs. Little recovered as best she could, gently moved Milton to the side, and returned to take Miss Mayhern's order.

Despite his less-than-positive opinion of Miss Finn, Milton felt slightly sorry for her. He knew the sting of Miss Mayhern's chilling blue stare well, but he knew better than to get involved. He decided it might be better to enjoy his tea at home today.

As Milton walked home and the shock of that scene wore off, he realized what that was all about, which made it even more ridiculous. Miss Trout er Miss Finn, whatever her fishy name was, apparently saw Miss Mayhern as a rival. He had no interest in Miss Finn whatsoever, even if Miss Mayrose Mayhern didn't exist. As for Mayrose, he had to admit that he was still more than a little intrigued.

Alpaca Finn went back to her table and sat down regally. This wasn't the first time she had been publicly humiliated. It probably wouldn't be the last. If Miss Mayhern thought Alpaca would turn tail and run, she had better think again. She would outshine that chilly lady. Alpaca had lots of sleeves and lots of tricks.

15
HAL AND TAMMY'S HONEYMOON SWEET SUITE

Meanwhile, as Alpaca was scheming to find a husband, Hal Hendrix had found someone he wanted to make his bride. Tammy Miller was the one for him. Her father had left her mother when Tammy was only two. She had no memory of him. Her mother died when Tammy was 18. Hal was very sweet to her when she made her mother's funeral arrangements. Tammy was alone in the world, and after the funeral, he helped her to settle her mother's affairs, what little there was to be settled. He spent a lot of time with her, comforting her when she cried. Tammy told him she didn't know what she would do without him. And she meant it. She was vulnerable, but he didn't want to take advantage. A year after her mother's death, he offered to marry and take care of her for the rest of her life. In her fragile, naive state, she agreed. She was only thinking of security, not what happened between a husband and wife.

Almost a year after Tammy's mother's passing, they had a simple civil ceremony officiated by Lily Lawson, Justice of the Peace. They went to Chicago on the train for their honeymoon. Tammy had never been out of Chanceville, and Hal seemed like a man of the world to her. He had been to many funeral director conventions in the Windy City, so he knew his way around. They took a cab to the Drake Hotel. Tammy was overwhelmed by the grandeur of it. When she saw the room with the beautiful bed, it dawned on her that they would occupy the same bed in a few hours.

"Shall we freshen up and get ready for dinner?" asked Hal. "I've made reservations in the best restaurant in the hotel."

"There's more than one?" she asked.

"Oh, sweetheart. There are several restaurants and private clubs. We will dine well tonight," Hal answered. "And in the morning, I suggest room service for breakfast," he said as a big smile appeared on his face.

Tammy wondered why he was looking at her that way. What was so amusing about room service?

Tammy had no idea what most of the items on the menu were, so Hal ordered for her. He was enjoying his role as mentor and didn't make her feel like a hick. He loved having someone special to spend his money on.

She was hoping he wouldn't order anything too exotic for her. He asked her if she liked chicken, and when she said yes, he ordered something called cocoa van for both of them. She didn't think chicken and cocoa sounded like much of a combination, but she would have to trust him, as she did in most things. To her great relief, it turned out to be chicken and vegetables. She could manage that. He ordered a dry white wine with dinner. Tammy had never had wine before.

"Are you enjoying the coq au vin, sweetheart?" he asked.

"It's delicious. Thank you for making that choice for me."

"I think there's something wrong with this, Hal. It tastes sour," she said as she tasted her wine.

"It's not sour, it's dry," Hal said.

Puzzled, she stuck her finger in the glass to test its "dryness." This served to endear her to him even more.

"Sorry. Dry means not sweet," Hal said without judgment. Tammy didn't see much point in a drink that wasn't sweet, but she kept that to herself. She would have been happy with a Coca-Cola. It was clear to her that Hal was trying to make the evening special.

Hal ordered Baked Alaska Flambé for dessert.

"What on earth is Baked Alaska Flambé?" she asked him.

"Well, it's basically baked ice cream," he said as her blue eyes opened wide.

"Come on. Stop teasing me," Tammy said. "I'm no great cook, but even I know you can't bake ice cream. Sounds like we'll have to drink it."

"That's what I thought, too, when I first heard of it."

At this point, they brought out the most beautiful thing Tammy had ever seen. The church ladies' merengue could never hold a candle to this artfully sculpted delight. Tammy clapped like an enchanted child when they poured the rum over it and lit the match.

"Oh, Hal. This tastes as luscious as it looks," she said, almost forgetting to swallow that first bite before speaking.

Hal suggested they return to their room when they finished their coffee. He was thinking that the evening was just beginning.

Tammy was thinking that she wasn't ready for their dinner to end.

Hal opened the door to their suite, carried her over the threshold, and placed her gently on the chaise lounge. He put the Do Not Disturb sign on the door and flipped the locks firmly. Then Hal went to the phone and ordered breakfast from room service for 8 a.m. without consulting her about what she would like to eat or what time. Hal thought she seemed to like it when he took charge of a situation that was new for her.

While Hal was in the bathroom, Tammy looked in her suitcase to see what he had packed for her. He had insisted on buying her all-new clothes for their honeymoon. She mostly had cotton print blouses that she had sewn herself and blue jeans. The first item she pulled out was a pale pink peignoir set. She held it up to the light. She could just make out the chandelier through it. She started to tremble. Just then, Hal emerged from the bathroom dressed in pajamas, over which he wore a maroon silk dressing gown. Tammy had only seen men wear dressing gowns in movies. Her idea of Hal from Chanceville, Indiana, didn't fit with the sight she was seeing now. Tammy started to giggle nervously. She was glad the dressing gown wasn't monogrammed. She was not having much luck suppressing her giggles. She thought he was handsome in an understated way with his hazel eyes, dark hair, and lashes. But he was no David Niven. This was all just too much. Tammy realized, too late, that it probably wasn't good to laugh at your husband as he prepared for their wedding night.

"What is so funny?" he asked.

"Sorry, I'm just nervous. You look handsome," Tammy said, looking at the floor.

"Oh," he said, unconvinced. "Why don't you go in the bathroom and get changed?

Tammy draped the peignoir set over her arm and took her cosmetic bag into the bathroom. The big tub in the bath and the wonderful smelling bath salts made her decide to take a long, very long, hot bath. Meanwhile, Hal kept tapping on the door, checking on her, and pacing on the expensive carpet impatiently. When she finally emerged from the bathroom, Hal was the one who started laughing and shaking his head.

"Oh, Tammy. How dear you are to me," he said.

When Tammy had put on the flimsy peignoir set, she felt so exposed that she put the thick terrycloth robe provided by the hotel over the diaphanous ensemble.

Hal had ordered champagne while Tammy was in the bath. He was hoping this would settle her nerves. He was willing to be patient for as long as it took but hoped he wouldn't have to be for too long.

Tammy jumped straight into the air when he popped the cork on the champagne. Hal poured them each a glass, handed hers to her, and gently led her over to the bed.

"To my beautiful wife and many years of married bliss," he said as they clinked their glasses.

She took a hesitant sip and decided she liked the bubbly sweetness. (Hal had learned his lesson and ordered a sweet Spumante.) After

Tammy had finished her first glass, he took it from her; he didn't want to take advantage. He sat it on the night table and gently began to ease that blasted heavy robe off her shoulders. Tammy was feeling warm and friendly and didn't resist. Hal took off his dressing gown, and they sat down on the edge of the bed together. Things progressed nicely until Tammy got to thinking about all the dead people Hal had touched, and she suddenly had her own case of rigor mortis. Well, at least that would feel familiar to him.

16

TAMMY AND PEGGY
MEASURE UP

The newlyweds spent another two days in Chicago, sightseeing by day, long leisurely dinners in the evening, and quiet lovemaking at night. Hal was gentle and patient with Tammy. He never made the connection that his profession caused Tammy's reticence in bed. He assumed it was his age. Tammy learned to love Hal for many reasons. Still, even with her previous non-existent experience, Hal seemed a little unimaginative in that department. But it was mainly the dead who seemed to follow him everywhere that she couldn't get past. She was careful with his feelings and would never tell him that his work put her off. Because, really, what could he do about it? To Hal's delight, his bride could relax and enjoy their lovemaking after a few months.

After their honeymoon, they settled into their quiet new life upon returning to Chanceville. Tammy, who had been raised by a very superstitious mother and grandmother, was always on alert in their home/funeral home. It didn't feel like she and Hal lived there alone. It seemed the dead not only followed Hal, but they followed her. The whole place was filled with spirits and chatter. Even when she played

Hal's stuffy old classical music loudly, it still didn't drown out the ghostly conversations.

When Tammy and Hal got married, she quit her job as a cashier at the Only Grocery Store, owned by Daniel Only. Still, Hal was very busy with work and his community activities. Tammy helped in the office and was a greeter during funerals and visitations. She also started spending more and more time in the Wax Museum. The wax figures were so poorly rendered that they weren't life-like enough to be creepy to her, closer to comically rendered. Put a long wig, reading glasses, and 18th-century clothing on the figure of Alfred Hitchcock, and you had Benjamin Franklin, which, theoretically, doubled their inventory. All they had to do with most of them was change their costumes. Hal had proudly told her that the wax museum had been his mother's life work. Tammy didn't believe that the oddities of the figures were from lack of talent but a reflection of her mother-in-law's worldview. Fuzzy at best.

Hal's mother, Peggy Hendrix, was currently residing at the Sally Forth Home for the Elderly and Infirm. Owned and run by former exotic dancer Sally Forth. Hal and Tammy visited Peggy every Sunday after church. They used to take her out for a meal, but Peggy kept trying to go back to the kitchen at the Tip Topp Diner, thinking she should be cooking Sunday dinner. They would stop by the diner on the way and bring chicken dinners for the three of them.

"I don't think I got a good do on the mashed potatoes. They seem a little runny," said Peggy with a mouthful.

Tammy reached over with her napkin and tenderly wiped her mother-in-law's chin. She reminded Peggy of her own grandmother.

"No, Mother," said Hal. "The meal is perfect, especially the potatoes. Thanks for making them; you know they're my favorite."

Mrs. Hendrix smiled a wide mashed potato smile at the two of them.

Tammy visited her mother-in-law a couple of days a week. If the old lady was having a good day, Tammy would sign her out and take her back to the Wax Museum. The two of them would putter around in amiable silence as they fussed with the figures. Peggy showed Tammy how to delicately clean the surface of the wax figures without damaging their skin color, which mostly seemed tinged with green, giving them all a slightly bilious look.

If Peggy was having a perfect day, they would stop at Prissy Paulson's Hem and Haul Fabric Store and Trash Removal Service to buy material to fashion new outfits for some of the wax figures' more tattered ensembles. Tammy's Grandmother Vera had taught her how to sew. She had been a firm taskmaster, so everything Tammy sewed was expertly done.

Tammy didn't like to think she was superstitious herself. Still, she found that she automatically tried to stem the tide of any bad luck that might come her way and observed rituals that brought good luck to her and those she loved.

"Now Tammy, always thread your needle from right to left for even-handed stitching. If you thread left to right, it will look like the cat sewed it," said Grandmother Vera. Tammy was always curious to know where her grandmother got these ideas. Still, she would never have been so rude as to question her beloved grandmother. Grandmother Vera had what, to Tammy, seemed like a million of these superstitious rules for every facet of life.

One day, when Tammy went to pick up Peggy at the Sally Forth Home for the Elderly and Infirm, Peggy seemed really excited to see her.

Before Tammy even got a chance to greet her, Peggy said, "It's time we spruced up Mrs. Clark, Pioneer Woman. Peggy alternately called Pioneer Woman, Mrs. Clark, or Mrs. Lewis. Can we go to the Hem and Haul and get some new fabric? I know exactly what I want."

"Of course, Mother Hendrix. That sounds like fun," said Tammy.

Peggy already had her jacket on and was so hurried to get out the door that she almost knocked Tammy down. As Tammy turned while laughing, she and Peggy tried to get through the door at the same time. They simultaneously snapped their fingers first on the right, then on the left to ward off evil doorway twins, saying be gone, Evil Doorway

Twins! They both burst out laughing, surprised that they knew the same superstition.

When they arrived at the Hem and Haul, Prissy Paulson greeted them warmly, asking what she could do for them on this fine day.

"We want to spruce up our pioneer woman, Mrs. Lewis," said Peggy.

Prissy looked at Tammy and winked. Tammy suppressed a giggle. One of Chanceville's worst-kept secrets was that Mrs. Clark/Lewis resembled Mae West, Dance Hall Girl, more than a hardscrabble, worn-out Pioneer Woman wearing a dress with a provocatively scooped neckline.

"We have some new feed sack prints that I think would be just the thing," said Prissy as she led them to the back of the store.

"That sounds perfect," said Peggy and Tammy simultaneously.

"Jinx, you owe me a Coke," said Tammy and Peggy.

Peggy picked out a soft pink and green flowered print for Mrs. Clark/Lewis's dress and some bright blue sequined rickrack for the trim around the scooped neckline. Perfect, thought Tammy.

Tammy treated to lunch at the Tip Topp Diner, where she managed to keep Peggy out of the kitchen for once. Then, they headed back to the Wax Museum to begin what could possibly be the finest effort of their partnership to date.

If only everyone in Chanceville were as nice as Peggy, Tammy, and Hal.

17

HIGH HORSE HARRY

Summer was fading into Autumn in Chanceville, and for about a year, High Horse Harry had stood, rain or shine, six days a week at the northeast corner of Main Street and Main Avenue, in front of the Blind Poodle Sisters' house, shouting to the world his thoughts on everything. No one knew what his name really was or where he came from. He appeared one day and began yelling. Tarsal had dubbed him High Horse Harry, and the name stuck.

Harry never talked to anyone or answered any questions. He stood and shouted at the world for two hours every morning and then disappeared back into the woods to an abandoned cabin at the back of old Mrs. Burl Tree's property. The cabin was so old that she couldn't remember much about it. Mrs. Tree let Harry stay there. He was harmless, and she hated the thought of him not having anywhere to live.

The cabin had a well but no running water and never had electricity; even so, Harry always appeared pretty clean. He looked to be over six feet tall. He wore bib overalls that were a little too short, a plaid shirt, a greasy-looking cowboy hat with metal beads in the hatband, and a leather poncho in bad weather. His dark hair and beard were long but not unkempt. If you got close enough to look, which few people did, you could see piercing green eyes under shaggy black eyebrows.

Most days, people tolerated or just plain ignored Harry, but today was not going to be one of those days because Tarsal Henley was nearing the corner of Main Street and Main Avenue. Tarsal had never been known for his patience or tolerance of other people getting attention, and today was no exception. He usually managed to avoid that particular corner, but he woke up spoiling for a fight, and High Horse Harry seemed like a good place to start.

"Never plant an elm tree near a maple," yelled Harry. "They are sworn enemies and will uproot each other given half a chance."

"You're an idiot, High Horse Harry," said Tarsal in a vain attempt to out yell Harry.

"And about as bright as those morons who think dogs have souls. You'd better get the hell out of here 'cause I'm getting real close to slugging you."

You need to plant an oak between the maple and the elm because acorns are known far and wide as peacekeepers," said Harry. "There will be no warring tree shenanigans in their presence."

"Did you hear me, Harry? Did you HEAR me?" yelled Tarsal.

"Some folks think the dogwood is the peacekeeper, but they'd be wrong.

Dogwoods stir up as much trouble as elms and maples. They're just sneakier about it so people don't catch on."

With that last statement, Tarsal had had about all he could take. He was clenching his fist in preparation to deck Harry when the clock on the courthouse struck twelve, Harry's quitting time. He stepped down from the rickety old crate that served as his soapbox, walked away from Tarsal, and headed for the woods. That was when Tarsal jumped on Harry's crate and smashed it to smithereens. Later that day, Ned, who had witnessed the whole thing, replaced the smashed crate with another one from his barn. He placed it upright near the hedge where Harry stored it so it was out of the way of people using the sidewalk. He was happy to help Harry but was tired of cleaning up Tarsal's messes.

Tarsal headed straight for the Tip Topp Diner, where Mrs. Tree happened to be having lunch. Everybody was complaining about everything. The whole town had been cranky since that dang feud over dogs' souls had caused the church to split. Mrs. Tree, who was usually sweet, was starting to feel a little on the snappish side herself.

Sid Topp was behind the counter as usual. As soon as he saw Tarsal Henley come in the door, he could tell he was fired up even more than normal, which was considerable.

"Anything besides coffee today, Tarsal?" asked Sid as he sat a mug of strong black coffee in front of Tarsal, who flopped down on the stool with a thud.

"High Horse Harry is getting on my last nerve. I've a good mind to run him out of town," said Tarsal between coffee slurps.

"Oh, shut up, Tarsal Henley, you big blowhard," said Mrs. Tree.

Every head in the diner snapped to attention. For a few seconds, it seemed as if all of the air had been sucked out of the room. A chorus of throats cleared as everyone waited in high anticipation of what Tarsal's response would be. Sid looked at Mrs. Tree and mouthed, Thank you. Most of the citizens of Chanceville had wanted to tell Tarsal Henley to shut up for years. But they didn't think it would do any good.

For once in his life, Tarsal has the good sense to zip it. He knew that if he talked back to lovely old Mrs. Tree, he might be the one run out of town instead of High Horse Harry. But, typical Tarsal style, he couldn't leave without making some sort of statement. He slammed his mug down, sloshing coffee everywhere, stood up, threw his money at Sid, and stomped out. Everyone burst out laughing.

About a week later, a shellacked wooden box mysteriously appeared at the northeast corner of Main Street and Main Avenue. On each side was painted a beautiful carousel horse. A crowd was gathering to examine the box and take bets on whether High Horse Harry would actually stand on this work of art. They all stepped back as Harry approached. And stand, he did. Harry walked right to it, stepped up, and stood on the box as if it were the same old rickety crate he had used all those months.

Two weeks after that, High Horse Harry was standing at his corner shouting about the evils of marshmallows. The sky was a menacing color of purple. People were passing by faster than usual, scurrying to escape the impending storm, not noticing that Harry had moved on to a new topic.

"Rabbits are the spawn of the devil," yelled Harry. "Their slimy little noses twitch out Morse Code messages from Satan. Yesterday, a little white rabbit told me the devil is holding Abraham Lincoln hostage."

He said this just as the rain hit and a loud thunderclap rattled the Poodle house's windows. It was about that time that Tarsal Henley was scurrying by. Zap! A lightning bolt struck the metal beads on the High Horse Harry's cowboy hat band. Poof! He was gone. All that was left were Harry's smoldering ashes.

The rain stopped as suddenly as it had come. As a crowd began to gather, Tarsal was still standing there. He seemed dumbstruck, but everyone knew that wouldn't last long. The Blind Poodle Sisters hurried down their sidewalk to find out what all the commotion was about. They were waving their white canes around, hitting Tarsal on the shins, causing him to come out of his stupor.

"What the heck?" said Tarsal as he blinked in an attempt to focus his eyes. "Stop hitting me!"

"Is that you, Tarsal Henley? You smell like a wood stove," said Babbette, or was it Annette Poodle? Before Tarsal could answer, the sisters' maid, Poppy, came out to herd the sisters back in before Tarsal started fighting with them. The news about what happened to Harry spread quickly. Everyone wanted to stand around and gawk at the smoldering pile of ashes.

Finally, Sheriff Yesper Orange came along and dispersed the crowd. He always carried a bucket and shovel to clear road kill off the county roads, so he grabbed them out of his trunk and scooped up the remains of what was left of High Horse Harry. Sheriff Orange borrowed a garden hose and a broom from the Poodle sisters, and with Poppy's help, they got the sidewalk cleaned off.

The Sheriff took the bucket of ashes back to his office and placed the remains in a shoebox. He taped it up with duct tape, wrote HHH on it, and locked it in the small closet he called the evidence room. He would soon place an identical box labeled BBB beside HHH.

18

A MYSTERIOUS STRANGER APPEARS AND MORE THEORIES AT THE TIPP TOPP

Sheriff Yesper Orange may not have seemed like the sharpest knife in the drawer. That was a clever ruse. His hooded eyes, with their wrinkled lids, gave him a sleepy turtle look. But they didn't miss a trick. While scooping up what remained of Harry, he noticed some sort of academic medal. He would have to check that out later. For now, Harry's remains were safe, and Yesper could sift through the ashes for clues when all the fuss died down.

A few days after High Horse Harry died, a stranger had been walking past the Blind Poodle Sister's house several times a day. As the sisters headed to town one day, the stranger approached Annette and Babbette. He had been waiting for them to leave the house without their maid, Poppy. He had a quiet conversation with them as they walked along.

"Hello, Lovely Ladies," he said.

"Oo, I like your voice," said Annette. "Who might you be?"

"I'm the man who would like to ask a favor," said the stranger.

"What kind of favor?" asked Annette, giggling into her hand.

"I'd like permission to erect a life-size carousel horse in your front yard in honor of High Horse Harry," he told them.

"Did you know him?" asked the sisters in unison.

"Let's just say I was an admirer of his," answered the stranger.

"Will it have lots of color?" asked Babbette?

"Of course, that's the beauty of carousel horses," he answered.

"Deal," said the sisters in unison again. "Just make sure there's lots of color." Even though they couldn't see it, it made them smile to think of all the color in the world.

"Much obliged, ladies. I promise you won't be sorry you agreed to this. One more thing," said the stranger. "If I find out that you mentioned this conversation to anyone, and believe me, I will know, you will not get a colorful horse, and we will never meet again. This must be an anonymous gift." The ladies only nodded in agreement.

With that, the stranger kissed each of the ladies' hands, his fingers lingering a moment on the twins' matching opal and diamond rings, a gift from their father on their sixteenth birthdays. The sisters continued down the street, twittering into their freshly kissed hands, not caring a fig about the carousel horse but really hoping they would meet the stranger again and hear his melodious voice once more. Sadly, it was not to be. That voice would be stopped forever in a few days. He would end up in the box marked BBB.

The folks of Chanceville couldn't talk about anything else but the shocking demise of High Horse Harry. Sid Topp had to order extra coffee because so many people hung around at the diner long after they'd finished their meals to dissect, so to speak, not only what happened to Harry but also who he actually might be.

Geraldine Nurse supposed he might be an army deserter hiding behind that beard. His long hair and cowboy hat seemed like a good disguise to her.

Hubert Patterson reckoned that Harry might be his long-lost Uncle George, who had run away with the circus 30 years ago. Clearly, Hubert had forgotten his Uncle George was only about 5'6" tall, had curly red hair, and would be almost a hundred years old by now.

"The last time I remember hearing Harry rant was a couple of weeks ago," said Mr. Williams the Younger. "He was going on about crossing a buzzard with a butterfly. His new creature would look much more beautiful than a dirty old buzzard as it pulled out the guts of an opossum lying on the side of the road."

"Well, I say, Harry was just a crazy old buzzard himself and not too pretty to look at," said Tarsal, loudly slurping his coffee.

Maxine Crabtree, Zealous Hospital Volunteer, announced loudly that Harry paid the ultimate price for being an unrepentant sinner. Although, when pressed by the diner's patrons, she could not say precisely what Harry's sins might have been.

"I don't rightly know. Harry just had the look of a sinner about him," said Mrs. Crabtree defensively. Everyone in the diner knew Mrs. Crabtree believed the whole town was teeming with sinners.

Chanceville was not exactly teeming with sinners, but there were a few lurking about.

19

NED AND BURL BECOME CHANCEVILLE'S NEWEST DETECTIVES

B
y now, Sid Topp had heard all he ever wanted to hear about High Horse Harry. Sid wasn't an unfeeling man; he did feel sorry for poor old Harry. But enough was enough. When the good people of Chanceville started chewing on a bone, they wouldn't let go. Besides, if he had to keep filling up all the "bottomless" coffee cups, Harry's death could become a losing proposition at the Tip Topp.

Fern Oldhat, who loved a good fugitive from justice story, reckoned High Horse Harry was a Nazi war criminal who never made it to South America.

"I still can't believe it. I guess I ought to count my blessings that I wasn't hit too," said Tarsal Henley. He had thrown out the clothes he wore the day the lightning hit Harry, but no matter how many times Tarsal bathed, he thought he could still smell that scorched stench.

"I'm sure Harry wasn't too thrilled about it either," said Sid as he poured Tarsal another cup of coffee.

"I wonder what Sheriff Orange did with the ashes?" asked Hal Hendrix, owner of Hendrix Funeral Parlor and Wax Museum, having a vested interest in the remains of the people of Chanceville.

"I saw him sweep them up in a bucket," said Charlie Towne, the train station master. "You'll have to ask him what he did with them after that."

"That I will," answered Hal as he perused the menu, hoping for something new, only to be disappointed but not surprised.

"It's just too weird," said Tarsal as he headed out the door.

A few minutes later, Ned Cochran and Mrs. Burl Tree entered the diner at the same time and took a seat at the counter. Everyone was glad that Tarsal had left before Ned arrived. They'd had enough drama lately. Tarsal could never resist poking Ned.

"How you doing, Mrs. Tree?" asked Ned.

"Not too bad, thanks," she replied. "Still in shock like everyone else, I 'spose."

"True. Harry came here as a mystery and left here in another one. Sure, it would be interesting to find out who High Horse Harry really was and where he came from. I guess we'll never know," replied Ned.

"We might be able to find out something," said Mrs. Tree as every head turned toward her.

"What do you mean?" asked Sid as he served both Ned and Mrs. Tree the meatloaf sandwich special they had ordered.

We could go have a look in his cabin. I haven't been in there since he moved in," said Mrs. Tree. "Would you consider taking me over there, Ned?"

"Of course," he answered quickly. "When would you like to go?"

"How about after we finish eating? It's too far back in the woods for me to walk, but I think we can get there in your truck," she said.

Cora Jean Mitchell, the gum-popping, snappy-talking waitress at the diner, said, "Hey, I finish my shift in half an hour. How 'bout if I go with you guys?"

To Ned's relief, Sid reminded Cora Jean that she had promised to work an extra shift that day because Jenetta Joyner, the other waitress at the Tip Topp, had told Sid she was going to see Doc Ivory to have her *bicuspidor* removed that afternoon. Ned didn't think he could stand listening to Cora Jean's gum popping the rest of the day.

Mrs. Tree said she thought it was best for now if just the two of them went. She promised to let everyone know if they found anything interesting.

"Sounds good to me," said Ned as he shoveled in another mashed potato mouthful.

That's how they discovered some interesting but puzzling clues about High Horse Harry.

Ned picked Mrs. Tree up at her house after they finished lunch. It was a good thing he had running boards on his truck, or he might never have gotten that tiny lady up in the cab of his truck. They bumped along an old logging road for about a mile. He parked in a small natural clearing in front of the cabin and helped Mrs. Tree get down from the cab. It was a sunny day, but the tall oak trees around the cabin heavily shaded it, so Ned retrieved a couple of flashlights from his toolbox.

What Ned didn't notice was a dark Ford sedan following him almost all the way to Mrs. Tree's. The stranger dressed in black had parked about a mile past her property and walked through the woods, following them at a safe distance.

"I know High Horse Harry is gone, but it still doesn't feel right entering this cabin, even though it's on my property," remarked Mrs. Tree.

"I know what you mean," said Ned. "It feels kind of spooky here. Those crows are having a fit about something."

Mrs. Tree didn't seem to notice the crows, but Ned always paid attention to their calls. It was never idle chatter. As Mrs. Tree went ahead, Ned stood stock-still, looked around, and listened for other sounds besides the raucous cawing. Nothing. He thought maybe they were spreading the word that a hawk was in the area.

They entered a surprisingly clean and tidy cabin. It was apparent by the spareness of the cabin that High Horse Harry owned very little, which would make their search easier but probably not too fruitful.

It hadn't taken long for the mice to move in after Harry Died. As soon as Ned and Mrs. Tree walked in, mice scattered everywhere.

"I had forgotten that my late husband, Woodrow, and I had used this place to store stuff that we didn't know what to do with. That's why there's a few pieces of furniture in here."

"I'll look high, and you look low," said Ned. Mrs. Tree nodded, and they began their search in silence to the backdrop of the crows.

They looked in all the usual places: in the one cabinet in the kitchen, under the nasty old mattress on the floor, and in the tall and surprisingly solid old chest of drawers in the sleeping room. The chest did not contain clothes; every drawer was filled with books. As Ned and Mrs. Tree took a few books out to sample Harry's reading tastes, they were surprised to discover he apparently loved great works of literature if, indeed, these were his books. His copy of War and Peace was filled with marginalia. They found the works of Voltaire, Dumas, and Descartes in the original French. In those volumes, the marginalia was in what they thought was French. So far, they had not been damaged by the mice.

"I guess there was way more to Harry than met the eye," said Ned, scratching his chin.

"It would be a shame to let the mice get to these wonderful books," Mrs. Tree replied.

"I'd be happy to store them if you want to load them in your truck and take them to my house. Maybe we can donate them to the Loone County Library."

"Good idea. I'll come back tomorrow with some help, and we'll bring the books to your house," said Ned.

"Okay, but pick someone who's not a gossip. It doesn't feel right to have nosey nellies snooping around in here," Mrs. Tree said as Ned nodded in agreement. Ned didn't really need the help, but he had an uneasy feeling and wanted to get Mrs. Tree safely back home as soon as they finished searching the cabin. Besides, he wanted to bring Sid Topp out here and get his take on the situation.

Mrs. Tree went back into the kitchen to have one more look around. She even lifted the handles on the old wood fired cook stovetop. She was about ready to give up when she decided to check the ash pan under the stove. At first glance, it looked like just a thick layer of ash, but she wanted to be sure. She went outside and got a stick so she wouldn't have to touch the ash as she moved it around. The stick hit something solid.

She called Ned from the sleeping room. "Look at this," she said as she carefully lifted an ash-covered envelope from the pan.

"Lay it on the table," said Ned.

He pulled a shop rag from his hip pocket and carefully removed the envelope's contents. They took the pages from the packet of papers and laid them on the rickety old table. They looked like legal documents. They decided to take the papers back to Mrs. Tree's, where they could look at them more comfortably and in better light. As they headed to the truck, Ned heard a rustle and saw a shadow move around the corner of the cabin. He ran around the corner to check it out but found no one there.

"I thought I saw someone sneak around the corner. But I didn't find anyone," Ned told Mrs. Tree.

She just shrugged her shoulders, ready to get back to her house.

When they pulled into Mrs. Tree's driveway, her beagle Junebug came running out of the barn, barking and yipping at Ned's truck.

"She's a great watchdog. She always lets me know when someone's around. She'll stop barking when she sees you're someone she knows," said Mrs. Tree. Sure enough, as soon as Ned stepped out of his truck, Junebug came running up, wagging her tail.

While Ned was laying out the papers on Mrs. Tree's dining room table, she made coffee and sliced up some pineapple upside-down cake for them to nibble on. Two people were named in the documents: Porter Pander and Joshua Moot. It appeared they had entered into a business partnership producing a product called Quacks, which neither Ned nor Mrs. Tree had ever heard of.

"It looks like this one here is something about a lawsuit," said Ned, holding up a yellowed page.

"It's hard to make out, but it looks like the name Bertram Benedict Bunnington, Attorney, or some such. They sat and discussed the possibilities of what these papers could mean over their cake and coffee. Ned sure did love Mrs. Tree's pineapple upside-down cake.

"I'd best be on my way. I've got to go back into town and stop by Steele's Hardware Store. I don't want to get into trouble for being late getting home. It's not good to get on the bad side of Gardenia. She might be named after a fragrant flower, but she can be as prickly as a cactus," said Ned

"What should we do with these papers?" asked Mrs. Tree, stifling a yawn. She had missed her afternoon nap, and even the coffee wasn't perking her up. It had been a big day for her.

"Boy, that's a good question," said Ned, taking his cap off and scratching his head. "Why don't you keep them until we have more time to read all of this legal mumbo jumbo and decide if there's someone else who should know about this."

"Sounds good. I'll put the papers in my box of photographs I keep under the bed in the spare room," Mrs. Tree replied.

"Great. When I come back for the books tomorrow, we'll decide what our next step is going to be," said Ned

"That's fine. See you tomorrow," said Mrs. Tree.

Ned didn't notice the tall figure lurking in the shadows of the barn as he headed to his truck. He thought maybe Junebug was barking at one of the barn cats, who seemed to enjoy hissing at her. They had not learned to live in harmony.

20

BURL TREE AND JUNEBUG
TAKE A NAP

T he next day was a Thursday, and Ned knew that was Sid Topp's afternoon off, so he asked Sid to help him retrieve the books from Harry's cabin. Even though the Tip Topp diner was gossip central in Chanceville, he knew Sid was reluctant to gossip about his customers behind their backs, a quick way to lose customers. Ned had known Sid since they were kids, and he also knew Sid could be trusted to keep a secret when need be. When he told Sid they were going to move some of Harry's belongings and that he and Mrs. Tree thought it best to keep their mission quiet for a while, Sid agreed without asking questions.

"Yeah, no need to give people anything else to chew on," said Sid.

"You got that right," said Ned.

Sid saw several cardboard boxes in the back of Ned's pickup. He said, "I can't imagine he had enough stuff to fill more than one box."

"You'll see why when we get to the cabin," Ned replied.

"Okay," said Sid, looking skeptical.

When they pulled up, Ned had that uneasy feeling again. The crows were gathered at the top of the old sycamore, cawing loudly to each other and possibly to the two men. Ned signaled Sid to be quiet as they walked up to the cabin's front door, which was slightly ajar. Ned was sure he had closed it firmly. He slowly opened the door as it creaked loudly on its rusty hinges, alerting anyone inside to their presence, causing the crows to rev up a decibel or ten. Ned and Sid stepped inside, but no one greeted them except the mice. Ned led Sid immediately into the sleeping room.

Damn it all to hell," he said as he saw that the drawers had all been pulled out and were empty. "This chest was full of books, and they're all gone."

"Ned, I don't think I've ever heard you curse before, even when Tarsal Henley was yanking your chain," said Sid.

"Something's not right. We'd better go check on Mrs. Tree," he replied.

Ned and Sid hightailed it to Mrs. Tree's to tell her about the missing books and ensure she had no problems during the night. On the way, Ned filled Sid in about the books and documents they found in the cabin. He was worried about all of the noise the crows had been making both times he had walked up to the cabin. When they pulled into Mrs. Tree's drive, nothing looked out of the ordinary, but that didn't help to alleviate Ned's uneasiness.

"That cabin gave me the creeps. Those crows were trying to tell us something. I'm sure of it. When we went inside, it felt like someone was watching us. I'm still feeling that way," Sid told Ned.

"I know what you mean," replied Ned. "Something's going on, or those books wouldn't be missing. Speaking of missing. I wonder why Junebug didn't come running out to greet us?"

"That is strange. Sometimes, if I've heard that Mrs. Tree is under the weather, I'll bring out a plate from the diner for her supper. Junebug always comes out to make sure who's on her property," said Sid.

"You check the barn, Sid. I'll go and check on Mrs. Tree," said Ned.

'Righto," said Sid.

Sid headed for the barn, calling out for Junebug. Ned walked up to Mrs. Tree's back door and started to knock, but he could see the door wasn't closed all the way. There were marks around the lock as if it had been forced open. He stepped into the kitchen and called out to Mrs. Tree. No answer. All was quiet except for the grandfather clock ticking in the living room.

"Mrs. Tree?" Ned called again. Still no answer.

He went down the hall, checking doors until he found her bedroom. Mrs. Tree was still in bed, unheard of at nine o'clock in the morning for this farmer's widow. She appeared to be sleeping soundly and was snoring lightly. He didn't want to scare her, so he said her name again and gently patted her shoulder. Mrs. Tree slowly opened her eyes and then closed them again. He noticed a pungent odor in the room and looked to see where it came from. He saw the corner of a white handkerchief sticking out from under the bed. He didn't have to hold it too close to recognize that smell when he leaned over to pick it up. Years ago, Old Doc Ivory had to pull an abscessed tooth and used chloroform on him to put him out. Ned had never forgotten that sickening smell.

"This explains why Mrs. Tree is still asleep in the middle of the morning," Ned said, holding out the smelly hanky toward Sid as he came into the room.

"Junebug is snoring away in the barn, said Sid. "I'd better go back out and see if I can rouse her."

"Good, take that thing outside, would you, Sid?" said Ned, handing him the handkerchief. "Lay it on the back steps so the sheriff can take a look at it. Would you mind making some coffee when you come back in? We need to get this lady to wake up, and I don't want to leave her alone."

"Sure will," said Sid, "after I've checked on Junebug."

Ned opened Mrs. Tree's bedroom window to get some fresh air in there. Then he went into the bathroom and got a cold cloth to use on her forehead. He might have to call old Doc Trueblood if he couldn't bring her around soon.

Ned returned with the cold, damp cloth and wiped Mrs. Tree's face. She opened her eyes and looked questioningly at Ned.

"What's going on? What are you doing here?" she asked, her eyes were cloudy.

About that time, Sid came in with a cup of instant coffee for the old lady. "Here you go, Mrs. Tree. Maybe this will perk you up a bit," he said as he set the mug on her nightstand. "Sweet and milky, Tip Topp Diner style, just the way you like it."

Ned helped her to sit up in the bed, propping her back with pillows against the headboard.

"Do you have any recollection about last night?" Ned asked her.

She held the cup with both hands, sipping the coffee gratefully.

"No. What has happened to me? Did I have a stroke?" she asked as she shakily sat the mug on the nightstand and pulled the covers around her neck.

"Nooo," said Ned. "It looks like you and Junebug were chloroformed last night."

"Junebug!" cried Mrs. Tree. Sid leaned over and patted her hand, "She's fine. I brought her to the kitchen. She had a good long drink of water. Now, don't you worry, she's coming around nicely."

"Why would anyone chloroform my Junebug and me?"

"Someone took all of the books out of the cabin. I had Sid check under your guest bed, and the papers you hid in your box of photographs are gone also," said Ned. "I noticed the dresser drawers were left open in the guest room and the dining room china cabinet. That's when I looked under the bed in the photograph box."

"That is where you put them, right?" asked Sid.

"Oh, yes. I laid the papers right on top. Are my photos still there?" she asked.

"Seem to be. I'll fetch the box, and you can take a look," Sid answered.

"I wouldn't do that yet," Ned cautioned as he got up to leave the room. "Sheriff Orange will probably want to come out here to take a look around. We need to find out what is going on. I'm going to call him now."

"Good idea," said Sid. "Meantime, Burl, why don't you come into town and stay with me and the missus until we figure out what's going on around here?"

"Good, Lord. I'm not lettin' anyone scare me out of my own home," she said. "And, besides, I can't leave Junebug."

"Not up for debate," Ned told her when he returned to the room. "The phone was dead. I went outside and found the wire had been cut. We're going to pay a visit to Doc Trueblood and then on to see Sheriff Orange."

"Yes, and I'll call Tippy from the doc's office to let her know you'll be staying with us," said Sid, holding up his hand to fend off any protest from Mrs. Tree.

"And I'll take Junebug home with me," said Ned. "She'll feel at home on the farm. Are you up to getting yourself dressed?"

"I think so. If you can help me stand up, we'll see how wobbly my legs are."

Mrs. Tree stood up and asked Ned to hand her the clothes she had laid on the chair the night before. "Okay, Ned. I can take it from here. Thanks."

They helped Burl into Ned's pickup and loaded a still groggy Junebug into the back. Sid rode in the back with her so she wouldn't be scared and try to jump out. They dropped her off at the farm and briefly filled Gardenia in about the latest events.

"Now, don't say a word about this to anyone, honeybunch," said Ned, already knowing he was wasting his breath.

Sid winked at Mrs. Tree. They both knew full well that there was no threat big enough to encourage Gardenia Cochran to keep her mouth shut. Since Ned had only given her a couple of facts, they also knew that she was quite capable of filling in the blanks where she felt it was needed. The gossip train was about to be overloaded.

21

DOC TRUEBLOOD AND SHERIFF ORANGE HAVE SOME VISITORS

Doc Trueblood listened to Burl Tree's heart and lungs, took her blood pressure, and checked the dilation of her pupils.

"Everything checks out just fine, Burl," said Doc. "The best thing you can do is stay active this afternoon and drink lots of water to flush out your system. I'm going to give you a vitamin B12 shot to boost your energy a bit. You should be right as rain by tomorrow, but I'd rather you didn't go back out there in the middle of nowhere all by yourself until Sheriff Orange finds out what's going on."

"Taken care of, Doc," said Ned. He and Sid had gone into the exam room with Burl to explain to the doc what had happened to her since she had no memory of it.

"Thank goodness," said Mrs. Tree. "I got to admit, I was pretty scared when I woke up and saw Ned standing over me."

"Thanks a lot," Ned replied.

"You know what I mean, Ned Cochran," said Mrs. Tree. "I'm not used to waking up to see any man standing over me, let alone you, and I still don't remember being drugged last night. Do you think my memory of it will come back?"

"It might," said Doc as he opened the door and asked Nurse Trachea Carmichael to prepare a B12 syringe. "If it does, it may take a few days. Sure, it would be helpful to the sheriff if you could remember who came into your house. Nurse is ready to give you your shot, then you can be on your way."

"Roll up your sleeve as far as you can, please, Mrs. Tree," said Nurse Carmichael. Mrs. Tree watched the whole process, but Ned and Sid turned their heads, exclaiming they hated needles.

"Nurse, please make Mrs. Tree an appointment a week from today," said the doc. "Burl, if you still feel poorly, don't wait a week to come in."

"Tippy and I will keep a close eye on her, doc," said Sid.

When Ned, Sid, and Burl had entered Doc Trueblood's office, his waiting room had been empty. By the time they left, it was full of what looked to be healthy people peering over the tops of their magazines as the three walked past them.

"News travels fast," grumbled Sid.

"Looks like Doc's opened a Chanceville Grapevine Branch," replied Ned as he held Mrs. Tree's elbow and guided her to the truck.

Sid Topp and Burl Tree looked at each other, knowing full well who the founder of this branch was. Gardenia Cochran was quick on the gossip trigger. Next stop, Sheriff Orange's office.

As Ned drove them the few short blocks to the sheriff's office, people who never paid attention when Ned drove by any other day stopped and waved as if Ned was leading the Founder's Day Parade. They were hoping he'd throw some candy their way. More fodder for the grist mill.

"I can't wait to get back to work tomorrow and hear all the brilliant theories about what happened to you, Mrs. Tree," said Sid, shaking his head slowly.

Ned pulled into the parking lot, and Maxine Crabtree appeared before he could shut the engine off.

When Sid opened the passenger side door and helped Mrs. Tree out, Maxine insinuated herself between him and Mrs. Tree.

"I'm here to pray for you, my dear," said Maxine.

"Why would you need to do that?" asked Burl.

"Well, uh, you know, after your ordeal," answered Maxine.

"That won't be necessary. It would be hard for you to know what to pray for since you have no way of knowing what her ordeal is," said Sid as he tried to loosen Maxine's surprisingly strong grip on Mrs. Tree's arm.

"Well, I, uh, you know," sputtered Maxine. "How about just a general prayer?"

Sheriff Yesper Orange came out of his office just in time to help Ned and Sid get Mrs. Tree into the office. Doc Trueblood had had Trachea call ahead to alert the sheriff that they were on their way.

"I'll take it from here, Mrs. Crabtree. Thanks for your help," said the sheriff, who had been watching for them and had seen Maxine Crabtree swoop down on poor Mrs. Tree.

" Can't we have just one little prayer before you go in?" pleaded Maxine.

No one bothered to answer her. They circled around Mrs. Tree and ushered her inside as fast as they could, her feet almost coming up off the sidewalk.

"Well, I never!" shouted Maxine.

"And you never will," muttered Ned as he closed the door behind them.

"If it isn't the Three Musketeers!" shouted Pearly Ringwald, the dispatcher. Sheriff Orange privately thought that the dispatch microphone was the most useless item in the department. He was sure Pearly could be heard all over town without it.

"You three go on in my office. I'll be right back," the sheriff said as he headed down the hall.

The phone began ringing, and Pearly shouted, "Sheriff's office. No, he can't come to the phone right now. He's down the hall taking care of business if you know what I mean."

Even though Mrs. Tree was a little hard of hearing, Pearly's voice made her jump. That was the last thing she needed today. This day had been jumpy enough already.

The sheriff came in from down the hall, shutting the office door with a definite click. He then closed the Venetian blinds to the window that looked out into the hall.

"Seems like a lot of precautions," said Ned. "We're the only ones in here, 'cept for Pearly."

"Pearly has ears like a bat. Sometimes, I think she can read lips, too," replied the sheriff.

"I don't think she's figured out how to listen in through the intercom, but I'm going to switch it off just in case." He turned on the radio that sat on a bookshelf by the door, hoping that the music would help to drown out their voices.

"Boy, do I sound paranoid," said the sheriff, shaking his head. "How you doing, Mrs. Tree? When Trachea called ahead to say you were on your way, it sounded like you've had a rough night and day."

"I'm okay. Doc gave me a B12 shot and said I need to drink lots of water," she replied.

"Let me go ahead and take your statements so you can get some rest," said the sheriff.

"That sounds good, but I'm supposed to stay active this afternoon. I don't think that's going to be easy. I'm feeling a might tuckered out," said Mrs. Tree, yawning.

The sheriff went to the door to ask Pearly to bring Mrs. Tree a glass of water. When he opened it, Pearly nearly fell into the room.

"Please get Mrs. Tree some water, Pearly," said the sheriff.

"See what I mean?" he asked. Ned, Sid, and Mrs. Tree nodded in unison. "Okay, let's get down to business," said the sheriff as he turned up the radio. "Nurse Carmichael told me on the phone that Sid is taking you home to stay with him and Tippy for a few days. I think that's a great idea. I'm hoping we can get this resolved pretty quickly. I know you want to get back home as soon as possible. I will check the Pawn It Off and the That's The Ticket pawn shops here in town and a few others in the vicinity. Maybe this yahoo has tried to pawn or sell those books. Though how he knew they were there is beyond me."

"Both Sid and I felt like we were being watched when we were at the cabin," said Ned. At that moment, Pearly barged into the office without knocking and handing a cup of water to Mrs. Tree.

"Thanks, Mrs. Ringwald," said Mrs. Tree. Pearly nodded, not budging.

"That's all for now, Pearly," said the sheriff. "I'll let you know if we need anything else."

At that, Pearly nodded and mumbled something under her breath, closing the door a little too forcefully and faked stomping down the hall.

After Sheriff Yesper Orange took the statements of Ned, Sid, and Mrs. Tree, he got up, motioned for the others to stay seated, walked quietly to the door, and quickly pulled it open, causing Pearly to lose her balance and nearly fall over. Despite themselves, Ned, Sid, and Mrs. Tree all burst out laughing.

Pearly dwelt in a constant state of frustration when her attempts to find out what was going on were thwarted, which was most of the time. It was probably a good thing she didn't know what was behind the stolen books. She may not have slept a wink for weeks.

22

THE TRANSFORMATION OF PORTER PANDER

Joshua Moot had yet to fully form his plan of how to steal the formula from Porter that he would eventually discover hidden in one of the books he had taken from the cabin. He was the person lurking in the woods around the cabin and had followed Ned and Mrs. Tree to her house, waiting until Ned had left to chloroform that barky dog and the old lady. Moot always kept chloroform in his trunk to quiet pesky dogs when he was breaking into houses under cover of darkness. Once he saw the papers he took from the old bat, he knew who to call to get his hands on the formula mentioned in the papers.

"Pander, Moot here."

"What can I do for you?" asked Porter, who didn't like to beat around the bush like Joshua, who was always working an angle. Get to the point, he thought.

"I saw something in the contract that Bunny drew up and wanted to ask you about it. Can I come over in a few minutes to talk?"

"Can't we do this over the phone?" said Porter, losing patience already. He had never trusted Moot since their high school days. Bunnington had been none too pleased when Moot have moved to Indianapolis and looked him up. He was becoming more and more suspicious of his motives. Even though Mr. Bunnington, whom Porter never called Bunny because he knew Bunnington hated it, had recommended Moot as an investor, there was something inherently shady about that guy. He was sure any money Moot had to invest would be ill-gotten gains.

"Not really," said Moot.

"Fine, come over then."

Soon, Moot was knocking on Porter's door.

"What's so important, Moot?"

"I think you know what I want." Again, beating around the bush.

"I have no idea what you're talking about."

"I want the Quacks formula. I'm cutting Bunny out of the deal, and now I'm cutting you out."

"What do you mean you're cutting me and Bunnington out of the deal?"

"Permanent like. You know."

"You can threaten me all you want. I'm not giving you that formula."

"Now look, Pander. Don't make me rough you up. Hand it over."

"I don't have it."

"Bunny said you did."

"That's a lie. I don't have it, and even if I did, Mr. Bunnington wouldn't tell you its location."

Moot walked over to Pander's desk and started going through his papers, wondering what the formula would look like.

"I told you it's not here. I think you'd better leave."

I'm not leaving without the formula," Moot growled, causing Pander to take a few steps back toward the wall phone. He reached for it.

"Don't even think about calling the police," said Moot, pulling a revolver out of his inside jacket pocket. We're going to your car and take a little drive, and you will keep your mouth shut.

"I'm not going anywhere with you."

Moot grabbed Pander's arm and twisted him around, pushing the gun into his back. "Now calm down and walk to your car like we're just going for a drive. Lock the door. Is your apartment key on your key ring?"

"Yes, but why...?"

"You don't need to know. Let's go."

Pander decided it would be smarter not to resist. This wasn't the brightest choice, as Moot wouldn't likely shoot him in his apartment. But that gun made him too nervous to think straight, so they walked down to his car, where Moot told him to get in the driver's seat.

"Where are we going?"

"Shut up and drive," said Moot, all business for once. "Head east on Brookville Road."

"Where are we going?" What's going on?"

"Shut up and drive until I tell you to stop." They drove to an abandoned farm in Hancock County east of Indianapolis that Moot knew about. "Pull behind that old barn."

"What are we doing here?" asked Porter.

Moot got out and went around the car, aiming the gun at Porter the whole time. He yanked the driver's side door open and pulled him out of the car. He poked Porter in the side with the gun and told him not to make another sound as he marched him over to the barn.

"Turn around, Pander. Hands against the barn wall. I'm giving you one more chance."

"I'm not giving you the formula without Mr. Bennington's permission."

"Don't say I didn't warn you."

Moot then pistol-whipped him until he fell to the ground, trying in vain to protect himself. Moot bent down to feel for a pulse after Porter stopped moving. He detected nothing. Good. Moot didn't want to have to shoot him. Shooting was too quick. He removed Porter's wallet and watch, dragged him deep into the woods, covering him with dead leaves and branches, and then headed back to Porter's apartment to leave his car and search for the formula.

"Goddammit." Moot cursed under his breath, not wanting

Pander's neighbors to hear through the paper thin walls. He had been searching the tiny apartment for two hours without finding the Quacks formula. He went out to Pander's car and searched it. Nothing. While there, he wiped everything he had touched in the car.

Joshua Moot searched three more nights and found nothing resembling a recipe for marshmallow treats. He didn't want to give up, but he had to earn money, and as luck would have it, he'd gotten a call about a job in Nicaragua. He would have to be out of the country for a few months, which didn't make him happy, but it paid well, and he couldn't afford to pass it up, no matter how shady the work might be.

Meanwhile, in the dark woods in Hancock County, a mound of leaves began to rustle, and a wobbly figure crawled to a log and sat on it. Porter held his head in his hands, unable to remember exactly what had happened. His head was pounding so hard he couldn't think. Porter laid down on the log, drifting in and out of consciousness for a whole day. On the second day, the fog had lifted enough for Porter Pander to remember a little bit of what happened, and he knew he had to get back to his apartment and retrieve the formula.

He made his way out of the woods and back to State Road 52, where he stuck his hand out to hitch a ride. Despite his apparent injuries and the disheveled "left for dead" look, a kind couple gave him a lift back to his apartment. They really wanted to take him to an emergency room, but he refused to do that. Since they didn't know him or how he got so beat up, they decided it was best not to argue.

When he entered his apartment using a spare key he kept in his shoe, it didn't take him long to figure out who had ransacked it and what that person was looking for. Still, he was surprised to see his car on the street outside his building. He remembered getting in his car with Moot, but everything got fuzzy afterward. He retrieved a spare set of car keys from the drawer in his bedroom nightstand. You're not as smart as you think you are, Moot, he thought as he loaded up his books and a few personal items and placed them in the trunk of his car, leaving Indianapolis for good. As he was driving south, his head started hurting like it never had before. A little way outside

Chanceville, he saw a narrow grass-covered lane and decided to check where it led. It took him back into thick woods, branches noisily scraping the sides of his car as his vision blurred. He had a hard time staying in the lane. He saw a dark shape ahead that turned out to be an abandoned old cabin. He parked the car, looked around inside, then unloaded his belongings. Some deeply buried instinct of self-preservation told him to drive his car as deep into the woods as he could.

By the time he returned to the cabin, his head was throbbing, and he could hardly see. He felt a tiny pop in his head and thought oh damn, and that was the last thought he had as the man named Porter Pander. His career as High Horse Harry was about to begin.

A hunter reported to Mrs. Burl Tree that he saw an abandoned car in the woods. She called Sheriff Orange, who had it towed and impounded. No one ever claimed it, but the VIN they used to trace ownership helped them solve the mystery later.

23
JOSHUA MOOT FIGURES THINGS OUT

By the time Moot returned to the United States in the spring of 1951, he had found out the owner of Pander's apartment, who assumed he'd abandoned it, cleaned it out, and rented it to someone else. Moot cursed Pander for hiding the formula so well that even God couldn't find it. He still had most of the cash that he'd earned in Nicaragua. He was saving up to retire in Florida someday.

Meanwhile, he got a job driving a Milky Day dairy truck. It paid the bills and allowed him to save a little each payday and add to his retirement fund. His route took him to Mooresville, Martinsville, and Chanceville.

He pulled up to the stop-and-go light at the intersection of Main Street and Main Avenue. Lo and behold, there stood a louder, hairier version of someone who looked much like Porter Pander, but that wasn't possible. Pander was dead. How could anyone survive that beating? Moot parked his truck down the street and returned to the corner where the man he would find out had become High Horse Harry stood.

Moot stood across the street, hoping to get a good look at this fellow's eyes. He would know for sure. Porter Pander had those piercing green eyes. Mr. Jimmy James, one of Moot's milk route customers, happened to be passing by and stopped to say hi to Joshua and ask what he thought of High Horse Harry?

"Who?"

"That's High Horse Harry across the street there, at least that's what we call him. Been here about a year, I guess," said Mr. James. "We have no idea where he came from; he showed up one day and started shouting."

"Interesting," said Moot noncommittally.

"He's spooky looking when you get up close. I guess it's those green eyes," said Mr. James. "Some of us have tried to talk to him, but he doesn't seem to hear us. He's here six days a week from ten in the morning until noon. In his own little world, I reckon."

"I 'spose he seems harmless enough. Guess I'd better get back to my route. Nice talking to you."

"Yep, see you next week," said Jimmy James.

"Sure thing," answered Joshua. He thought the sure thing was that "High Horse Harry" was, indeed, Porter Pander. And that put a smile on his face. It was almost noon. All he had to do was follow Pander wherever he went when he quit shouting on the street corner. Moot got in his truck and moved it to a spot where he could watch Harry's movements. Luckily, Chanceville was the last stop on his route, so he wasn't keeping anyone waiting for their milk order.

Like Mr. James said, promptly at noon, Harry stepped off his crate and started walking toward the west edge of town. Moot put the idling truck in gear and slowly followed Harry out of town. Harry kept walking and walking until he reached a wooded area. It would be hard for Moot to stay out of sight, although Harry didn't seem to notice his surroundings. He only looked straight ahead and paid no attention to barking dogs or kids on bikes. At last, Pander turned down a narrow lane. He made a mental note of where it was and drove on by.

A week later, when Joshua Moot made his stop at Jimmy James' Stop Shop and Pay Market, he heard all about Harry being zapped by lightning.

When he heard about Harry's demise, he returned to the lane he had seen Harry walk down. He drove slowly back and soon came upon the cabin. The first time he went, he was almost caught by a middle-aged man and some old lady. They carried out an official-looking envelope. Maybe those were the contracts he couldn't find in Pander's apartment. As soon as they left, he went into the sleeping room. All he found were those damn books, lots of them stuffed in drawers in the sleeping room. He decided that that was all Pander had bothered to bring along. They must be important or at least worth selling. He put them in some old boxes he had in his truck.

He asked one of his customers about the old lady he saw at the cabin and found out where she lived.

Four days after Harry went up in smoke, a beautiful, brightly painted carousel horse was installed in the front yard of the Blind Poodle Sisters' house. No one in Chanceville ever found where it came from. The sisters were strangely tight-lipped about the whole thing and said it was a "gift." To their everlasting sadness, they never heard from the stranger again.

The last piece of the High Horse Harry Puzzle was the stranger with the melodious voice. It was never discovered that it belonged to Bertram Benedict Bunnington, who had been Porter Pander's attorney. He had quite a fondness for the eccentric inventor. He never trusted Joshua Moot, whom Bunnington was sure had something to do with Porter's transformation into High Horse Harry. He had happened upon him during a business trip to Chanceville, and the voice sounded hoarser (probably all the shouting). Those flashing green eyes under the black, shaggy brows cinched it for Bunnington. Harry was, indeed, what was left of Porter Pander.

He wished he could have saved Porter. Now that that was no longer possible, the least he could do was honor him in the only way he knew how. And that's how the carousel horse that resulted from Bunnington's hobby came to live in the front yard of the Blind Poodle Sisters. Moot had spotted BBB leaving the vicinity of that pink poodle house late one night.

A few days after the horse appeared in front of the Blind Poodle Sisters' house, BBB was found in a burnt car parked next to the woods near the cabin where High Horse Harry lived. The registration in the glove compartment had not been burned. His name was Bertram Benedict Bunnington. Before long, Sheriff Orange would have to decide what to do about tracking down Harry's true identity and who BBB was.

24
BIG TEDDY'S TIP PAYS OFF

Meanwhile, Joshua Moot was lying low for a few days after nearly being caught by Ned and Sid when they came to get Harry's books. He had just pulled out on the highway with his trunk full of books when he saw them turn onto the old lane that led back to the cabin. Moot pulled off at the spot where he had left Bunnington's charred remains in his burnt car and walked back to the woods to spy on the two men. He didn't know who they were and wanted to know if they had suspicions about what was in those books. He couldn't get close enough to hear because of all the racket those damn crows were making, so he decided to go back to his crumby apartment and come up with a plan. He didn't know he was being followed by Big Teddy, who Moot sometimes did "jobs" for. Teddy believed that Moot most likely had done away with Bertram Bunnington, whom Teddy had used as his attorney for his many property holdings.

Big Teddy's twenty-dollar tip to a barmaid who worked at the Down the Upstairs Tavern, where Moot hung out most nights, gave him the scoop on Moot's plans, which he had told the barmaid after one beer too many. Moot was heading up towards northern Indiana, known as the Region, in two days, some malarkey about finding a quiet motel to research a book he was writing. Guess he thought that would impress the barmaid. This would give Big Teddy time to put his plan into action.

25
JOSHUA MOOT FINDS A ROOM

Joshua Moot was ready to get the hell of Dodge. The rent to his furnished apartment was paid through the few days left in the month, so he could walk out with just his personal belongings, which weren't much, and never look back.

Moot had tried several other motels on the lonely stretch of highway connecting Indianapolis to The Region, and strangely, they all seemed to have their no vacancy signs lit up. He got out and went into them anyway, but despite their abandoned look, they all claimed to be full up. So, when Moot pulled his dusty 1930 Studebaker Champion into the parking lot of The Grouse Inn, he was happy to see its vacancy sign lit up. This place could be just the ticket, way out in Nowheresville, he thought as he locked the car, stretched his long legs, and went inside to register for a room.

Joshua pulled off his sunglasses, but it was so dark in the motel office he still couldn't see much. The dust-mote-filled light coming in through the one grimy window made him realize that might be a good thing. He banged the rusty service bell on the counter. No response. He thought he could hear the radio coming from somewhere in the back. He banged on the bell again and waited. As his eyes adjusted to the darkness of the office, he could see all manner of stuffed birds on rickety-looking shelves and a pheasant under a glass dome on a shelf above the Exit sign. Joshua Moot was about to go behind the counter to knock on the door marked Private when it swung open with a rusty creak.

He moved a few steps back as a short owl-like creature emerged from behind the door.

The creature shuffled out, looking as surprised to see Joshua as he was to see her.

"Hi, I'm P-tess Ptarmigan. The second P is silent, and that is the only thing silent about me," she chirped.

"Nice to meet you," said Joshua, pretending to be looking for something in his pockets to avoid shaking her pointy-nailed hand. "Can I get a room?"

"Take your pick. You can probably guess by the looks of the parking lot that we're not exactly chock-full. How long will you be with us, er me?"

"Uh, not sure. Maybe a week?" Moot said, hoping, not too optimistically, that she wouldn't start asking a lot of nosy questions.

"Shouldn't be a problem," she said as she turned a coffee-stained (he hoped those were coffee stains) register around for him to sign.

He had decided to use the name James Morton when he registered and gave his address as the one in Gary where he grew up, never mind that the old house was torn down years ago. He used his own license plate number for now because she might be nosy enough to make sure the plate number matched what he wrote in the register. Anyway, he planned to ditch that old junker as soon as he got the hell out of Birdtown.

"Here you go, Miss Ptarmigan," said Joshua as he turned the register back around.

"Actually, it's Mrs., but you can call me P-tess," she said as she carefully read the information he had filled in.

"This all seems to be in order *James,*" said P-tess, turning her head to one side as she peered up at him through the thick lenses of her glasses.

Was he imagining he heard quotes when she said, "James?" He couldn't afford to let his nerves get the best of him now.

"Now, let's see what room would suit you best," she said as she turned to peruse the pegboard holding the room keys. The board was a sight in itself. Each key was on a fob made of several feathers, beads, and bones.

"I'd like your most private room. I'm researching a book I'm writing and need peace and quiet. Too many people in the house I live in at the moment," said Joshua.

"We have The Fowl Room, The Duck Down Room, The For the Birds Room, The Feather Your Nest Room, and The Come Flock with Me Room. Any one of those would be most suitable for your needs," she said.

"Which one is the farthest away from the main parking lot and office? I don't want to seem anti-social, but it seems to me if there were any noise around here, those two places are where they would be coming from," he said, not holding out too much hope that she would buy any of that story.

P-tess looked up at him and blinked slowly, twice. This trance-like state only added to the uncomfortable but unnamable feeling she gave him. Creepy was the best he could come up with, but that didn't quite capture it. He just wanted to get to his room, close the door behind him, find the formula, and get the hell out of Birdtown for good.

"Oh," said P-tess, seeming to come out of her trance. "Then you might want The Cuckoo Cabin behind the motel at the edge of the woods. It'll cost you more, though. It's $30 a night instead of $20. It has a kitchen, which you might like since you may be here a few days, and the Where It's At Diner is over in Wattsville, about 20 miles down the road."

"That sounds like just the ticket," said Joshua, starting to feel a little more hopeful about things. "Can you give me a special deal if I take it for five days?"

"Hmm," said P-tess, back to blinking again.

"How about $125, cash up front?" asked Moot.

"Okay, but no refund if you leave before the five days are up."

"You drive a hard bargain for someone who seems to be running an empty motel," said Joshua, and as soon as he said that, the room got a whole lot chillier.

"I guess that's okay," she said.

"It does sound like it's just what I need, but I thought I saw another cabin out back. Is it any cheaper?" said Joshua.

"Oh, you mean the Rook's Roost. It would be a little cheaper, but I don't have a bed in there right now. Mice got into the mattress. And we haven't repaired the water pipe that sprung a leak after a hard freeze last winter, so there's no water. Even with your fancy cowboy boots, it's pretty obvious that you're a city slicker," she said as she assessed his get-up.

Joshua was over six feet tall, slender, and always dressed in black. He liked the dramatic effect it gave him.

None of what P-Tess said about Rook's Roost was true. She wouldn't be able to keep an eye on him if he stayed in that cabin. After Big Teddy, who P-tess worked for when he needed some discrete job done, had found out Moot was heading north, he made sure the signs for every motel on the highway between Indy and The Region except for the Grouse Inn all said No Vacancy, which wasn't hard to do because he owned them all. He needed a few legitimate business interests to hide his illegal operations behind. He sent Butch Bird, the great-great-grandson of Robin Bird, founder of Birdtown and the guy who ran the Grouse Inn for him, on a paid vacation to Florida and put P-tess in place as the manager of that crazy motel.

I guess it'll have to be The Cuckoo Cabin, then," said Joshua, reaching for his wallet. He still had most of the three hundred dollars he had taken off the chloroformed Bunnington before setting his car on fire.

Her mood seemed to brighten, and P-tess turned around to get the key marked Cuckoo Cabin.

"Good choice. Pull your car around back to the cabin, and I'll meet you there," she said. Joshua nodded and went to his car, thinking that Little Miss Ptarmigan, with the one silent P, had better be careful not to shit in her nest. He wouldn't have a problem silencing both Ps for her, just like he did with Bunnington and Pander.

He parked the old Studebaker in the small parking spot and followed P-tess up the weedy crushed stone path that led to the cabin. The cabin itself didn't look too bad from the outside. He would be satisfied if it had a bed and a table where he could work. He watched P-tess waddle up the three steps to the cabin's porch.

Joshua Moot stepped inside the cabin behind her and was immediately assaulted by wall-to-wall ticking and cuckooing clocks at asynchronous intervals. Apparently, this woman had no concept of peace and quiet.

"Isn't this something?" asked P-tess.

"It's something all right," answered Joshua. "Remember five minutes ago when I said I needed peace and quiet to do my research?"

"You mean you don't find these cuckoos soothing? You know, like you're in a nice big forest?" asked P-tess, seemingly incredulous at this news.

"In a word, no. Would you allow me to silence all the of the clocks if I promise to start and reset them before I leave?" Moot asked, knowing full well he would stop them but would never start them again. He would be long gone before she discovered that fact.

She was back to the slow blinking again and scratching both double chins as she pondered his request as if he'd asked to cut a hole in the roof to let in more light. While P-tess pondered, Joshua took the opportunity to look around the cabin to see what other treasures it might hold. There was a comfortable-looking double bed in the bedroom and a serviceable-looking kitchen complete with a fairly sturdy-looking table and chairs, which would work fine for his research.

"Do you solemnly swear to wind and reset every single one of them?" said P-tess when she finally stopped blinking and scratching.

"I solemnly swear," said Joshua. He didn't even bother crossing his fingers behind his back. After all, he was way more comfortable with lying than telling the truth.

"Deal," she said.

And at that, he turned quickly on his heels to go outside and get his suitcase and food supplies, wanting to avoid another awkward handshake moment.

P-tess handed him the gigantic key fob with what looked like a turkey feather attached to it and began her waddle back to the office, telling him she would be right back with fresh towels. He was a little skeptical about how quickly "right back" actually meant, as she seemed only to have one speed. Slow.

When he had brought in his food supplies, put them away, and returned to fetch his suitcase, he saw her come moseying back around the corner and ran out to meet her to speed up the towel delivery process.

"Thank you very kindly, Mrs. Ptarmigan," Joshua said as he took the dark brown towels from her. He turned around and quickly returned to The Cuckoo Cabin, trying to avoid another conversation with her. Still, he didn't make his escape fast enough.

Suddenly, she was able to shift into high gear and was right on his heels on the front porch. He tried to block her way to the screen door to the cabin. She was spryer than she looked and managed to zig when he zagged and got her hand on the screen door handle. Still, Joshua could lean against it at an awkward angle and keep her from opening it.

"Sooo, what kind of book are you writing?"

"What? Book? Oh, yeah. Um, it's a history book about Gary, Indiana," he answered, hoping that wasn't a subject she would warm to.

"Oh, I was hoping it would be about birds of Indiana or some such. I'm not from around here but from Chanceville in the southern part of the state. My late husband and I inherited this motel from his Uncle Albert Finch a few years back, so I don't know much about the area," she said. She noticed his eyes narrow a bit when she mentioned her hometown.

"Thanks for the towels. I've got lots of work to do tonight. Got to carry in my research books and cook myself some dinner. Like I said, I've got lots to do," he said when she didn't seem inclined to move off the porch. He didn't want to arouse her suspicions or answer any more of her questions, but he thought Jesus, lady, take a hint. He didn't believe it would be good to ruffle her feathers, so to speak. There was something about her cluelessness he didn't entirely trust.

"Oh, sorry. It's just that I don't often have anyone to talk to since Mr. Ptarmigan died. Guess I kind of got carried away," she said, still not budging.

He was smart enough not to take the bait, giving her the silent treatment, not budging either. He hoped this standoff didn't last all night. Finally, she took the hint.

"Right, yes. I'll just be going. Almost time for my evening programs anyway." And with one last blink, she turned and made her way back to the motel office. She had an important call to make.

26

MOOT UNWINDS

It took Joshua Moot almost half an hour to stop all the cuckoo clocks in the cabin. There were eight clocks alone in the tiny bathroom. After dinner, he began carrying in the boxes of books, ready to start the hunt for the Quacks recipe. Moot cursed out loud when he found those books in "High Horse Harry's" cabin because he remembered seeing them in Pander's apartment and hadn't even thought to look in them. Now he knew that had to be where that crazy s.o.b. had hidden the formula. Moot sat at the table, opened a beer, and began searching. If only Porter Pander had written down the recipe on a piece of paper that he could shake out of the book he had hidden it in, but so far, the shaking had been unproductive. By midnight, he had looked through the first of eight boxes. This search was turning out to be way too tedious. His bleary eyes couldn't focus on the mostly fine print for another minute.

Joshua Moot was asleep almost as soon as his head hit the pillow. Next thing he knew, cuckoo, cuckoo, cuckoo!

"What the hell?" he shouted as he jumped out of bed.

According to the cuckoo clock, it was three in the morning. Moot turned on every light in the cabin as he searched for the offending clock. If he had missed one, it would have still been ticking and cuckooing before he went to bed. He knew he would have heard it. He stood still for a minute and listened. The ticking sounded like it was near the window he had left open by the front door. Sure enough, the biggest clock on the wall was ticking away. Joshua strode over, yanked it off the wall, and stomped it into the floor. At that point, he could have cared less about what that nut case P-tess Ptarmigan thought.

He smoked a cigarette on the front porch to settle his nerves. It took him a while to calm down and get back to sleep. He slept through until morning light when a real bird, a mourning dove, sang its woeful song. He made himself a hearty breakfast for energy and a pot of strong coffee to last the morning. He opened a new pack of cigarettes, put box number two by his chair at the kitchen table, and began day two of his search. After a couple of hours, he took a bathroom break, stepped out on the porch for a stretch, and got some fresh air. He immediately regretted that decision.

P-tess was walking toward the trash cans in the back of The Grouse Inn when she spotted him.

"Good morning. Sleep well?" P-tess asked, looking over the top of her glasses.

"Like a rock," he answered, not wanting to mention the incident with the cuckoo clock.

"Funny. I thought I heard a noise and looked out about three this morning, and all of the lights in the cabin were blazing," said P-tess as she pushed her glasses back up on her nose.

"Oh, yeah. I thought I heard something, too, and got up to have a look around. I didn't see anything, so I went back to sleep. Must have been a raccoon or something."

"Probably," she answered, not seeming too convinced. She was sure she had heard a clock cuckooing and the stomping that followed.

She called Big Teddy last night to let him know "James Morton" was most likely the guy they were looking for. Big Teddy told her to stay in touch and be careful. He told her that "James Morton" would probably have bumped off Porter Pander if lightning hadn't done the job. A few months back, when Teddy was in Bunnington's office to talk about some of his properties, the attorney had to take an urgent call from a client and asked him to step out of the room. He stayed close to the door and thought he heard something about a secret formula and money making plan. Teddy heard just enough to jump to his own erroneous conclusions. He didn't know the attorney suspected Teddy was eavesdropping. When his client got off the line, he kept talking and made up a story about Ruskies and secret formulas, letting Teddy finish the jumping. This small-time crook also didn't know that Bunnington had long been an FBI informant and a plan to catch Big Teddy would soon be in place. They had been on his trail for years, and the net was finally tightening.

"I'll be careful." She promised Teddy as she used a pencil to scratch under the hated, itchy wig she was wearing. She didn't tell Big Teddy that she messed up and mentioned Chanceville or that she planned to do some snooping tonight after dark. She would have to ditch those stupid fuzzy yellow house slippers she was wearing as part of the disguise that Big Teddy insisted she wear. She couldn't skulk around noiselessly in those scuffy things. Big Teddy wouldn't have liked her plan, not one single bit.

It took Moot the rest of the afternoon and most of the evening to go through two more boxes. Still nothing. Three boxes down, five to go. He wondered if good old Porter had made the whole thing up, and that recipe might have gone up in smoke, like High Horse Harry.

Moot was never known for his patience, and what little he had was drying up quickly. He was going to step out on the porch for one last smoke and call it a night, start fresh in the morning. If another clock went off in the middle of the night, he thought he might lose it altogether.

It was almost midnight when P-tess saw the lights go out in the Cuckoo Cabin. She decided to wait another half an hour to make sure James, or whoever he was, was sound asleep. She couldn't stand wearing that itchy wig for one more minute, so she took it off and tied a headscarf tightly beneath her first chin so that none of her bleached blond hair peeked out, but not until she had a good scratch. As P-tess was changing out of her fuzzy slippers and putting on her Keds, the phone in her living quarters rang. She decided not to answer it. It was probably Big Teddy, and she didn't want to have to tell him that she still had nothing to report, so she just let it ring. She stood up and wiggled her toes in the Keds. It felt good to have that support. Throwing those stupid house slippers in the trash also felt immensely satisfying. They were over the top, like most of Teddy's ideas.

There was a full moon tonight, but it was cloudy, so she decided to take a small flashlight just in case things got interesting. On second thought, she could take the big one in case she needed to defend herself if James caught her snooping around. She had hoped to be able to snoop if he went out for supplies, but he came pretty well stocked up, so no such luck. She would have to wing it, so to speak.

P-tess started by checking out the car. She used the flashlight to check out the trunk. Nothing unusual there: a ratty old blanket, a bald spare tire, and a tire iron. Closing the trunk lid as quietly as possible, she used the flashlight to peer into the car's back seat. She was afraid if she opened the door, the dome light would come on, and he might see it. There was not one single thing in the back of the car. She did the same with the front seat. All she could see was a crumpled cigarette package on the passenger floorboard.

She could see a matchbook on the dash in front of the steering wheel, so she tiptoed around to get a better look. That was when a hound dog started baying, probably at a treed raccoon. She quickly knelt beside the driver's door, out of the line of vision from the cabin, and held her breath. After what seemed like an hour, she slowly rose up just enough to peer over the car's hood to see if there were any lights on in the cabin. It was still dark inside. Thank goodness that dang hound had stopped its baying. When she stood all the way up, her knees started popping, sounding like firecrackers going off in the silence of the night.

When she could get the light's angle from the flashlight just right, she could see the matchbook was from Tony's 24-Hour Mechanic and

Roadhouse down in Chanceville. Aha! She nearly exclaimed out loud. She knew she had been right about him shifting uneasily when she mentioned her crazy hometown. P-Tess turned the flashlight off and pondered whether she should try to go inside and see if there were actually books in all of those boxes he had carried in, as he claimed. Something told her not to risk it. One close call a night was enough for her. She kept hearing Big Teddy's voice in her head, telling her to be careful. She would have to wait for another chance; maybe he would go into town for more cigarettes soon. Then, she could look around in the cabin while he was gone.

P-tess didn't realize that Moot was awakened by that damn dog and had gotten up to look out the window. He saw a light fluttering around his car. Oh, she was cruisin' for a bruisin' for sure. He continued to look out the window until he saw her stubby figure waddle back to the motel before he went back to bed. God, he hoped he would find that recipe tomorrow.

Joshua Moot finally gave up returning to sleep at 4 a.m. He got up and made a pot of strong coffee. While the coffee was perking, Moot turned on the porch light, stepped outside, and peed on the pine needles beside the steps. He hoped the old coot was watching. If she said one word to him, she was a goner. He could probably hide her body in the woods where no one would ever find her. But this time, he would make sure his victim was dead. He wouldn't make the same mistake he'd made with Pander.

Was there anyone out there who would even care if she went missing?

He resumed his place at the table armed with coffee and his last pack of cigarettes. He would have to make a trip into town soon. But he hated giving P-nosy a chance to return to the snoop train. He decided to wait for breakfast for a while. His stomach was churning up a lot of acid, so he poured extra milk into his coffee. The next box he opened had fewer books than the others. But the books it held were huge. His head began to throb as he opened the first one.

27
P-TESS TAKES A P-TUMBLE

wo hours later, he got up from the table to take a break. He rubbed his temples, then his aching back, and cursed Porter Pander to hell and back. He thought that if Pander weren't already dead, I'd kill you again, hoping he would not go blind from all this reading. He picked his pack of cigarettes up off the table and realized he'd already smoked the last one. He crumpled it up and threw it across the room, hitting the pile of the smashed cuckoo clock on the floor.

He knew he couldn't function without cigarettes, so he would have to go into Birdtown and pick some up. He had undoubtedly underestimated his nicotine needs. Come to think of it, he'd better get some more coffee, too. Before he left, he strung a piece of thin wire from the smashed-up cuckoo clock on the screen door handle, connecting it to the latch on the inner door so he could tell if old Snoopy Drawers had tried to take a look-see.

The minute his car disappeared down the highway, P-tess high-tailed it to the Cuckoo Cabin. She had been watching when he peed off the front porch. She allowed as how he was taunting her and decided not to take the bait. She was also smart enough to figure that he had rigged the door to test for intruders. She made her way around the back of the cabin and brushed the leaves off an in-ground door leading to a cellar. She had brought her flashlight and switched it on as she closed the cellar door above her.

She crossed the dirt floor to the rickety stairs, hoping they would hold her weight. It took all her inconsiderable strength to push up the door in the cabin's floor. She had begun to think that character had put something on top of the door. Huffing and puffing, she could finally push the door up enough to wedge her body between the door and the floor to find some leverage in opening it all the way. She ended up on her hands and knees on the cabin floor.

She crawled over to a chair and pulled herself up, then walked over to the table and began looking through the box that was open. Books? Maybe he wasn't lying. Perhaps he was doing research. She pulled a book out of the box and looked at the title. This was a Russian novel, Crime and Punishment. Didn't look much like an Indiana history book. Maybe Big Teddy was right. Perhaps he was a commie spy looking for the formula for invisibility and radar-repelling paint to coat the Ruskies' spy planes. Big Teddy had "associates" in Chicago who would pay big money for that formula.

She heard a noise. She hadn't heard the car return. But the hair standing on the back of her neck told her someone was out there, and that tall drink of water seemed just sneaky enough to have doubled back to spy on her – spying on him. She laid the open book on the table and scampered to the open cellar door. She tripped over the throw rug and plunged headlong into the darkness, hitting the dirt floor and knocking herself out cold.

Joshua felt the ker-thud as he was quietly stepping onto the porch. He yanked open the screen door, forgetting about the wire. Moot saw the open cellar door and rushed to peer down into its gaping maw. He grabbed the flashlight on the floor and shone it into the cellar.

There lay P-tess in a crumpled heap. Joshua cautiously made his way down the steps. When he shined the light on her face, she didn't move. Out cold. The cellar ceiling was so low he couldn't stand up straight. She looked different to him. He couldn't quite place what it was until he saw what he thought was a big furry rat by the steps. He realized it was a wig. She was actually a blond. Her own hair was twisted around and pinned flat to her scalp. Weird.

Joshua shined the flashlight around the cellar. He found what looked like the outside door to the cellar. He stepped around P-tess and made his way over to that door, pushing on it, testing to see if he could open it. It opened easily, and behind him, he heard a groan. P-Tess was moaning and trying to get up. He shuffled over and put his cowboy boot on her chest. Her eyes flew open in a panic, unable to understand what was happening to her. In the aftermath of the blow to her head, she passed out again.

Joshua realized she wasn't going anywhere, and even if she tried, she was no match for him, concussion or not. He found a shovel leaning against a wall. He carried it up the stairs to the outside and slid it through the handles of the double cellar door. He felt his back pop as he stood straight up again and returned to the cabin's front door. He rightly assumed that the throw rug had tripped her up. He closed the door in the floor to the cellar, spread the carpet over it, and then set the kitchen table on top of it, effectively trapping her.

As badly as he wanted those cigarettes, Joshua had made a U-turn after driving a few miles down the road. He was itching for a chance to catch P-tess in the act of snooping. He had parked the car down the road and was quietly stepping on the porch when he heard what he now knew was P-tess hitting the cellar floor.

This should work out fine. Moot didn't have a problem leaving her down there to rot. He would move into one of the other cabins or rooms and search for the Quacks recipe. He went back outside, found a wheelbarrow full of wood, and parked it on the outside door to the cellar just for good measure. That would keep her down there.

Joshua returned to the road to get his car and the cigarettes he craved. When he returned, he decided to move into Rook's Roost, even if he had to drag a mattress over there. It was more hidden than the Cuckoo Cabin. He didn't want to be there when P-tess came around and had to listen to her begging him to let her out. And he didn't think it would be a good idea to stay in one of the other motel rooms. He stopped at the office to be sure the "No Vacancy" sign was switched on, got the key for Rook's Roost, then pulled around the back of the motel next to it and went inside to check it out.

There was a fully made up bed. Moot walked over to the kitchen sink and turned on the water faucet, which, after a few seconds of sputtering, let forth with a clear, sparkling stream of water.

"Well, that little liar," he muttered to himself.

Best of all, there were no damn cuckoo clocks. Moot realized that P-tess hadn't wanted him in this cabin because she couldn't keep an eye on him from the motel. He returned to the Cuckoo Cabin and brought his clothes and supplies to Rook's Roost.

Joshua wasn't paying enough attention to realize that Crime and Punishment was open, and he hadn't opened it when he finished looking through War and Peace. He stuck a napkin in for a bookmark, threw it in the box, loaded it in the car, and returned for the rest of the unopened ones he still had to go through.

28

JOSHUA AND BIG TEDDY MAKE DISCOVERIES

After he returned with cigarettes and coffee, Moot was able to pull the car back into a small clearing on the far side of the cabin where it would be hard to see from the motel or the road. By the time he finished all of that, he was starving. He heated up two cans of Hormel's Chili and ate a whole row of crackers from the Nabisco Saltines tin. He finished that off with two Hostess Twinkies and a second glass of milk. Of course, all of that made him sleepy. He needed a nap after having lost sleep the night before. He cleared the dishes off the table, placed Crime and Punishment, unopened, on top of the stack that he unloaded from the box, had one more cigarette, and went to lie on the bed *that didn't exist*. He was quickly out like a light.

He didn't see that he was being watched while moving, although P-tess was still lying motionless on the cellar floor. Big Teddy had gotten worried when he could not reach her last night or this morning. He decided to drive down from Chicago and see for himself what was going on. He left his Caddy at the Where It's At Diner (another one of his holdings) over in Whatsville and borrowed the manager Slim Jimmy's car. He didn't want to leave a trail.

Big Teddy couldn't see Joshua Moot's car tucked away in the woods, and all seemed quiet around the motel. He began his search for P-tess in the office and the private quarters of the motel. Nothing. Again. Nothing. No P-tess. He noticed the keys to Rook's Roost and the Cuckoo Cabin were missing. He knew James had been staying in Cuckoo Cabin, so why was the key to Rook's Roost not hanging there? He walked back out to the highway and entered the woods so he could come up behind Cuckoo Cabin. This may not have been his best idea because even though it was summer, many fallen leaves covered the woods' floor, and his footsteps sounded pretty crunchy. The first thing he saw was the shovel Moot had placed through the door handles and the wheelbarrow of wood parked on top of the outside cellar door. Great. He would move it and sneak into the cabin that way. As soon as he opened the door, he wished he had brought a flashlight from the motel office. He crept down the steps, closing the outside door behind him. In the darkness, the first thing he did was trip over P-tess.

Umph," she said, waking up for the first time since Joshua had left her there to die.

"What the hell?" said Big Teddy.

"Is that you, Teddy?" asked P-tess.

"P-tess?"

"What are you doing here?" she asked as she struggled to sit up, her head throbbing.

"I came to check on you. You weren't answering the phone," said Big Teddy as he reached down to help her get on her feet. With her padding P-tess was built like Big Teddy who was as short as he was wide, so they could stand up quite comfortably in the cellar.

"Jesus God, my head is pounding," she said, gingerly feeling for bumps on her head. "Ouch! There is a big knot on the back of my head."

"How in the Sam Hill did you end up down here?" asked Big Teddy.

"I remember climbing the stairs and pushing up the door into the kitchen. I managed to pull myself up, and then I walked over to the table and looked through Morton's so-called research books. When I heard him stepping onto the porch, I turned around to get back into the cellar. I think I tripped over the rug and fell down the stairs. I remember someone shining a light in my eyes, but I must have passed out again. I had a flashlight with me. I'm not sure what happened to it."

"Maybe Morton found it, and he shined the light in your eyes," offered Big Teddy. "I'm pretty sure he found you because someone parked a wheelbarrow full of wood on the outside cellar door." Even though he didn't have a lot of practice, sometimes Big Teddy could come to the correct conclusion.

"Thank God you found me," said P-tess.

Big Teddy moved over to the cellar steps that led up into the cabin, climbed a few steps, and pushed on the cellar door in the cabin floor. It only budged a little.

"I think we should go out the outside door and move that wheelbarrow and shovel back, so James won't suspect you're not in the cellar anymore," said Big Teddy.

"I'm pretty sore all over. I hope I can make it up those stone steps," P-tess said.

"I'll go up first. That way, I can help you up," he said.

After much huffing, puffing, tugging, and pulling, Big Teddy extricated P-tess from the cellar. Even though it was hazy, she squinted in the daylight after being in the cellar for several hours. Big Teddy replaced the wheelbarrow and shovel, and then they checked out the cabin, finding it empty.

" Let's go out on the porch so you can get some fresh air. Wow, that's quite a shiner you've got there, honey," said Big Teddy when he finally got a look at P-tess, who had grabbed her wig from the cellar floor and was gingerly trying to put it back on her head.

"Let me have that damn thing," he said as he grabbed it from her hands and threw it into the trees. "I think the time for disguises has come and gone."

"Good. I hate that thing," P-tess said, wincing; even smiling hurt. "Maybe some birds can use it to make nests."

Before returning to the office, they set up Cuckoo Cabin the way they needed to carry out their plan.

While all this was happening with P-tess and Big Teddy, Joshua Moot had awakened from his nap with a belly full of gas and a sour taste in his mouth. He opened a bottle of beer, took a big, long swig, and let out a long, satisfying belch. Then Moot lit a cigarette as he went outside to take a big piss off the front porch. Feeling better, he returned and sat down at the kitchen table. He guessed he'd better get back to work. He glanced at his watch and realized he'd slept for two hours. This day was turning out to be a total bust.

He opened Crime and Punishment, where he had shoved the napkin between the pages, and started to read.

"Son of a bitch!" he shouted as he pounded his fist on the table. "There it is. That's it!"

Pander had written the recipe in the marginalia of the enormous tome. Hiding it in plain sight. Moot carefully tore out that page of the book and jumped up from the table. He hadn't unpacked his suitcase, so he pitched it in the car, along with his beer and cigarettes. He tucked the recipe safely in his front shirt pocket. He forgot to grab the contract that Bertram Benedict had drawn up for him and Porter Pander to form a company and share the profits for Quacks, which Joshua Moot was sure would be worth millions of dollars. He left the boxes of books in the cabin and threw the ones still in the Studebaker into the woods. No one would connect them to him. He didn't ever want to read a book again. Besides, he would have enough money to hire someone to read for him as soon as the Quacks marshmallow treats shaped like little ducks started selling.

After everything was loaded in the car, his curiosity got the better of him, and he walked over to the Cuckoo Cabin to see if he could hear any commotion coming from the cellar. He wasn't particularly quiet, so P-tess and Big Teddy heard him coming. They could see Joshua heading around to the back of the cabin, presumably checking out the wheelbarrow, and then heading back to the front of the cabin and went inside.

Big Teddy whispered his plan to P-tess, and they quietly made their way to the back side of the cabin and peeked around. They saw the man who called himself James, who Big Teddy knew as Joshua Moot, step up onto the porch. Teddy drew his own stub-nosed pistol and motioned for P-tess to follow him.

When they stepped on the porch, they could see him looking at the rug placed over the opening to the cellar in the kitchen.

"Hold it!" growled Big Teddy.

While Joshua stared wide-eyed at Big Teddy's gun. Teddy kept poking him in the chest with it until he took one step back too many and landed at the bottom of the cellar stairs with a satisfying thud.

"You stay up here," said Big Teddy to P-tess, grabbing the flashlight from the table and carefully descending the cellar stairs. Joshua was lying on the floor with his neck bent at an awkward angle. Teddy felt for a pulse. Nothing. While holding the gun on Joshua's still body, he searched his pockets for some identification. He found that page from the book and kept Moot's wallet, which had the last of his cash. Moot was a goner, all right. Too bad.

"He's okay. Just out cold. We'd better get out of here. He'll probably come around soon," he lied, closing the cellar door and putting the rug and table back over it. "We'd better get out of here before that happens. Let's go back to the office, and I'll pay you." As he was reaching into his inside jacket pocket, he realized she could be a witness to murder if any of this came to light.

"This is for you with much thanks," he said, handing her an envelope nicely stuffed with cash. "There's a little extra there for "hazard" pay.

"Thanks, Big Teddy. It's been a wild ride. Give me some time to settle my nerves, and I'll be ready for another assignment if you need me," she said, caressing the envelope as if it were a beloved pet.

"Maybe we should go back and check on Moot," suggested Teddy.

"Good idea," said P-tess, smelling a rat. "I'm right behind you." Teddy thought she was falling right into his plan.

"First, I'm going to check on that cellar door around back," he said.

The minute he went around the back, P-tess ran down the porch to her car. She'd had the foresight to leave a spare set of keys under the floormat. All of her actual identification was safely locked away in her trunk. She sped away just as Teddy was coming around the corner of the office. "Damn you! I'll find you," he yelled, shaking his fist at the car as it screeched onto the highway. He'd never find her. Her real name was Sharon Martin, FBI Field Agent, and the car she was driving belonged to the FBI.

Big Teddy didn't have any time to waste. He picked up the copy of *Crime and Punishment* and stuck the page with the recipe on it back in the book. He was satisfied that he wasn't leaving anything behind to incriminate himself. Still, he'd call his "cleaners" to take care of the "item" in the cellar. Then all would be in readiness for Butch Bird's return to his hotel from Florida in a couple of days after Big Teddy gave him the green light to come back to Indiana. Meanwhile, the NO VACANCY sign would stay lit, and the office would remain closed.

He was itching to return to Chicago and peddle his recipe to the highest bidder. His big plan was to sell his holdings here in the good old U S of A and retire in Cuba.

The minute Sharon Martin got to Indianapolis, she stopped for gas. She used the station's restroom to change from her costume into her "civilian" clothes, which she kept in her trunk. She found a pay phone, reversed the charges, and called her contact, Agent Russell Ruby, at the FBI Chicago Headquarters. It took quite a while to debrief him. Now he knew Big Teddy would soon be shopping that formula around, and they could bust him with espionage charges and, from what Sharon Martin had said, possibly the murder of Joshua Moot. They hadn't been able to pin him down on any of his other illegal activities. He had learned a lesson from Al Capone and always paid his taxes. When they later found out that the invisibility and radar-repellent paint was actually a recipe for some kind of gooey marshmallow candy, that fact was irrelevant, though pretty hilarious. Big Teddy thought he was selling a valuable secret to the Ruskies. Unbeknownst to him, he would be shopping his formula to Russell Ruby, whose name and number P-tess had given to him as a possible buyer.

Before she got back on the road to Chanceville, she stopped at Al Green's Drive-In. She treated herself to their famous giant breaded tenderloin sandwich. Feeling proud of what she had accomplished, she enjoyed every self-righteous bite. She doubled her pleasure by imagining Big Teddy calling Agent Ruby, and effectively setting his own trap.

29
BIG TEDDY MEETS THE RUSKIES

Back in Chicago, Big Teddy met his associate, as he thought of him, in a greasy spoon on the Southside.

Big Teddy had wanted to meet in a little hole-in-the-wall place in Chinatown near where the Dan Ryan was being constructed. He loved Chinese food almost as much as he loved his Cuban cigars. His associate nixed that idea immediately, reminding him that it would be best for them not to stick out like sore thumbs when they had their meeting.

I've got your grandma's long-lost recipe," said Big Teddy, who always talked out of the side of his mouth as if the walls had ears. In his line of business, that could very well be true.

"Here's a book I think you would find interesting," said Big Teddy after the waitress brought their blue-plate specials of Beef Manhattans. He shoved *Crime and Punishment* with the handwritten copy of the recipe tucked inside over toward his colleague. He kept the torn page out of the book for himself as extra insurance.

"Mmm," said Russell Ruby, his mouth full of mashed potatoes. Big Teddy avoided looking at Russell when he ate; his manners were not up to Big Teddy's fastidious habits, who wiped his mouth with his napkin after every bite he took, preserving the tidiness of his pencil-thin mustache.

Russell did not look at the book until he had wolfed down his meal, after which he let out a huge and personally satisfying belch.

"I thought we were supposed to be inconspicuous," said Big Teddy.

"Everyone belches," said Russell, neglecting to wipe a glob of gravy off his untrimmed mustache. He leaned back and loosened his belt a notch. Russell opened the book and picked up the copied recipe. He stared at the paper for a long time, feigning interest in what he was sure was some sort of candy recipe. It really didn't matter what the recipe was for. It only mattered that Big Teddy believed it to be something valuable he could sell to the Russians.

"This looks like the real thing, all right," said Russell after slurping up the last drop of his strong black coffee. "I need to call my business partner, but I feel confident telling you we have a deal."

Big Teddy let out a long, low sigh of relief. Sold on his first try! He couldn't wait to make his flight reservation to Cuba.

"So what's the next step?" he asked.

"I'm going to go out to the phone booth and call my boss," said Russell, pointing out the window. "If he trusts my personal authentication of this recipe and we can agree on a price, then we can make the sale today."

"Terrific," said Big Teddy, already mentally spending the money.

"You give me a price, and I'll run it past him," said Russel Ruby.

Big Teddy had thought about this a lot. He knew from his friends in Cuba that the Cuban peso had the same value as the US dollar. He would still have his properties as security. If things went well, he could sell them off gradually to supplement his income, sort of his retirement plan. He didn't want to seem greedy but knew he had something valuable and wouldn't settle low. If they didn't want to meet his price, he had other associates who knew people who also knew people.

"Come on, don't take all day. I got other fish to fry," said Russell, eyeing the pie case and thinking a big slice of apple pie would go down good about now. Instead, he just had his coffee cup refilled, wanting to avoid causing any delays and making Teddy suspicious.

Big Teddy was beginning to sweat. He took out his linen handkerchief and patted his forehead.

"I think this recipe is worth half a million cool ones," said Big Teddy.

Russell spit his coffee all over the table and onto Big Teddy's spotless white shirt. He thought he should get an Oscar for this. It didn't matter what price this schmuck named, he wasn't getting one red cent, but still, it was fun to play it out. There was something about the arrogance of this guy that made Russell enjoy reeling him in. He was especially looking forward to seeing the look on the face of this chump when he realized he was busted.

"You have got to be pulling my leg," said Russell. "Seriously, what is your rock bottom price?" He watched Teddy assess the damage to his shirt.

Big Teddy knew he would have to come down, but he wasn't willing to come down much.

"I'm not happy about this, but I'll settle for $475,000, rock bottom," he said with more bravado than he was actually feeling.

"Get serious, buddy," said Russell.

Big Teddy examined his well-manicured nails, pretending to be agonizing over his next move. His actual rock bottom was $400,000, but why go there too soon?

"Okay, $450,000," he said, sighing heavily.

Russell was tired of toying with this guy. He was ready for the unveiling, so to speak.

"Fine, I'll run it past Vladi... er, my boss. Don't get your hopes up. You'll probably be able to hear him laughing from here," Ruby said.

Russell went out to the pay phone to call his boss to give their approximate arrival time in a pre-arranged location. He also called his wife to ask if she needed him to bring anything home for dinner. Mrs. Ruby was expecting their fourth child and requested chocolate ripple ice cream for dessert. With each child, she craved a different flavor of ice cream. They had a nice chat about the best place to buy said ice cream. Might as well let the gangster sweat a little longer.

He could see from the phone booth that Teddy was watching from the diner, so he made a big show of gesticulating and yelling after the missus had hung up. He slammed the phone down, lit a cigarette, and stomped back in.

"It was a hard sell, but he's willing to go $425,000. We have to go meet him; he wants to see the goods. Of course, he wants to verify the recipe before laying out that much moolah," said Russell. "Leave your car here; I'll bring you back to get it later. We're going to the west side."

"Is that the bottom dollar?" said Teddy, not too successfully hiding the smirk on his face.

"I had to fight like hell to get that. He was about ready to call the deal off," answered Russell. "Let's go. He won't wait around forever. He's on his way to pick up the cash and will meet us in half an hour."

They got in Russell's beat-up sedan from the FBI's carpool for undercover ops and headed for an industrial district. He pulled into an abandoned warehouse lot and shut off the engine. As soon as Big Teddy stepped out of the car, two more undercover agents stepped out of a black limousine.

Big Teddy was thinking about the money, making him slow on the uptake. He said, "Guess it takes a lot of people to carry that much cash." He shifted nervously from one foot to the other when he realized no one was laughing at his joke.

Russell handed the recipe to a tall blond man in an expensive-looking suit, who stared at it for a long time. He then snapped his fingers for one of his associates to hand him a battered-looking briefcase.

"And what exactly are you claiming this recipe is for?" asked the blond man.

"It's a recipe to make fighter jets invisible and allow them to go undetected on radar. I think the Commies will find it quite valuable," answered Big Teddy out of the side of his mouth. He didn't realize that answer said in front of witnesses would help to seal the deal in more ways than one.

"Count the money," Russell told him after the blond put the recipe in his inside jacket pocket and handed the briefcaseover to Teddy.

Teddy had no idea how much $425, 000 weighed, but the briefcase had a nice heft to it. As soon as he opened the briefcase and saw it was filled with newspapers cut into bill-sized chunks, he dropped it. Agent Ruby grabbed his wrists and cuffed him.

"Theodore Munson, you are under arrest for acts of espionage against the government of the United States of America and the murder of Joshua Moot," said Agent Ruby.

Big Teddy had counted on the cleaners to take care of any evidence he might have left behind at the Grouse Inn. Thanks to Sharon Martin, the FBI got there first, his fingerprints were everywhere.

Of course, Teddy yelled and sputtered as they put him in the back of the limo driven by the tall blond agent. But in the end, Big Teddy knew that his career as a spy was over. He would have plenty of time in jail to figure out who had snitched him out. But luckily for Sharon Martin, he was small-time and didn't have the outside connections to retaliate the way he would have liked. The Quacks formula would have a very different future than Theodore "Big Teddy" Munson had imagined.

30

THE SECRET OF THE QUACKS

Sheriff Orange was contacted by FBI agent Russell Ruby, who filled him in about HHH being Porter Pander and that Joshua Moot had invested some money so Porter could develop his recipe for the yellow duck-shaped marshmallow candies. They were going to call them Quacks. They were able to figure out some of this information on their own from the contract they had found in Mrs. Tree's cabin and, thanks to Sharon Martin's good work, had recovered more evidence from Moot's car trunk. The contract also showed that BBB was the attorney for this enterprise. That's all they really knew. Russell Ruby, Sharon Martin's supervisor at the FBI, had filled Sheriff Orange in on what happened to Moot, whom they had found dead in the cellar of the Cuckoo Cabin before Big Teddy's cleaners got there, just as Sharon Martin had suspected. Agent Ruby asked that the sheriff not share it with the people of Chanceville. He didn't want to take a chance on blowing Sharon Martin's cover. The good, the not-so-good, and the mediocre citizens of Chanceville didn't need to know everything. Besides, they were good at filling in the blanks simply by starting with a fact or two.

31

GOSSIP CENTRAL STRIKES AGAIN

As soon as her black eye healed enough to be covered up with makeup, Sharon and her husband, Marten Martin, went for breakfast at the Tip Topp Diner. It was time to find out what the people of Chanceville thought they knew. They were never disappointed at Gossip Central. She was happy to be back home with her husband and be rid of the prosthetic makeup, wig, and the "fat suit" that made up her disguise. She was actually a petite, quite attractive blond.

Everyone was talking about the burned-out car with the charred remains inside. And Mrs. Tree's mysterious visits to Doc Trueblood and Sheriff Yesper.

"Hiya, Sharon. Hiya Marten," said Cora Jean, managing to pop her gum between every word. No one in the Tipp Topp could figure out how she never bit her tongue. "Good to have you back, Sharon. You've missed all of the excitement."

"Sounds like it," said Sharon, exchanging sly looks with her husband. "I heard about Harry from Marten, and the burned-up car that has appeared. Seems like lots of people are burning up around here."

"Sure is weird. I'd better take your order. Sid's giving me the evil eye. Looks like lots of people are waiting to get their coffee refilled," said Cora Jean, adding another stick of Juicy Fruit before she took their order.

About that time, Ned Cochran and Sheriff Orange came in and sat down at the counter. They had just come from the meeting at the sheriff's office, where they had looked at the documents with BBB's name on them that were also in the glove compartment and the possible connection to High Horse Harry. In that meeting, they had just started talking when the sheriff received a call from Russell Ruby, who filled him in on the connection between Joshua Moot and HHH, whose name was actually Porter Pander, the other name on the contract. Agent Ruby did not reveal the name of his field agent who had been on the case. He was sending someone else to collect the remains of BBB and HHH from the sheriff's evidence locker.

Ned and Sheriff Orange were taking their first sips of coffee when Tarsal Henley walked in. Great, thought Ned. But he knew he couldn't escape Tarsal forever.

"What can I get you?" asked Sid as Tarsal sat down at the opposite end of the counter from Ned.

"I'll have the #2 eggs over-easy, venison sausage, and coffee. Thanks, Sid. I heard you found a mobster in that burnt car out on Old County Road."

Sharon and Marten's ears perked up.

"Not exactly," said the sheriff. "Here we go," he side-mouth whispered to Ned, who nodded.

"It's true. That's what I heard," said Tarsal.

"I'm not saying you didn't hear that, Tarsal. It's just not true," said the sheriff, who knew Tarsal was fishing.

Marten took the sugar shaker away from Sharon, who was so intent on the conversation that she kept pouring sugar into her coffee cup. She took a sip and made a face.

"Cora Jean, can you get me a new cup of coffee? There's something wrong with this one," said Sharon.

"Sure thing," said Cora Jean. She winked at Marten. She had seen him take the shaker away from Sharon.

"Who was it then?" asked Tarsal, slurping his coffee loudly. He knew that irritated Ned to pieces.

"No one from around here," said the sheriff, knowing full well that would not satisfy the ever-curious Tarsal Henley.

"I heard he was from Chicago," said Tarsal, giving Ned the triumphant look of a know-it-all. But Ned could care less about what Tarsal thought he knew, which was never as much as he thought it was.

"You need to find another source for your information," said Sheriff Orange. "Come on, Ned. I'll give you a lift to your car."

"Hey, Sheriff O, I heard you found out who High Horse Harry was," shouted Tarsal as the sheriff followed Ned out the door.

"Sure did," the sheriff answered, closing the door behind him.

Everyone in the diner burst out laughing. That was the second time that week Tarsal Henley had been cut down to size. Tarsal's track record indicated that it probably wouldn't be the last.

"Shut up," said Tarsal to no one in particular.

32
AUNT PINEY

Sam Chance, owner and publisher of the Chanceville Examiner, hadn't had time to think about the anonymous letter he had received a few weeks ago when all this High Horse Harry business was happening. He was kept busy reporting on the mystery of Harry.

On an October morning chilled by rain, Mr. Chance, great grandson of Arnold Chance, found another envelope slid under the door of the newspaper office. It contained a letter reminding him of the lovelorn column idea. This time, it included a number for a post office box over in Carp, a little town about twenty minutes east of Chanceville. He was asked to send a reply addressed to Aunt Piney. He made himself a strong pot of coffee and sat down to mull it over. It wasn't a bad idea. Circulation had been up since Harry's gruesome demise. This could help keep the numbers up, even keep them going up.

He wrote back saying he would put a notice in next Wednesday's paper announcing "Aunt Piney's Advice to the Lovelorn," which would start in two weeks. He asked that Aunt Piney contact him so he could set her up on payroll, but he also said there would be a two-month trial period to see if the column worked out. He was extremely curious about who Aunt Piney was, but he didn't have time to drive over to Carp and stake out the post office boxes.

True to his word, Sam put an announcement in the paper on Wednesday asking people to send their letters in care of Aunt Piney to the Chanceville Examiner. The first letters came in on Friday. There were fifteen of them. He read them all for content. He couldn't take a chance of having anything inappropriate appearing in the paper, especially since he didn't know who Aunt Piney was. The letters were all anonymous, but he could make some good guesses about the identity of the writers. No one in Chanceville believed a secret was meant to be kept.

Aunt Piney had not made an appearance, so he sent the letters to the post office box over in Carp, telling her to have her answers back by the following Friday. He would run the column every other Monday which was usually a low pick-up day for non-subscribers.

The first column was a big hit. How could it not be with letters like this?

> *Dear Aunt Piney,*
>
> *Three months ago, my husband went out for a loaf of bread. The day after he left, I went to the store and bought my own bread. I wanted to make a damn sandwich. Do you think he will be back?*
> *Signed,*
> *Tired of Waiting in Chanceville*

———

> *Dear Tired,*
> *Yes, I believe he will definitely be coming back. Sometimes, it's hard to find just the right loaf. Leave the light on.*
> *Best of luck,*

Aunt Piney

———

Dear Aunt Piney,
I'm in love with my handsome boss. I'm sure he loves me
too, but he's very shy. I leave him little notes written in my
signature red ink with little hearts dotting the eyes, so I'm sure
he knows who the notes are from, although he's never
mentioned them. He is single, so don't think I'm a home
wrecker. I occasionally see him at the Tipp Topp Diner with a
woman I assume is his cousin. He doesn't have a sister. They
appear to be very close as they seem so affectionate with each
other. I keep searching the drawers in my desk in the
desperate hope I will find a note from him. He must be hiding
them really well. What should my next step be? I don't want to
lose my job or make it awkward between us.

Signed,
Love Sick at Work

———

Dear Sick,
You should ask him directly if he is in love with you. He
must be the shyest man on earth, and you don't want to wait
forever. My guess is you're not getting any younger. I'm sure the
woman you mentioned is indeed his cousin, and he is probably
asking her for advice about confessing his love for you. Don't
worry about your job. I predict a happy ending.
Hearing Wedding Bells
Aunt Piney

———

Dear Aunt Piney,

It's no secret that this town is full of sinners. I've made it my life's work to pray for this town and its citizens on every possible occasion. My problem is that these sinners won't cooperate. Can you help me figure out how to get them to let me pray over them at every possible opportunity? I'm praying for you too.

Signed,
Praying in Chanceville

———

Dear Praying,

Your problem is a tough one. And I agree that this town is full of sinners. I suggest you ask the town board to make it a law that a prayer must be given at every gathering of more than one person or face arrest, jail, and a fine.

Praying for Success

Aunt Piney

———

These are a small sampling of the first letters that appeared in the Chanceville Examiner. The Tipp Topp was abuzz with speculation about who was writing the letters and who the heck Aunt Piney was.

"I think I know who Aunt Piney is," said Tarsal.

156

"Who would that be?" asked Sid Topp, unsurprised that Tarsal thought he had the answer.

"I think it's Sadie Stenner," said Tarsal as he stirred way too much sugar into his coffee.

"What on earth would make you think that?" asked Sid.

"She has a lot of time on her hands, and she always looks like she's up to something," answered Tarsal with his usual obnoxious certainty.

"That's not a lot to go on, Tarsal," said Frank Stenner, Sadie's husband, whom Tarsal hadn't seen walk up behind him. And that's all Frank said. He had learned a long time ago that the best way to deal with Tarsal was to limit conversations with him as much as possible. Frank chuckled as he went to his usual booth in the back and waited for his wife to meet him there. He winked at Ned Cochran, who was also sitting in a back booth, smiling and shaking his head at Sid on his way.

"Alpaca Finn is always asking a lot of questions about the folks of Chanceville," said Cora Jean. "Maybe she's Aunt Piney."

Several diners nodded, thinking Cora Jean might be on to something. However, there was one particular person who smiled, knowing better.

Everyone in the diner smirked as Sadie Stenner walked in. It didn't take Tarsal long to get the heck out of there.

33
MRS. LITTLE, INVISIBLE
MATCHMAKER

I t was a rainy Thursday morning in October when Milton
Matthews decided to stop in at the Jasmine Tearoom. He told
himself he just wanted to warm up with a steaming cup of tea,
but really, he wanted to see Mayrose Mayhern. He had missed the last
couple of Thursdays because he had to fill in for sick employees at
Steele's Hardware.

Milton arrived at 10:15. He knew Miss Mayhern always arrived at
10:00 on the dot. He wanted to give her time to order and get settled in
before he approached her. Milton realized he was a little nervous about
speaking to her, which wasn't like him. Maybe it was how she had put
the hard freeze on the Fishy woman the last time he was in the
tearoom. He had experienced a certain amount of frostiness from Miss
Mayhern. He was familiar with how that felt.

When Milton arrived, Mayrose was in her usual spot, primly
sipping her tea and eating her bran muffin with her ever-present
precision. If she took notice of Milton, she did not let on. He walked by
without nodding and took a chair at a table behind her.

"Good morning, Milton," said Mrs. Little as she pulled her pencil from behind her ear to take his order. Unlike Mayrose, Milton rarely ordered the same thing. "What'll it be this morning?"

"A pot of your Orange Pekoe tea, my dear. I'm feeling adventurous this morning. How about a slice of lemon with that?"

"Wow, you are living dangerously!" laughed Mrs. Little. "Anything else for you?"

"Any banana bread left."

"It's your lucky day. One slice left with your name on it."

Milton planned to do the crossword puzzle, so he unfolded and refolded his copy of the Chanceville Examiner as quietly as possible. However, he noticed Miss Mayhern's shoulders still scrunched up at the slightest rustling of the paper. He thought she must have been scared by a runaway newspaper as a child.

"Here you are, Milton," said Mrs. Little as she placed his tea and banana bread in front of him. "Looks like you've recovered from your surgery."

"I sure have. Feeling fit and frisky as ever," Milton replied.

At that, Mayrose cleared her throat with a definite sound of disapproval of such personal talk. As she got up to leave, she turned and looked directly at Milton. He could sense she was looking at him, but he didn't look up or acknowledge her presence. Two could play the *I'm denying your existence game.*

For some reason, this totally puzzled Mayrose. She wanted him to feel the full force of her disapproval of such talk in the tearoom, and when he wouldn't look up, she didn't know how to react. How dare he ignore her when she was trying to make a point.

It was no puzzle to Mrs. Little what was going on between Milton and Mayrose, or, more accurately, what was not going on that should be for two good people such as them.

When she returned to Milton's table to clear the tea things, she just looked at him and shook her head.

"What?" said Milton as he wiggled his eyebrows and chuckled softly.

"I'm afraid you're spinning your wheels, Milton," said Mrs. Little.

She hated seeing him wasting his time, but she was fond of the man and didn't want him to get hurt. She had never seen anyone pay any interest in Mayrose, even though she was an attractive lady. It must have been that steely armor she wore that kept possible suitors away. She saved all of her softness for her first graders.

Mrs. Little thought Milton would be quite a catch for someone. She hoped it wouldn't be Alpaca Finn, whose claws were too sharp for the tenderhearted Milton. She was sure Alpaca annoyed him like she did almost everyone in Chanceville. Mrs. Little had never played matchmaker, although she was tempted to try with Mayrose and Milton, but where to begin? Mayrose was far too clever and was not a gullible person who could be tricked into talking to anyone she was not naturally inclined to speak with. It was fun to think about getting those two together, though. She thought they would make a good match with their love of reading if Mayrose would let herself thaw out a bit.

It was Mrs. Little's natural tendency not to meddle or gossip. Like Sid Topp, she knew those things didn't play well when you ran a business in a small town. She wanted her tearoom to feel warm and welcoming for everyone. And she thought she had accomplished that, so she didn't appreciate Alpaca's shenanigans with Mayrose last week. She wouldn't mention her matchmaking ideas to her husband because he would tell her to mind her own beeswax.

That was probably a good plan.

Then, the opportunity to matchmake without seeming to matchmake dropped into her lap. She remembered a customer telling her that Milton had joined the Loone County Library Board when his brother James decided to retire from it. It was a good fit for Milton, a lover of books, and a way for a newcomer to get to know the community. As a former teacher, Milton wanted to promote reading for young ones.

About a month after he joined, Alpaca Finn had just started working at the library. Mrs. Little hoped she wouldn't try insinuating herself into Milton's life through his board work.

The day after Mrs. Little had thought about and decided against matchmaking, that same customer who had told her about Milton joining the board told her that she and her husband were retiring to Florida and that she would soon be leaving the library board. She asked Mrs. Little if she knew someone who would be interested in sending them her way. Yep, thought Mrs. Little, I think I know just the person.

On the following Thursday morning, when Miss Mayhern made her punctual appearance, it so happened that the same customer was in the tearoom also. Mrs. Little sent her over to speak to Mayrose, and that's how she came to be on the library board with Milton, and Mrs. Little served as a totally innocent bystander.

34
MILTON PLAYS IT SMART WITH MAYROSE

The Loone County Library Board met on the first Tuesday evening of every month in the library's conference room. The board members were the board chairman, Doc John Ivory, town dentist; Nurse Trachea Carmichael; Milton Matthews, retired history teacher; newly appointed member Hal Hendrix, owner of Hendrix Funeral Parlor and Wax Museum, Mayrose Mayhern, retired elementary school teacher; Gardenia Cochran, school art teacher and wife of Ned Cochran, and Mr. William Williams the Younger, co-owner with his brother Wallace Williams the Elder of Williams Brothers Stationery Store and Haberdashery.

Milton and Mayrose could not have been more surprised that they were on the board together than if they had found a tiger sitting in the board chairman's chair. The Chanceville Grapevine wasn't really falling down on the job. Everyone was just obsessed with Aunt Piney.

Doc Ivory called the October meeting to order. Since there were two new members to the board, he asked them to introduce themselves and give a little of their background. Doc Ivory asked Trachea Carmichael to read the minutes of the last meeting. Then Mr. Williams, the Younger gave the library budget report, which was pretty healthy after a nice donation from an anonymous benefactor. Mr. Williams explained that this was a perpetual trust with interest being paid out to the library on a quarterly basis. The money was to be used as the board saw fit, but a minimum of one-third was used to promote reading for young children. Thanks to Gardenia Cochran, the whole town knew about this godsend, and everyone was twisting their brains like pretzels, trying to figure out who the benefactor was. No one in Chanceville knew of anyone with that money except maybe Muddy Poodle. He had left all of his moolah to his daughters, Nanette and Babette, who had no trouble spending it on themselves. It was almost as mysterious as the identity of Aunt Piney. With these two things happening simultaneously, the whole town was in an uproar. Business was booming at the Tipp Topp, and Sid had to hire another waitress and order even more coffee because everyone gathered at the diner to try to figure out those puzzles. It had almost become like a game of Clue.

After the old business was taken care of, Doc Ivory opened the floor for a general discussion of new business. During the old business portion of the meeting, Milton kept his eyes on whoever was speaking. This meant he only looked at Mayrose when she introduced herself to the group. It was hard for him to keep his eyes off her. She looked lovely, as always, so well put together. He knew zero about fashion, but she always struck just the right note, tasteful and elegant for him.

As for Mayrose, she found herself strangely unable to keep her eyes off Milton despite her best efforts to completely ignore the man. What WAS it about him that was so maddeningly compelling to her? That was more mysterious to her than the identities of Aunt Piney and the Library Benefactor. She suddenly realized that everyone was looking at her.

"Sorry, what was the question?" asked Mayrose as she busily looked in her handbag for a handkerchief.

"We were wondering if you would be willing to help us make up a summer reading list for the children of Chanceville categorized by age groups. We could use some of the money donated by our benefactor to buy the books for the children," said John Ivory, puzzled by Miss Mayhern's unexpected lack of attention. She was usually so focused. He couldn't remember ever seeing her so flustered.

"Oh, I do apologize," she said as she daintily dabbed at her nose with her hand-embroidered linen handkerchief that matched her oat-colored suit perfectly.

"I realize it's only October, but I was thinking we might do a Christmas and a summer reading list. The Christmas reading list might get them excited about the summer reading program," said Mr. Matthews.

"That's a wonderful idea," said Gardenia Cochran. She thought Mr. Matthews would be a valuable addition to the board.

"I would be most happy to do that. I'll get to work on it right away. What is the deadline for the Christmas reading list?" asked Miss Mayhern.

Everyone thought privately that she would have both lists done in a week. She never one to procrastinate when there was work to be done.

"How does November 30th sound? I can have Principal Masters announce the program just before the children leave for their two-week Christmas break," said Gardenia. "And I'll be happy to make colorful posters for the library and Chanceville Elementary."

"Maybe we should also include the junior high and high school. Don't want anyone with children in all three schools to feel left out," said Nurse Carmichael sensibly. "Siblings can be quite competitive; this might have a side benefit of motivating them to complete the list."

"I like that idea. The more the merrier," said Doc Ivory.

"Shall we make it a goal to give a prize to each child who completes the list?" asked Milton.

"I'd be happy to go around to our business owners and solicit prizes. There will be a lot of children vying for these prizes, so I think we need to keep it simple, like a free sundae at Sudsy's Soda Shoppe," said Gardenia. "If I've remembered enrollment numbers correctly, and I can verify that with the school board, we have approximately 300 students at Ernie Pyle Elementary, 450 at James Whitcomb Riley Junior High, and 600 at Chanceville High School.

"Come in my store, and we'll pick out some bookmarks and colored pencils that I will donate," offered Mr. Williams the Younger. At the same time, his brother Wallace nodded in agreement. "We can also print completion certificates at no cost to the board. Consider it part of the Williams Brothers' contribution."

"That's so kind of you, and bookmarks and colored pencils as prizes is a wonderful idea. Thanks so much," replied Gardenia as she pulled a little gold notebook with an attached pen (most certainly purchased at Williams's store) out of her giant handbag and started a list of prize donors.

"Anyone else who thinks they can donate something or knows someone who will speak with Mrs. Cochran after the meeting," said Doc Ivory.

"Does the committee think three books in two weeks is reasonable for the two-week Christmas break?" asked Mayrose. She had addressed her question to the group, but for some reason unknown to her, she looked directly at Mr. Matthews.

"I'm sure you know more about the capabilities of younger students than I do, Miss Mayhern. I taught high school history, so my students were much older. I'm interested in getting them into the habit of reading at an early age," said Milton. He hoped what he just said made sense because all the time he was speaking, he was thinking how extraordinarily blue Miss Mayhern's eyes were.

"I agree with Mr. Matthews. I'm sure you're best qualified to know the reading habits of our young children," said Trachea.

" I don't want it to be too ambitious, but I do want it to feel like a competition so they will want to keep reading and win those coveted prizes," answered Miss Mayhern. "I feel like three is a reasonable number, given the busyness of the holidays. The books they read at each grade school level shouldn't be long for this competition. Mr. Matthews might know better about junior high and school readers' capabilities. I think one short novel or work of non-fiction might suffice. My hope is that they will learn to love reading for the sake of reading, not just for a prize."

Will we do this on the honor system?" asked Mr. Hendrix.

"I don't know how else to do it. I don't want to burden the parents with monitoring their children's reading when they're already busy getting ready for the holidays," said Mayrose.

"I think that sounds reasonable for the grades seven through twelve," Miss Mayhern said.

Everyone nodded in agreement, and the committee finished working out the contest details. Then Doc Ivory adjourned the meeting after everyone agreed to assemble the following Tuesday for an extra meeting so they could report back on everyone's progress. Miss Mayhern was given permission to give the reading list to Geraldine Nurse so that she could order the books for the children using money from the donor's fund. There would be four levels of reading: grades 1-3, 4-6, 7-8, and 9-12.

Doc Ivory was thinking to himself as he put his coat and hat on that this was going to be a very congenial and productive group. Especially since Tarsal Henley had resigned because he would not sit on the board with Ned Cochran's wife. Fine, so be it, thought John Ivory. He was never all that helpful anyway. Mostly, he liked hearing the sound of his own voice. Yes, he felt good about the work this board could accomplish.

As the group headed toward the front doors, a figure popped out from behind the nearest stack. No one was surprised that it was Alpaca Finn. Not even Mayrose.

"I hope your meeting was productive. I'm so impressed with the good work this library is doing in the community," Alpaca said, looking directly at Milton Matthews.

Mayrose was surprised to hear Milton utter a tiny sigh, which resounded in the quiet library because no one responded to her comment. Mr. Williams, the younger, tipped his hat at Miss Finn as the committee passed her. Everyone kept going, mumbling good evening as they filed out past her. Something about that woman set most people's teeth on edge or put them on guard.

Milton wanted to walk Miss Mayhern to her car but decided that if he had made even a little headway with her, he didn't want to blow it. So, he bid a general goodnight to everyone and headed down the sidewalk toward his home, only a couple of blocks from the library.

At the same time, Miss Mayhern wondered if Mr. Matthews would walk her to her car. She was surprised that she was disappointed when he did not, but she had to admit that he had played it smart. If anyone had been watching, they would have seen more than her usual upturn at the corners of her mouth.

Mayrose found herself thinking about what she would wear to the next library board meeting. This led to her wonder again what was familiar about Mr. Matthews.

35
HIRING NEW PASTORS DESPITE HUBERT PATTERSON

As if the townspeople didn't have enough to occupy their minds and tongues, there was still the business of building two new churches and selecting a pastor for each church. The citizens of Chanceville watched the building of the two new churches as if it were a spectator sport. Rumor had it that there was even a pool for which one would be done first.

The names for each church had been selected, and each church board was in the process of choosing their new pastor. Ned Cochran was the head of the search committee for "his" church, Main Avenue Christian Church, along with Geraldine Nurse, town librarian, Fern Oldhat, owner of The Lovely Locks Salon, and gum-popping waitress at the Tipp Topp diner, Cora Jean Johnston. Hubert Patterson had somehow managed to get himself on both hiring committees, but that wasn't working out so great for either committee. The interviews for the pastor of the Main Avenue Christian Church began.

"Meeting called to order for the first candidate interview," announced Ned. "Our first candidate for today hails from Bedford, Indiana. Reverend Sam Stonecut."

"Welcome, Reverend Stonecut," opened Ned. "Thanks for sending your credentials ahead so we would have time to look at them. Everything seems to be in order. If we choose you for a second interview, we will call the references you kindly provided. I will ask the initial questions, and then the committee members can ask follow-up questions." Then, he introduced the members to the candidate.

"I want to thank you all for this opportunity," said Reverend Stonecut in a bellowing voice that nearly knocked them out of their chairs. His voice didn't bother Hubert, whose hearing aids didn't seem to be working. Everyone else scooted their chairs back a few inches in preparation for the next onslaught. Ned addressed the reverend first.

"Can you tell us a little bit about yourself and why you'd like to become—"

"What is your favorite color, Reverend Stonecat?" Hubert asked before Ned could finish his question.

"Mr. Patterson, is it? Actually, the name is StoneCUT, not StoneCAT. My favorite color is gray, but I'm not sure what relevance that—"

"Green is my favorite color, too," said Hubert, looking pleased with himself.

The reverend appeared to be thinking of correcting Hubert again but thought better of it as Ned made a futile attempt to get back to the interview.

"Once again, can you just give us a little background on—"

"I understand you're from Bedford, Massachusetts. Did you know there's a Bedford, Indiana?" asked Hubert.

"I'm not from Bedford, Massachusetts. I AM from Bedford, Indiana," shouted the reverend, looking like a rat caught in a trap. The frustration of dealing with Hubert was causing him to bellow even louder.

"And when did you move from Bedford, Massachusetts, to Bedford, Indiana?" asked Hubert, still gnawing on the same erroneous bone.

Reverend Stonecut looked at the committee members for guidance. They all shrugged their shoulders.

"Let's let the reverend answer my first question, Hubert," suggested Ned.

"If you'd quit talking to me, Ned, maybe he would have a chance," said Hubert, effectively shredding Ned's last nerve.

"Cora Jean, will you please, for the love of God, stop popping your gum!" shouted Ned, causing everyone to jump.

"I... I'm sorry, Cora Jean. I didn't mean to yell at you. It's been a long afternoon."

Everyone nodded in agreement, even though, in reality, they'd only been there for about fifteen minutes.

Reverend Sam Stonecut took his cue from Ned and just shouted through any further questions that Hubert tried to interject.

And so it went. Reverend Stonecut may have been a perfectly fine pastor, but the bellowing quickly disqualified him to Ned's mind. They adjourned for the day, all but Hubert going home to take some aspirin and try to calm their jittery nerves.

After two more candidate interviews that went pretty much the same as Stonecut's, with Hubert asking different but just as irrelevant questions, the committee was getting somewhat discouraged. Not just because of Hubert but also with the quality, or lack thereof, of the men who had applied. Chester Young, son of Oblivia and Henry Young, fresh out of high school, had applied. Ned called him to let him know that they needed someone who was actually a pastor. His mother answered the phone.

"Hello, Mrs. Young, it's Ned Cochran. Is Chester home?"

"Why no, he's at the Get Out of the Gutter Bowling Alley setting pins. Can I take a message?" Oblivia asked eagerly and naively, hoping Ned would offer her son the job on the spot.

"Could you just tell him that we appreciate his application, but since he hasn't actually had any training as a pastor, he might not be the best candidate for the job," said Ned, trying to be as diplomatic as possible.

"But, Ned. He's such a fine young man and a quick learner. We've taken him to church his whole life, and I'm sure he knows the Bible as well as anyone around here. Of course, you know we'll be attending the Main Avenue Christian Church as soon as it's ready to hold services."

Ned had heard that Oblivia had been telling Tarsal Henley they would be attending the MAIN CHURCH of the Righteous that the other faction was building. He suspected Chester had also applied there and probably only did so at his parents' urging. The handwriting on his application looked suspiciously neat. As far as Ned could tell, that young man wasn't too swift on the uptake and seemed highly unmotivated.

After as many diplomatic refusals to interview Chester as Ned could muster, he finally caved in, mainly because he wanted to get off the phone before midnight. The Youngs had always been generous contributors to the church fund, and even though he wasn't sure which church she would choose, he didn't want her running over to Tarsal Henley's MAIN CHURCH complaining about him, so he set up the interview for the following evening meeting. He called a stunned Geraldine Nurse to notify the committee who the interviewee would be.

Since Geraldine Nurse was on the committee, she had reserved the Paul V. McNutt Reference Room in the Loone County Library for their meetings. Ned was thankful for that because Tarsal had rushed over to Mother Mary's Pool Hall and reserved the back room every night for the rest of the month. Typical, thought Ned. There were only so many spaces to use in Chanceville that were free and private, and neither committee wanted to spend money on meeting rooms.

The committee secretary, Geraldine, had "forgotten" to notify Hubert of the meeting. But as if by magic, the old man appeared just in time for the meeting. Great.

Ned waited by the front door for Chester to arrive at the library so he could show him back to the McNutt Reference Room. Geraldine had reported that Chester Young had never stepped foot in the Loone County Library as far as she could remember.

Paul V. McNutt was the 34th governor of Indiana. Ned had always secretly thought that the McNutt Reference Room of the Loone County Library had a nice ring to it. He glanced at his watch. Chester was ten minutes late, not a good sign. Hubert Patterson came shuffling out to find out what the holdup was like. He had somewhere else important to be. About that time, Oblivia pulled up in the sleek, black Fleetwood Cadillac she was so proud of.

"Sorry we're late," said Oblivia as she huffed her way up the steep stone steps of the building, Chester trailing along sullenly behind her.

"Well, at least Chester's here now. Thanks for dropping him off," said Ned. This puzzled him because the Youngs lived only a few blocks from the library. Maybe she was afraid Chester would get lost on the way.

"Oh, I'm not dropping him off," she said, sounding surprised. "I thought I'd stay for the interview."

"That won't be necessa–" Ned tried to say.

"Sure, come on in!" said Hubert, suddenly appearing and taking her arm as if she were the candidate.

Geraldine, Cora Jean, and Fern looked equally surprised to see Oblivia being escorted into the room by Hubert. They most likely realized later they should have suspected she couldn't stay away and leave Chester to his own devices. Oblivia had barely let that poor kid out of her sight since the day he was born. She motioned Chester to take a seat. Ned thought if God wanted to play a trick on them by letting Chester become the pastor of the Main Avenue Christian Church, his mother would probably stand at the pulpit right beside him. They all saw her poke Chester in the ribs and whisper to him to sit up straight.

"Chester, tell us why you would like to be the pastor of our church," said Ned.

"Ask my mom. It was her idea," said Chester, slouching even further down into his chair.

"Chester Charles Young! That's not true. All my son has talked about is being a pastor his whole life," said his mother to the committee as she gave him a good swat to the back of his head. "I told you to sit up straight," she hissed in his ear.

"Ma, cut it out! You must have another son 'cause I've never said anything like that. Isn't there something you're always quoting about not being a liar in that Bible of yours?"

"Weeell, Chester just loves people and is so good with them. I always believed he would be a wonderful pastor," said Oblivia, trying not to notice that her son was slouching in his chair again, examining his none-too-clean fingernails. He was tall and gangly, never seeming to fit comfortably into his surroundings.

"Mrs. Young, we appreciate your hopes for your son, but we really need Chester to answer the questions himself," said Ned, thinking they didn't need the Young's

contributions to the church had enough to go through this rigmarole. "Chester, do you want to be our pastor. Yes or no."

"Who are your favorite people in Chanceville?" asked Hubert before Chester or Oblivia could answer Ned's question.

"That's not an appropriate question, Hubert. Remember we agreed after the last meeting to let Ned lead the interview?" said Fern Oldhat, trying half-heartedly to get this runaway train back on its bumpy track.

"We did? Nope, I don't remember that. If Ned's going to ask all of the questions, then why are we here?" said Hubert.

"We agreed that Ned would ask the questions, the rest of us would take note of the answers, ask only relevant follow-up questions, and then work together to select the best candidate," Fern told him, who was thinking of taking out her hatpin and poking both Chester, his mother, and Hubert.

"Hmph," said Hubert. "I'm pretty sure I didn't agree to that stupid plan. I have lots of questions I need to ask."

"Trouble is, Hubert, none of them have anything to do with hiring a pastor," said Cora Jean, nervously chipping off her bright orange nail polish. She had to do something to calm her nerves if she couldn't pop her gum without getting yelled at.

Hubert wrote I vote for Chester on a piece of paper and slid it across the table to Ned.

"We're not voting yet," said Ned.

"What? It's anonymous. I didn't sign it." Geraldine, Cora Jean, Fern, and Ned shouted in chorus. "Not yet!"

Among Hubert, Chester, and Oblivia, Ned couldn't pinpoint the source of his headache. Still, it felt like it would be a doozy, he thought as he rubbed his temples. Meanwhile, Oblivia was whispering vehemently in Chester's ear. "Ma, you're spitting on me," said Chester, wiping his face.

"Let's try this again. Chester, I want you and only you to answer my question. NO interruptions," said Ned, already wondering if he was wasting his breath.

"He's talking about you, Mrs. Young," said Hubert, missing half the point.

Ned shot a look at Cora Jean, who had returned to popping her gum. Cora Jean bit her tongue when she tried to stop popping too quickly. Fern decided the contents of her handbag were suddenly fascinating. Geraldine, who had had about all of this she could take, held out her hand covered with a tissue and told Cora Jean to deposit her gum. Now!

"Chester, do you or do you not want to be the pastor of the Main Avenue Christian Church?" asked Ned. Everyone leaned forward, beyond curious to hear how Chester would answer.

"Nope," he said, sitting up straight in his chair.

"Chester!" screeched Oblivia as she prepared to swing her handbag at her son.

Ned jumped up to rescue Chester, who clearly didn't need it.

"I joined the Marines today. Time to blow this one-horse town," said Chester as he stood up from his chair and to his mother. "I'm outta here on Friday."

Upon hearing Chester's news, Oblivia fainted, sliding out of her chair. Her son stood there and stared down at her. Geraldine went to the water cooler and got her a cup of water while Cora Jean kneeled down and patted Oblivia's face none too gently. Finally, as she showed signs of coming around, Chester bent over and helped his mother back into her chair. Hubert shuffled over with an encyclopedia, trying to use it as a fan.

"Put that down, Hubert!" said Ned. "You'll knock her out with that thing. Chester, take your mother home."

They all wished Chester well as he ushered his long-suffering mother out the door. All were privately thinking it was a good thing for Chester to get out from under his mother's iron grip but weren't quite sure the Marine Corps was a good option for a boy as bone idle as Chester Young.

Ned reminded them of the interview they had tomorrow night at 7:00 with a candidate named Chuck Peevish from Greentown, Indiana. "Please, God, let this one be the one," Ned prayed out loud as he walked to his car.

The next night, they had all arrived at the library except for Hubert. Ned was afraid to hope that maybe the old man had forgotten all about it. In truth, he was actually worried about the old man who had always been a bit off the mark. Still, his behavior seemed weirder than usual lately. He hoped Hubert wasn't losing it altogether.

Ned had already welcomed Reverend Peevish into the McNutt Reference Room. He was getting ready to make the introductions to the rest of the committee when Hubert Patterson came shuffling in. The air seemed to deflate from the room as if it had been pricked like a balloon.

"Sorry I'm late," said Hubert, looking at the only empty chair as if trying to decide where to sit. "I've been at the Youngs trying to persuade Chester to be our pastor. He'd make a lousy Marine but a great pastor."

They couldn't argue with half of that statement.

Everyone else's jaws dropped wide open. The Reverend Peevish looked (and rightly so) puzzled. Ned knew if he even attempted to reply, he would lose it with Hubert. He could feel the veins in his temples throbbing. Actually, they were still throbbing from last night.

"Welcome, Reverend Peevish. Let me introduce the committee to you. We have prepared a short list of questions that I will ask. And then each committee member will ask ONE follow-up question," said Ned, pointedly looking at Hubert.

"Can I ask my follow-up question now?" asked Hubert.

"No, you can't. You do know that a follow-up question is asked AFTER all of the main questions have been asked, don't you, Herbert?" said Fern Oldhat.

"But it's important. I need to know now."

Ned wouldn't have been surprised if Reverend Peevish had bolted for the door at this point. Ned asked the first question, ignoring Hubert's request.

"As I said, Reverend, welcome to the interview. First, we'd just like you to tell us a little bit about yourself and why you've applied to be the pastor of our new church," said Ned, trying to sound like a civilized human being.

"Thank you all so much for inviting me to this interview. I've been pastoring the Greentown First Christian Church for the past ten years. A developer has offered to buy the land the church sits on. Because it's an elderly population with ever-diminishing attendance, the board has decided to sell. They'll give the money to the Greentown Second Christian Church. We call it The Second, doesn't need two pastors, so I'll soon be out of a job. My wife, Paula Peevish, is related to Peggy Hendrix, Hal Hendrix's mother. Peggy's sister, Nellie, was Paula's mother. My wife spent summers here and has fond memories of Chanceville. When Hal heard of our dilemma, he wrote and suggested I apply."

Hubert had apparently lost interest when he couldn't ask one of his, by now, infamous follow-up questions and was snoring quite loudly. He awoke with a snort when Cora Jean tapped him on the shoulder.

"I remember Paula Robinson! We used to spend time with Peggy in the Wax Museum and play dress up with the costumes," said Cora Jean. "Paula was a few years older than me but didn't seem to mind hanging out with a little kid.

"She's a wonderful person. I'm sure she'll be thrilled to know you're still in Chanceville," said the reverend, smiling.

Cora Jean was happy to hear she might be seeing her childhood friend again, and it would also be nice to have someone good to look at behind the pulpit; to her mind, the reverend was quite handsome. Well, anyone would be an improvement over Reverend Trout Finn and his slovenly ways. Cora Jean's job as a waitress gave her the skills to observe and learn how to deal with people. She didn't miss a detail. This candidate was of average height, not too skinny, but slender, his dark hair combed straight back, dark eyes, thick lashes. He had a neatly trimmed mustache, which gave him a distinguished look. He wore his clothes well, almost like a model. Cora Jean had a thing for hands, and she always noticed them. Reverend Peevish bit his nails to the quick, which did not fit with the rest of his dapper look. Could be he was the nervous type.

After the reverend had answered quite satisfactorily, to Ned's mind, all of the questions on the list, Ned asked the rest of the committee if they had any follow-up questions.

Of course, Hubert was the first to raise his hand. "Why are you leaving Greentown?"

'Hubert, he answered that question already," said Ned.

"Well, maybe he wasn't telling the truth the first time," said Hubert, folding his arms across his chest.

"I have a question," said Fern before things got out of control again. Fern, who liked to hang on to a dollar, asked, "What is your policy on tithing?" Finally, a relevant question thought Ned. Reverend Peevish didn't even squirm in his chair.

"I do believe in tithing. Here is my policy. I believe each family or person should tithe according to their ability. I don't want families to do without. I would rather see them volunteer their time to the church and the congregation's needs," he answered.

It was most likely that was the moment when each board member said to him or herself, you're hired!

There were some questions about living arrangements since the parsonage would be sold and other pertinent questions. Hubert had fallen asleep again. They decided to talk over the snoring and not disturb him. All questions were answered satisfactorily. Ned told Pastor Peevish he would be hearing from them.

Hubert woke up and said, "Why did he refuse to answer our questions?"

Ned sighed heavily and said, "Hubert, he answered every question, to my mind and I think the rest of the board, quite satisfactorily." Everyone nodded in agreement. "You slept through it all."

"You need to bring him back. I have lots of questions. I don't believe that whole cockamamie story about his wife being from Chanceville."

"It is true. I know Reverend Peevish's wife," said Cora Jean as she dug in her purse for her pack of gum. She didn't care if Ned yelled at her.

"Let's take a vote so we can get out of here," said Ned. Everyone except Hubert raised their hands in favor of hiring Reverend Peevish. Ned asked all opposed to raise their hands as a mere formality.

"I'm not voting. You can't make me, Ned Cochran."

"We don't need your vote, Hubert. We have a majority. I'll call Reverend Peevish and invite him to preach for us on Sunday. We'll see how that goes and take another vote after that," Ned told the group.

The following Sunday, the Reverend Peevish gave a sermon to the congregation in the VFW Hall, which the church used as a temporary sanctuary. As he began to speak, Hubert asked quite loudly, "Who's that?" Geraldine Nurse, who was sitting next to him, poked him in the ribs with her elbow and shushed him.

The committee observed at coffee time after the service that the reverend mixed well with the congregation, many of them giving committee members the okay sign behind Reverend Peevish's back. Those who knew Paula Peevish were quite happy to see her again.

The vote was nearly unanimous, with only one no-vote turned in with the question Why didn't we interview this guy? We all know who had asked that question.

Ned left the meeting wondering how the interviews were going for the MAIN CHURCH of the Righteous.

36

HUBERT HAS MORE QUESTIONS

On the other side of town, in the back room of Mother Mary's Pool Hall, Tarsal Henley and his committee consisting of Hubert Patterson (who, as you will remember, managed to get himself on both committees), Maxine Crabtree, fervent hospital volunteer, nurse Trachea Carmichael, and Frank Stenner, county engineer were holding their first interview for the new pastor of the MAIN CHURCH of the Righteous.

"Hey, Tarsal. I hear Ned Cochran is putting window boxes on the front of his church," said Hubert.

"Where'd you hear that?" growled Tarsal. Just so you know.

"I'm not revealing my sources," sad Hubert, not looking Tarsal in the eye. Just so you know. He's fillin' 'em with marigolds.

"Shouldn't we call the meeting to order? Don't want to keep our candidate waiting," said Trachea Carmichael, seeing where this was heading.

"Yes, we should," said Tarsal clearing his throat and thinking he'd better get started on boxes for The MAIN CHURCH of the Righteous.

Mrs. Crabtree insisted on opening the interview with a prayer. She proceeded to offer one that was way too windy for the occasion.

The committee had looked through the applications, which were basically letters, and selected Reverend William Dollar from Greenfield as their first candidate.

"Welcome to Chanceville, Reverend Dollar," said Tarsal, the self-appointed head of the committee.

"I appreciate the invitation," replied the reverend, adjusting his faded blue tie.

Tarsal had heard about Hubert's high jinks when he had breakfast at the Tipp Topp Diner, so he was prepared to head the old man off at the pass.

"Here's how this works, Reverend," explained Tarsal as he held his hand toward Hubert's open mouth. "First, we will ask you to tell us a little about yourself and why you'd like to be our pastor, then each committee member will have one question. You'll also be able to ask us any questions you might have of us. So, please tell us about yourself. Then we will have the opportunity to ask follow-up questions."

"Do you ever wear bowties?" Hubert interjected before the reverend could begin speaking. The rest of the committee sat shaking their heads.

"You don't need to answer that, Reverend. Hubert, that was not a follow-up question. It's not even a relevant question. Wait your turn," said Tarsal.

"As I said on my application, I've been the assistant pastor at the Greenfield Christian Church for about five years now. With six kids to feed, I've been working a part-time job to make ends meet. To be perfectly honest, I was hoping that a full-time position would pay more than I'm making now. I want to devote more time to pastoring and to my family," answered Reverend Dollar as he watched the unknown to him, a parsimonious committee, squirm in their seats.

"Do any of you have a question?" said Tarsal, cutting to the chase.

They all said "NOPE" in unison, even Hubert. And that was the end of Reverend William Dollar's interview and any chance of him being hired by the MAIN CHURCH of the Righteous.

The second candidate they interviewed that evening was Reverend

Leslie Lincoln from Brookville, Indiana. The committee had assumed that Leslie was male and was quite surprised to see a middle-aged woman walk into Mother Mary's backroom. They all stood up to greet her, even the women.

"Please, have a seat, Mrs. Lincoln. It is Mrs., isn't it?" said Tarsal.

"Yes, it is. By the stunned look on your faces, I can see that you were expecting a male candidate," Leslie Lincoln said, trying too successfully to hide a smile. This wasn't the first time this had happened to her.

"I must admit I was a bit surprised," said Tarsal. He introduced her to the board and explained their interview process to the reverend. "So, please tell us a little about yourself and why you'd like to pastor our new church.

Before she could even open her mouth, Hubert asked one of his infamous follow-up questions. "Will you be planting a garden?" he asked, peering over his permanently smudged glasses.

Hubert! Let the lady speak." Hubert thought about telling Tarsal he was just as bad as Ned Cochran but thought better of it. He really wasn't supposed to be on both committees.

"Thank you, Mr. Henley and committee members, for inviting me to this interview. Currently, I'm the lay pastor at the Brookville Country Church. It's a fine job where I mostly minister to the elderly residents of Franklin County. I do enjoy it, but I would really like to have a church of my own to pastor."

"Will your husband be standing behind the pulpit while you run the bake sales and Ladies Luncheons Committee?" asked Hubert.

Even though Tarsal was not too keen on having a lady pastor, he still wanted to punch Hubert Patterson for being so rude.

"Actually, I'm a widow. My children are grown. When I said I would like to have a church of my own to pastor, I meant that I would be the pastor. No one else. I can see this might not be the right town for me. Mr. Henley, Mrs. Crabtree, Miss Carmichael, Mr. Stenner, and Mr. Patterson, I thank you for your time," Leslie Lincoln said.

And with that, she was out the door before Hubert even could say a word. They all sat there, stunned. Stunned that a woman had applied and that she turned THEM down.

"Hubert, what is wrong with you?" asked Trachea. "You refuse to follow procedure and ask rude or ridiculous questions."

"I think we just didn't pray hard enough," said Mrs. Crabtree. "If we had, God wouldn't have sent us a woman who clearly doesn't know her place in this world. Hasn't she studied her Bible? Clearly, it states in 1 Timothy 2:12 – But I suffer not a woman to teach, nor to usurp authority over the man, but to be in silence".

"It doesn't matter now. Pastor Lincoln is gone. Maybe we don't want a woman as our pastor, but you never gave her a chance. Especially you, Hubert, with your rude question. You could have worded that a little more diplomatically. I'm about ready to kick you off this committee if you can't stick to the rules," said Tarsal.

The other members on the committee thought it was funny that Tarsal was giving Hubert advice on finesse. Tarsal went at most things as if he were wielding a hammer.

"You can't do that, Tarsal. And if you do, I'll go back to Ned's Main Avenue Christian Church," replied Hubert, looking triumphant. He was tired of Tarsal yelling at him.

'The ladies couldn't wait to hear Tarsal's answer to this "threat."

"Do it, Hubert. If you're trying to threaten me, that's not the way to go about it. Go annoy Ned Cochran. I can't think of anything that would make me happier," said Tarsal, hoping that would get rid of Hubert. No such luck. At the next interview, Hubert was the first one there, after Tarsal.

"I thought you were going over to the Main Avenue Church," Tarsal said in a none-too-friendly tone.

"My work with the Main Avenue Church is finished. Ned's group has made their choice. I'm needed here," Hubert replied. All ears perked up at this news.

"Who did they choose?" asked Tarsal a little too eagerly. Nonchalance was not his strong suit.

"Some guy from a town with green in the name. His wife is from here. I forget his name. Reverend Something or Other seemed like a nice enough fella," said Hubert. In Indiana, a town with green in its name was a wide field. As usual, Hubert Patterson was little help. At least he was consistent.

"Now listen, Hubert," said Tarsal. "Keep quiet. Do NOT ask any questions until I tell you to. Nurse Carmichael, you have my permission to pinch him if he so much as opens his mouth."

Hubert thought Nurse Carmichael looked a little too eager at having the power to hurt him. About that time, their next candidate arrived. His name was Edgar Beagle. The irony of his last name was not lost on a committee formed because of an argument over whether dogs had souls.

"Welcome, Reverend," said Tarsal, shaking the pastor's hand and guiding him to a chair at the table. He then introduced the committee, giving Hubert a look that said don't do anything but nod. The threat of being pinched by Trachea prompted Hubert to keep his mouth shut. She had given him shots before. He knew she didn't have a problem inflicting pain.

"Good evening, everyone. Thank you very much for inviting me," said the reverend in a gruff, clipped tone.

His voice may have been a little gruff, but he had soft brown eyes, which somewhat warmed up his pointy-nosed face. His gingery brown hair was parted down the middle and side-swept back. His neat but inexpensive-looking suit was brown, light beige shirt, brown tie, and brown shoes, overall a brown effect. When he smiled, he showed two elongated canine yellowed teeth. It looked as if the good reverend may have been a smoker or at least a heavy coffee drinker. Mrs. Crabtree had the un-Christian thought that someone should tell Edgar Beagle not to smile.

"Can I offer a prayer?" asked Mrs. Crabtree.

"A very short one," answered Tarsal, not feeling too hopeful. Maybe he should have Nurse Carmichael pinch her, too. But she kept it short, and Tarsal quickly asked the reverend to answer their standard "getting to know you" questions.

"As you know from my application letter, I'm from Greensburg. My church's elderly population is sadly dwindling, and my wife and I feel the time is right for a change of scenery. Our children are grown and gone, both to San Francisco, California. We would never move that far away from Indiana, and, besides, there are too many kooks in that part of the country," said Reverend Beagle, cocking his head to one side and scratching behind his ear. "We're also tired of being asked about that dam- er, that tree growing out of the courthouse tower."

Tarsal didn't think that was much of a reason to move, but he didn't comment.

"We like the looks of Chanceville. Last Saturday afternoon, the missus and I drove over and had coffee and pie at the Tipp Topp Diner, a friendly place in this town. I'm also excited to have the opportunity to start with a brand new church and congregation."

The committee wondered how Mr. and Mrs. Beagle's visit to Chanceville had missed the grapevine news. Someone was falling down on the job.

"Frank, would you like to ask the reverend a question?" asked Tarsal.

"Yes, I would. What's your stand on dogs having souls?"

Luckily for Edgar Beagle, he had heard all about the feud from a member of his congregation who had a cousin in Chanceville. He knew it was a question designed to trap him.

"I don't believe it's possible to know if any animal has a soul since they don't have the power of human speech. Don't get me wrong, I love dogs, cats, and animals of all kinds. But they are just that, animals. Why do you ask?" Reverend Beagle hoped that would be a vague enough answer to not come back to haunt him.

"Just curious," said Frank. "That's my only question."

"Nurse Carmichael?" asked Tarsal.

"Since we have such a small church, will you be acting as our music director or appointing a member of the congregation?" asked Trachea. Reverend Beagle sensed that this was another loaded question. It was a good instinct. Trachea had always wanted to be choir director. Still,

Reverend Trout Finn had somehow managed to avoid that mistake, as Trachea couldn't keep time to save her soul.

"I would have to assess the situation of how I'm able to manage my time, but in the past, I've always appointed an eager volunteer from the congregation," he told the committee, both answering and not answering the question.

"What kind of car do you drive?" asked Hubert as Trachea promptly pinched him hard on his cheek. "Ow! Stop that, Trachea!" The rest of the committee didn't even try to hide their smiles.

"Uh, a 49 Packard. But I'm not sure what that has to do with anything," said the puzzled pastor.

"You'll figure it out," said Hubert as he flinched when he saw Trachea's hand snaking toward him. Even the committee members who were used to Hubert's nonsensical questions were puzzled by Hubert's reply.

Tarsal jumped back in and gave the nod to Mrs. Crabtree to ask her question.

"Could I say another prayer before I ask my question?"

"I think your earlier prayer covers the whole interview," answered Tarsal, getting aggravated but trying not to sound like he was against prayer per se because he wasn't.

"Humph. Very well, Reverend Beagle, this is a two-part question. How many prayers do you usually offer during the Sunday morning service? Do you ever ask a congregation member to offer prayers?"

The reverend was a good observer of people. In his line of work, that was essential. This was another loaded question if he ever heard one. He bought some time by leaning back in his chair, scratching behind his ear with his somewhat pointy fingernails, and giving himself time to think it over.

"I usually have a minimum of three and a maximum of four prayers during a regular service. I typically ask congregation members to offer prayers during holiday services. Still, I might be persuaded to consider revising that practice to add more participation from the congregation." Again, he manages to answer without actually committing himself. Mrs. Crabtree wasn't thrilled but guessed that might be the best answer she could hope for.

"We have a parsonage that is being sold, and the money will be split between the two new churches. This money will be used to purchase a new parsonage. In the meantime, we will find a suitable rental for the pastor we choose," said Frank, head of the finance committee. He liked taking care of practical matters. No foolish feuds could be made up of black-and-white numbers. "This, of course, will be considered part of your pay, as is standard with most churches nowadays."

"That sounds very satisfactory," said Reverend Beagle.

"I don't believe I have any more questions," said Tarsal. He pointedly looked at Hubert and said, "I'm sure no one else does either." With that, everyone stood up, thanked the reverend for coming, and shook his hand.

"We'll be in touch," Tarsal told him as he guided him out the back door of Mother Mary's Pool Hall.

"I certainly do appreciate the opportunity, as I said before," replied Reverend Beagle, looking bright-eyed. "I look forward to hearing from you."

The committee unanimously agreed that Edgar Beagle was the man for them. Tarsal would call and invite him to preach at the next Sunday service. The committee hoped that the congregation would approve of hiring him. They did.

Now that the new churches had hired their pastors, the town could get back to the serious business of who Aunt Piney is.

37
ALPACA FINN FINDS A NEW HOME

Now that both new churches had their pastors, Ned and Tarsal each had to find suitable properties for their respective parsonages. Miss Alpaca Finn had been given written notice that the old parsonage was being put up for sale and that she should begin her search for a new residence. She received a written notice because Tarsal would not agree on a date for them to go together to give her the news in person. Alpaca was not surprised by this news. She had been told the parsonage would be sold in due time.

One church could have bought the other church's interest in the old parsonage, but it needed a lot of work, and both boards agreed that a fresh start would be best all around. They planned to sell the house as is because they didn't want to spend money to get it ready to sell, money the board knew they could not recoup. Both factions hoped some young couple would come along looking for a fixer-upper. And that's sort of what happened.

After Alpaca moved out, a smart, recently married couple new to Chanceville bought it. Most of the furnishings were taken to the Loone County Dumping Grounds, and the usable and cleanable items were divided and stored, awaiting the churches' purchases of parsonages.

The couple immediately tore the parsonage down and built their new house on the property, which was in a prime location. Tarsal blamed Ned and Ned felt stupid for thinking of the house's value and not the land it sat on.

Miss Finn hadn't seen any point in wasting time waiting for the old parsonage to sell. It was a good thing she could find something so quickly because the couple who bought it had been the first to look at it as soon as the "for sale" went up. They wanted immediate possession but would consider two weeks. They had cash, and the church didn't want to take a chance on losing a quick full-price sale, so they agreed to the terms.

A couple of weeks before Alpaca received the letter, she was in the Lovely Locks Salon when Fern Oldhat, the owner, was there working on the books for the shop. She happened to mention that her boarder, Mrs. Cooper, had to go to the Sally Forth Home for the Elderly and Infirm. When Alpaca heard that, she told Mrs. Oldhat she was looking for a room since the parsonage would be sold. They made an appointment for Alpaca to look at it later that day.

She liked the looks of the place from the outside. It was a sprawling two-story white Victorian-style house with gray trim and shutters, an ample front porch lined with rocking chairs, and huge ferns on antique plant stands.

The furnished room Fern showed her suited Alpaca as well. It was large enough that Mrs. Cooper had made a cozy sitting area by the tall windows. The Murphy bed gave it extra floor space. The closet was smallish, but there was a nice wardrobe for her to hang the clothes that didn't fit in the closet and a chest of drawers for the rest of her clothing.

"The furniture belongs to Mrs. Cooper, but she's leaving it here in exchange for her last month's rent since she can't take furniture to the nursing home," said Fern.

"That's wonderful. Good to be able to save some money," said Alpaca, who had not brought furniture from Minnesota. To her dismay, Grandmother Chagrin's money had gone to the nursing home where she had resided for the last fifteen years of her life. So, money was tight as she was still waiting on the pending sale of her family home in Saints of the Lakes.

"My cousin, Corning, boards here. He works nights at the Sprocket Factory, so we don't see much of him. Sadly, Old Ned passed away a couple of weeks ago, so I've got that room to let as soon as we spruce it up. My daughter Bonnie cooks and cleans for me since I'm busy at the salon most days. She has her own home, so she doesn't live here. We provide breakfast and dinner as part of your rent; lunch is on your own. You have use of the kitchen and the refrigerator that's on the back porch in case you want to keep food for your lunch in there. There are two full baths here on the second floor. You'll have use of the one closest to your room. Only the women use it. Everyone has a designated shelf in the linen cupboard for their toiletries. A coin-operated washer and dryer is set on the back porch for everyone's use. We get the Chanceville Examiner every morning. It's kept in the living room for everyone to share.

"You have been to my tea parties, Mrs. Oldhat. I would like to continue to hold the parties. Would you mind if I hosted them here?"

"I would love it!" said Fern. "I even have an extra china cabinet in the dining room that you could use to store your beautiful tea service and china. The china in the cabinet belongs to Mrs. Cooper, but her daughter is taking it to her house. I can also have my boy Sonny bring over your belongings if you think the room suits you."

I do believe that it is very suitable. The rent seems reasonable, and I like the proximity to the library and the town square. How soon could I move in?"

"Um, let's see. Two weeks from today? Mrs. Cooper leaves at the end of the week. That should give me plenty of time to have her china moved and for Bonnie to give the room a good cleaning."

"Will I be permitted to entertain a gentleman caller in your living room?"

"Of course, my dear," answered Fern, thinking that based on the gossip about the library board she had been hearing, there wasn't much chance of that if Milton Matthews was the gentleman. caller Alpaca had in mind.

"Perfect. I'll let Mr. Henley and Mr. Cochran know I've found a place to live and will move out soon. And if you can arrange for your son to transfer my trunks here, that would be much appreciated."

"I'll do that. I look forward to having you as a part of our little family here."

38
AUNT PINEY ANSWERS
ANOTHER LETTER

Dear Aunt Piney,

There is a certain gentleman in town I would like to get to know better, but he seems uninterested. Any suggestions as to how I can get his attention? He seems interested in someone else, who I think is not the right choice for him. I would appreciate any advice you can give me.

Signed,

Looking for Love in Chanceville

———

Dear Looking,

Honey, you came to the right place. Attracting the opposite sex is my specialty. I have three excellent suggestions for you.

If you aren't already dressing provocatively, start doing so right now!

Follow him *EVERYWHERE*.

Tell him every reason why you think this other woman is no good for him.

You will be surprised and amazed at the immediate results you get! I can practically guarantee it.

Good luck to you. (Not that you need it.)

Aunt Piney

39
ALPACA MAKES ANOTHER MOVE

After seeing that look of dumbstruck puppy love on the face of Mr. Matthews when they were all leaving the board meeting, Alpaca Finn decided it was time to make another move toward that handsome gentleman before he made a move on that Mayrose person.

But what to do? She'd already dropped huge hints to Geraldine Nurse that she'd like to be on the library board, to no avail. It was Geraldine's years of working in the library where people only spoke in hushed tones that made her able to tune out any conversation that didn't interest her. Besides, Alpaca would prefer Milton all to herself and not have that snooty Mayhern woman anywhere near them.

Since she now lived in a boarding house, she had no reason to frequent Steele's Hardware to purchase home repair items. The Church Ladies' teas were becoming a real bore and hadn't gotten her anywhere. She wasn't sure how much longer to keep up that charade. She needed to mix it up a bit. She remembered something that Fern had mentioned a few times. Her landlady loved to play a card game called Euchre, a game that Alpaca had never played because her parents were dead set against card playing. Fern always complained that she couldn't get people to play anymore, so Alpaca talked her into arranging a card party night at the boarding house. She offered to prepare the refreshments in her sly, skillful way and recommended who should be invited.

Fern knew Alpaca well enough to know that Alpaca never did anything without a reason, a reason that most likely would help her get a man. That particular plan of Alpaca's was one of the worst kept secrets in Chanceville, which was not that much of an achievement in a town that had no intention of letting a secret go unrevealed. Fern allowed herself to be manipulated because she was curious to see how all of this would play out.

At Alpaca's request, Fern sent invitations to James and Celia Matthews, Milton Matthews, Sadie and Frank Stenner, Ned and Gardenia Cochran, Mr. Williams the Younger, Trachea Carmichael, and Geraldine Nurse, with Fern and Alpaca that would make three tables of four. All had accepted, mostly out of curiosity, because they knew where Alpaca was living now and suspected she was up to something. They couldn't wait to find out what that might be.

The Thursday before the aforementioned card party was to take place, Milton had made it a point to stop by the Jasmine Tearoom at 10:00 a.m., just as Mayrose was arriving. He saw her coming and opened the door for her.

"Good morning, Miss Mayhern. I hope that you're well this morning." He stopped short of bowing like he usually did with the tearoom owner, Mrs. Little, who had rightly mentioned that it would most likely annoy Mayrose.

Mrs. Little had heard through the ever-present third-party line that Milton and Mayrose were warming up to each other quite nicely, so she wasn't surprised to see how Miss Mayhern responded to Milton. She was letting Milton see her softer side that she usually reserved for her first graders.

"I am well, thank you. It is such a bright, crisp day. And you?"

"Fine as fine can be. Would you like to take tea together this morning? I have some ideas about the reading program I'd like to run past you."

Mayrose's reply surprised Mrs. Little since she had never known her to take tea with another living soul, even people she had known for years.

"That sounds lovely. I've had some ideas, too. I'm very enthusiastic about this program, as you can probably tell," said Mayrose, shocking herself when she realized she had come close to batting her eyelashes as she looked up at Milton, a thing she had never done in her life.

Milton noticed an ever so slight blush on Miss Mayhern's cheeks. He hoped it was caused by her pleasure at the prospect of having tea with him.

"Your usual table?" Mrs. Little asked, looking at Mayrose.

"Yes, please," answered Mayrose.

Mrs. Little led them back to Mayrose's usual table in the cozy alcove. They didn't need menus and quickly gave her their orders. She discreetly left to give them some privacy instead of engaging in the usual banter she enjoyed with Milton.

After exchanging ideas about the summer reading program, reviewing what a success the Christmas reading program had been, and some small talk, their tea had been drunk, scone and muffin eaten. Milton decided to get to the real point, which, frankly, Mayrose suspected there must be another point because the ideas Milton shared with her were not all that new or possibly just had a slight twist to the ideas the board had already agreed upon.

"Miss Mayhern, have you ever heard of a card game called euchre?" he asked after much throat clearing.

"Oh, yes. My parents played it with a group of friends every Friday night for years. On occasion, they would recruit me if someone couldn't make it. It's quite easy. Do you know it?"

"Never heard of it," he said.

"I think it might be an Indiana or a Midwest thing. Why do you ask?" she said as Mrs. Little silently took away the tea things.

"Fern Oldhat is having a euchre night at her house this Saturday evening, and she invited James, Celia, and myself. I was hoping you might accompany me." Then he held his breath, waiting for her to answer. Everyone in the tearoom held their breath because even though he had tried to keep his voice low, the citizens of Chanceville had keen hearing and were especially attuned to conversations that were none of their business.

And then, as if those kinds of conversations were an everyday occurrence for her, Miss Mayrose Mayhern said yes. She said YES. And the White Jasmine Tearoom patrons let out a collective sigh of relief. Some had to restrain themselves from applauding.

Mayrose surprised herself as much as she did the patrons of the tearoom when she accepted Milton's invitation. She had seen another side of him on the board. Maybe he wasn't just a silly man with too much time on his hands after all. She had to admit that now that she was retired, she did get a bit lonely on occasion. And it was becoming harder to pretend she didn't need anyone's company.

"Yes, Mr. Matthews. I would like to accompany you," she said, a bigger than usual but still tiny smile appearing at the corners of her mouth. Milton noted that the Arctic ice in her eyes had changed to a tropical warm blue. The writer in him especially liked that phrase. He really wanted to jot it down but thought better of it. He hoped he could remember it when he got home.

"Perhaps you could call me Milton now that we are on the library board together and will be attending a card party on Saturday night," said Milton, hoping that he hadn't pushed his luck too far.

"Thank you, Milton. And please call me Mayrose," she said without any awkwardness at all. They left the tearoom, and Milton walked her home with the promise of calling for her promptly at 6:45 on Saturday night. He whistled the whole way as he walked back to his house.

40

MILTON PULLS A CARD OUT OF HIS SLEEVE

Finally, it was Saturday night. And because it was the fifties, Milton wore a shirt and tie, gabardine dress pants, and a sport coat. Mayrose looked put together, as she always did: light pink wool suit with a tailored ivory blouse, pearls with matching earrings, flat shoes, and because it was a party, she decided to dress more casually than usual and wore no hat. Milton had never seen her without an always-fashionable chapeau. He quite liked the softened look it gave her silver blonde hair.

"You look very lovely as always, if I may say so," said Milton.

"Thank you. And, yes, you may say so," Mayrose answered.

"Well, who's this then?" asked Milton as a calico cat wound its body around his ankles.

"That's Kitty. She adopted me last year after she came to my back door, and I fed her."

"She's a beauty. Well, if you are ready, we can go. I told James and Celia we'd pick them up because I thought it was silly to take two cars," he said as he reached down to scratch Kitty's ears.

"How sensible. I'm ready. Just let me put Kitty out the back door," she said as she scooped the cat up and headed out of the living room.

When she returned, Milton helped her with her wool suit coat and caught a scent of something like violets. He tried not to linger too long, but he enjoyed being close to her for a moment.

Meanwhile, at Fern Oldhat's home, last-minute preparations were underway. The coffee was percolating, and Alpaca's coconut cookies were about to come out of the oven. There was a vegetable tray with the newly popular sour cream and dried onion soup mix for dipping, potato chips, and the ubiquitous punch with orange sherbet floating in it. The tables were set up and covered with Alpaca's pale blue linen tablecloths that she had used for her bridge parties when the wives in Saints of the Lakes were still speaking to her.

Fern had always considered Alpaca a cool cucumber. Still, she seemed a little wound up and fussed continuously over every detail. Fern was pretty sure it was because Milton had accepted her invitation. Milton had asked Fern when she was in the hardware store if he could bring a guest. She told him that would be fine because she was pretty sure who that guest would be. And she was also sure that would not fit in with Alpaca's plan for the evening. Yes, this could be a very interesting evening.

The guests started arriving at around the same time. They all came in chatty and chilled from the cold November night. Alpaca took their coats, and Fern started filling punch cups for everyone and directing them toward the refreshments. When Alpaca returned from depositing coats in Fern's bedroom, Mr. Williams the Younger rushed over to her as fast as someone pushing eighty could rush.

"You look lovely, my dear," he said as he tried to gaze into her eyes.

"Thank you," said Alpaca as she looked over his shoulder, wondering where the Matthews and Milton were. Everyone else had arrived. Then the doorbell rang, and Alpaca nearly knocked the frail Mr. Williams over as she ran to the front door. He grabbed the edge of the dining room table to steady himself in her wake.

James came in apologizing that they were late because Celia had taken a call from her brother over in Columbus, Ohio, and couldn't get him off the phone. "It's not my fault. I couldn't get a word in to tell him we were going out the door," said Celia.

"I told you not to answer the phone," her husband said good-naturedly.

Alpaca opened her mouth to say that none of that mattered just as Mayrose Mayhern stepped in through the door with Milton right behind her. And before she could stop herself, she blurted out, "Miss Mayhern, you weren't invited."

All the happy chatter suddenly stopped. No one spoke.

"I was told I could bring a guest," said Milton, trying to help Mayrose off with her coat without too much success. She was holding it closed at the top button, not wanting to be where she wasn't welcome. Alpaca shot a look at Fern, who shrugged her shoulders.

"Of course, you're welcome, Miss Mayhern, said Fern. "The more the merrier, I always say."

"What difference does it make?" said Trachea, not liking the turn this was taking. This was supposed to be a fun night.

"Give me your coats, and let's play cards!" said Fern.

Because there was an odd number, Fern offered to sit out the first round. Alpaca immediately sat down at the table Milton and Mayrose had chosen. She sat across from Milton, which made her his partner. Mr. Williams, the Younger, sat down across from Mayrose so their table was complete. Fern had given Alpaca a couple of quick lessons on the rules of the game. James and Celia had learned the game and taught Milton in the week before the party. He and Alpaca were both quick studies and caught on immediately.

They intently studied their cards after Mr. Williams declared hearts as trump when Milton suddenly shifted in his seat. He kept shifting and seemed distracted. At the end of the next round, when Mr. Williams and Alpaca took their second trick, Milton jumped up quickly, his face red.

"Alpaca, would you show me where the bathroom is? I need a quick break," said Milton.

"I'd be happy to," she answered as she led him down the hallway.

Milton stopped outside the bathroom door and whispered, "What do you think you're playing at, Miss Trout?"

"It's Miss Finn, and I don't know what you mean," she replied, all wide-eyed.

"You know exactly what I mean, Miss FINN. You really need to stop playing footsie with me under the card table," said Milton, his face growing red all over again.

"Maybe it's Miss Mayhern."

"You and I both know better than that. In the first place, Miss Mayhern has more class than that, and in the second place, I saw your foot. You were rude to her when we first arrived. I'm sure you're a fine person, and I don't want to be rude, but you might want to find someone else to give your attentions to. I don't want to waste your time or cause any further embarrassment for either of us." Milton said, trying his best to keep his voice down.

With that, Alpaca abruptly turned and returned to the card table where Mr. Williams and Mayrose were discussing the summer reading program. When Milton returned, Alpaca asked Fern to sit in for her, saying she had a headache and was going to go to her room. Fern and Milton exchanged looks as she sat down across from him. Mr. Williams stood up, looking disappointed, telling Alpaca he hoped she would feel better soon. She didn't reply. The rest of the evening proceeded smoothly.

Everyone agreed that the party was a great success, and they all wanted to make it a regular thing. James and Celia offered to host the next one. "I do hope Miss Finn is all right," said Mr. Williams to Fern. "Do you think I should go check on her?"

"I'm sure she's fine. I'll check on her myself," said Fern, trying to suppress a smile. She didn't know precisely what had happened, but she would be willing to bet that Alpaca did not have a headache. After everyone left, Fern was about to go upstairs to check on Alpaca when she heard her coming down. "I hope you're feeling better, dear," said Fern as she busied herself tidying up.

"Yes, I took some aspirin, and my headache is almost gone," she said as she sat at one of the card tables Fern was trying to clear. "Oh, I should help you," said Alpaca, firmly planting her elbows on the tablecloth that Fern wanted to remove.

"Oh, no. You keep me company while I finish up," said Fern, and with that, she decided to cast out a net to see what she could catch.

"Your headache seemed to come on quite suddenly. I've never known you to complain of headaches before."

"I think it was Miss Mayhern's overpowering perfume," said Alpaca, turning her nose up and demonstrating smelling something offensive.

"I didn't notice any fragrance strong enough to cause a headache when I handed her a cup of punch."

"Oh, trust me, it was definitely Mayrose."

"James and Celia offered to host the next card party. Perhaps I could suggest that no one wear perfume or aftershave," suggested Fern. At that, Alpaca sniffed, thinking she would unlikely be invited after the conversation with Milton earlier. As Fern finished cleaning up the kitchen, Alpaca admitted to herself that it was time to mark Milton off her list. She had given it what she thought was her best shot. He couldn't have made it more clear that he was not interested in her and most likely never would be. He couldn't even get her name right, for Pete's sake. The problem, as she saw it, was that her list of possible future husbands had dwindled to zero, which made her head hurt for real. She sat back in her chair and began rubbing her temples, which gave Fern the opportunity to gather up the tablecloth and put it in the laundry hamper. She could fold up the table before church in the morning.

"I'm going to bed, dear. If you want to stay up a while, would you turn out the lights and make sure the front door is locked?" said Fern as she hung her apron on a hook by the door.

"I'm going up now too. I feel my headache coming back."

"I hope you sleep well, Alpaca. I'll see you in the morning."

Fern ascended the stairs wondering what scheme Alpaca would come up with next.

41

MR. WILLIAMS THE YOUNGER
HAS STARS IN HIS EYES

About a week after the euchre party, Alpaca went into Williams Brothers Stationery and Haberdashery Store to buy some note cards. She wanted to let the Tea Ladies know she didn't know what else to do but keep hosting her monthly teas at Fern Oldhat's, where she was now residing. She needed to keep mining what was turning out to be slim pickings in Chanceville. She wouldn't waste her time inviting Celia Matthews; the door to Milton felt permanently closed.

Mr. Williams the Younger was at his usual station by the cash register. If he had been wearing a hat, he would have tipped it to Alpaca. "I'm happy to see you, Miss Finn. I do hope you're feeling better," he said as he came from behind the counter to be nearer to her.

"Oh, I'm quite recovered, thank you. I hope I wasn't rude, but that blinding headache took me by surprise."

"Oh, not at all. You could never be rude. I'm just happy you're feeling better. Now, what can I help you with this morning?"

"I just need some note cards that are blank inside."

"Come with me," said Mr. Williams, crooking his finger and

motioning her to follow him. He selected a plain ivory card and envelope set with dainty scalloped edges.

"How about these? They look like something a lady with your refined taste might like."

"You're too kind, Mr. Williams. Actually, those are the exact ones I had in mind," Alpaca answered as she noticed how perfectly his suit was tailored for the first time. She caught a subtle scent of a cologne that smelled very expensive.

After completing her transaction, Mr. Williams felt reluctant to see her leave the store. "How are you finding Chanceville, Miss Finn? I hope our good people are making you feel welcome."

"Oh, yes. I'm very much enjoying my job at the library, and I quite like the hominess of my room at Mrs. Oldhat's." And that was all she was going to reveal. Even though Mr. Williams seemed like he might have a sympathetic ear, what she had heard about him led her to believe he would disapprove of her plans to land a man. But at least he got her name right.

"Good to know. I feel I've been remiss in welcoming you to our fair town. My family has lived here for generations, and I can't imagine what it would be like to move to a new town where the only person I knew had met an untimely death," said Mr. Williams, laying the groundwork to ask her to tea. Mr. Williams had never married, and at seventy-five, he felt his own mortality. He thought Alpaca Finn was the most exotic creature he had ever seen. And since laying his eyes on her, he had known true loneliness and something that felt like longing for the first time in his life.

"It's been quite an adjustment. But the ladies of the church, Geraldine Nurse and Fern Oldhat, have helped to make Chanceville feel more like home."

"I was wondering if you'd care to take tea with me sometime soon."

Alpaca was caught totally off guard. For once in her life, she was speechless. Then she thought, tea. Yes, tea at the White Jasmine Tearoom with this prominent citizen of Chanceville would help her wounded ego, hoping she could get him to agree to meet on a Thursday morning.

"I would love to have tea with you, Mr. Williams, " she answered in the affirmative, much to his surprise. "I'm off on Thursday mornings, but I would imagine you are working here at that time.

"Thursday morning would be fine. My brother, Mr. Williams, the Elder, who is retired, is always happy to man the store when I need a break. Shall we meet this Thursday morning at the White Jasmine, then?"

"That would be lovely. How about 9:30?" Alpaca asked.

"It's a date!" he blurted out before he thought. She smiled politely, took her purchase, and glided out the door. And so, it came to pass that Miss Alpaca Finn and William Williams were conspicuously seated two tables away from what Alpaca knew to be Miss Mayhern's usual table. Alpaca made sure they were engaged in deep conversation when she saw Mayrose pass in front of the window of the White Jasmine Tearoom. And to her utter delight, Milton Matthews was accompanying Miss Mayhern. Double revenge!

Mrs. Little was outside watering her prize-winning marigolds when Mayrose and Milton approached the tea room. The two of them to her mind, looked like the perfect couple, she entered with them and escorted them to what she now thought of as their table and smiled as Milton winked and nodded slightly toward the table where Alpaca and Mr. Williams were seated. Mayrose seemed oblivious to anyone else's existence when she was with Milton.

Milton's first thought when he saw Mr. Williams with the Fishy woman was poor devil.

Alpaca could not catch Mayrose looking her way, no matter how hard she tried.

Milton was another story. He couldn't resist a good wind-up. "Excuse me, Mayrose. I'd like to say hello to Mr. Williams and tell him how much I'm enjoying my new typewriter before our tea comes."

"Good morning, Mr. Williams, Miss Trout," said Milton as the older gentleman stood up to shake his hand.

"It's Miss Finn," said Alpaca, even though she corrected him, she now suspected he was getting it wrong on purpose.

"My tea is on its way, so I won't interrupt you too long, except to say I'm really enjoying my typewriter, sir," said Milton, which seemed to puzzle Mr. Williams.

Mayrose merely smiled to herself. She knew he had already spoken to Mr. Williams about his love affair with that typewriter. Her blue eyes, no longer icy, twinkled at the prospect of what Milton might say to the couple. She had to admit to herself that she wasn't above a bit of pettiness when she felt it was deserved.

"I'm glad you're happy with it. We like satisfied customers at Williams Brothers."

Alpaca decided to play Milton's game and become wholly absorbed in Mr. Williams. And much to her surprise, she found that wasn't so hard to do. Life could be funny sometimes. Perhaps the best revenge was living well after all.

Milton returned to his table as the tea was arriving. Both Mrs. Little and Mayrose were looking at him and shaking their heads. Some people never grow up, thought Mayrose, and to her surprise, she realized she quite liked that quality in Milton.

She was enjoying the time they had been spending together. It wasn't too much, and it wasn't too little. It was just right. They were both delighted at how much they had in common and how much they liked introducing each other to new horizons.

Spring was coming and bringing romance with it. More grist for the gossip mill at the Tipp Topp.

42

MAYROSE REMEMBERS

Mayrose had finally figured out why Milton's presence felt like a comfortable old sweater. He reminded her of a young professor who taught English Literature at Ball State University, Dr. Thomas, the first man to whom she had felt the stirring of attraction. He made her favorite subject come to life in his classroom. He was handsome and dynamic, and she had to rein herself in continually to keep her mind on the discussion.

He had been attentive and kind which gave her every reason to believe he was highly interested in her. He made her feel as if she were the only one in the world when he talked to her. They met several times for coffee in a discrete coffee shop off campus. After one such meeting, he drove her home, and some heavy petting ensued. She knew it was wrong to be going out with her professor, but she had fallen in love with him. He led her to believe they would go public when she was no longer his student. In her mind, she had planned a whole future together. She quite liked the idea of being a professor's wife. But it was not to be, as she found out when her classmate Helen came to her dorm room one afternoon.

"Can you keep a secret?" asked Helen, who was in tears.

"Of course," said Mayrose, and she could.

"You have to promise because I don't want to get anyone in trouble," said Helen.

"Cross my heart," answered Mayrose.

"I've been secretly going to coffee with Dr. Thomas. I thought it could turn into something serious. He promised me things," whispered Helen, even though Mayrose's door was closed.

"What kind of things?" asked Mayrose as she felt a knot forming in her stomach.

"Marriage, a life together."

Mayrose couldn't even speak. Her ears were buzzing.

"I succumbed to his advances. When I found out I was pregnant, I went to him to tell him. That's when he told me he was engaged. He walked out of the coffee shop. I haven't stopped crying since. I will have to drop out of school and go back home. My parents are going to kill me,"

"I'm so sorry, Helen. I don't know what to say. How horrible." She stiffly let Helen sob on her shoulder.

A few weeks later, Mayrose received a letter from Helen. She had miscarried and lost the baby. She would transfer to a small college near her home and lick her wounds.

Mayrose realized she could have easily been Helen. That's when her wall went up. She quit trusting her instincts and kept herself from letting anyone in until she met Milton, bless him. It had taken her a while to realize that Milton reminded her of the good qualities she had admired in Dr. Thomas: their warmth and intelligence. The difference, and it was a big one, was that everything about Milton was genuine. His interest in people was real because he cared about the people themselves, not just what they could do for him. He was a man comfortable in his own skin, which in turn had, to Mayrose, the magical effect of helping her to feel comfortable in her own skin as we do. They hadn't gotten around to discussing their pasts, and he hadn't told her why he had never married. Perhaps he'd had a similar experience.

As it happened, Milton did not have a similar experience. He had never met the right woman for him. He believed he had been waiting for Mayrose most of his life. To that end he began making plans.

43
LOVE COMES TO CHANCEVILLE

No one was more surprised than Mr. Williams the Younger that at seventy-five, he had at long last found love. Inside, he felt as smitten as a schoolboy. Still, Mr. Williams, the quintessential gentleman, always held himself in check.

Equally, to her surprise, Alpaca Finn felt something that she could only guess was love for Mr. Williams. He was almost thirty years her senior, but he was young at heart and so vital, a charming man of the world who had traveled extensively. He opened up new worlds to her. Her only travel had been through books.

That's not to say that Alpaca had made an overnight transformation. Her fondness for William was genuine, but she was honest enough, with herself at least, that being seen around Chanceville with him was highly satisfying after Milton's total rejection of her. She knew how word got around town and felt quite embarrassed that she was sure everyone knew that she had set her cap for Milton and that he only had eyes for that Mayrose person. She also knew they would assume she was only out for Mr. Williams' money. Admittedly, that was a bonus, but her heart told her there was so much more to him than a healthy bank account. His attentions would bring her the respectability she had craved since leaving Saints of the Lakes. She would never understand how Milton could find that plain woman more attractive than herself. Alpaca decided to enjoy this triple victory to the maximum.

Alpaca and William had been meeting for tea (not always on Thursday mornings) or lunch for about a couple of months when Mr. Williams asked to take her to dinner at St. Elmo Steak House in Indianapolis. She had heard about St. Elmo and knew this most likely was not a casual dinner invitation.

Mrs. Oldhat answered the door and welcomed Mr. Williams in. "She's on her way down, William," said Fern as Alpaca made her entrance down the stairs, looking elegant in a black linen dress accessorized with pearls. Mr. Williams appeared dapper as always in a new charcoal gray pinstripe suit. "You both look wonderful," said Fern. They made a striking couple, both being tall and slender.

They had a pleasant hour-long drive to Indianapolis. Alpaca had never been there and enjoyed seeing Monument Circle and the bright lights of this Midwest city.

They ordered dessert and coffee after a delicious dinner of filet mignon, baked potato, and a small house salad with blue cheese dressing. Mr. Williams liked that Alpaca, who was usually a light eater, thoroughly enjoyed her steak.

She noticed he had become quiet, except for frequently clearing his throat. They finished their dessert and coffee with minimal talk, agreeing on the excellent quality and service of their meal.

After clearing his throat one more time, Mr. Williams covered Alpaca's hand with his and looked into her eyes. She met his gaze directly, hoping she was right about what might be coming.

"My dear Alpaca, even though we've spent a short time together, I find I have fallen in love with you."

Alpaca squeezed his hand and felt her once cold heart beat a little faster.

"It has been a delightful surprise for me to realize that I have fallen in love with you, William,' she replied with a slight catch in her throat.

"But I was afraid to hope that a gentleman like yourself would ever be interested in someone like me."

"Oh, my dear, you have no idea how much you have brought into my life, but I'm hoping you'll allow me to demonstrate my love for years to come."

With that, Mr. Williams released her hand. He pulled a small black velvet box from inside his jacket pocket. He opened it to reveal a large round European cut antique diamond set in antique platinum. It sparkled brilliantly, even in the low candlelight of their table. As he took it from the box, he said, "My dearest one, would you do me the great honor of becoming my wife?"

Alpaca struggled to keep her emotions in check in this public place. Still, she could not keep her large obsidian eyes from tearing up. "It would be my honor to become your wife, William," she said as he glided the diamond onto her ring finger. When she looked up, she saw that he was tearing up, too.

"This was our beloved mother's ring, and my brother Wallace agreed it should be your engagement ring. Since neither of us have ever married, we were in despair that the ring would remain in the box until we died and then sold off to a stranger. He will be quite happy that you have accepted my proposal. I am thrilled beyond belief."

Alpaca withdrew her hand from Mr. Williams's. She moved it at different angles to see how the diamond reflected the light. "It's stunning. And it fits me perfectly."

"That just confirms it was meant to be," said William, returning her smile. "I don't think we should delay the wedding given my advanced age. Besides, I'm anxious to start our life together as man and wife."

"You don't seem like a man of advanced age to me. You're so young at heart, and I, too, am anxious to begin our life together." Of course, Alpaca, being Alpaca, was already envisioning showing off her expensive ring all over Chanceville. We all know where Alpaca will be at 10:00 next Thursday morning.

"Do you want a large wedding, my dear?" he asked, hoping she would say no because that would take longer to plan.

"I don't think so. It would have been nice to have my brother officiate our wedding, which makes me sad. They don't have the two churches quite finished yet, saving us from choosing between the two congregations. I think a justice of the peace would do nicely." It didn't really make her sad that Trout wouldn't be officiating their wedding, but she thought it was the right thing to say to her genteel fiancé.

"Excellent idea. We can spend the money on a long honeymoon. How does touring Europe sound to you?" Despite herself, Alpaca clapped her hands together and said, "Oh, William, that would be wonderful!"

Mr. Williams summoned the waiter and asked for their finest bubbly. When it was brought out, and the waiter was told what the occasion was, he announced it to the other diners. Everyone clapped and tipped their own drinks to the happy couple.

The breakfast crowd at the Tipp Topp was abuzz with the stunning news of the Finn and Williams pending nuptials. Little did they know that was only the beginning in the Williams' lives.

44
BON VOYAGE AND REVELATIONS

The following week, Alpaca and William were married by Justice of the Peace, Lily Lawson. The bride wore an ivory silk suit with pink mother-of-pearl buttons down the front of the jacket. She wore her hair in a French twist, secured with a comb covered in matching pink mother-of-pearl beads. Mr. Williams, who wore the same charcoal pinstripe suit that he wore the night he asked her to marry him, thought he had never seen such a lovely sight in his whole life as his bride.

After the wedding, Fern's son moved Alpaca's few belongings from the boardinghouse to the Williams' home. She finally sold her house, including all its belongings in Saints of the Lakes, to her cousin. Her husband and his brother had no need of her furniture in the stately old home that the Williams family had built in the late 1800s. It was three stories covered in southern Indiana's ubiquitous limestone with a long tree-lined driveway. Mr. Williams, the Elder, lived there also, but the home was so large that each brother had his own wing. The home was fully staffed. She could think of no other way to describe how she felt other than the clichéd, died and gone to heaven.

The happy couple embarked on a two-month European excursion

a week after the wedding. Alpaca had no idea what to expect from the physical side of her marriage to William. Still, she was happily surprised at his enthusiasm and stamina at seventy-five.

Alpaca rose especially early one morning in the middle of their Atlantic crossing. They strolled the deck, waiting for her husband to join her. It was a little cool due to the brisk ocean breeze. As she strolled, she pulled the collar of the mink coat William had given her as a wedding gift closer around her neck. She couldn't believe her luck had changed since leaving Saints of the Lakes. Alpaca felt bound to silently thank her brother for his timely demise. She had never loved him more in life than she did in his death. She would always wonder if he knew what had taken place in their hometown that had made her so happy to get out of there. They hadn't spoken in a couple of years when she phoned to let him know of Grandmother Chagrin's death. His letters became less frequent after that, but she knew how news like that traveled, and she still had a couple of cousins in Saints of the Lakes who might have written Trout to fill him in.

It had all started when Darrell Davis took an interest in her. She knew he was married and had quite the reputation as a lady's man. She was so bored with her life in Saints of the , beyond caring about her reputation, which had lost its luster over the years. Prim and proper was getting her nowhere. Why not have a little fun? Besides, Darrell was good-looking in a greasy Clark Gable kind of way. His wife appeared to be oblivious to his shenanigans.

Darrell would drive into the alley behind the family home she had inherited from her parents. They would drive over to a roadhouse on the outskirts of St. Cloud, about twenty miles west of Saints of the Lakes, where they could get cheap drinks and dance to the jukebox. One night, a friend of Darrell's came in with a woman. Alpaca was initially worried, but Darrell said Smitty wouldn't squeal on him because he wasn't with his own wife either.

Their luck was about to run out. About a month later, Lydia Burger, the wife of Saints of the Lakes mayor, was driving through St. Cloud and was having car trouble. She pulled into the parking lot and came in to use the pay phone. The first thing she saw when her eyes adjusted to the dark was Darrell and Alpaca on the dance floor. All the time she was talking on the phone to her husband, she glared at the couple slow dancing alone. As soon as they saw her, they knew they were in trouble. Lydia was friends with Donna Davis, Darrell's wife. The illicit couple grabbed their coats and exited as fast as they could when they saw the mayor's wife. Before he pulled out on the highway, Darrell lit a cigarette, and she could see by the light of the dashboard that his hands were shaking.

The ride back to Saints of the Lakes was quiet. Darrell dropped Alpaca off in the alley with a "see ya" before he drove off, screeching his tires as if he couldn't get away fast enough. She was sure that would be their last evening out, and she was right. It soon became apparent that word had spread quickly because she got the evil eye from most of the women she came across as she went about her daily routines and at work at the library.

A few days after Lydia's discovery, Donna Davis came into the Snow County Library with a stack of three books, which she slammed down on the counter, causing everyone, including Alpaca, to jump. "Stay away from my husband," she hissed. Then, she promptly spun around and stomped out. Alpaca could feel her face reddening.

It was the day after that embarrassing incident that Alpaca received the news that her brother had died, and her help was required to settle a delicate issue. She promptly gave notice at the library and bought her train ticket to Chanceville, Indiana. She would sell the house and deal with its contents later. It didn't take long for the news to get to Darrell. The night before she left, he arrived at Alpaca's unannounced and gave her the cash to tide her over until she could settle in and find a job. Thanks for nothing, Darrell.

Mr. Williams startled Alpaca out of her reverie when he came up beside her at the railing, putting his arm around her. "Didn't mean to startle you, darling. You seemed deep in thought," he said, attributing the tears in her eyes to the brisk sea air.

"I was just thinking how lucky I am to be your wife. And my

morning walk has made me hungry. Shall we go in to breakfast?" she asked, putting her arm through his as they walked to the dining room.

"I'm suddenly ravenous myself," he said, blinking back tears of joy.

Nothing could phase the couple's happiness, even if they knew that was awaiting them when they returned.

45
A FLY IN THE WILLIAMS' FAMILY OINTMENT

Wally Williams, the son of the Williams brother's late sister Wilma, was, in the vernacular of the day, a ne'er-do-well. Wilma was quite a bit younger than her brothers and had married late in life. When she was pregnant with Wally, her husband, whose surname was also Williams but no relation to the Chanceville Williams, died in an automobile accident, leaving her to raise the boy alone. It wouldn't be hard to guess she had spoiled him rotten. Wilma had died when Wally was 20, and he had been adrift in the following 15 years.

He had moved into his uncles' home about six weeks after William and Alpaca had left for their honeymoon after he lost yet another job and was evicted from his apartment in Greenwood. Wallace the Elder didn't want to do anything to spoil their trip, so he didn't communicate that news to his brother. They couldn't do anything about it anyway. When the newlyweds returned, they would have a family meeting.

It didn't take long for Wally to create a problem with the family's long-time housekeeper, Mrs. Clara Broom. She had been with the family so long that everyone felt she was part of the family, giving her quite a bit of autonomy. Clara oversaw a staff of three, and things ran perfectly. In actuality, she liked the new Mrs. Williams, who treated her kindly and respectfully. Mrs. Broom hadn't been quite sure what to expect after all the rumors she had heard about the former Alpaca Finn being on the hunt for a man. But, as far as she could see, the new bride genuinely loved her husband.

Before they left for the honeymoon, Alpaca made it clear to the housekeeper that she would not implement any changes because she saw no need when things were already running smoothly. Alpaca also acknowledged that she understood her presence would create extra work for the staff and would try to make it as minimal as possible, thereby earning extra points with Mrs. Broom.

Every Thursday, the housekeeper did an inventory of household supplies and groceries to prepare a shopping list and do the shopping as they headed into the weekend. She had weekends off, so she prepared dishes they could warm up in the oven for themselves. Soon after Wally arrived, Mrs. Broom noticed that many things were missing from the pantry: whole bags of cookies and candy. This only happened when Wally was in residence, so she knew exactly who the culprit was. After about three weeks of replacing everything, Mrs. Broom set a trap, literally. She put a mouse trap between two bags of candy. The Williams brothers enjoyed their sweets, but not bags at a time. All she had to do was wait. Instead of going home that Thursday night she would bunk with Billie, so she could wait in the darkened kitchen for Wally to appear. Sure enough, about midnight, he crept into the kitchen. He started feeling around on the dark shelves, not wanting to risk turning a light on.

When Mrs. Broom heard the SNAP, she jumped up and switched on the kitchen light as the young thief ran out of the pantry, trying vainly to release the trap. He was yelling so loud that he awakened the housemaid Billie, who came running in to see what all the commotion was about. Mr. Williams the Elder, a light sleeper, also came down to the kitchen, tightening his dressing gown around him, looking bleary-eyed.

"What in the world is going on, Mrs. Broom? Why are you still here?" asked Wallace.

"Young master, here, has been helping himself to the pantry. He's cleaned out all the sweets several times. It's getting costly to replace them. I didn't want you to think I was mismanaging the household funds," she said, knowing that Mr. Williams the Elder went over all of the household accounts with a fine-toothed comb.

The housemaid was trying to get Wally to hold still so they could pry the trap off his rapidly swelling fingers. Mrs. Broom was filling an ice pack. After the trap was removed from his hand, she directed him to sit down so she could examine it for broken bones, even though it was only a mouse trap not a bear trap as Wally's crying and complaining might make one think.

"Wiggle your fingers," she told him. He wiggled his fingers without wincing but was able to keep the crocodile tears coming. "I don't think anything is broken. Keep this ice pack on tonight, and keep it elevated. You should be fine by tomorrow."

"But it hurts!" Wally wailed.

"Stop bellowing, you big baby," said Wallace, rough language for the genteel Wallace.

"Serves you right. How dare you steal from me. Mrs. Broom, I want a full inventory of the silver and any other valuables you think he might try to pawn. If even so much as a teaspoon is missing, Wally, you'll be out on your ear before you can say, Baby Ruth!"

Mrs. Broom and Billie snapped to attention. They had never heard their employer speak to anyone that way, even when they deserved it. They loved working for the Williams brothers, who treated them so well. Wally must have tromped on his last nerve.

"Uncle Wallace! How could you think such a thing? I'd never steal from you."

"I believe you just got caught in the act by the very clever Clara Bloom. You're lucky I don't throw you out tonight. Now, let's all go to bed and try to get some rest. Since you've all had your sleep disrupted, let's have breakfast at 9:00 instead of 8:00. We could all do with a bit of a lie-in.

Everyone except Wally murmured their thanks and shuffled off to bed.

"Good night, all. Wally, I'll speak to you after breakfast," said Wallace.

"Can I have breakfast in bed earlier? I'll be starving by 9:00!" asked the clueless young man. Mr. Wallace, the Elder, shook his head and said, "That question doesn't deserve an answer. I don't want any of you giving him any special treatment."

The next morning, his uncle reminded Wally he wanted to see him in his study after breakfast. Wallace made a big show of favoring his injured hand even though the swelling had nearly disappeared.

"It doesn't look like your injury has hurt your appetite," said Wallace as he watched his nephew shovel in scrambled eggs, fried potatoes, and sausages.

"Mmph," said Wally with a mouthful of toast and jam. "It shtill hootz."

"Be that as it may, we will meet after breakfast." Wally only ducked his head closer to his plate and kept shoveling.

Wallace seated himself behind his desk and indicated one of two chairs on the other side when his nephew entered the room. He flopped down in the opposite chair that his uncle had indicated. The old man was getting way too bossy. This was all going to be his one day anyway. All he had to do was wait them out. They couldn't live forever, could they? He didn't like the idea of sharing any inheritance with this Alpaca person. He hoped she was as ancient as his uncles.

"Wally, your uncle and your new aunt will be arriving home the day after tomorrow. I want the household to be running with its usual efficiency in preparation for their return. I don't want anything to spoil their homecoming. Do you understand me?"

"I guess," Wally sniffed. "Don't know what you want me to do about it."

"I don't want you to DO anything. I want you to quit causing trouble and more work for the household. I have a report that your room is full of trash and dirty clothes. Go to your room, take the trash out, and carry your dirty clothes to the laundry room. Am I making myself clear?"

"I suppose," mumbled Wally, not budging.

"I hope we understand each other. Things will be changing around here in a very short time, so don't get too comfortable." Wally was afraid to ask what that meant. He decided he'd better be on his best behavior before his uncle got some crazy idea about making him get a job. The nerve.

46
WALLY "FINDS" A JOB

The perpetually unemployed Wally was fond of saying he was "between jobs" and didn't seem in any hurry to find one so he could get a place of his own. His uncles didn't want him working in their store. They had hired him one summer while he was between college semesters (before he was expelled for plagiarizing an English paper.) Money had gone missing from their cash register. They couldn't prove Wally did it and didn't want to upset their sister, so they never hired him again. It wasn't like they really needed the help; they had made the mistake of trying to help someone who only took advantage of people.

Wally had held several jobs, but they lasted only a short time. It always seemed his boss had it in for him, or his co-workers were slackers and got him into trouble. Never Wally's fault. He appeared to be good with plants. The housekeeper had asked Wally to water the many houseplants in the home. To her surprise, the plants thrived under his care. This gave Wallace Williams an idea.

Upon their return, the new bride and groom were surprised to find Wally in residence. Wallace said they would have a quiet word to determine what could be done about this awkward situation. Alpaca didn't like seeing her husband and brother-in-law upset. She would go along with whatever plan they came up with. She was not a stranger to resentment aimed at her and could feel it oozing off Wally.

Wally had been in a real funk when he saw how much younger Alpaca was than his Uncle William. He would be an old man himself before she kicked the bucket. Well, he would have to see what could be done about that.

One evening, while the five of them were having dinner, Mr. Williams, the Elder, cleared his throat several times. He said, "Wally, dear boy, I've noticed our potted plants have flourished since you came to visit. Mrs. Broom told me that it is thanks to you. I talked to Sal Seedy this morning, and he said there is an opening at The Seedy Garden Center. I told him you would come in tomorrow and fill out an application. He said that was a fine idea."

Wally, who had just taken a mouthful of consommé, sputtered the broth all over the previously pristine ivory lace tablecloth. "Uh, thank you, Uncle Wallace, but I'm not sure what my long-term plans are yet," said Wally after recovering from his choking spell.

Even though Alpaca knew what was coming, she touched her linen napkin to her lips to suppress a smile. Wallace and William had discussed their plan with her. Unlike his fastidious uncles, she had not been impressed by the slovenly young man.

"I imagine that hanging around here with the old fogies, Mrs. Williams company excluded, might get a little boring for you, and you'd like to get a place of your own. That job would help you to save up for an apartment. You're welcome to stay here rent-free until the end of the month, which gives you about three weeks to save up. I'm sure you'll have found a place by then. William and I will be happy to chip in with a deposit," offered Wallace the Elder gently. Alpaca and William responded in the affirmative, nodding their heads vigorously. They were all tired of his sloppiness that seemed to spill out of his room all over the vast house. And they couldn't believe how much that boy could eat.

Wally quickly realized he was outnumbered and, with a put-upon sigh, agreed to go down to The Seedy Garden Center in the morning. Later that night, tossing and turning in his bed, he decided this was all Alpaca's idea. Wally had her pegged from the start. His Uncle William was a great guy and all, but for Chrissake, he was as old as the hills. Why get married at his age? Yuck. They had all gotten along fine before she came along. He would get that job if only to get a little dough and hire someone to look into what was sure to be Alpaca's shady past. Gold digger came to mind.

Indeed, Stan Seedy did hire Wally Williams. The salary could have been better, but he thought he could get extra money from his uncles. He erroneously believed that he could still play the sympathy card, what with him being an orphan and all.

Finding an apartment was another matter. Wally didn't want to stay in a stuffy old boarding house with some nosy widow. Luckily, another youngish co-worker who was new to Chanceville told Wally about a house he was renting from his cousin, and they were looking for another roommate to help with the rent. Wally moved in the next week. And even though his new friend hadn't asked for it, he told his uncles he needed one hundred dollars for his part of the deposit. They gladly gave it to him since he was a week ahead of his month-end deadline. And for a time, all seemed well in the Williams household as the family and staff breathed a sigh of relief that Wally was out of the house and finally on his own. Peace was restored. At least for now.

47

CITIZENS OF CHANCEVILLE CONTINUE TO CHEW THE SAME FAT

Meanwhile, back at the Tipp Topp, the people of Chanceville were still abuzz with the news of The Marriage over their breakfasts as no new gossip was available to dissect.

Geraldine Nurse asked Fern Oldhat if she had any idea that Alpaca had set her cap for Mr. Williams the Younger.

"Honestly, I think it was the other way around. Miss Finn appeared to be interested, um, elsewhere and seemed to be oblivious to Mr. Williams' attentions. But I noticed the night of the euchre party that he couldn't take his eyes off her," said Fern.

"I think we all know who she was after, especially after her disastrous behavior at the card party. I was so entertained that I didn't even see what Mr. Williams was doing," said Geraldine.

"I don't think he thought he stood a chance until that night," said Trachea Carmichael, who had witnessed the embarrassingly awkward situation first-hand.

"True. Due to the age difference and Alpaca's not-so-subtle attentions toward Milton, he didn't think she would even notice him," said Geraldine.

"I just love great love stories," said Cora Jean as she poured coffee into the ladies' cups.

"Not sure how I feel about Alpaca and William's story being a great one, but it sure qualifies as interesting," said Trachea in her straightforward manner. "To my mind, the great love story is Mr. Matthews and Miss Mayhern's. Now that seems like a match made in heaven."

"I heard Mayrose put up quite the resistance to Mr. Matthews' charms, which, to my mind, are quite considerable," said Fern as the ladies nodded in agreement.

"I saw her start thawing out during our library board meetings. I think she finally saw that they had a love of books and learning in common. And that Milton had a caring, serious side," said Trachea.

"Isn't it about time for another Aunt Piney letter?" said Cora Jean. One patron in the diner jumped at that question, thinking the waitress could read minds.

48

AUNT PINEY BITES THE DUST

Soon after Cora Jean's question, and right on schedule, Aunt Piney's column appeared in the Chanceville Examiner. Unfortunately, Sam Chance was on vacation, and his rookie assistant was filling in as editor. He published the column without really reading the letters.

> *Dear Aunt Piney,*
> *I suspect someone has buried an animal in the graveyard of the MAIN Church of the Righteous. I noticed a suspicious mound of dirt near the gate when I was on my nightly rounds this week. We need to get to the bottom of this. Ned Cochran, if you don't meet us at the graveyard tonight, we will start digging ourselves.*
> *Signed,*
> *Concerned Anonymous Citizen*

———

Dear Anonymous,

This is a public notice for Ned Cochran. Either show us what you've been burying at the MAIN Church of the Righteous graveyard, or we'll dig it up for you. Is anyone in town missing any pets?

Aunt Piney

———

Dear Aunt Piney,

My parents MADE me go to summer camp, and I fell in love with a boy named Tim from Jeffersonville. He kissed me one night after the bonfire. A rat-fink counselor caught me sneaking out of my cabin one night to meet him by the lake. She told my parents, and now I'm grounded for a whole MONTH!!!! So not fair!!!!

I wrote a letter to him, which I could give to my friend Cathy when she visited while my parents were at work. She mailed it for me. That was two weeks ago. I put Cathy's return on it. But she hasn't been to see me lately.

I'm DESPERATE to see Tim. What should I do?

Signed,

Miserable in Chanceville

———

Dear Miserable,

I couldn't agree more. Your parents are being extremely unfair. Here's what I recommend. As soon as you're not grounded anymore, go to the bus station and get a ticket to Jeffersonville. Go see Tim! I'm sure he misses you as much as you *miss him.*

Don't give up. True love always wins, and your parents are too old to remember what it was like to be young and in love.
Hugs and Kisses,
Aunt Piney

───────

This created such an uproar that Sam Chance had to return from his fishing trip early to deal with it. The first thing he did was cut the column permanently from the paper. This quickly became the hottest topic at the Tipp Topp. Everyone wanted to know who that idiot Aunt Piney was.

"I just can't imagine who would be that irresponsible," said Mrs. Burl Tree, who had recovered from her ordeal and was glad to be back in her own home and enjoying a quiet life again.

"I don't know what the big deal is," said Tarsal, who had heard all he wanted to hear about Aunt Piney. "I don't think anyone took Aunt Piney seriously."

"You don't know that Tarsal," said Frank Stenner. "What if that young girl had taken Aunt Piney's advice?"

Before he knew it, Tarsal blurted out, "Some of those letters to Aunt Piney weren't even real!"

Ned Cochran, who had been sitting quietly at the other end of the counter, couldn't ignore Tarsal any longer and said, "You have got to be kidding me, Tarsal Henley. YOU are Aunt Piney and an even bigger idiot than I already thought you were!"

At that revelation, pandemonium broke loose in the Tipp Topp. Everyone was talking at once and yelling at Tarsal.

Just when I thought you couldn't get any worse, Tarsal!

You could have lost Sam Chance the paper!

What if some kid out there had taken you seriously?

"Ah, you're all crazy," said Tarsal as he slammed down his cup, sloshing coffee everywhere. He stomped out the door, leaving the buzz behind him.

Tarsal Henley had loved being Aunt Piney. Writing this column might be the only way anybody would ever seek out his advice or listen to him. He was sick of Ned Cochran and the whole lot of them. Animals with souls. Humph, they're all crazy. Well, now look who's having the last laugh. He couldn't remember the last time he'd had so much fun. He had thought giving horrible advice to the lovelorn would be the best part of being Aunt Piney. He hadn't counted on the bonus of sitting around the Tipp Topp listening to everyone try to guess who Aunt Piney really was. That was over now. Those dummies always spoiled his fun. How many idiots can one village have?

49
MAGNUM PALTRY, P.I.

Magnum Paltry had been a private investigator for twenty years. He learned not to assume he had seen it all a long time ago. So, when lumpish Wally Williams shuffled into his office on the west side of Indianapolis, he didn't think anything unusual was about to happen. The best he could see through his cigar smoke haze was an average-looking looking, slightly overweight man who appeared to be in his early thirties.

"Is this the office of Magnum Paltry, the private detective?" asked Wally as he came through the door marked Magnum Paltry Private Detective.

Got a livewire here. "It is. Have a seat. What can I do for you?"

'I'm Wally Williams from Chanceville. I'm sure you've heard of my uncles' business over there, Williams Brothers Stationary Store and Haberdashery," said Wally as he stuffed himself into a narrow, rickety chair.

"Can't say that I have. Is that relevant as to why you're here?" asked Paltry, thinking he sure would like a swig of that Scotch he had stashed away in the bottom drawer of his desk. This could be a long afternoon, he thought while listening to the slow as molasses- talking Wally.

"It's relevant, all right. My uncle, Mr. Williams the Younger, just got married, and the bride might be a gold digger."

"Maybe we should go over my rates before we get started," said Paltry, thinking this kid didn't look like he could afford much. First, they had to agree on a retainer and a billable hourly amount. Wally had the cash for the retainer. (He wanted to use cash instead of a check that could be traced.) The day before, everyone in the household, including the housekeeper, was out when he stopped by. His mother had foolishly given him the combination to the safe years ago. And his uncles, who didn't know Wally had the combination, hadn't changed it. He helped himself to some jewelry that had belonged to his great-grandmother. Wally pawned the pieces when he got to Indianapolis for a tidy sum. Wally didn't know that he was about to be found out. At that very moment, his Uncle William opened the safe to return some of the jewels his bride had worn on their European excursion. He had just picked them up from the jeweler, where he'd had them cleaned and the stones checked.

Wally gave what little information he had about Alpaca to Paltry, who promised to start working on the case immediately. Paltry was happy to send the slobby young man on his way. As soon as Wally closed the door behind him, the detective sprayed the room with Lysol, hoping that the definite scent of BO left behind would spoil Paltry's favorite fragrance of cigar smoke.

The first thing Paltry did was contact a pal on the Indianapolis Police Force to find out if Wally Williams had a record. He didn't trust that kid for a minute. The second thing he did was call his friend, Jerry, in Chanceville to get the scoop on the Williams brothers and Alpaca Finn Williams. He was not surprised to find out that the brothers had an excellent reputation in that small town, were good businessmen, and were good citizens who contributed generously to their community.

Alpaca Finn was another matter. He learned how she came to be in

Chanceville and her rocky start with her quest for a man. But Paltry's friend said she seemed to have turned over a new leaf now that her future was secure, and by all accounts, her new husband was over the moon happy. His friend suggested he call the police department in Saints of the Lakes, Wisconsin if he wanted more background information on her. Rumor had it she left there under some shady circumstances. Jerry said that he would hate to see Mr. Williams the Younger be hurt by his bride and by Wally's shenanigans and filled him in on what he knew of that lazy young man.

Later that afternoon, Paltry's contact in Chanceville, Jerry, a retired detective, called him back. Some news had just come in that a warrant was out for Wally's arrest, and the theft of the jewelry had been discovered. When William told his brother Wallace of his discovery, they both knew what had happened to it. This was the last straw. The jewelry was worth tens of thousands of dollars. They couldn't let him get away with this, family or not. They immediately called Sheriff Yesper, reported the theft, and told him who the likely culprit was. Since Jerry knew Wally had been in Indianapolis that day and had paid Paltry in cash, a quick check at the local pawn shops turned up the jewelry. Wally was quickly apprehended at the Seedy Garden Center, where he was filling trays with potting soil for seedlings of what seemed like a never-ending array of marigolds. Spring would soon be coming to Chanceville.

The Williams brothers were sad that things with Wally had taken such a bad turn. They were relieved that their sister had not lived to see her son go to jail, even if it was only for a year. This could be a wake-up call for the young man. He would be put on a work release program at the end of the twelve months. He was jailed in the Marion County Jail in Indianapolis since he had pawned the item there. Still, it would have been a hardship for the elderly brothers to make that trip on a regular basis. They were, however, faithful letter writers and made sure he had money in his account for the items he could buy at the commissary.

Because Wally was lazy didn't mean he couldn't sum up the energy to cook up a new scheme.

50

THE NEWLYWEDS ARE ENTERTAINING

The Williams family and their staff had settled into a nice, quiet routine since Wally had been incarcerated and taken all the chaos with him. Alpaca and William were blissfully happy with each other. The hard predatory lines that had been forming on Alpaca's face had softened, giving her a more serene look. William had a spring in his step, and on some days, he might even go so far as to say he felt spry. Wallace enjoyed the couple's company. They brought life to the old house, and his new sister-in-law added lovely feminine touches to their old fusty home.

After a quiet winter, the three decided it was time to open the house up for a party. A garden tea party at the end of April sounded nice. Tea parties were Alpaca's specialty, and she felt that she and Mrs. Broom could handle it quite nicely. They would have to hire extra serving staff and a few additional lawn people. They decided to put an invitation in the newspaper to avoid leaving anyone out of the festivities. Their grounds and gardens were extensive and could accommodate all who might want to attend. Of course, that would be nearly all of Chanceville. As soon as the invitation was published in the

Chanceville Examiner, the Tipp Topp was abuzz with gossip about the big event.

"I wonder what the catch is," said Tarsal to Sid Topp from his usual spot at the counter.

"What are you talking about, Tarsal?" What is wrong with you? Only you could find fault in a party invitation," said Sid as he poured Tarsal his third cup of coffee. Sid always secretly switched Tarsal's third cup to decaf. He was bad enough without over-caffeinating him.

"We've never been invited there before. I'm not opening up my wallet for those old men."

"The Williams brothers could probably buy and sell Chanceville. Why on earth would they be asking their guests for money?"

"Still don't trust 'em," said Tarsal as he loudly slurped his coffee as usual. Sid believed that Tarsal always sat at the counter so he wouldn't have to leave a tip, believing that you didn't need to tip the owner of an establishment.

"Guess that means you won't be going," said Frank Stenner, who was sitting a few stools down from Tarsal.

"Course I'm going. Just leaving my wallet at home." Sid and Frank shook their heads and exchanged grins, not surprised by Tarsal's answer. He would never miss free food.

"I'm going to call and ask if I can say a prayer before tea is served," said Mrs. Crabtree to Cora Jean, who was serving two blue plate specials to her and Geraldine Nurse in a booth at the back of the diner.

"Not sure that's appropriate for this occasion," said Geraldine. "Besides, we have two new reverends in town who might want to perform that function if needed."

Hubert Patterson ambled in about that time, holding up the newspaper with the invitation in it. "Look, everyone! Invitation to a tea party," he shouted as if no one else in town ever read the paper.

"We know, Hubert. We all read the paper," said Trachea Carmichael. "I plan on being there. Good excuse to buy a new dress."

"I wonder who all is invited," said Hubert, missing the point, as usual.

"Hubert, you idiot," said Tarsal, ever the tactful conversationalist. "The whole damn town is invited," he told the old man as he snatched the paper out of his hand and pointed to the part where it said: TO ALL THE TOWNFOLK AND BOTH CONGREGATIONS OF THE MAIN STREET CHURCH OF THE RIGHTEOUS AND THE MAIN STREET CHRISTIAN CHURCH.

"Zip it, Tarsal," said Ned from his perch at the opposite end of the counter. "No need to be hateful all of the time."

"Like you're an angel, Ned Cochran. I'm not speaking to you anyway."

"Good. Start not talking to me now." With that, everyone in the diner smiled at the snappy comeback. Ned paid his bill and left. It took only a short time to get his fill of Tarsal Henley.

"Well, I'm looking forward to it. I think it's a nice gesture," said Fern Oldhat, privately thinking it would be good for business because everyone would want a new "do" for the party.

"I can hardly wait," said Cora Jean, popping her gum even louder with the exciting prospect of seeing the Williams's home and garden.

The White Jasmine Tearoom was also atwitter with the prospect of the garden party. Milton and Mayrose were quietly discussing the idea of attending. They had settled into a comfortable companionship and went almost everywhere together. Mayrose was too old to change many of her habits of a lifetime. She still ate with precision and dressed immaculately, no matter the occasion, but she felt so at ease with Milton that she could relax and be a little more spontaneous. And now that Alpaca was happily married and no longer on the prowl, Milton felt more relaxed in general, not fearing that she would jump out from behind a bush or a library stack.

"I must admit I'm quite impressed with the idea of a garden party. Although I was never tempted to attend, I heard from some of the ladies in town that Alpaca knew how to serve high tea. I'm sure everything will be done first class, especially now that she has the wherewithal to do it without worrying about the expense," said Mayrose between dainty sips of tea.

As different as they were, Milton seemed to embrace Mayrose's idiosyncrasies instead of being annoyed by them. He felt his laid-back approach to life was an excellent complement to her military precision. Together, they achieved a happy medium.

"I suspect you're right, my dear," said Milton. "Will you do me the honor of accompanying me to the garden party?"

"Of course, I would love to," said Mayrose, who still sometimes blushed at the attentions of the handsome Mr. Matthews.

"Before the party happens, I like to propose an idea to you," said Milton.

"Oh?" said Mayrose, trying not to appear too curious.

"A little bird, we'll call her, 'Mrs. Little' told me you have a birthday in early April. I would love to celebrate it with you, if I may. What is something special you would like to do on your birthday?"

"Milton, that is very sweet, but I don't usually celebrate my birthday."

"Well, it's high time that changed. You deserve to be celebrated. Isn't there something you've always wanted to do but didn't want to do on your own?"

"There is one thing. But it might be too much to ask," she replied after thinking about it for a minute.

"Nonsense. All you have to do is ask."

"I've always wanted to take a riverboat ride on the Ohio River."

"Done. Leave it to me." This was perfect, fitting into his plan quite nicely. Now, all he had to do was purchase the ring. Proposing was the exact thing he had in mind. And for that, he would ask for his sister-in-law, Celia's help to pick out the ring. She had excellent taste and was a great admirer of Mayrose and would know exactly what would please this wonderful lady.

Milton had been thinking of asking Mayrose to marry him for a few months now. After Mr. Williams, the Elder, at his advanced age, took the plunge, he thought, why should he let a little thing like age stop him? Besides, he and Mayrose got along on every level. They liked many of the same things and enjoyed each other's company. Still, the prospect of popping the big question set butterflies loose in his stomach. If she said no, he could handle it, but he didn't want that to end what they had now. He had never been a gambler, and this seemed like a considerable risk. That afternoon, Milton stopped by Celia and James's, ready to throw the dice.

"Celia, I need your help with something very special," said Milton.

"You want me to help you pick out a ring for Mayrose," said Celia with a twinkle in her eye.

"Why on earth would you think that?" asked Milton, nearly choking on the iced tea she had just served him.

"That's it, isn't it?" she said.

"Well, yes, but I haven't said a word to anyone about it. I know the Chanceville grapevine is good, but not that good."

"Celia's been saying you've had that look in your eye for a while now," said James from behind his newspaper. "She knows these things. I've learned there's no sense in fighting it." Milton just sat there stunned, speechless.

"Of course, I'd love to help you," said Celia. "I assume you want to go out of town to purchase the ring, given the determination of most of Chanceville citizenry to never keep a secret."

"Yes," said Milton. "I thought we might drive to one of the finer jewelers in Indianapolis."

"How about tomorrow?" said Celia. "You're not getting any younger." The three of them laughed. James offered to drive them, and they made their plans for their trip on the following day.

The next morning, the three Matthews set out early for Indianapolis. They stopped at Steak n Shake on the city's east side for breakfast to fortify themselves for some heavy-duty shopping.

They also bought an Indianapolis Star to look for ads for upscale jewelry stores. They decided on Harrison Jewelers on Washington Street. It sounded classy, and Milton knew that Mayrose was first class all the way. He wanted the best for his, hopefully, new bride.

It didn't take long for Milton to find a ring. He and Celia (James was waiting next door in a small diner) were drawn to simple solitaires on a slim gold band with a wider gold band wedding ring. The diamond was a quarter-carat, not too big nor not too small. Just right. They decided on the one with the highest quality diamond.

"We'll take this one," Milton told the gentleman waiting on them.

"We can size it for you now since your future bride is here with you."

"This is my sister-in-law," said Milton.

"Oh," said the clerk, his face reddened, unbidden. "Well, I guess it's good to keep it in the family."

"I'm only here to help him pick out the ring. I'm not marrying him, although he is quite the catch," said Celia, who immediately picked up on the clerk's discomfort.

"I'm so sorry. I can't apologize enough for being so presumptuous."

"No need. I should have realized how that sounded. Please don't give it another thought. Nothing can ruin this day for me," Milton said graciously.

"Shall I gift wrap it for you? Free of charge, of course."

"Thank you, no," said Milton, nearly bouncing up and down, not having much luck containing his excitement.

Their mission complete. Celia and Milton joined James at the diner, where Celia told Milton perhaps he should have a mild tea since he was already jittering at top speed.

"Good idea," said Milton. "The clerk thought I was buying the ring for Celia. When I said she was my sister-in-law without further explanation, he jumped to the wrong conclusion."

"Hey, get your own girl, brother!" said James, chuckling.

"I will if Mayrose says yes."

"Not funny, Milton," said James.

"Boys, boys, settle down. Don't make me choose," said Celia.

"Not funny, Celia," James repeated.

"Aw, come on. Lighten up, honey," Celia said to her husband. You know I would choose you. Yes, I'm pretty sure I would. Uh-huh."

"That's it. Time to go. You two are way too giddy for me," said James, pretending to be grumpy. "Time to get this show on the road. Milton has to get home and write his big proposal speech."

"I've been rehearsing what I would say in my head for weeks," said Milton. "Maybe writing it down would help me get my thoughts together. Good idea, James." And with that, Milton paid their bill, and they headed back to Chanceville with their precious cargo on board.

The three were quiet on the way home, each with their own private thoughts. Milton was thinking back on the time he first saw Mayrose. He was definitely intrigued, but he never guessed that within a relatively short time, he would be buying her an engagement ring. Whether she would accept it was another matter.

He used to think of her as the Ice Lady, but he always believed that deep down, she had a warmth he wanted to bask in. The Great Thaw began when they were appointed to the Loone County Library Board. As retired teachers, they both believed in getting as many children to read as possible. They were the future of the country. And their reading campaign had been quite a success.

Celia hoped that Mayrose might let her help plan the wedding or at least stand up with her if they went to a justice of the peace. She mentally took inventory of her wardrobe and decided she might need to go shopping. Celia wouldn't go crazy. She could wear the new dress for the wedding and the garden party.

James was thinking about getting home, taking off his tie, and perhaps napping in his Barcalounger.

As for Mayrose, who was thinking about Milton at that very moment and remembering when she realized that he was willing to work hard and had great ideas on how to achieve the board's goals, she began to see there was more to him than a simple court jester. Once she was able to get the memory of Dr. Thomas out of her mind and saw Milton as a genuine person, she could relax and stop worrying about being hurt. She had never been a creature who embraced change, but her wall would come down slowly, brick by brick, as she allowed herself to enjoy his company.

Milton didn't know what had caused her change in attitude about him. It really didn't matter. He was grateful that there had been a change and could feel the warmth he always knew was there. The big question was had she warmed up enough to accept his proposal.

51

MAYROSE AND MILTON FLOAT DOWN THE RIVER OF LOVE

On the morning of Mayrose's birthday, she awoke early in anticipation of her riverboat trip on the Ohio River with Dear Milton, for that is how she thought of him, Dear Milton. When she opened the back door to let Kitty out, she stepped onto the back porch to see what kind of day they had ahead of them. The weather, to her satisfaction, was lovely. The sky was a deep blue dotted with stark white clouds moving lazily above the trees. It's a perfect day for a drive and a riverboat ride.

For some reason, she couldn't quite decide why. She felt a little nervous. She thought about this as she drank her orange pekoe tea and ate her three-and-one-half-minute egg and one slice of lightly buttered toast. She was comfortable with Dear Milton. He liked to tease her, which, to her surprise, she had learned to quite like, but he was ever the gentleman. He was always kind to her and everyone he met. Granted, they had never gone out of town together; it was only a day trip to celebrate her birthday, but those butterflies wouldn't go away. She would never in a million years have guessed what this day had in store for her. It's as well, or Milton may have found her fainted on the floor when he arrived.

She took special care with her attire and hair, hitting just the right note between casual and elegant. An ice blue linen dress belted at the waist, pearl earrings were her only jewelry, and flat, comfortable shoes. She wasn't a vain woman but believed one should look one's best. And she was aware that Milton especially liked it when she wore blue that accentuated her eyes.

"Look at you, Mayrose Mayhern, dressing to please a man. What have you come to?" she said to her image in her full-length mirror. She went to the back door when she heard Kitty meowing to be let back in.

Kitty perpetually lived in the false hope that Mayrose would feed her a second breakfast after a hard morning of patrolling the yard for cheeky squirrels who chattered at her just out of reach. She sashayed around her bowl a few times, meowing loudly, and finally gave up to take her post in the bay window, keeping watch on the street but mostly napping. Kitty jumped in the window just in time to see Big Man parking his car. She liked him and greeted him with a friendly mew when Lady let him in the front door.

"Mayrose, you are a vision in blue," said Milton, kissing her lightly on the cheek.

"Oh, Milton. You are quite the flatterer."

"I only speak the truth, dear lady. Are you ready for our great adventure?"

"I believe I am. Just let me get a sweater and let Kitty out." They walked to the car, where he opened the door for her, making sure she was securely tucked in. Mayrose noticed his hands were shaking when he put the key in the ignition. She hoped he wasn't ill or had some bad news for her. He seemed to relax as he started driving, and they made easy conversation as they drove through the scenic hills of southern Indiana toward Cincinnati and the Ohio River. They would be cruising on the Delta Queen, a paddlewheel boat that had been in operation on the river since the 1920s.

Milton parked the car, and as they made their way to the ticket booth, Mayrose noticed that Milton started to seem nervous again.

This was so unlike him. She was really beginning to worry. He kept patting the left side of his sports jacket. What if he was having chest pains?

"Would you like to sit up on the top deck, sweet pea?" asked Milton once they had boarded the boat. "It's probably the best vantage point."

"Let's try it. It looks like we have the option of being outside, or we can go inside the enclosed portion of the top deck if the wind and sun get to be too much," answered Mayrose, ever the practical one.

They quickly found seats with beautiful views all around and settled themselves. Soon, the boat was underway, and the captain began his commentary on the history of the area and the Delta Queen. They both found it interesting, but Mayrose noticed Milton becoming restless again.

The captain had taken a break, and Milton asked Mayrose if she would like a lemonade.

"That would be lovely."

"Let's go inside for a bit of a break from the sun." He returned with a tray with two lemonades, two grilled cheese sandwiches, and two slices of white cake with pink icing. His hands were trembling so badly that she feared he would spill the lemonade before he reached their table. She wanted to know what was going on but didn't want to embarrass him. She took the things off the tray as he went back for napkins.

"This lemonade is refreshing. And the cake looks delicious. Thank you, dear," said Mayrose in her newly found comfort with terms of endearment.

"My pleasure, sweet pea. I thought you should have cake on your birthday," he said, attempting to be casual but failing miserably. When they finished their lunch, they returned to the outside deck. The captain had yet to resume his commentary, and Milton decided it was now or never.

After much throat clearing, Milton turned to Mayrose, who looked at him with concern. "Are you all right?" she asked, her brow furrowed.

"I'm about to be the best I've ever been or the worst I've ever been," he said, patting his left breast again.

"I'm sorry, Milton. I don't take your meaning," she said, still not knowing what was about to happen. He reached into the inside pocket of his sports jacket and pulled out the black velvet box.

"Milton, you didn't need to buy me a birthday present. This lovely trip was more than enough."

"This isn't exactly a birthday present," he said, sweat appearing on his upper lip.

"What is it then?" She's not making this any easier, thought Milton. I don't believe she has guessed what I'm up to.

"Mayrose Mayhern. I've fallen for you, head over heels, to be precise. And I want you to be my wife more than anything in this world. I don't want to be apart from you. Ever. Please accept this as a promise of my deep affection for you," he said, shakily handing her the ring box.

It felt like it took an eternity for her to open the box. Milton thought he would scream. When at last she opened it and saw the sparkling diamond, to her utter and everlasting dismay, she burst into tears. Not just tears but loud, noisy sobbing and all the attending effluvia.

"Oh! I didn't mean to make you cry," said Milton, patting her arm a little too forcefully. Mayrose shook her head vehemently, unable to speak as she reached into her extremely organized pocketbook for a handkerchief. She pulled it out without looking. She was still Mayrose Mayhern, after all. Some things would never change. "I guess that's a no, then," he said, his disappointment scraping the sub-bottom of the bottom of the barrel.

"No!" was all she could say.

"It's all right. I know I sprung this out of the blue."

"No!" she said again.

"You don't have to keep saying it. I get it. You're turning me down."

"No!" By this time, people were starting to stare, and the captain was on the loudspeaker again, talking about the Indians who originally lived in the Ohio River Valley. This was not how he had envisioned this day.

Mayrose blew her reddening nose in a most unladylike fashion. Which only endeared the brokenhearted suitor to her even more.

"No! I mean, yes. It's not a no. It's a yes," she said, taking his hand. "I find I want more than anything to marry you. Yes. Yes. You took me completely off guard. You were so nervous and kept patting the left side of your chest. I thought you were having chest pains or going to tell me bad news of some sort. Now I realize you were making sure the ring was still in your jacket pocket." And with that, Milton removed the ring from its nest, and with still shaking fingers, he placed it on Mayrose's equally shaking ring finger of her left hand.

"Look! It fits perfectly!" she said louder than she had intended. And everyone around them started clapping, causing Mayrose to burst into tears again, which caused Milton to follow suit. "What a right mess we are," he said to his betrothed. To which she sniffed in agreement.

She lightly dabbed the tears from her eyes so she could get a better look at her ring. "It's beautiful. I love it," she said as she moved her hand this way and that, admiring its sparkling in the sunlight.

"Are you sure? We can always exchange it."

"Absolutely not. I'm never taking it off, " uncharacteristically bordering on the sentimental.

"I admit I had some help picking it out. Celia went along with me, and we both liked this one immediately."

"How did you keep it a secret? You know what Chanceville is like. I'm surprised that Mary Ann at Lucky Charm Jewelers hasn't told everyone in town."

"James drove us to Indianapolis to avoid that very thing."

"Well, you certainly took me by surprise. I just realized what an understatement that is," Mayrose said as they shook their heads and chuckled. Finally, she took her eyes off her ring and looked into his still teary brown eyes.

"I do believe we have some plans to make," said Milton, taking both her hands in his. As they discussed the plans for their future, they lost track of time. "Why is the boat slowing down?" asked Mayrose. They were at the end of the river cruise, and the boat was docking. Then, the happy couple strolled off the ship hand in hand and headed back to Chanceville, but not before engaging in a long, leisurely kiss once they got into the car.

52
CALLING GOSSIP CENTRAL

The first place Mayrose and Milton went the following day after she had accepted his proposal was the White Jasmine Tearoom.

"Don't you two look pleased with yourselves?" observed Mrs. Little as they headed for their usual table. They smiled at each other and kept walking with Mrs. Little on their heels. She sniffed a change in the air surrounding these two.

As we know, Mayrose always wore gloves and was always deliberate in how she took them off. Today, she was extra deliberate for the benefit of Mrs. Little, who actually gasped when she saw the ring on Mayrose's finger.

"It looks like congratulations are in order," she said. "I'm bowled over."

"Not as bowled over as this lovely woman was," said Milton with a grin as wide as the sky. This caused Mayrose to blush, her cheeks feeling hot.

"This is cause to celebrate. You two order whatever you'd like. It's on the house today." Of course, Mayrose never ever changed her order, but Milton said, "I feel like living dangerously. How about some cinnamon in my hot chocolate?"

"Wow, that is living dangerously. Next, you'll tell me that you two are eloping to Las Vegas."

"Don't think we haven't thought about it," said Milton as Mayrose smiled her best smile and shook her head. After they finished their drinks and muffins, they headed to the Tip Topp Diner to spread more cheer.

The diner wasn't someplace Mayrose typically frequented. She told herself it was because she preferred tea to coffee. Still, if she was honest with herself, it was because she wasn't comfortable with the gossip and the presumption that everybody was great friends with everybody. Milton had convinced her to make an appearance because he knew that would be the quickest way to get the news of their engagement out short of putting an announcement in the newspaper, and he wanted the world to know.

He was sure he heard several pins drop when they walked in the door together.

Sid couldn't remember the last time he had seen Miss Mayhern in his diner. Probably when she used to bring her mother in for dinner after Mayrose's father died several years ago. Everyone watched as they strategically seated themselves at a booth about halfway back in the diner.

"What'll it be for the two of you?" asked Cora Jean, almost swallowing her gum as she remembered Miss Mayhern always making her spit out her gum in the trash can when she entered her classroom.

"Why is everyone smiling at Milton and Miss Mayhern?" Tarsal asked Sid.

"Because they just got engaged," said Sid, who had already heard about it from his wife Tippy, who was in the tearoom when the couple had shown Mrs. Little the ring. And with that announcement, Tarsal swallowed his mouthful of coffee, got off his stool, and approached the happy couple.

"Sid just told me a funny story," he said, looking at Milton.

"What's that?" asked Milton.

"He said you two just got engaged, which I guess means you're getting hitched."

"What is so funny about that?" asked Mayrose, shooting him her blue dagger stare.

"At your age? Why bother? That's just as embarrassing as Mr. Williams, the Younger, getting hitched to that Finn woman." Everyone quickly lost interest in their food, and all heads turned toward Milton and Mayrose's booth. This was going to be choice.

What Milton really wanted to do was to punch Tarsal Henley. Instead, he spoke in measured tones.

"Not that it's any of your business, Mr. Henley. But allow me to provide you with a list," said Milton, enumerating loudly for the benefit of everyone in the diner.

1. I love the lady.

2. She loves me.

3. We don't want to be apart.

4. We will enjoy as many years as we have together, much like Alpaca and William.

5. When you start paying my bills, you can have an opinion on how I run my life.

6. Last but certainly not least, go back to your perch and mind your own business."

And that was the day the first standing ovation was awarded to a patron of the Tipp Topp Diner.

Tarsal stomped out of the diner without paying for his lunch. And Milton, being the class act he was, put a ten-dollar bill on the counter beside Tarsal's plate.

"There's no need to do that, Milton. And besides, that's way too much money. And your lunch is on the house today."

"Thank you, Sid. Then consider it a tip. That's a drop in the bucket when it comes to compensating you for the abuse you've suffered from Mr. Henley over the years." On their way out, other people dropped change or bills on top of Milton's ten as a show of support for the long but quietly suffering Sid.

"Thanks, folks. I have an idea about what I will do with the money," said Sid with a impish gleam in his eye.

A week later, a plaque appeared on the gate of the graveyard of the MAIN Church of the Righteous (Tarsal Henley's church).

It read:

"Who teaches us more than the beasts of the earth and makes us wiser than the birds of the heavens?" Job 35:11

All the people who had been in the diner that day knew exactly who had placed that plaque on the gate of the graveyard.

No one wondered who placed that plaque on the gate of the graveyard. But they all wondered who would be invited to the wedding.

53

DID WE MISS THE WEDDING?

At last, the big day for the Williams' garden party rolled around. Practically, the whole town of Chanceville was buzzing. The Williams were supplying finger foods, desserts, and the tea. New dresses had been bought, croquet sets were dusted off, picnic blankets were washed, and some men even sported new straw hats. The weather cooperated quite nicely. The last Saturday in April dawned bright and clear. The clouds against the marble blue sky were as white as cotton balls.

The party was to start at 11:00 am, but the road to the Williams's house was lined with cars by 9:00. "At this rate, it will be noon before we get there," Ned Cochran said to his wife, Gardenia.

"Oh, I hope not. I don't want to miss anything," said Gardenia as she lightly dabbed her forehead with her best embroidered handkerchief.

"You mean you don't want to miss any gossip."

"I don't know what you're talking about, Ned Cochran."

Ned was the kind of successfully married man who knew when to change the subject. "Well, it looks like we're moving a little faster. Maybe it won't be much longer." They were soon directed into the freshly mowed field that served as a parking lot since even the Williams brothers' expansive drive could not accommodate almost the whole town of Chanceville.

Everyone was being directed to the back gardens, dashing Gardenia's hopes of getting a tour of the house. "Guess we'll be staying outside," she told her husband.

"You couldn't expect them to let the whole dang town traipse through their home."

"I guess not," she said, sticking her bottom lip out.

"Now, don't pout. Let's have a nice day."

"You're right. Oh, there's Geraldine! Yoo hoo! Geraldine! Yoo hoo! She knows all the best goss... er stories." Gardenia was never one to pout or be angry for long. Soon, she returned to the sunny self her husband knew and loved.

Much to Frank and Sadie Stenner's chagrin, they saw Tarsal and Scapula Henley heading toward them.

"Mind if we put our blanket next to yours?" asked Tarsal as he placed their blanket next to the Stenners, who just rolled their eyes at each other.

"Have you heard the latest?" asked Scapula.

"The latest about what?" asked Sadie, looking at Scapula, who in turn looked at her as if she were the stupidest person on earth. "Old Maid Mayrose and that foreigner got engaged."

"Foreigner?" asked Frank. He didn't like to gossip, but he was curious about who Scapula thought was a foreigner in Chanceville."

"That Limey," answered Tarsal. The Stenners were mentally scratching their heads. Still having no idea who they were referring to. Suddenly, a light went on above Sadie's head.

"Do you mean Milton Matthews, who was born in England but was raised in this country?" she asked.

"Hmph. Still a foreigner to my mind," said Scapula as her husband nodded in agreement.

"Yes, we heard that he and Miss Mayhern became engaged," said Sadie, who did not want to continue this conversation and tried to ask

Frank if he wanted to go through the buffet line. Before she could finish her sentence, Scapula interrupted.

"Well, I think it's scandalous. They're over the hill," Scapula said.

"I wouldn't say that in front of William and Alpaca if I were you," said Frank.

"I think they're ridiculous, too," muttered Tarsal.

"Why can't you just be happy for them?" asked Sadie. "What difference does it make to you anyway? Come on, Frank. Let's go get some food." After they were out of earshot, she said to her husband, "Wonder if they're talking about us now."

"I'm sure they are. At least they'll give Milton and Alpaca a rest." And speaking of the happy couple, the Stenners saw Milton and Mayrose's blanket next to Fern Oldhat's.

"It's so good to see the two of you. Congratulations on your engagement," Fern said to Mayrose and Milton.

"Actually, you're a little late on the engagement. Congratulations," said Milton.

"I don't understand," said Fern. "Are you still engaged?"

"A little more than that," answered Milton, Mayrose smiling mysteriously by his side.

"We went to the justice of the peace yesterday morning. This lovely lady is now my bride." Fern screeched so loud that everyone in the immediate vicinity rushed to her side. Alpaca reached her first.

"Fern, are you all right?" she asked. It took Fern a minute to catch her breath.

"Yes, I'm fine. Did you know Milton and Mayrose are already married?" Much to Mayrose's dismay, Fern yelled as more people gathered around. "Who married you?"

"We went to the Justice of the Peace," answered Mayrose.

"You mean Lily Lawson?" asked Fern.

"Yes," the newlyweds said in unison.

"She's a personal friend of mine. She was in the shop yesterday afternoon and never said a word," said Fern.

"I doubt if Miss Lawson goes around making announcements

about everyone she has married," said Milton, as William the Younger, who joined the group when he heard Fern scream, nodded in agreement.

"She has always been discreet... She married us, you know," said William, taking his wife's hand, who smiled lovingly at him and squeezed his hand back. About that time, Ned and Gardenia Cochran strolled up with Tarsal and Scapula hot on their heels. Tarsal pushed past Ned and bumped into Gardenia.

"Scuse me, Gardenia. I need to see what's going on here," mumbled Tarsal as he pulled Scapula along with him.

"Nothing much to see. Just an old married couple," said Milton.

"Well, I think it's just- Ouch! What did you do that for?" Tarsal asked his wife, who had poked him hard in the ribs.

"Just say congratulations, Tarsal," said Scapula, knowing they were outnumbered.

"Yeah, great. I guess," he mumbled, rubbing his side.

"I wish both couples a very happy and long life together," said Scapula. "Come on, Tarsal. I think you've spread enough joy for one day." She might be a gossip, but she wasn't stupid. It's not good to insult the guests of your hosts, or your hosts, for that matter. The rest of the group just smiled at each other and shook their heads. Just when they thought they were safe, Hubert Patterson ambled up to the group.

Milton decided it might be good to take the bull by the horns where Hubert was concerned. He took Mayrose's hand and said, "I'd like you to meet my new bride, Hubert."

"What happened to that other lady I saw you with at the library last week? Does she know that you're married?" asked Hubert.

"This is that other lady you saw me with. This is Mayrose, whom you talked with when you told her how to check out a book."

"No. I don't think so," said Hubert. "That lady had silvery hair and blue eyes."

"Yes, just like Mayrose here," said Milton. The rest of the people who were gathered around were shaking their heads and walking away. They had known Hubert long enough to see this conversation had nowhere to go but down.

"Well, I just hope that other gal never finds out you're married," said Hubert as he walked away like Moses parting the Red Sea, people turning their backs on him and scuttling away as quickly as possible.

Hubert's ridiculous idea about who the woman beside Milton was would shrivel and die on the Chanceville Grapevine. He would soon jump to another erroneous conclusion.

54

THE BLIND POODLE SISTERS
SPLIT UP

The first Sunday after the Williams's garden party, the Reverend Edgar Beagle was eager to preach his first sermon at the MAIN CHURCH of the Righteous, as was Reverend Chuck Peevish at Main Avenue Christian Church. The buildings were constructed in similar styles and finished that same week.

The new churches and their pastors were the main topics of conversation around town, mainly at the Tip Topp Diner and over the fresh produce at the IGA. The two camps were not defined by who believed whether dogs had souls or not. Their church affiliation was mainly determined by whether they liked Ned Cochran or Tarsal Henley, or in Tarsal's case, whether they could tolerate him for more than five minutes because "his" church asked for the least amount of tithing.

The week before, at the garden party, the Blind Poodle Sisters, Annette and Babbette, had talked to Reverend Peevish about the upcoming services.

"I'm very much looking forward to hearing your service this Sunday," said Annette.

Before the reverend could respond, Babbette interrupted. "What are you talking about, Annette?" she asked.

"Well, of course, we'll be going to Ned's church. I can't stand that Tarsal Henley," answered Annette.

"Have you forgotten our last name is Poodle? The pastor at Tarsal's church is named Edgar Beagle. We HAVE to go to a church whose pastor's last name is a dog breed. How could you even think of attending anywhere else?" said Babbette. At this point, Reverend Peevish quietly walked away. Knowing this was a conversation he should not get involved in.

"That doesn't make any sense, Babbette. You can't base your choice of church on the pastor's name. We have to go to the same church. We've done everything together our whole lives, gone everywhere together, dressed alike, and agreed about most things," said Annette.

"Well, I'm not going to any church whose pastor isn't named after an animal. It's just a rule of mine. Remember Reverend Trout Finn? We went to his church," Babette rebutted.

"That's because it was the church Daddy always took us to. It had nothing to do with the name of the pastor. I think you made that rule up on the spot," said Annette.

"Nope, I'm going to the MAIN CHURCH of the Righteous, and you can't change my mind," said Babette, crossing her arms for effect. She knew her sister couldn't see her, but it made her feel more powerful and sure of herself. Babbette felt so powerful that she just walked away from her sister, the other half of herself. Something she'd never done before. Of course, they'd always had their little tiffs, but nothing like this. Annette soon realized her sister had walked away; she was so downhearted that she couldn't enjoy the party. She just wanted to leave. She caught a ride with Geraldine Nurse.

"Where's your sister?" asked Geraldine. She assumed she was talking to Annette because she was wearing a sundress with a large sunflower print, but she didn't want to chance getting it wrong.

"Oh, Babette wasn't feeling well and went home early."

"I'm sorry to hear that," Geraldine said, glad to know she was talking to Annette. "I need to run into the library for a quick second. Do you mind waiting in the car for a minute?

"I'll just get out here. I'll walk the next few blocks," said Annette, not wanting to take a chance on Geraldine seeing Babette and revealing the lie she'd told about her sister not feeling well. She thought her sister Babbette was losing her mind. And that's what really scared her. The twins had never walked anywhere without each other since they had become blind at ten years of age. This must be what loneliness feels like, thought Annette as she walked alone, feeling almost naked.

Even though they were in their early forties and lived in a many-roomed mansion, the sisters still shared a bedroom. Annette immediately went to their room to look for her sister when she got home. She wasn't in there and felt for the door to their dad's old room, which was closed. She tried to open the door. It was locked.

"Babbette, you open this door immediately," yelled Annette as she pounded on the door.

"Nope. You can't make me. I'm not speaking to you," said Babbette, who was tired of being bossed around by her "older" (by ten minutes) sister.

"You just did speak to me," answered her twin, who always enjoyed a good quibble. This made Babbette really stop speaking to her sister. She knew how much Annette enjoyed quibbling and was determined not to give her that pleasure EVER again, or at least for the rest of the night.

About this time, Poppy came running up the stairs to see what all the commotion was about. She had never heard a cross word between the sisters since she came to live with them after their daddy died. When Annette filled her in, she just shook her head and walked away, saying to no one in particular, "What is it with this town and their silly feuds?"

Sure enough, the next morning, the sisters did the heretofore unthinkable and went to separate churches. Both congregations, for the most part, were happy with their choice of pastor. And if they weren't totally thrilled, all seemed to be willing to give Reverend Beagle and Reverend Peevish a chance before they rushed to judgment, which seems a little out of character for the people of Chanceville, whose collective hobby was judging people. But they were so tired of the whole silly feud that they just wanted to get on with it and enjoy their beautiful new churches.

The churches were very close to the twins' house, and they reached the gate at the same time upon returning from the separate services. "After you," said Annette to Babbette, hoping this would help to make amends. She hadn't slept much the night before. She kept dreaming that she was falling off a cliff and her twin wouldn't save her. She never wanted to spend another night without Babbette, even though they had only been a few doors apart.

"Thank you," said Babbette, hoping this was a good sign. "Would you like to sit on the porch swing for a while?"

"Yes, I would. I'll let Poppy know we're home and to call us when lunch is ready."

"How was Reverend Beagle's sermon?" asked Annette, venturing into dangerous territory.

"Very disappointing. Reverend Beagle didn't mention one single animal. How can you have the last name of Beagle and not at least mention a lamb or a donkey? They're in the Bible."

"I'm sorry to hear that," said Annette, feeling vindicated but thinking better of mentioning that. Does this mean you'll be attending church with me next Sunday?"

"Oh, yes. I'm never going anywhere without you again. It's just not natural. Anyway, even if the Reverend Beagle had told an animal story, I'm not sure I could go back there again."

"Why not?" asked Annette.

"That Tarsal Henley. Bragging about "his" church, as if he built it single-handedly," Babbette answered, taking her sister's hand when Poppy called them into lunch. They went into the house together again.

We can all guess what the topic of conversation was at the Tipp Topp the following day. And you know who got the ball rolling.

"One of those Blind Poodle Sisters came to my church yesterday morning. I've never seen one without the other. Wonder what that was all about?" said Tarsal while adding way too much sugar to his coffee as usual. Sid took the sugar dispenser out of Tarsal's hand. No one wanted Tarsal hopped up on sugar. The caffeine in his coffee was bad enough. As was his usual practice, Sid would slip decaf into his cup if Tarsal had more than two cups to save wear and tear on all of their nerves.

"I gave Annette a ride back from the garden party yesterday. She said Babbette wasn't feeling too well," said Geraldine Nurse, not wanting to admit that she didn't know which twin she was giving a ride to. "Maybe it was Annette at your church service."

"I don't think so," said Doc Ivory. "Annette was at the Main Street Church service. I knew it was Annette because she always wears clothes with sunflowers on them, and Babbette wears sunflowers."

"Hmm, that is puzzling. I can't remember ever seeing one without the other," said Mrs. Crabtree. "Maybe I should go over and offer a prayer."

"NO!" Everyone in the diner shouted at once without even looking up.

"I'm sure they're fine and can work things out for themselves. Besides, Poppy is there to take care of them," said Ned Cochran, always the Chanceville Voice of Reason.

"A lot you know about it, Ned," said Tarsal. "Why don't you mind your own business?"

"You mean like everyone else in this town?" asked Doc Ivory, which caused everyone to chuckle and nod in agreement, which caused Tarsal to harrumph out of there. This was fine with everybody.

"Watch where you're going," said Tarsal as he bumped into Hubert Patterson coming in the door of the diner.

"What new bee is in his bonnet?" Hubert asked Sid as he took a seat at the counter.

"We were talking about the Blind Poodle Sisters going to separate churches yesterday morning," Sid answered, pencil at the ready to take Hubert's order. "What'll it be for you today?"

"The number one, eggs over easy, with a side of bacon and coffee," said Hubert, looking at a menu he had memorized. "No, make that scrambled eggs, Sid. You make the over easy too runny.

Sid decided it wasn't worth correcting the old man.

"What do you mean, Blind Poodle Sisters?" said Hubert.

"As far as I know, blind means they can't see," answered Sid as he poured Hubert his coffee.

"I know what blind means, Sid. Why are you calling them blind?"

"Because they can't SEE," said Sid, already losing his patience with the old man.

"But they're not blind," said Hubert as everyone looked his way in shock. "They can see. They walk and shop all over town on their own. They can't be blind."

"Why do you think they use white canes?" asked Ned.

"I thought they just went with those outlandish get-ups they wear, always wearing sunglasses like they think they're all Hollywood movie stars or something."

"I honestly don't know how you can live in the same town with those girls who have been blind for about thirty years and not know they can't see," said Doc Trueblood, who had been quietly listening to all this palaver from his front corner booth. "They had high fevers we could never determine the cause of, and they both lost their sight at the same time."

"Oh, have you checked them lately?" said Hubert. Maybe they're faking it."

"I check them every year. The damage was permanent. And what on God's green earth would they have to gain by faking something like that?"

"For the money?" mumbled Hubert.

"WHAT money? Their daddy left them a bundle. As usual, Hubert, you don't know what you're talking about," said the doc, uncharacteristically impatient, along with Ned Cochran, known for his patience. If they had a contest in Chanceville to see who had the most patience, Ned and Doc Trueblood would probably tie for that honor.

"Can I have a refill on that coffee, Sid?" asked Hubert, losing interest in a conversation in which the error of his ways was pointed out.

"Maybe I should go over and pray to get their blindness healed," offered Mrs. Crabtree again.

"NO!" shouted everyone in the diner, even Hubert.

55
THE CASE OF THE QUACKS

The following spring, after she had finished the Big Teddy case, Sharon Martin, a.k.a P-tess Ptarmigan, received quite a shock while shopping at the Woolworths for treats for her grandkids' Easter baskets. Stacked up on a center display were boxes of Quacks marshmallow treats shaped like ducks. She grabbed a box, paid for it, and hot-footed it to Sheriff Yesper Orange's office.

"Is Yesper in?" she asked Pearly Ringwald, the dispatch operator for the sheriff.

"What's this about?" shouted inveterate shouter, Pearly.

"I just need to talk to the sheriff," Sharon said, trying to catch her breath.

"I'll need to tell him what it's about."

"No, you don't, Pearly. Come on back, Sharon. Sorry about that. Pearly thinks she needs to know everything that's going on. It's like she thinks she's my personal bodyguard," said the sheriff as he shut the door and did his usual trick of turning up the radio so that Pearly couldn't hear conversations that were none of her business, which were most of them. "What can I help you with?"

"Look what I found at the Woolworths just now," answered Sharon as she pulled the box of Quacks out of her giant purse. "Do you remember that "recipe" that Big Teddy thought was paint to make military planes invisible but was really a recipe for marshmallow treats?"

"Yeah, looks like someone started making them."

"Teddy gave that recipe to Agent Russell Ruby. It was evidence. It should have stopped there. And if anyone will make money off it, it should be relatives of High Horse Harry, er Peter Pander," she said. "I don't want to go to the agency with this until I know more. Don't want to get anyone in trouble needlessly. First, I need to find out who is making these. Can you help me with this?"

"The package says they're manufactured in Gary. Let's give them a call and see what we can find out." After getting the operator to get him the number, the sheriff rang them. It rang and rang and rang. Finally, someone picked up.

"Yeah," said a gruff-sounding man.

"Is this the plant where Quacks are made?

"Who wants to know?" said the voice.

"Who am I speaking to?" asked the sheriff.

"Not important."

"Am I speaking to the owner?"

"Nope."

"I'm the manager of a small grocery store down in Jasper. I'm hearing good things about your product. I'd like to learn a little more about it and maybe order some for my store," said the sheriff, making big eyes at Sharon, who was having a hard time keeping a straight face.

"Where'd you hear about 'em?"

"From my daughter, she bought some for my granddaughter, who is begging for more."

Where'd your daughter get 'em?"

"Dunno. I didn't ask."

"We don't sell just to anybody. We'll need a credit reference from your bank. Once you give me that, I'll check it out and call you back."

"Can't you just answer a few questions? Like who owns the

company. I like to know who I'm dealing with. I hope you're run by a good Christian family," said the sheriff, quickly running out of ways to improvise.

"You ask a lot of questions. Don't see what being a Christian has to do with selling candy."

"Well, it's sort of a rule of mine. Doesn't look like we can do business together," said Sheriff Orange, hanging up quickly. "Wow, something's fishy about this whole thing. Makes me wonder if it's a front for something else. Whoever this guy was, he asked all the questions, didn't answer one."

"Stinks to high heaven as far as I'm concerned," said Sharon. "This gets more puzzling all the time."

"I know a private detective in Indianapolis, name of Magnum Paltry. Let me give him a call. I may not give him all the details. Just ask him to do a little digging. Meantime, I think we should sample the wares. I'll buy some more later to send to Mr. Magnum."

"Ooo, yes!" said Sharon, never one to turn down a sweet treat. She quickly opened the package and handed it to Yesper so that he could pick one out. Then, she chose one for herself. They both bit the heads off their ducks first.

"Pretty tasty," said Sharon after consuming the whole duck. "What do you think?"

"Pretty sugary. I think kids will love em. Somebody's got a hit on their hands, which makes it all the more important we find out who's manufacturing these since people died and went to jail over it.

"Well, I've taken up enough of your time, Sheriff Orange. Keep me posted, and let me know if you or the detective need any help." The sheriff was amused to note that Sharon hadn't offered him another Quack.

"You can help. Here's some petty cash. Will you go back to Woolworths and buy up the rest?" said the sheriff as he whipped the door open, nearly causing Pearly to topple over.

"Pearly, are you all right?" he said after she righted herself.

"Yeah, just chasing down a damn dust bunny."

"Sharon, thanks so much for bringing this to my attention. You have no idea how important this could be."

"Oh, you're welcome," she said as he shook her hand enthusiastically.

By the time Sharon got to the Woolworths, she was almost out of breath from all this rushing around. The Quacks supply was dwindling already. She grabbed the five remaining boxes and headed for the cash register.

"Do you think you'll be getting more of these before Easter?" she asked Babs, possibly the oldest cashier ever but still sharp as a tack. No one knew how old she was or could remember a time when Babs hadn't worked there. After all these years, she couldn't care less what people bought or why. She wasn't deaf. She just pretended to be. Saved her a lot of unwanted chit-chat.

"That'll be $10," said Babs without looking up as she took a 20-dollar bill from Sharon. Another ploy of hers is never look them in the eye. No sense in sending a signal that you might be open to conversation. "I have no idea. Next!"

While Sharon was on her mission, the sheriff called Magnum Paltry to fill him in on the Quack situation. The sheriff told him it might be safer for Sharon Martin if Paltry did the initial leg work. The detective was eager to take the case. He hadn't had an interesting case for a while. Lately, he'd mostly been taking divorce cases, his least favorite. He suspected there was more to this than met the eye in the case for the sheriff. He couldn't wait to start snooping. Soon, he was on the phone with some contacts he had in the money laundering business, which he guessed this whole thing was about.

56
PALTRY PLAYS A HUNCH

About a week later, Pearly was standing in the sheriff's office discussing her vacation schedule when the private line he had installed for some privacy rang.

She grabbed the phone before he could pick it up, as usual, ignoring the things that were meant to exclude her. He would have fired her a long time ago, but she was his wife's niece, and the trouble he would have been in at home would be much bigger than the aggravation Pearly caused him at work.

"Sheriff's office," she yelled as Yesper tried to grab the phone from her. "Who's calling?"

"Tell him it's Buddy," said Paltry, puzzled that someone answered the sheriff's private line. He used the code name they had agreed upon in the event of situations just like this one.

"Just give me the damn phone, Pearly. Go answer the phone you're assigned to." This time, he successfully wrested the phone from her iron grip. As she stomped out of the office, the sheriff told Buddy to hang on a second while he walked over to the radio and turned it up. After that debacle, the two men agreed that Yesper would drive to Indianapolis to Paltry's office so they could meet in private. The sheriff filled Paltry in on what he knew about Quacks. "I know Agent Ruby, who was in charge of the case, and I really don't believe he was involved, so I think it would be best if you do the initial asking around. The detective agreed to make some calls and get back to the sheriff when he knew something."

The following week, they settled themselves in Paltry's smoky office. Yesper thought the only way to be safe from Pearly's ears was to meet in Paltry's office.

"What have you got for me, Paltry?"

"I think this might be a money-laundering operation," said Paltry.

"Don't tell me you think Agent Ruby is involved with this. I thought he was a good guy."

"No, no. Ruby's clean. He worked with an agent named Sigmund Colon, known as Siggy. Apparently, he has a gambling problem and got in debt to the wrong people. They got him to steal a formula that was confiscated from a small-time crook named Theodore "Big Teddy" Munson. They got the bright idea to produce these things up in Gary as a way to launder drug money. Apparently, the product is in demand, so they've made this profitable even though it's a front. What's our next step?"

"Do you think Agent Ruby is aware of this?"

"It's my sense that he doesn't know. From what I know of him, he would have been all over this," said Paltry.

'You answered my question. I'll contact Russell. He'll take care of it."

"Sounds like a plan. Let me know how it all plays out. I hear these guys are some tough customers."

They had previously agreed on the detective's fees, and the sheriff said. "I brought your paid invoice and a check. I added a little extra for your discretion on this job." *Glenfiddich here I come.*

"Hey, that's great, thanks," said the detective, already thinking his first purchase would be a bottle of single malt Scotch rather than the cheap stuff he usually had to buy.

"Oh, I have a question for you. How do I get to Al Green's from here? Ever since I was told how delicious their tenderloins are, that's all I can think about. We don't have tenderloin sandwiches in Chanceville. Maybe after I check it out, I'll talk to Sid Topp, who runs our local diner, and get him to add giant tenderloins to his menu."

"I'll do you one better. Are you parked in the garage?" The sheriff nodded yes. "Me too. Follow me in your car. We can have lunch together. I must admit I'm hooked on those sandwiches myself," he said, patting his slightly rounded belly.

"Terrific. On one condition. It's my treat. You did a bang-up job on this and got to the bottom of it way quicker than I would have been able to."

"Deal!"

Yesper Orange was so impressed with the giant tenderloin that the first thing he did upon his return to Chanceville was stop by the Tipp Topp. He was on a mission.

57
THE HENDRIX CELEBRATE
GOOD NEWS

As it does everywhere, time had a way of passing without notice in Chanceville. Tammy and Hal Hendrix had settled quite well into married life. They were happy with each other and the life they had built together. Hal continued to run the funeral parlor, and with the help of her mother-in-law, Peggy, Tammy had made the Wax Museum quite successful. It was now a regularly scheduled field trip for many schools in southern Indiana due to Tammy's efforts to add Chanceville and Indiana history exhibits to the museum.

On the day of their third anniversary, Tammy had big news for her husband. She had prepared his favorite meal of rib eye steak, baked potato, and salad with Wishbone French dressing. Hal had taught her a lot about wines, and she had chosen a nice Burgundy to go with their meal. There would also be candlelight and soft music.

Hal had brought her a beautiful non-funereal bouquet of long-stemmed red roses at lunchtime.

"These are a small, but not the only token, of my love for you," said Hal, who had become quite the romantic, much to Tammy's delight.

"What do you mean not the only token?" said Tammy. "You've got that mischievous look in your eye, Hal Hendrix." The more she fell in love with her husband, the younger he looked to her. Even the good people of Chanceville had noticed that the once stodgy-looking and acting gentleman had a more vibrant air about him. Marriage to Tammy indeed agreed with him. He woke up surprised every morning at how lucky he was to have a wonderful woman like Tammy to love and to love him back.

"Don't be so nosy, darling. You'll find out this evening."

"You may not be the only one with a surprise up your sleeve," she said with a matching twinkle in her eye. "I will tell you that we're having a lovely dinner. I have everything planned, even a special dessert."

"Can't you give me a little hint, sweetie cakes?" said Hal, putting his arms around her waist.

"Nope. Don't you have some work to do? I know I do."

"Fine. I'll go, but only because the sooner I get my work done, the sooner I can get back to you." Promptly at 5:00, Hal finished the paperwork, arranging two funerals required for the coming week. He unlocked his desk drawer and pulled out a narrow box that held a necklace with three diamonds for their three years of wedded bliss. He couldn't wait to present it to her with all the love it symbolized.

Tammy had the wine opened and breathing and had prepared Hal's pre-dinner cocktail, dry martini with extra olives ready for him when he entered the residence, which was upstairs over the funeral parlor. She had gotten over her uneasiness about the business her husband was in, no longer thinking of the cold bodies his hands touched so often. His hands were so warm and loving that they banished those thoughts from her mind. She also loved the way he was with the bereaved families who came to him for his services. They received so much more than caskets and organ music. He was kind and supportive without giving them platitudes that were often unhelpful. And he only tried to sell them what they could afford.

"Is that a new dress?" Hall asked as she handed him his martini and kissed him on the cheek. "You look lovely."

"It is. Bought it, especially for this occasion. Glad you like it. Come to the kitchen and talk to me while I finish our salads." They talked of how their days went, both bursting at the seams to reveal their surprises to each other but staying cool on the outside. They enjoyed their meal, Hal commenting on how his steak was done to perfection.

"I hope you saved room for dessert. I've made something special."

"I might have a little room left. Here, let me help you clear the table."

"No, you sit still and finish your wine. I'll be right back." She took their plates into the kitchen, started the coffee, and brought the Baked Alaska to the dining room.

"Wow, don't tell me you made that beautiful confection."

"I did. In honor of our honeymoon and all of the things you've introduced me to," said Tammy as she flambéed the meringue. Hal couldn't stop himself from clapping like a young child.

"The coffee should be ready in a minute. Would you do the honors of slicing?" she said, handing him the cake knife. As she sat down, she saw the jeweler's box on her placemat.

"What's this?"

"Open it and see," said Hal, grinning from ear to ear. "I hope you like it."

Tammy's eyes filled with tears when she saw the three sparkling diamonds on a thin gold chain. "Oh, Hal! It's beautiful, three diamonds for our three years together. Help me put it on. My hands are shaking."

"I'll try. My hands are shaking, too," Hal said through his own tears. He finally managed to hook the clasp, then went to the bedroom to fetch a hand mirror so Tammy could see how his gift looked on her. "While you're admiring yourself, I'll get the coffee."

"You certainly have this Baked Alaska thing down pat. So delicious. Didn't you like the wine? I noticed you hardly drank any. I thought it was an excellent choice."

"I actually didn't even taste it."

"Really? Why not?"

"My stomach's been feeling a little queasy lately."

"Why didn't you tell me you weren't feeling well? We could have postponed our celebration to another night or gone out to eat."

"I don't think I'll feel that much better in a day or two."

"What? Have you been to the doctor? How serious is this?" said Hal, panic in his voice.

"About nine months' worth of seriousness," said Tammy, smiling broadly.

It took a minute for his brain to comprehend what his wife was telling him. "

"OH! Really? OH! Tammy!" he cried as his wife nodded vigorously while shedding more tears. Then they were both full-on sobbing, laughing, sobbing.

"Hal, where are you going?" she asked as he ran into the bedroom. He returned with two clean handkerchiefs; things were getting a little messy. "When did you find out? When are you due? Oh, God, I'm so happy."

"I found out for sure this morning. Doc confirmed what I've been suspecting for a while but was afraid to hope. I've been bursting to tell you all day. I'm two months along. The baby is due in April."

"Are you feeling alright? All of this cooking and baking you did today. Should you be working that hard?"

"I feel pretty good so far, just a little queasy in the mornings. Doc says I'm healthy as a horse. Not sure I like that comparison, though," she said, laughing through her still-flowing tears.

"Oh, my darling. You've made me so happy in so many ways already. This is the icing, no, the meringue on the Baked Alaska." And with that, they both burst out laughing without the tears.

Tammy's pregnancy progressed smoothly, for the most part. She had to work hard at keeping Hal and his overprotectiveness at bay. However, there was some sadness lurking about. Hal's mother, Peggy, was in declining health. The couple hoped she could hang on until the baby was born. Hal was an only child, and Peggy was excited about her first grandchild. Years ago, she had given up hope that, at his age, 35, he would ever find a wife or have a family. Then her beloved Tammy came along and made Hal's life complete and, by proxy, Peggy's.

Peggy was worn out and no longer had the energy to go on the outings to the Hem and Haul Fabric Store and Trash Removal Service that she had enjoyed so much. Her daughter-in-law still spent time with her, but she missed going to the Wax Museum to refurbish the costumes for the wax figures. On good days, Peggy kept busy knitting baby clothes and blankets. Since they didn't know if they were having a boy or a girl, she knitted tiny sweaters in all colors, sometimes in the same sweater. When she tired of knitting, she got creative and started crocheting little outfits in the shape of different fruits. She was especially proud of the yellow one with a hood that made it look like a banana.

Tammy honored her mother-in-law by keeping a few of the more bizarre wax figures as Peggy had envisioned them. They were always a good draw, but she wanted the museum to become more educational. She was having success along those lines and invited local schools to include the wax museum in their field trip schedules.

In early April, Tammy gave birth to a healthy baby girl. They named her Elizabeth Margaret Hendrix after both of their mothers. When the doctor gave the okay for the new parents to take their baby out, the first thing they did was dress her up in her crocheted banana outfit to see her grandmother.

As luck would have it, Peggy was having a rare good day and was thrilled to see her granddaughter dressed in the outfit she had so lovingly made. Hal took lots of pictures with Peggy holding the baby banana. He realized his daughter would have no memories of this remarkable woman. He wanted his daughter to have these photos included in the baby book they were making for her. Peggy lived long enough for them to make several visits to the nursing home with Lisbet, as they called her. The day after they visited Grandma Peggy when her granddaughter was wearing the last of the fruit-themed outfits that she could fit into, Peggy passed away quietly in her sleep.

58

PEGGY GETS WAXED

Tammy and Hal would miss Peggy terribly, but it was hard to stay sad now that they had Lisbet, the happiest baby they had ever seen. To Tammy's relief, Hal was a relaxed father who loved caring for his baby girl. He didn't even mind changing diapers. They had the perfect business where, between the two of them, they could take care of the baby without having to find a sitter while they worked.

Hal had asked a funeral director over in Liberty to prepare his mother's body for burial. He knew he wouldn't be able to do it himself. Tammy asked if she could do her hair and makeup, which she had been helping her mother-in-law with since she married her son.

A few days after the funeral, Hal was going through his mother's things that they had brought back from the Sally Forth Home for the Elderly and Infirm. He sat a box marked "Papers" on the floor in his office and kind of forgot about it until things had calmed down after the funeral and the luncheon after.

Everyone in town knew and loved Peggy, so her son knew they would need a big venue for a dinner that neither of the new churches was big enough to accommodate. Besides, he didn't want people to have to choose one and take a chance of losing some people who would like to attend. He secured the community building at the Loone County Fair Grounds. It was perfect. Many citizens thought this was the most well-attended funeral they ever had in Chanceville. There were so many flowers they were able to give a bouquet to each room in the Sally Forth Home for the Elderly and Infirm and a lovely big bouquet for the reception area of the Loone County Hospital. Of course, Mrs. Crabtree insisted on being in charge of distributing the flowers that went to the hospital. She tried to make each patient pray before she would reward them with a bouquet without much success. However, some patients were just too sick to resist and agreed to pray with the determined volunteer to get her to go away and leave them in peace. Many of them believed in the power of prayer, but didn't appreciate having it foisted on them.

When Hal finally looked in the box of his mother's papers, he found a manila envelope marked private and confidential in his mother's scrawled handwriting. Inside was a set of legal documents from the firm of Tort, Lawson & Venue. It was Peggy Hendrix's last will and testament. Everything looked straightforward, with her son being her sole beneficiary. It had been updated since his marriage to include Tammy and any issue of the union in the event that Hal died first. There was one last request that nearly knocked Hal Hendrix off his chair. His dear, sweet mother wanted to be memorialized by having a wax figure of herself in the museum made by her beloved daughter-in-law, Tammy. She had even included a photo of her as a young bride that she wanted to be used as her likeness.

First, he went into his den and poured himself a Scotch. His hands shook so badly that he nearly splashed that precious amber liquid out of the cut crystal glass. All he could think about was how he was going to tell Tammy this. Fortunately, she had taken Lisbet to the park and would be out for a while. He needed time to sort his thoughts out. He lived with the dead in his home daily. He didn't spook easily, but this felt too creepy to have a likeness of his mother watching them all the time. After he downed the Scotch and his hands had mostly stopped trembling, he returned to his office to call Terrence Tort, his and his mother's attorney.

"Hello, Hal. Glad to hear from you. I was going to contact you in a few days. Just wanted to give you time to try to get back to normal before we went over the will. I don't foresee any problems. It's all pretty standard," said Terrence.

"Really, Terrence? Standard? What's standard about having a wax figure of your mother staring at you every day?"

"Well, I understand this is a bit er... unusual, but she was very insistent on this point."

"Sooo, I have to honor it?"

"Your inheritance is not contingent on this clause if that's what you mean, but I'm afraid you'll be haunted either way you go. If you don't do it, you might have a lot of guilt about not following her wishes, or you will be haunted by having to look at her visage every day."

"I'm just so flabbergasted. We were very close, and Mother never said a word about this."

"Maybe she was afraid you'd try to talk her out of it."

"Hmm, maybe. I dread telling Tammy. She and Mother were very close; she loved my mother like her own, but she's in the museum nearly every day. I'm not sure she wants to be that close to her. "

"Why don't you two talk it over and come in tomorrow morning at 10:00, and we'll go over everything."

"Okay. See you in the morning." Hal spent the rest of the time until Tammy and the baby came back staring at the wall. Tammy didn't call out when she went in; instead, she headed straight upstairs to the residence. That told him the baby was probably asleep. He padded up the stairs and waited for his wife in the kitchen, where he put the water on to make her a nice cup of calming chamomile tea.

Tammy came up behind Hal, standing at the counter, and put her arms around him. "Your daughter was the hit of the park. Everyone stopped to admire her, charming all with her big blue eyes and ear-to-ear smiles. I saw Mayrose and Milton Matthews. They offered to babysit anytime we need a night out. Let's take them up on it when things settle down."

"Mmm... yes. Settle down. That could be a while. Here, have a seat," Hal said as he pulled a kitchen chair out for her. "I've made you a nice cup of tea."

"What's going on, darling? You look like you've seen a ghost," she said, taking his hand after he shakily set down her cup and saucer.

"In a way, I have," he said, having a hard time looking his beloved in the eye.

"What are you talking about?" As we know, Tammy is very superstitious, and her curiosity level rose immediately. "Don't tell me you saw your mother here."

"No. It's not that, but we may be seeing more of her than we ever thought we would," he said, finally looking at her. Tammy took a big gulp of tea. It wasn't like her husband to have trouble getting to the point. When she carefully placed her cup back in its saucer, he took both of her hands in his.

"Hal, you're beginning to frighten me. Just tell me what is going on."

"I read Mother's will while you were gone. It contained quite a surprise," he said, handing her the document and pointing to the troublesome addendum. "Here, read this part."

As Tammy read, her big blue eyes grew larger and larger. Hal had gone into the den to get another Scotch to fortify himself for the most likely to ensue argument. He heard a strange noise coming from the kitchen. When he came up behind his wife, he saw her shoulders shaking. Oh, dear. This is going to be worse than I thought. As he sat down in front of his wife, he saw that she wasn't crying at all. She was laughing. She looked up at Hal. No tears.

"What is so funny?" he asked, seeing nothing funny about this situation.

"Oh, sweetheart. This is so Peggy. I'm not the least bit surprised."

"She must have told you. You're taking this way too well."

"Peggy never said a word. You know I would have told you if she had. I'm not surprised because it just seems like something she would do. I'm sorry you were here alone and were shocked." And then she began giggling all over again. "I'm sorry. I'm just so tickled about this."

"You mean you won't mind having her stare at you daily? You'll be around her more than me."

"I think it will be a comfort, having her watch over me. We had so many happy hours together in the museum. It's been lonely in there ever since she wasn't able to join me anymore. I'm already thinking about the fabric I'll choose for her dress," Tammy said as she looked at the photo her mother-in-law left for them. "She was so beautiful."

"Well, I guess if you can handle it, so can I," said Hal, finishing off the last of his drink. "We have an appointment with Terrence in the morning to go over the details of the will. I guess we'll sort everything out then."

"I can call Mayrose and see if they're ready to make good on their offer to babysit."

"Let's take her with us. Terrence asked me when he was going to get to meet her."

"Will you check on her while I start dinner?" Her husband nodded as he headed for his daughter's room. His wife never ceased to amaze him. And for that, he was eternally grateful.

Lisbet woke up just as they were finishing dinner. Tammy nursed her while she watched Hal wash the dishes. "Peggy taught me how to pour the wax and sculpt. She said I had the touch. I'll start sketching tomorrow when we return from the lawyer's office. I know I can find a suitable fabric for her dress. I have an appointment at the Lovely Locks next week to get my hair cut. I'll talk to Fern about wigs."

"You sound excited about this."

"You know, I am. What better way to honor your mother?"

"I know you're right. It may take me a while to get used to the idea, but I'll try. Thank you for being so understanding about this."

"It's not about understanding. It's about love. I love you, and I adored your mother. It's just that simple." That night, they fell asleep wrapped in each other's arms.

The next morning, Hal and Tammy met with Terrence Tort, who was relieved to hear that Tammy was on board with the wax figurine of Peggy.

She had left them a tidy sum from her years of saving. The couple was doing quite well financially, so they decided to put this money in a college fund for their daughter. This would please Peggy, who firmly believed women should have their own careers.

It didn't take Tammy long to find a suitable ivory Duchesse Satin for Peggy's wedding dress at the Hem and Haul Fabric Store and Trash Removal Service.

"Looks like you're going to have a bride at the museum," said Priscilla, the owner of the store, as she expertly unrolled the bolt and cut a little more than the amount Tammy had requested. She and Peggy had been good customers over the years, and she sensed this was going to be a special project.

"Uh, huh," said Tammy, not wanting to reveal just yet who the bride would be. It would be all over town soon enough. "This really is beautiful fabric." She handed Priscilla the pattern, thread, and pearl buttons to cover what she needed.

"Hmm. This pattern reminds me of a dress I made years ago. Can't remember who it was for."

"Oh, well." Tammy paid quickly and escaped before she had to answer any more questions. As she strolled Lisbet home in the baby buggy, she began to think maybe she should have Hal take her to Indianapolis to purchase the wig she needed for the figure of her mother-in-law, who had kept her light blond hair tinted pink. She could manage the tint herself, but Peggy wore a tousled Marilyn Monroe style do that Tammy wasn't sure she could manage. Once the ladies who patronized the Lovely Locks saw that, it would be all over town. Yes, that would be best. There was no such thing as a secret in Chanceville. She would talk to Hal about that tonight. She wanted to have an event for the surprise unveiling of Peggy's figurine.

Tammy worked every spare moment on the figure and the dress for the next two months. Thank goodness, Lisbet was such a good baby and played happily in her playpen while her mother sculpted and sewed. She had hired Sara "Sugar Pants" Peterson to run the museum while she closed herself off in the workshop every afternoon. Sara had successfully made it through menopause and felt quite happy about life. She loved greeting all the people who came through the museum. She knew a lot about the history of Chanceville, so she gave an added value to the tours.

Even though school was out, they were busy all summer. Tammy had convinced Hal to put up a billboard outside of town to advertise. It had brought travelers in from all over the country as they drove across the Midwest heading for their mountain vacations. She hadn't even let her husband in the workshop. She wanted to have the figure complete before the unveiling. She was pleased so far but was nervous about what Hal would think of the facsimile of his mother. Peggy had been quite a beauty in her time, and Tammy wanted to do her justice.

When she felt like there was no more she could do with the figure, she said, "Hal, are you ready to see the figure of your mother? If you're not up to it, I'll certainly understand." She had realized that she would never be fully satisfied with the wax figure of her mother-in-law. She feared she wouldn't get it right, especially since her husband was still struggling with the idea.

"I know you've worked hard on it, and I've been thinking a lot about this whole thing. This really has nothing to do with me. This was Mother's dearest wish. I want to honor that, be a good son, even after she's gone. Also, I hate to admit it, but I'm curious about what you've done. I don't think anyone else would have been up to the task or wanted to do a better job than you, darling. So, that's the long answer to your question. Yes, I want to see it."

"Great, let's do it now, then. Lisbet is down for the night; even if she wakes up, we won't be there long. You can stay as long as you like. I'll come back in after you tell me what you think of her to give you some time alone. Let me go in first and get the right lighting on."

Tammy had set the museum lights on low, with a soft spotlight on the figure of Peggy. Holding his wife's hand, Hal slowly walked into the hushed space. It had a feeling of reverence. Okay, so far, he thought. The closer he came to the figure of Peggy, the less anxious he felt. As soon as he stood before the figure and saw his mother's face, gentle tears slid down his cheeks. Tammy also teared up when she went to get a folding chair for him to sit on. She could see his knees shaking and was afraid they would buckle under him.

"Here, honey. Sit down," Tammy said, afraid to ask him why he was crying. Did he love it or hate it? She wasn't sure she wanted to know. Hal pulled a handkerchief from his back pocket and loudly blew his nose.

"Do you want to be alone?" Tammy whispered. Hal reached out for his wife's hand, taking it tenderly. He sat there for a minute or two, trying to compose himself enough to speak. It seemed like forever to her. Then he stood up and took her into his arms.

"I've never seen anything so beautiful. I can't believe how you were able to capture not only Mother's likeness but her essence. As I said, I knew you would do a good job, but this is above and beyond. I think I know part of your secret."

"My secret? I don't have any secrets from you."

"That's not what I meant. The secret to your artistry is love. You put so much love into this, and it shows. She positively glows."

"It probably also helps that she's not green," said Tammy, and then they both began to laugh, their tears drying up.

"I'm so happy I didn't disregard Mother's wishes. As usual, she was right, especially when she said I had the best wife in the world. She died knowing I was happy. What a gift that was."

"Oh, Hal. I adored your mother and miss her so much," said Tammy, trying not to dissolve into tears again.

"I think I was so busy missing her myself that I didn't even think about you missing her also. I'm sorry for that."

"It's okay. We're both feeling that loss. Whenever I look at Lisbet with her blonde tousled hair like her grandmother, I think about how much she would have loved spending time with her only grandmother and how much fun Peggy would have had with her."

"I think about that a lot, too. I'm just grateful that Mother got to see her. And we got pictures of her in all those fruit costumes she made. I've noticed she's already outgrowing them."

"You stay as long as you want. I'm going to get up and check on the baby," said Tammy, kissing Hal on the cheek.

"I'll be up in a few minutes."

As Tammy climbed the stairs she wondered what the townspeople would think of Peggy's wax figure. One thing she knew for sure. Everybody would have an opinion. Some would surprise her.

59
HUBERT VISITS THE WAX MUSEUM

The next day was a free day at the museum. A few months ago, Tammy had started making the first Friday of the month a free day to show appreciation to their customers and, hopefully, to bring more people in. It was working. They had solid bookings for the next six months.

The museum opened at 10:00 a.m. When Tammy went to unlock the doors, there was already a long line. She realized that word must have gotten around about a new wax figure on display despite her best efforts. It was Chanceville, after all. She and Hal hadn't wanted to have a formal viewing thinking it would be too much fuss. Let people discover Peggy on their own.

Tammy had placed Lisbet in her playpen, so people who knew the Hendrix family made that their first stop.

"She's such a darling baby," said Mayrose Matthews, her husband, nodding in agreement.

"Thank you. We are quite proud of her, I must admit."

"This could be a long day for her. How about we take her to the park in her stroller after we see the exhibit? It's a lovely day," Mayrose offered.

"Oh, that is so kind of you. I'll take you up on that offer. That way, Hal won't have to take off work to take care of her this afternoon." About that time, Alpaca and William Williams walked over to the group gathering around the baby, who managed to stay sound asleep through all of the commotion. And speaking of commotion, Hubert Patterson was the next person to peer in at the baby.

"She looks so life-like," said Hubert.

"That's because she's alive," said Milton, shaking his head and chuckling.

"I'm pretty sure she's part of the exhibit," said Hubert, reaching in and poking Lisbet before anyone could stop him. Lisbet looked up, saw all the people staring at her, and began wailing.

"Wow, she's even animated. Great job, Tammy!" yelled Hubert above the crying as Tammy picked up the poor little thing.

"Hubert, shut up!" said Doc Ivory. "She's not an exhibit. Why don't you move along?"

"You're not fooling me," mumbled Hubert as he shuffled off to find "another" exhibit.

"What's going on? I could hear the baby crying from my office," said Hal as he came rushing over to his wife and baby. Tammy managed to calm the baby down, but she still looked sleepy. "Here, I'll take her. I finished my paperwork, and I can answer the phone in the residence. I think she needs her bed right now."

"Thanks, honey. The Matthews have offered to take her to the park later. Shall I send them up when they've finished the exhibit?"

"Sounds good. Now go enjoy your admiring public."

She kissed her daughter on the cheek and handed her over to her daddy. Tammy was secretly grateful that Hubert had caused a distraction. She was still nervous about what people would think of Peggy's figure. She could see several people gathered around the figure and decided to bite the bullet and find out what was being said.

"Geraldine Nurse was the first to comment. "Peggy looks so lovely. Is this all your work?" she asked, taking Tammy's shaking hand.

"Yes, I did it all. We were a little nervous about this at first, but this wish was in Peggy's will, and I'm too superstitious not to honor something like that."

"Well, it shows it was a labor of love. I'm sure she's looking down at you, beaming with pride," said the librarian.

"Thank you, that means a lot to me." Next, Alpaca and William came over to Tammy.

"I can't keep my eyes off her. I only briefly met Hal's mother when you brought her to our garden party, but I've heard what a lovely person she was," said Alpaca.

"She was, both inside and out," Tammy replied as she looked at the enlarged framed photograph she had used as the likeness her mother-in-law requested.

"And look at her artistry with the dress," said Prissy Paulson, the Hem and Haul Fabric Shop and Trash Removal Service owner. "I thought you were going to make a wedding dress with that fabric, but I had no idea it would be for Peggy. It's gorgeous. Now I remember where I'd seen that pattern before."

Everyone gathered around nodded in agreement, even Tarsal Henley, who rarely agreed with anyone. As everyone was admiring the wax figure of his mother, Hal came into the room holding Lisbet, who had quit crying after her rude awakening by Hubert, refreshed from her little nap.

"Hal, she is so beautiful. Your wife has done a terrific job honoring your mother," said Trachea Carmichael. "I'm sure you're very proud of her."

"Indeed, I am. Mother would be, too," he said as tears gathered in his eyes. "Oh no!" he said as he spotted Mrs. Crabtree making a beeline for the group gathered around the figure. Everyone turned to look at him. He started to say maybe they should all move on, but he was too late. The infamous Prayer Offerer descended upon them, waving her well-worn Bible. It wasn't that the people of Chanceville didn't believe in prayer, but they were an independent bunch and didn't like to have things forced on them.

"What's going on over here?" shouted Mrs. Crabtree. "For where two or three are gathered together in my name, I am there among them. Matthew 18:20. I count about a dozen. Looks like we have enough for a prayer group or at least a prayer."

"No!" they shouted as one.

"What kind of prayer would you offer?" asked Hubert, much to everyone's dismay. No one had seen him slip into the back of the gathered group.

"Um, you know just a general prayer for the success of this new display. That kind of thing."

"Oh, my God. They've stuffed Peggy Hendrix! Maybe you would want to pray for the person who stuffed her for forgiveness," said the old man as they started yelling at him all at once, except for Mrs. Crabtree, who was dumbstruck, a rare occurrence.

"Just when I thought you couldn't get any dumber, Hubert. You never cease to amaze me," shouted Tarsal. "I should learn never to be surprised by your ignorance." Even the most diplomatic citizens of Chanceville couldn't come up with an argument in Hubert's defense.

"Now, Hubert, what on earth would make you think the Hendrixes would do something like that? This is a WAX MUSEUM. The figures are made of WAX, not actual humans," said Ned, still trying to be the voice of reason but fearing he was wasting his breath as usual with the old man. He feared Hubert was really losing it.

"But this one looks so life-like. I think Peggy is real. I thought the old green-skinned ones that Peggy made were Martians," said the old man.

"Come here, Hubert," said Hal, motioning the old man to approach the figure. "Give me your hand." Hal took him behind the figure and pushed up the wig, and taking Hubert's hand, he told him to scratch the back of "Peggy's" head. "Now, what is that underneath your fingernail?"

"I guess it does feel like wax, but that could just be a cover-up layer."

"Sometimes I wonder why we even try with him," said Doc Ivory. The group all shook their heads and walked away, tacitly agreeing that there was no point in trying to talk sense to the old codger. He was going to think what he was going to think. They had better things to do with their time than argue with the likes of Hubert Patterson.

Despite that unfortunate event, the day was a huge success, as Mayrose and Milton found out when they returned from taking the baby to the park.

The next morning at the Tipp Topp, Mrs. Tree, who had not heard about Hubert's idea concerning Peggy's figurine, patted her tiny stomach after eating a larger-than-usual breakfast, declaring, "I'm stuffed!" to uproarious laughter.

"What? What did I say?" asked the puzzled lady.

"You had to be there," said Doc Ivory.

Hubert may never learn a lesson at his late stage of life, but Wally Williams was about to learn a big one—actions have consequences.

60

THE SHADY RETURN OF WALLY WILLIAMS

Wally had done his time in the Marion County Jail. His family hoped he had learned some lessons while he had time to think about his life. Indeed, he had learned a lot, but unfortunately, it was not what his family had hoped for.

He learned that "work was for suckers," which particularly appealed to this basically lazy young man. He realized that he could get others to work for him. This appealed to him because he enjoyed bossing people around. His mother had made him believe he was better and more intelligent than everyone else. We all know that neither of those things was true. This should have become clear to him when his actions landed him in jail. However, his mother had also instilled the belief in him that nothing was ever his fault. He repeatedly told his cellmate that it was the police who were stupid. The cellmate believed that his real punishment wasn't simply being locked up. It was being locked up with Wally Williams. Luckily for the cellmate, his stint as a captive audience only lasted a couple of weeks. The day he was released, he vowed never to return to jail. No more life of crime for him. If only that had been the lesson Wally learned.

The Williams family sent their driver to pick Wally up the day he was released. None of the family were up for the drive to Indianapolis, nor were they that anxious to see their nephew, a harsh reality for his uncles, but true. William, Wallace, and Alpaca had agreed that they didn't want Wally to live with them, so they had to devise a plan to help the lad support himself. They knew no one in Chanceville would hire him. This was true, no matter how much they thought of his family.

"What can we do? I don't just want us to give him money to support himself. He'll blow through it," said Wallace, his brother and sister-in-law nodding in agreement.

"Even if we bought him a house, he wouldn't take care of it or he'd sell it and blow that money, but we certainly don't want him living here. I think our whole staff would quit," said William. "I'm at a loss."

"What if you give him a lump sum? Tell him that is the last dollar he'll ever get from you. From now on, he's on his own," offered Alpaca. The brothers agreed that might work, but it still didn't seem like the ideal solution. They were growing weary of the seemingly unsolvable problem of Wally.

Little did they know that Wally was way ahead of them. He had run a booming black market operation while incarcerated with his last cellmate. With the money they earned, they entered into a partnership to buy some rigged arcade games and set up their own business. The two cellmates were released on the same day, and the cellmate's girlfriend picked them up. Wally knew his uncles were sending a car, but he had no intention of going back to that one-horse town and his selfish family. He called his uncle collect from a phone booth down the street from the jail.

"Hey, Uncle Wallace. It's Wally," said the newly freed prisoner, as if his uncle hadn't just accepted the charges from his only nephew. "Just calling to let you know you don't need to send a car. I've caught a ride with a buddy of mine. Won't be coming back to Chanceville." And with that information, he hung up the phone, leaving his uncle staring at the receiver in shock. Their driver, Andrew Handy, should be arriving at the prison about now, so it was too late to save the man the trip. Typical, he thought.

"You're not going to believe the phone call I just received," said Wallace as he entered the sun porch where Alpaca and William were enjoying their mid-morning coffee.

"Must have been from Wally," said Alpaca, guessing correctly.

"You mean he didn't even ask for money?" asked William after his brother had filled them in about the brief content of the phone call.

"That's what really struck me as odd. We've had very few conversations that didn't involve that boy asking us for money. I can't imagine where he would go if he's not coming back here," said Wallace.

"I can't imagine he had an actual buddy," said Alpaca. "I'm sorry. That was unkind. I know he's your flesh and blood."

"Don't remind us, my dear. And you're quite correct on the money issue," answered Alpaca's husband. "I must admit to being relieved that he's not coming back here, but it feels like we're waiting for the other shoe to drop, not knowing what he's up to."

"If he's true to form, I don't think it can be anything good," said Wallace. "At least we don't have to listen to Wilma; God rest her soul, defend her son's actions. Those were arguments nobody won."

It wasn't long before the Williams family got wind of what Wally was up to. He and his partner had set up their arcade business over in Carp, just east of Chanceville. Of course, it was Tarsal Henley, who loved delivering bad news at the Tipp Topp diner, who dropped the bomb on the three members of the Williams family as they were having lunch there as they always did on Saturday when they closed their shop at noon.

"Too bad that nephew of yours is back in jail," announced Tarsal loudly from his perch at the counter. Of course, all heads turned toward the Williams.

"What are you talking about?" asked Sid before Wally's family could even form a question.

"He was running some phony arcade with rigged machines over in

Carp. Police got wind of it from complaining customers and sent an undercover cop in to check it out. They were rigged, alright. He arrested your nephew and his partner on the spot on suspicion of fraud. The seized machines were proof of fraud. They're waiting on a hearing."

"When did this happen?" William was finally able to ask. The other patrons of the diner sat in stunned silence, feeling embarrassed for the Williams and angry at Tarsal.

"Yesterday afternoon. Got a cousin who lives over there. He called me last night to tell me," answered Tarsal. "What are you all staring at? It's the truth."

"That's not the point, Tarsal," said Sid Topp. "Why did you feel you needed to announce it here?"

"I figured it was common knowledge. Can't keep news from getting around in this town."

"Not with you around," said Ned, mentally chalking up another mark on his list of reasons why he could never like Tarsal again.

"Shut up, Ned," said Tarsal.

"He's right," said Doc Trueblood. "Did you ever hear of letting a family have its privacy? How would you feel if it was someone in your family who'd been arrested?"

"That would never happen in my family," said Tarsal, holding up his cup for a refill.

"Oh, for God's sake. That's it, Tarsal. You're banned for life from this diner. Don't even try to pay. I don't want your money," said Sid. And as has been happening of late, when Tarsal was taken to task for his behavior, all the diners, particularly the Williams family, broke into applause.

"Ah, who needs ya?" said Tarsal as he stomped out, slamming the door as hard as he could.

Sid came from behind the counter and walked to Williams's table. "I'm so sorry for this. I know it's not much, but lunch is on me."

"No need to apologize or buy our lunch. That was all the Tarsal Show," said Wallace.

"I insist. Lunch is on me. I hope you know that you have the support of the whole community," said Sid.

"Well, minus one Tarsal Henley," said William, shaking his head. Everyone in the diner nodded in agreement.

The Williams family didn't have much time to feel guilty about being relieved that Wally was locked up again. There would always be new drama lurking around the corner in Chanceville.

61

THE QUACKS LAY A GOLDEN EGG

When Sheriff Yesper contacted Russell Ruby and told him about the Quack factory up in Gary, the agent knew precisely who had stolen the formula.

"Confidentially, I have a feeling Agent Sigmund Colon is the culprit. I heard he had a gambling problem, but we never had any reason to suspect he was breaking the law," said Ruby. "I'll go to the Evidence Lockup and see if I can find the formula. Thanks for the tip." He leaned back in his chair, feet up on his desk, and admired the baby picture of his fourth child. At last, he had a son.

"That's what Paltry, the private detective I hired, found out. The agent got in debt to the wrong people, so he stole the formula. When the "businessmen" saw what they had, they figured it was a good way to launder money. After it became so successful as a product, they cleared Siggy's debt," said the sheriff.

"I'm definitely on it. Will follow up with you later. How's everything in Chanceville?"

"Normal. Everyone minding each other's business."

"Sounds like situation normal all right. Thanks again. I'll be in touch." When he hung up the phone, Agent Ruby went to the basement level to the Evidence Lockup and requested the evidence for the Theodore Munson case.

"Hey, Mole. Has anyone else requested this file in the last few months?" asked Ruby.

Mole, the head of the Evidence Lockup, whose real name was Maynard Burrow, scratched his head, then his sloping chin as he tried to think back. Years ago, someone called him Mole, and the nickname stuck. Ostensibly, it was because he worked deep in the bowels of the FBI quarters in Chicago. Unfortunately, that was not where the comparison stopped. Maynard had tiny dark eyes, a long nose, prominent front teeth, and a non-existent chin.

"Hmm, let me look back at my records. Nothing comes to mind right now."

"I'd appreciate it. I know you have a lot of people who come down here. Couldn't expect you to remember everyone," said Agent Ruby.

"Right, and I'm not the only one down here. I think crime keeps going up and up. I keep having to hire more people. Be right back," said Mole as he disappeared into the darkness of the stacks. He returned with a box marked Theodore Munson, October 1950, Secret Formula. "Here's the box. I'll check the sign-out sheet for you."

Even with his thick glasses, Mole's vision was so poor that he had to hold the clipboard so close to his face that it almost touched his nose. "Ah, here it is. One person, Sigmund Colon, asked for this evidence on December 5th."

"Did he take it with him or look at it here?"

"He didn't sign it out according to the sheet. He took it over there," said Mole, pointing to a battered-up wooden desk. Guess he found what he was looking for," said Mole. "I'm glad that even though he didn't take it with him, he still had to sign the sheet. We need to track access to all files."

Russell opened the box and took out "Crime and Punishment." He leafed through the book and shook it, but nothing fell out. "Crime and Punishment." The formula was no longer in the book.

"I'll need to sign out the whole file box and take it with me. I have to take this to my supervisor. We may have some irregularities. I'll keep you posted on the status."

"Is something missing?"

"Looks like it. But this isn't your fault. It was a tiny piece of paper hidden inside this large book. You're not in trouble. Looks like you followed procedure."

"I've never been in trouble before. Don't want to start now that I'm a year away from retirement." Russell tried again to reassure him and took the elevator back up to the floor where his boss's office was located.

Al Mann had been Russell's supervisor for about ten years. He was a fair man and a good boss who put a lot of trust in his agents. Russell hated to take this news to him.

"Hi Gloria, is Al in? I've got some pretty urgent business."

"Yes, I'll tell him you're here," said Gloria as she called her boss to let him know he had a visitor. "He says for you to come right in."

"Thanks, Gloria," said Agent Ruby.He shifted the box to his hip, tapped on the door, and let himself in.

"What's all this?" asked Agent Mann, eyeing the box as Ruby set it on the chair next to the one he seated himself in. It was a relief to set it down. It felt much heavier than its actual weight. "You look very serious. I've got a feeling this isn't something I will be happy about."

"I'm afraid you're right, boss," said Agent Ruby as he braced himself to deliver the news that a trusted agent of theirs had broken the law. Agent Mann removed his glasses and rubbed his temples as he listened to his agent.

"Guess I'd better call my wife. Looks like it's going to be a long night," said Mann. "Let's get a team together since we'll need to perform a raid on the factory site and then get Agent Colon in here. Let's add Agents Smith and Remington to our team. Find out where Colon is, and let's convene back here in an hour. You'd better call your wife, too.

"Okay, if I leave the box here?" His boss nodded as he reached for the phone to call his wife, who was never surprised to get these calls after twenty years of marriage to an FBI agent.

The team assembled in Agent Mann's office, and were briefed by Russell Ruby. Smith and Remington were honored to be recommended to be on this team by their boss. Still, they were not looking forward to the conversation they were about to have with Agent Sigmund Colon.

"Let's plan our strategy about how we want to proceed. Then we'll have Colon join us. I've determined that he is in his office and asked Gloria to call and tell him to come up. I thought it would seem routine if she called him instead of me. Don't want to alarm him. I had her tell him I had a new case I wanted to run by him. Strictly speaking, that is true," said Agent Mann. About fifteen minutes later, Agent Colon tapped on the door.

"Come in, Siggy," said Al Mann.

"Wow, this must be a big case if you've got all of these guys here," said Colon, nodding at the already seated group. "What's going down?" Russell Ruby thought, while trying to keep his best poker face. The group had agreed that he would tell Agent Colon about his tip-off concerning the Quacks and the money laundering scheme without implicating anyone to start off with. As he told the tall, blond agent about his field agent bringing this tip to him and started laying out what they had discovered about this operation, Siggy paled, flushed, and squirmed in his chair.

"We are trying to figure out how they got this formula, which has been locked up in the evidence room since October. As far as we know, we had the only copy, which is now missing, and all the other parties are either locked up or dead," said Agent Mann. "Anyone got any ideas?"

"Does anyone think Big Teddy could have made a copy?" asked Smith as they had rehearsed.

"I'm sure that little toad made plenty of copies," said Agent Colon, hoping that would be the tack they would follow.

"He swore at the time that he hadn't made any copies. Besides, when you and I arrested him, we took him straight to jail. We didn't find any copies in his car or apartment. I'm not sure he's bright enough to think that far ahead. I think his greed got the best of him; he couldn't wait to get his hands on the money," said Russell Ruby, who thought that Teddy wasn't the only not-so-bright player in this game. Siggy should have copied the formula while sitting at the Evidence Room desk. It was a simple formula. It might have made his trail harder to follow if no evidence was missing.

"You may have missed something," said Siggy, hopefully.

"I don't think so. Even if we did, it doesn't change the fact that the one Teddy gave Agent Russell is missing," said Remington. "At any rate, we contacted him at the state prison in Michigan City. He's still swearing that he didn't make any copies. Not really something he would have any reason to lie about after all this time."

"Well, then I haven't a clue," said Siggy. "I have an appointment in about half an hour. I'm going to need to go." He got up to leave, but his boss waved him to sit back down.

"You can give us a couple more minutes," said his boss. Siggy turned pale once again and lowered himself slowly into his chair.

"We looked at the sign-out sheet. You signed it on December 5th. According to the log, you had it for about 5 minutes," said Agent Mann, handing him a mimeographed copy of the sign-out sheet. "You are the only one who has requested this evidence since it was originally logged in."

"That doesn't mean anything. Mole isn't perfect. There could easily be someone else who requested the box, and it just wasn't recorded," said Agent Colon, squirming visibly as hope faded fast for him that this would blow over.

"That's not going to fly, Siggy," said Mann. "Mole's reputation for meticulous record keeping is unblemished. How dare you accuse him of sloppiness." Mann was quickly losing his patience with his obviously guilty agent. Time to go in for the kill. "Agent Ruby, please tell us what you believe has occurred in relation to Agent Colon."

"Sure thing, boss. Here's what we think, Siggy. We think you got into serious gambling trouble and were indebted to some bad characters who began demanding payment and promising some pretty ugly consequences. You knew what the formula was actually for and offered it to them as a way to launder money and begin to pay off your debt. They agreed to give it a try as they were in desperate need of laundering the illegal money they were making from their lucrative numbers racket and "protection" plans for local contractors in the greater Chicago area. Fortunately for you, the product was so successful you were able to work off your debt more quickly than anyone had anticipated. How does that theory sound to you, Agent Colon?"

"Sounds like a fairy tale to me," said Siggy as he examined his cuticles but could not pull off his "disinterested" act.

"I'm buying it," said Mann. "When we raid the factory, I'm sure we'll find some people who will be happy to identify you. Who else is buying this theory? Let's take a vote. Agent Smith?"

"Bought it," said Smith.

"Agent Remington?"

"Sold. You don't even have to gift wrap it for me," said Remington.

"Agent Ruby?"

"Hook, line, and sinker, boss." Siggy sank even lower in his chair, wishing with all his heart that the floor would open up and swallow him whole. Prison was no place for a crooked FBI agent. He knew exactly what he was in for. They had him. There'd be no wriggling off the hook for him.

Sigmund Colon was precisely correct. The raid went off without a hitch, shutting the business down. Their forensic accountants traced the laundered money while all those involved cooled their heels in jail, seasoned criminals and new. After the professional crooks and the amateur ones were settled into their new accommodations, some local businessmen worked a deal to buy the factory and, with some testing, could figure out their own new and improved formula for Quacks, much to the delight of children and grownups everywhere. This windfall prompted the new owners of the Quacks formula to send a generous check to the Loone County Library.

This felt like a satisfying end to the Tale of the Quacks, but sometimes not all things remain in the past.

62

ALPACA SEES A GHOST

When food started to go missing in the Williams' home again, Alpaca, William, and Wallace suspected that Wally had broken out of jail.

"Should we call the jail?" William asked Wallace. "Nothing has changed around here. The staff is the same, and we haven't had this happen anymore since Wally's been gone."

"Maybe we should," answered Wallace from behind his newspaper. "I'm sure we would have been notified, but just in case." The newly formed Williams family had set in with a daily routine that worked for all of them. They especially enjoyed their habit of sitting on the sun porch after breakfast, enjoying more coffee or tea, reading the papers and magazines that they subscribed to, and mulling over their plans for the day. William Williams had semi-retired after that whole exhausting business with their nephew Wally. They had hired the highly reliable and competent Paula Peevish to manage the store for them. Paula, wife of Reverend Chuck Peevish, originally from Chanceville and niece of the late Peggy Hendrix, was more than happy with the job. She loved working for the Williams brothers, possibly the nicest bosses in the world. Working in the store was a nice boost to the modest income of a pastor.

"Alpaca and I are thinking of embarking on a Mediterranean cruise now that we have Paula to help out with the store, but I don't want to leave you with this mystery of the missing food hanging over our heads."

"You make it sound like a Sherlock Holmes story, The Mystery of the Missing Food," said Wallace, and they all chuckled.

"You do sound a bit dramatic, darling," Alpaca said, patting her husband's hand. "Do you have a deerstalker cap in stock at the haberdashery?"

"We might have one in my size," he answered good-naturedly.

When were you planning on embarking on your cruise?" asked Wallace.

Not until after Christmas. Our plan is to escape our cold Indiana winter, so there is time," answered Alpaca. "We don't want to leave until this is resolved, though. What do you think about us talking to Mrs. Broom and padlocking the pantry and the refrigerator at night? I don't want to insult her. I know it's none of our people, but it's costly and inconvenient to keep replacing food. More expensive items are starting to go missing lately."

"You make a good point, Alpaca," said Wallace. "I think we can approach Mrs. Broom in a non-accusatory manner. She's just as frustrated as we are. It's hard to prepare a meal when ingredients keep going missing."

"At least that much is settled. We can talk to her tomorrow morning since Mrs. Broom is off for the rest of the day. If it's all right with her, I'll get some padlocks when I go into work tomorrow afternoon," said William. And with that, they returned to their reading and sipped in comfortable silence.

When Mrs. Broom arrived for work at the Williams home the next morning, the first thing she did was check the pantry. She quickly discovered that a canned ham, a bag of chocolate chips, and a loaf of bread were missing. She was going to report to Mrs. Williams when the lady herself came into the kitchen, followed by William and Wallace.

"Mrs. Broom, I can tell by the look on your face that more things have gone missing overnight. We have decided upon a plan, so would you be so kind as to join us in the front room before you start breakfast?" asked Alpaca.

"Of course," said Mrs. Broom as she took off her apron and draped it over the back of a kitchen chair. "Something's got to be done. This is getting to be very costly for you when I have to keep replacing things."

"Alpaca, would you make the coffee and bring it in? Mrs. Broom, go ahead in the parlor and get yourself settled. This is a family meeting, and you're certainly a part of this family," said Wallace.

"Happy to," answered Alpaca, surprising herself at how much she enjoyed domesticity and how freeing it was not to be on the manhunt all the time. It gave her much more energy to devote to her beloved William. She realized now how much energy scheming had taken.

"Please sit here, Mrs. Broom," said William, indicating a comfortable chair by the fireplace. "You just relax. We're serving you coffee this morning." Wallace smiled in agreement. Mrs. Broom warmed her hands in front of the fire before seating herself. It was a chilly late fall morning, and William had lit a fire to make the cozy room even cozier. Even though some considered their house a mansion, the brothers and Alpaca gave it a lived-in, comfortable feel.

"We know you have been just as stressed as we have, Mrs. Broom," said Wallace when they were all settled with their coffee. "You must know that we trust all of our employees implicitly and think of you all as part of the family, as I said this morning."

"We are proposing that we will have you padlock the pantry and refrigerator before you leave for the night. You will have a key to keep with you even when you go home, and my wife will have a key," said William. "As you said, this is getting very expensive, and we have to get to the bottom of this. I even called the jail to make sure Wally hadn't broken out since he was the culprit the last time food went missing. He is still safely locked up, but he mostly stole sweet stuff. Whoever is our thief now has a more wide-ranging palate."

"We've also decided to alert Sheriff Orange and ask him to send a patrol car around here at night when they're making their rounds," added Alpaca.

"This all sounds very sensible. I'm happy to lock up and help in any way I can," said Mrs. Broom, enjoying the conviviality of having coffee with the Williams and helping to problem solve. She hated that the family was going through this. They deserved all good things.

After their meeting, William left earlier than usual to go to Steele's Hardware before going into the stationery store. He purchased two sturdy padlocks, a bracket for the pantry door, and two short lengths of chain to secure the refrigerator door and chest freezer doors. Luckily, they were very busy, and Lawrence Steele didn't have time to ask what he was locking up. William had their driver, Andrew Handy, put everything in the trunk before driving him to the sheriff's office to request nighttime surveillance.

"Hello, Miss Ringwald. Is the sheriff in today?"

"He's in, but he might be a little busy. Is there something I can help you with?" said Pearly, who always lived in the hope that she could find out what people want to talk to Sheriff Orange about. But most everyone in Chanceville was on to her and rarely revealed even the simplest thing they wanted to request from the sheriff.

"I just need to have a quick word of a personal nature; it won't take long," said William, rightly thinking that using the word personal would make Pearly even more curious. William Williams the Younger definitely had an impish side. About that time, the sheriff came out to get another cup of coffee.

"Well, hello, William. Do you need to talk to me about something?" asked the sheriff, sensing correctly that Mr. Williams wasn't about to tell his dispatcher why he was there. "Come back. Would you like a cup of coffee?"

"No thanks, I'm about coffeed out this morning; I just need a quick word." After the sheriff firmly closed his office door, he motioned to his guest to not talk until he performed his well-established routine of turning the radio up. William immediately understood that strategy.

"Now, what can I do for you?"

Mr. Williams leaned in close to the sheriff and, speaking quietly, explained the situation of the missing food.

"I'll be happy to do the extra patrol myself. The wife's folks are visiting, and I'll take any excuse to get out of the house. Pop Redenbacher likes to advise me on how to do chores that I've done all my married life. I'll stop by the house tomorrow morning to let you know if there's anything to report and find out if the locks did the trick."

"Thanks so much, sheriff. I feel better about things already. Best get to work; don't want Paula to fire me."

The sheriff walked William to the door and whipped it open. There was Pearly intently wiping non-existent dust off the top of the water cooler outside the sheriff's office. The two men smiled at each other and shook hands.

"Bye, Pearly," said William. "That Pearly certainly doesn't let any dust settle, does she, sheriff?" And with that, he winked at Sheriff Orange and headed off to work. Pearly harrumphed back to her desk, and the sheriff went back into his office, chuckling softly.

After dinner that evening, the Williams brothers' gardener and handyman, Rod Kurten, installed the bracket for the padlock on the pantry door and helped Mrs. Broom as she wrapped the heavy chains around the fridge and the upright freezer on the back porch.

"That should do the trick, sirs," said Rod as he returned his drill to the toolbox. "That's a good quality lock and a strong bracket. They'd have to be really determined to pry that off the door. Besides, that would make a helluva racket."

"Thanks, Rod," said the Williams brothers in unison. "And thank you, Mrs. Broom. Let's hope this works. Sheriff Orange will be patrolling tonight. We'll get to the bottom of this pretty quickly, I think," said Wallace.

"I've just had an idea," said Mrs. Broom, addressing her employers with a gleam in her eye. "Would it be okay if I sprinkled a little flour from the canister in front of the pantry door? Maybe we can get some footprints. See where they lead us."

"Mrs. Williams has started calling me Sherlock," answered William. "Perhaps I'll start calling you Watson, Mrs. Broom." They all had a good chuckle over that one, especially Mrs. Broom, who thought she would quite like that moniker. Even with everything in order, none of the Williams felt they would sleep well that night. They were too excited about catching the crook or at least foiling him. They were trying to keep their regular routine so as not to tip off the culprit.

The Williams were all up early and met Mrs. Broom as she let herself in the kitchen door. They all stood stark still, looking at the tracks in the flour that the housekeeper had sprinkled before she left the night before. They could see the locks were all undisturbed. The silence was broken as the sheriff knocked on the kitchen door. The four onlookers jumped and then laughed at their skittishness.

"Come in, Sheriff Orange," said Alpaca, stepping carefully around the flour to open the door.

"Nothing to report. I parked behind the garden shed to see any comings and goings on the road and your driveway. There was not one car all night. What's all this then?" he asked, pointing to the scuffled flour.

"Watson here had the brilliant idea to sprinkle flour in front of the pantry door so we might get some identifiable footprints," said William quite proudly.

"Watson?"

"Mrs. Broom is playing Watson to my Sherlock."

"Ah, do you have a camera we could take a picture or two with?" asked the sheriff.

"We have one of those new-fangled Polaroid Land Cameras that Alpaca and I purchased for our Mediterranean cruise," said William.

"Perfect," said the sheriff. "No negatives to develop. We all know how nosy Jeremiah down at the Rexall is. He always wants to discuss the quality of my photography." William fetched the camera, and the sheriff quickly produced two clear images of the soles of the perpetrator's shoes.

"Those shoe prints look very familiar to me," said Alpaca as she tiptoed closer to the pantry. "Can't quite place them."

"Is it okay if I sweep this flour up, sheriff," asked Mrs. Broom. "I'd like to get breakfast started, and I need to unlock everything."

"Sure. I think these photographs are clear enough," said the sheriff after examining them carefully.

"Won't you stay for breakfast, Sheriff Orange?" asked Alpaca. "You've had a long night. You must be getting hungry." The sheriff said that sounded great and asked to use the restroom to freshen up a bit. Wallace told him to join them on the sun porch.

"Have a seat, Yesper," said William as the sheriff entered the sunroom." Mrs. Broom will bring us some coffee shortly." The next thing they heard was a blood-curdling scream from the kitchen. They all jumped up and ran to see what the commotion was about.

Mrs. Broom was standing in front of an almost empty refrigerator. She had stopped screaming, but her eyes were bulging out. The sheriff walked over to her and guided her to a chair. Alpaca quickly fetched a glass of water and held it to the housekeeper's quavering lips.

"The lock wasn't open. How could all the food be gone?" asked Clara Broom, not typically given to hysterics. William used Alpaca's key to open the lock on the pantry door only to discover that the same thing had happened with the food stored there. "I simply don't understand how this could be," he said. "Mrs. Broom and my wife have the only two keys. No one else but the people in this room and Rod even knew what we were doing with the locks."

Alpaca, who was back to staring at the shoe prints, suddenly realized where she had seen them before and promptly fainted.

63

HE MAY BE DEAD, BUT HE'S STILL HUNGRY

Alpaca came around to her husband as he gently patted her on the cheek, and the housekeeper laid a cold cloth on her forehead.

"Are you all right, darling?" asked William. "What on Earth happened. You look like you've seen a ghost."

"In a way, I think I have," whispered Alpaca as she struggled to get off the floor, her usual grace failing her.

"What are you talking about?" said William as he and Mrs. Broom helped her to a chair. The housekeeper nodded and quickly set the water to boil.

"Those shoe prints. Look at this closely," said Alpaca, handing her husband one of the photographs the sheriff had taken. "My brother, Trout, had a pair of sneakers with that kind of zig zaggy tread."

"I'm sure many people could have the same shoe," said Wallace. "Are you trying to say you think your brother is our food thief?"

"You're not looking at the photograph closely enough," she answered, offering it to her brother-in-law.

Wallace had fetched a magnifying glass from his study and examined the photo closely.

"There appear to be initials carved into the sole," he said as he passed it and the magnifying glass to his brother, who took a long look and passed it on to the sheriff.

Mrs. Broom impatiently waited her turn.

"Looks like TCF," said Mrs. Broom. No one argued with her.

"Yes, Trout Chagrin Finn," whispered Alpaca. Then she sipped her tea and set the cup down shakily in its saucer.

"Anyone could be wearing those shoes. I'm guessing you gave away the reverend's things when you moved into the parsonage," said Sheriff Orange as Mrs. Broom poured more coffee for him.

"I can only offer you eggs for breakfast. Everything else is gone," Mrs. Broom said. "We need something besides coffee in our jittery stomachs.

Everyone agreed that was fine.

"I didn't keep any of his clothing. They weren't suitable for donation. I burned everything, including those shoes in the barrel in the backyard."

"I don't see how that can possibly be," said William, taking Alpaca's hand. "And why would anyone carve their initials in a pair of cheap sneakers? Sorry, dear."

"He had a childhood habit of carving his initials in everything. He got in a lot of trouble with Mother and Father when he carved them in his headboard that had belonged to our Grandfather Chagrin," she said defensively. "I WATCHED those shoes burn," answered Alpaca, withdrawing her hand from William's to take a long sip of her tea.

"I'm not saying you're not telling the truth," said her husband, trying to take her hand again. She folded her arms and looked around the room at all the shocked faces.

"You have to admit that it's pretty hard to imagine this happening," said the sheriff.

"But, you know, all of the foods that went missing were some of Reverend Finn's favorites," said Wallace. "We all were familiar with his eating habits, no offense, Alpaca."

"None taken. I'm aware that Trout's appetite was legendary. Apparently, that carries over into the afterlife. My brother's idea of heaven would be unlimited access to free food."

"It's true, said Mrs. Broom. "Ham, bread, puddings, cakes, chicken, potato chips, to name a few. No vegetables went missing. No fruits unless they were in a pie." Their eyes widened as the list of missing foods grew longer.

"Let's, just for a moment, assume Reverend Finn is our culprit. What can we do about it?" asked the sheriff, ever the practical one.

"An exorcism?" offered Mrs. Broom, warming to the idea of a ghost instead of a flesh and blood person.

"Well, he wasn't Catholic," said the sheriff, still being practical. "But an exorcism is not off the mark. Not sure there is a practical solution to this. We tried that with the locks and chains."

"I've got an idea I can check into," said Mrs. Broom as she served breakfast of scrambled eggs and cut fruit to the hungry gathering. "Can you give me a couple of days?"

"You're sounding mysterious, but I don't think we have many options," said Wallace. "We'll trust you. In the meantime, we can eat out or order meals from the Tip Topp."

"Sounds like a good idea," said William. "Give Mrs. Broom a break from the stress of constantly replacing food."

"Tonight, I'll go into town to seek the help I mentioned," said the housekeeper.

"I will go into town and get orders for our lunch and dinner at the Tipp Topp for you," offered Alpaca. You should go home after breakfast and rest. You deserve a break." Mrs. Broom had been skeptical of Miss Finn at first, but over time, she could see that Mr. William's new bride was genuinely fond of him. But she had been most worried about Alpaca lording her status over the staff, which had not happened.

"Thanks, Mrs. W. I think I will," said Mrs. Broom. "I'm feeling tuckered out." After leaving the kitchen in perfect condition, she went home and took an afternoon nap for the first time in years. It was the most satisfying sleep she had had in ages. She woke up feeling refreshed and ready to tackle the tricky problem of getting rid of a ghost. She made herself a light supper and then drove into town to speak to the person she thought could help them.

64

TROUT FINN MOVES ON TO THAT BIG RESTAURANT IN THE SKY

The person who could help with moving Trout Finn along to that Big Restaurant in the Sky was Babs, the cashier at the Woolworths Five and Dime. Clara Broom had always been a down-to-earth person. She was practical and independent. She had to be after her husband, Clarence Broom, had died, leaving her a young widow with an infant son to raise. Her mother, Henrietta Sharp, was getting ready to retire, and Clara immediately took her place with the Williams family. It was a smooth transition. Clara's mother took care of her grandson while Clara was at work. It worked out well for everyone. But Clara missed her husband desperately. She loved her son, mother, and job, but she was lonely. Through the Chanceville Grapevine, she had heard that Babs Haylo did tarot card readings and kept in touch with the spirit world through her crystal ball.

A few months after her husband died, Clara told her mother she was going to the library and asked if she could stay on after dinner and put the baby to bed. She hated lying to her mother, but she knew her mother would think she was tempting fate, playing with fire to consult Babs, who used the devil's tools as far as Henrietta was concerned. She went to the library first and checked out books for herself and her mother.

Babs lived in a quaint little cottage on the outskirts of Chanceville. She let Clara in immediately to a tiny candle lit living room.

"Come in, honey. Have a seat and tell me what I can do for you," said Babs. Clara was surprised at how different Babs was in her home instead of at work, a much softer version of her public self. Clara told her how much she missed her husband and said she would love to know how he was doing.

"I know how you feel, dearie. I've been widowed a long time, and I still miss my Ben," said Babs, patting Clara's hand. "Let's look at the crystal ball first, and then we'll see what's in the cards. Sit back and relax," she told Clara as she waved her hands around the shape of the crystal ball without touching it. The only sound in the room was the clock ticking on the mantle and the fire crackling in the fireplace. The room had felt warm when she first stepped inside from the cold November air, but now it felt cold. She was sure she felt a shift in the pressure of the air.

"Clarence is here," said Babs. "He says to tell you he misses you and your birthmark that only he has seen." Clara let out a little yelp. Besides Doc Trueblood, Clarence Broom had been the only man to ever see the tiny heart-shaped birthmark near the nipple of her left breast.

"It's him," she whispered, nearly unable to breathe. "Only Clarence would know about my birthmark."

"That's his way of letting you know it's really him," said Babs, nodding. "He says you're doing a great job with our son, and he's sorry he had to leave you." And with that, Clara began crying softly. Babs went to make her a cup of chamomile tea before they moved on to the tarot reading.

The cards were a guide for Clara, affirming that she was on the right path with how she was leading her life. She found it very comforting. Thus, I began a lifelong habit of monthly sessions with Babs. After her mother died when Clarence Jr. was a teen, she didn't feel like she had to keep it a secret anymore. She recommended Babs to anyone she felt would like that kind of guidance.

When Clara showed up at her door on a night that wasn't her regular appointment, Babs was surprised.

"Sorry, I'm not dressed for crystal ball gazing. Just got home from work," said Babs, a tiny bird-like woman, white-haired now, with long flowing locks with butterfly combs holding her hair away from her small-featured face.

"That's not why I'm here. I have a favor to ask. The Williams family desperately needs your help. They have a ghost they need to get rid of. Can you help with that?" asked Clara.

"I can sure try. Tell me what's going on."

Clara filled her in on the food-thieving ghost and who they believed it was.

"Think this will be an easy one. I can come out there on my day off tomorrow or tell you what they need to do."

"I think they would take it more seriously coming from you. You've quite a good reputation as a clairvoyant. I remember people were skeptical until you predicted the split in the church. Shall I let the family know you'll be out after breakfast?"

"Yes, that sounds fine. I'll bring along what I need. In the meantime, tell the Williams not to worry. Maybe give Reverend Finn one last meal as a send-off," Babs said with a smile and a wink.

"Will do. And thanks so much. You're a lifesaver." When Clara got home, she called and spoke with Alpaca, who sounded relieved and said she would leave some food out for her brother as a "going away" present.

As promised, Babs arrived at the Williams's home the following day. She knocked on the back door, and Clara promptly let her in. "I'll take you to the sunroom where the family is having their coffee. I'll add a cup of tea for you. I know you like chamomile." When they were all settled with their drinks and pleasantries exchanged, Babs explained what she would be doing.

"It's very simple," she said, pulling one of the two large box of rock salt from her huge cloth bag. "I will sprinkle this salt around the outside of the house, and we will all say some words to let the reverend know we are releasing him. Tell him it's okay, it's time to go, that sort of thing."

"You mean, that's it?" asked Wallace. "It's that simple?"

"I've never had it not work," answered Babs. "Don't see why it won't this time. Did you feed him last night?"

"Yes!" said Alpaca. I left out ham sandwiches and half a cake I had gone into the Tipp Topp Diner to buy for our dinner last night. Cake was always my brother's favorite. I knew if our thief was him, he wouldn't be able to resist it. It was all gone this morning, not even a crumb left."

"Great. Let's get started."

They all trooped outside and followed Babs as she sprinkled a thin line of salt around the perimeter of the vast old house, saying, "Reverend Trout Finn, if you still linger, your work here is done. Return to the stars from whence you have come. Go in peace." The house was so large and rambling that it took both large boxes of salt to complete the task.

"That should do it. Let me know if any more food goes missing. But I seriously don't think you will have this problem anymore."

"Let's go back in, and I'll write you a check," said Wallace, who took care of the bills the family had as a unit.

"Not necessary. This is a ritual I never charge for. If you ever have occasion to recommend me, that's all the pay I need."

"Well, whatever you purchase from the Williams Brothers store is on the house for life," said William, his brother nodding in agreement.

As they came in through the kitchen door, Alpaca remarked, "Do you feel it?"

"Feel what?" asked her husband.

"I feel it," said Clara Broom. "The air feels lighter in here. I agree with Babs. I think our troubles are over."

Indeed, their troubles were over. No food ever went missing again. Even though Alpaca was not particularly religious, she still enjoyed picturing her brother sitting on a substantial cloud, having his cake and eating it too.

The Williams were now free to embark on their Mediterranean cruise after Christmas. They enjoyed living with Wallace but were looking forward to some time to themselves. They both felt as if their honeymoon would last forever.

65

MRS. CRABTREE PRAYS ONCE TOO OFTEN

Determined Prayer Offerer Maxine Crabtree had been losing sleep after she got wind through the Chanceville Grapevine that Babs Haylo had done "black magic" at the home of the Williams brothers. Hank Wheatley, local farmer, had been driving his tractor past the Williams's house when he saw Babs leading the family around the house as she sprinkled some kind of "magic dust" around the perimeter of the old family home. All Hank had to do was mention it at the Tipp Topp, and the race to spread that juicy tidbit was on.

Mrs. Crabtree tossed and turned for about a week, trying to decide what she could do to undo this blasphemous behavior. It never occurred to Maxine to go to the involved parties and directly ask what was actually going on. To her, it was clear that the devil was at work here. There were souls that needed to be prayed over. It was an emergency situation if there ever was one.

The first thing she did after she decided on a plan of action was to head over to F. W. Woolworth to beard the lioness in her den. She wanted witnesses. Maxine wanted people to know that she was saving souls, not just of the citizens of Chanceville but quite possibly the very soul of her beloved town. To Maxine, every molehill was a potential mountain.

She took her largest cross off her bedroom wall. She held it high as she carried it down the sidewalks, marching like a Christian Soldier toward the dime store. People gave her a wide berth as she passed, wondering what cause she was going to pray over now. They thought it must be serious as they had never seen her marching with a cross before. This was erratic behavior, even for that old lady. People had noticed that she had been more eccentric than usual lately.

Mrs. Crabtree strode right up to Babs, who was at her usual spot at the register nearest the door. Babs, who, as we know, never looked up or actually looked at customers, didn't even see the old lady, let alone the huge cross she was carrying. It was hard to imagine because the cross was about three feet high with a tortured-faced Jesus hanging on it. Everyone else in the store stood stock still, waiting with bated breath to see how this would unfold. When they realized Babs was the target, they knew it wouldn't end well. Mr. Trinket, the store manager, could spot oncoming disasters and was skilled at heading them off. That skill would come in handy today. He had dealt with Mrs. Crabtree before when she used to come in and pray for the success of Christmas and Easter sale items and tried to get him to donate all of the proceeds to the church. He had thought about banning her from the store, but he felt that would make him the unpopular one, and it was only twice a year, after all.

"Babs Haylo, in the name of God and all that is holy, you will cease this witchcraft you are perpetrating on the Williams family," shouted Maxine as she waved the cross over Babs' head, nearly hitting her with it. It was not her intention to hit Babs, but the cross was unwieldy, and her eyesight had been blurry lately, so her aim to wave the cross over her target's head was way off.

At last, Babs looked up and ducked under the counter when she saw the cross coming at her. It came so close that she felt the whoosh of air over her head.

Mr. Trinket, who didn't want to wrestle a cross from the hands of a little old lady, yelled, "Mrs. Crabtree, will you PLEASE stop waving that about? You nearly hit Babs. I can't imagine anything Babs could have done to deserve being conked on the head with a cross. And I really can't imagine Jesus would want you to use His symbol of suffering as a weapon."

Mr. Trinket's words stopped Maxine mid-swing, which almost caused her to topple over. This was something she hadn't thought about. She reasoned that she needed to summon all the power she could for good to triumph over evil. She laid the cross down on the counter with a kerthunk. She was feeling a little woozy and started to sway. Mr. Trinket put his arm around the old lady to steady her.

"Can you get Mrs. Crabtree a glass of water?" Mr. Trinket asked Violet, his assistant manager. He then asked Kenneth, his sixteen-year-old stock boy, to get a chair for Maxine.

"What's this all about?" asked Babs as she peeked over the top of the counter prairie dog style, still afraid to stand up even though Mrs. Crabtree's weapon of choice was lying on the counter and the lady herself still looked a little wobbly, but no sense taking any chances. After all, Mrs. Crabtree believed she had the force of the All Mighty God behind her.

"Hank Wheatley saw you spreading magical powders around the Williams' family home with the family and their housekeeper in thrall as they followed you around," said Mrs. Crabtree as she began to feel stronger. "It was the work of the devil."

All eyes and ears turned toward Babs.

"Oh, for heaven's sake. The "magical powders" were common rock salt. I was performing a centuries-old ceremony as a blessing for the house and its inhabitants at the family's request," answered Babs. She was not about to tell the whole story. She was a firm believer in confidentiality. That news would have been all over town faster than you could say voodoo. "The brothers just wanted a little cleansing done after the shenanigans their nephew Wally had pulled on them." She would have to call Clara Broom as soon as she had time and tell her what to say in case she was asked the same question. And she would bet the last pack of her delicious Black Jack gum that it was only a matter of time because she thought she caught a glimpse of Gardenia Cochran lurking around the back of the store.

"See, there was never anything to worry about, Mrs. Crabtree," said Mr. Trinket. "Can you really think the Williams brothers would be up to anything even mildly sacrilegious?" Mrs. Crabtree answered by grudgingly shrugging her shoulders. "Okay, do you think you'll be able to make your way home, or do you want Kenneth to walk you?" At that suggestion, the poor teenager looked more horrified than if he had been ordered to eat worms.

"That won't be necessary," she answered. "Can I at least offer a short prayer, just in case?" Everyone knew that the old lady didn't understand the meaning of short.

"I don't think that would be a good idea. We have a line forming behind you," said Mr. Trinket, much to everyone's relief. Mr. Trinket hoped that she would understand that was an invitation for her to leave without having to come right out and say it to her. She sniffed, stood up, straightened her back, picked up the cross, and cradled it to her chest like a baby, much to Kenneth's relief. Babs, however, did not come up from behind the counter until Mrs. Crabtree was safely out the door.

Mr. Trinket told Babs to take her break, and she asked to use the phone in the office. He told her that was fine and closed the door behind him to give her some privacy. She called Clara Broom to apprise her of the situation, much to the amazement and gratitude of that lady. Then Babs decided she was too worn out from the day's excitement to cook her dinner; so after work, she stopped by the Tipp Topp for the Wednesday Blue Plate Special of Beef Manhattans. When she walked in, everyone stood up an applauded her. She was surprised they were applauding but not that they knew what happened at the Woolworths that afternoon.

"We're so glad you survived Mrs. Crabtree's cross swinging today, Babs," said Cora Jean. "Sid says your meal is on him tonight."

"He doesn't need to do that. I'm fine, just a little shaky still.

"I've found it's best not to argue with Sid," said Cora Jean, popping her gum as she poised her pencil to take Babs' order. "And he's right. You deserve to be treated today after what you've been through."

"I'm sure you know best. I'll have the Blue Plate Special and a Coca Cola, please, and since Sid's treating, maybe a piece of pie!"

By the time Babs had talked to nearly everyone in the diner and enjoyed her piece of fresh coconut cream pie (also on the house), it was almost dark. She was thinking about how nice a long soak in the tub with lavender bath salts would be as she walked up her sidewalk when suddenly a figure leaped out at her, yelling, "Jesus Saves!"

"For the love of God, Maxine Crabtree. You scared the holy hell out of me," said Babs.

"That's exactly what I'm trying to do," said Mrs. Crabtree, leaning on the cross, trying to catch her breath. "You have been taken over by the devil with all of your witchcraft. Let us pray. Get thee behind thee, Satan!"

"Come with me," said Babs as she pried the cross out of Mrs. Crabtree's shaking hands and took her, none too gently, by the arm, pulling her up the front steps and into the house. "Sit down and be quiet. I'm going to make you a nice cup of chamomile tea."

"Oh, no! I'm not drinking any of your voodoo potions!"

"Good Lord. I said be quiet," said Babs. "I'm not going to poison you. You need to calm down. Don't move. I'm going in the kitchen."

"I'm not afraid of you. I've got God Almighty behind me," yelled Maxine. Babs didn't answer because she was on the phone calling Doc Trueblood, who lived just two doors down. She had heard stories about how Mrs. Crabtree was going off the rails, but it was hard to tell if that was real with some people. Then, there was always the validity factor of the Chanceville Grapevine.

She made a pot of soothing chamomile tea, and when she went to answer the door, she saw that Mrs. Crabtree was asleep in the rocking chair.

"Thanks for coming so quickly, Doc," said Babs as she opened the door.

"Happy to. I heard what happened at Woolworths today. So she was lying in wait when you got home?"

"Yes, I went to the Tip Topp for dinner and didn't get home until about 6:00. She had to have been hiding in the shrubs for hours. Scared the daylights out of me."

Doc went over and gently patted the sleeping lady on the shoulder. "Wake up, Maxine. I'm here to take you home."

"What? Where am I?" she asked, blinking and looking around the softly lit room.

"You're at Babs' house. Remember? You were hiding in her shrubs." said Doc.

"I was?" she said, still trying to get her bearings. "Oh, I remember now. I had to try to get the devil out of her."

Doc motioned to Babs to pour the tea.

"Here you go, Mrs. Crabtree. A nice soothing cup of tea," said Babs.

"No! I'm not drinking that poison," she yelled as she swatted the cup and saucer out of Babs' hand. Babs caught the cup and saucer mid-air, but the tea spilled everywhere. She went into the kitchen to get a towel.

"Now, Maxine, you know Babs is not trying to poison you. Look, see, I'm drinking the tea," said the doctor, raising a cup to his lips. Before he could take a sip, the newly energized old lady jumped up and knocked the cup and saucer out of his hand. Babs was coming out of the kitchen and couldn't get there in time to save that cup and saucer, family heirlooms from her grandmother. She made a U-turn to go back to the kitchen to get the broom, dustpan, and more towels.

"I want to take your blood pressure. Let's go in the kitchen where we'll be out of the way," said Doc Trueblood as he steered her around the wet hardwood floor.

"Her blood pressure is dangerously high," he told Babs. "I've called the hospital so they can ready a room. I'm afraid she'll have a stroke if we don't get it under control. I think her sugar might be out of control also, which would account for her erratic behavior. You know, more than her regular style." A slight grin escaped his lips.

It took Doc Trueblood a couple of days to get Mrs. Crabtree's blood pressure stabilized and her insulin levels back to normal. She had no memory of assaulting Babs at the Woolworths or lying in wait for her at her house. Mrs. Crabtree being back to normal meant she was ready to pray over everything and everyone, which, of course, was met with the usual resistance.

"Good morning, Mrs. Crabtree," said Ivy Greenly, a hospital volunteer. "Here's your breakfast. Hope you're hungry. Looks like you're feeling better; nice color in your cheeks."

"Thanks, I am hungry, but I couldn't possibly eat until we pray over my food tray," said Maxine.

"Why don't you go ahead and pray while I deliver these other meals? Don't want the other patients' food getting cold."

"Hmpf. Guess I don't have much choice. Maybe tomorrow I'll feel like helping you deliver food, and we can pray together." Ivy didn't respond. She wheeled the food cart quickly into the next room, thinking she'd better tell Doc Trueblood about Mrs. Crabtree's plans for the future.

When she came back to Mrs. Crabtree's room after delivering all the breakfasts on the floor, she could hear the old woman still praying over her breakfast, her scrambled eggs long since gone cold.

As it turned out, Maxine had already told the doctor her plans, and he told her she was to rest and not get out of bed without help. And if she did what he ordered, she could go home in a couple of days.

"Well, okay. Can we pray for my speedy recovery?"

"You go right ahead. I have other patients to see here in the hospital and office hours this afternoon. I'll check in on you tomorrow."

True to his word, he released Mrs. Crabtree to go home with her promise that she would take it easy, rest most of the day, and stick to her diet.

When word got around that Mrs. Crabtree was ill, as we knew it would, the church ladies made sure she had plenty of healthy meals to help speed up her recovery. Of course, she was annoying, but she did a lot of good work in Chanceville, and people wanted to do the right thing by her.

Luckily for Babs and the Williams family, she had forgotten all about the voodoo magic she had heard about. Things were peaceful again for the moment in Chanceville. We all know that is a temporary situation.

66

TENDERLOINS AT THE
TIPP TOPP

The winter months passed without much fanfare, and in early spring, Sheriff Yesper Orange finally had succeeded in his bid to get Sid Topp to add an Al Green style tenderloin to his menu, which hadn't changed much in years. Most of the old timers couldn't remember when anything new had been added. Sid had taken the diner over from his dad, Sal Topp when he passed. Sid inherited the diner and the menu, which his dad had been disinclined to meddle with, and he thought he should honor his old man by continuing his tradition of simple fare born of the Depression.

He was beginning to tire of cooking the same dishes day in and day out. That was one of the reasons he had agreed to give the tenderloin sandwich a try. But the main reason was Sid had tried one of those sandwiches a few months ago and was still thinking about how delicious they were. All he needed was that nudge from the sheriff. On Sunday nights, when the diner closed early, Sid experimented with different types of breading and the thickness of the tenderloin itself, crucial elements to the success of this favorite Hoosier fare. After a month of Sundays, he decided he had hit on just the right formula. Sid introduced the sandwich as Monday's Sandwich Special on the chalkboard easel on the sidewalk in front of the diner. Mondays could be slow, and he hoped this new item would generate more business. Monday was the one day he didn't serve breakfast. There weren't enough diners to make it worth his while.

Well, that sign certainly generated lots of interest. This news spread all over Chanceville faster than a field fire on a windy summer day. Even people who didn't usually eat at the diner stood outside and stared at the sign as a crowd gathered to ponder this unheard-of change. Usually, Monday was Cora Jean's day off. Sid could usually handle things himself since business was so slow. He soon saw he could not handle it by himself today. He called Cora Jean and then his wife, Tippy, to come in and help out.

"Hello?" said Cora Jean, managing to pop her gum before, after, and in the middle of a two-syllable word. She lived just around the corner from the diner in an apartment over the Steele's Hardware. "What's going on over there? I can see people lined up around the block from my window."

"I added a new sandwich today, and everyone has lost their mind. Can you come in and help out with the lunch crowd?

"On my way," she answered, thinking of what she might buy with her extra tip money.

"Topp residence, Tippy speaking," said Sid's wife, answering the phone on the first ring as usual. He could never figure out how she managed to always do that.

"Honey, I'm rushed off my feet with this new sandwich. I've called Cora Jean in. Can you come in and help out through lunch?"

"I'll be there in a jiff." And she hung up before Sid could reply. Tippy wasn't the best waitress in the world. She tended to sit down and talk to the customers. There wouldn't be time for that today. He was afraid to hope Cora Jean wouldn't have time to pop her gum today. Thankfully, both women arrived quickly.

"Hey, you can't cut in line!" Hubert, who was first in line, yelled at Cora Jean. "Go to the back."

"I work here, Hubert, it's Cora Jean. Please move aside." Sid could see Cora Jean trying to get past Hubert so she could get in the door.

"Hubert, if you want to be served today, let Cora in," said Sid, taking her by the arm and guiding her past the old man. Hubert still looked skeptical, but he stepped aside long enough for her to enter the door. About that time, Tippy came rushing up the sidewalk.

"Now wait just a goldang minute there, missy," said Hubert as he put his arm out to block Tippy's entrance to the diner. "Your hubby doesn't have time to talk to you today. Can't you see this line?"

"Hubert, I'm here to work. Now kindly move your arm, or I'll have Sid put you at the back of the line," said Tippy Topp, who didn't take guff from anyone. Hubert immediately dropped his arm and opened the door for her. She tilted her chin upward and regally strolled into the diner.

Cora Jean was filling water pitchers and adding extra napkin-rolled silverware to all the tables, thinking people might have to double up. They would have to get cozy today, Sid had told her.

"What do I start with?" asked Tippy as she put on her apron, grabbed an order book, and sharpened her pencil.

"Can you make more coffee and fill the extra urn I brought out from the back? I think we're going to need a lot of coffee today," said Sid, kissing her forehead as he headed toward the grill. "Might not be a bad idea to make an extra batch of ice tea. Thanks for coming in, hon." His wife nodded and got to work. Sid turned around, leaned on the counter, and surveyed his domain. All looked to be in order. He had called Ned Cochran to ask if he would volunteer to come over and let only a certain number of people in at a time. Otherwise, with Hubert at the helm, there would have been a mad stampede.

"Okay, ladies. Are we ready?" They both nodded. "Ned gave me the high sign. He's got the first twenty people counted out. Then, he'll let more people in as others leave. I'm giving him the signal to open the door. Stand back, ladies; Hubert might mow you down even though he's first in line and guaranteed a seat.

"Outta my way, Cora Jean!" Hubert shouted at Cora Jean, who was behind the counter rolling more silverware.

"Get me one of them tenderloins right quick like before you run out!" shouted the old man before anyone could take his order as he took his seat at the counter.

"Since you're the first customer, I doubt we'll run out. My darling hubby has a little experience running a diner. What two sides do you want with that?" asked Tippy, pencil poised to make out Hubert's ticket.

"Hmm... "What are the sides again?"

"The same as they've always been," said Tippy, pointing to the Sides column on the menu.

"Gosh, I can't decide."

"Decide, or I'll decide for you. You're not my only customer."

"Okay. Okay. What's everybody so touchy about?" said Hubert, clueless as usual. "Guess I'll choose fries and slaw (the two sides he always chose) since you rushed me."

Tippy turned and clipped the ticket up on the order wheel, rolled her eyes at Sid, and moved on to the next customer at the counter. Cora Jean was managing the table service with her usual efficiency. With the exception of Hubert, everyone in line made it seem like they were attending a party. And then along came Tarsal.

"What's going on here, Ned?" asked Tarsal. He didn't like talking to his former friend, but he had heard about the new item on the menu, and his curiosity had gotten the better of him.

"Sid added a tenderloin sandwich to the menu, Tarsal. But you're banned for life, so move on. Too bad, I hear they're mighty good. He's promised to keep one back for me. Can't wait to try it," said Ned, unable to resist twisting the knife a bit.

"I don't think Sid was serious. He wouldn't turn away a life-long customer," said Tarsal, standing firm.

"Go ahead then. Get in line, although I think Sid was pretty serious. You insulted the Williams family in front of a lot of people. But since you always know best, you stand in line and waste your time. I could care less."

Of course, as soon as Sid saw Tarsal coming through the door, he signaled for him to make a U-turn and head right back out. Tarsal pretended he didn't understand and headed for an empty seat at the counter.

"Don't you know what banned for life means?" said Sid as he grabbed Tarsal's elbow and marched him back toward the door.

"That's what that idiot Ned told me, but I didn't think you were serious," grumbled Tarsal as he pulled away from Sid's grasp.

"Oh, I was serious. You can't keep on insulting people and expect to get away with it. Just so we're clear. Get out. Don't EVER come back. Got it?"

"This isn't over, Sid." Then Tarsal mumbled something that was just as well no one understood, considering the mixed company in the diner.

Ned managed the crowd as if he were a professional security guard. The lunch hour ended just as the tenderloin supply was nearly running out. As promised, Sid had saved one back for his new "security guard."

"I think you're going to have to make this a regular item on the menu," said Ned as he enjoyed the first few bites of his sandwich.

"I think you might be right. I don't think I can deal with this kind of rush every Monday until the newness wears off."

"That makes sense," answered Ned, savoring the last few bites of his sandwich. "How soon do you think you can manage that?"

"Mmm, maybe in a couple of weeks. I have to get supplies in and change the menus. I'll get to work on it as soon as I recover from today, and what a day it's been! You did a great job handling the crowd. Especially Hubert."

"To tell you the truth, I enjoyed bossing him around. He's such an old Scrooge," said Ned as he got up to leave. "Sorry about the whole Tarsal thing. I told him he was banned, but you know how he is. Can't tell him a damn thing."

"Like you dealing with Hubert, I enjoyed throwing him out again."

"That was pretty satisfying. I'd best be going so you can get out of here. See you soon."

"Thanks again," said Sid, handing him a twenty-dollar bill. "It's not much, but you were a lifesaver today. I'm hoping you can help me out on Mondays until I can offer it every day."

"I'd be glad to. The guys can handle the electrical shop for a few hours. Keep your money, Sid. I had fun and got a delicious sandwich, no pay necessary," said Ned, handing him back the twenty.

"Free tenderloins for life then if I can't pay you."

"Sold!" said Ned, patting his stomach as he strolled out into the sunshine. Ready for whatever Chanceville had to offer.

67
PEEVISH AND BEAGLE TEAM UP

It took about three weeks for Sid to organize everything so the tenderloin could be a permanent item on the everyday menu. The diner was as crowded as that first day for the next three Mondays. Ned continued crowd control duty and had fun keeping Hubert in line. Hubert was true to form and grumbled at everything.

"You cut in front of me," Hubert told Lawrence Steele, owner of Steele's Hardware, as he tapped him on the shoulder.

"No, I didn't, Hubert. I was here first."

"But I'm supposed to be first. I'm not gettin any younger," said Hubert, trying to play the sympathy card.

"You're still second in line, Hubert. You'll be let in at the same time as Lawrence," said Ned.

"I'd better be," harrumphed Hubert. Ned and Lawrence looked at each other, shook their heads, and chuckled.

A few days after Tarsal had been unceremoniously thrown out of the Tipp Topp for the second time, Gerald Nozay, Food Inspector for Loone County Health Department, made a sudden appearance at the diner.

"Hey Gerald, what can I get you," asked Sid, assuming Ted was there for breakfast.

"Not here to eat. Here to inspect," said the inspector, a grim man of few words.

"You were here two weeks ago, and everything was fine."

"Had a call. Someone said there might be a problem with your meat storage."

"Nothing's changed, and you passed it with flying colors last time," said Sid, really puzzled because he had never had a violation in all of his years as a restaurant owner. "Who called?"

"Anonymous." Gerald Nozay knew precisely who had called, even though "Anonymous" had tried to disguise his voice.

"It was Tarsal Henley. I know it was; he's mad because I kicked him out for life."

"As I said, Anonymous. Wouldn't say even if I knew who it was."

"Give it your best shot, Gerald. Don't think you'll find a problem," said Sid as the inspector headed back toward the cooler.

"Everything looks fine. Can't see a problem," said Gerald, handing Sid his clipboard so he could sign off on the inspection. "Honestly, I never worry about your diner, but I have to check out every complaint."

"I understand, Gerald. I try to keep up the same practices as my dad. Besides, I eat here, too." They both chuckled.

As Gerald headed toward the door, he noticed "Anonymous" peeking in the diner's window. He looked back at Sid, and they both just shook their heads.

The place was so crowded on the three Mondays that were tenderloin special days that people were happy to share tables if it meant getting a seat. That's how the two new pastors, Peevish and Beagle, ended up sharing a booth. They enjoyed each other's company so much the first time they made sure they sat together every time. After introducing themselves, the two men awkwardly danced around the reason that brought two new pastors to Chanceville. They talked about where they had come from and the situations with their former churches. By the third Monday, they had exhausted those topics.

"So, how's it going with your congregation?" asked Chuck Peevish as a way to maybe sidle up to the unspoken topic of the feud.

"Not bad. Good attendance, fairly generous giving, committees running smoothly for the most part," answered Edgar Beagle between bites of his now favorite sandwich.

"For the most part?" said Chuck, taking the bait as Edgar hoped he would.

"Yeah, um, Tarsal Henley can be. I guess the word is difficult," said Edgar, hoping he hadn't said too much.

"Difficult isn't the word I've heard bandied about," answered Chuck, feeling safe to talk to his new friend openly. "I won't use that kind of language, but I'm sure you know what I mean." Both men chuckled at that one.

"I promise, however you answer this, it won't go any farther," said Edgar as he looked behind him to see who might be listening. It was an old couple who were infamous for being stone deaf. Their conversation consisted of shouting at each other, so no worries there.

"Tell me honestly, Chuck. What do you think of this feud that split the churches?" The Reverend Peevish had just taken a big swallow of coffee; he laughed, got choked, and almost spit coffee toward Edgar.

"Sorry, Edgar. It's just so ridiculous that I can't take it seriously. Don't know what you think, but I don't get it," said Chuck as he wiped coffee off his chin.

"I agree, not that I'm complaining," Edgar agreed. "I probably wouldn't have gotten this job if they hadn't needed two pastors. I do like it here, but there are some things I'll never understand about a small town I didn't grow up in."

"I know what you mean. I like it here, too. I grew up in Elwood, south of Greentown, with its own set of small town quirks, but this one takes the cake. I'm glad we could talk about this. I've felt guilty, or maybe hypercritical is a better word, that I even think negatively about the reason for the feud," said Chuck.

"One reason I brought this up is I was hoping you'd agree and we could work together to bring about some peace. What do you think?"

"I'm ashamed to say that never occurred to me, but I like the idea. I've heard that Tarsal is the one who is driving this. From what I've seen of Ned, he's had it with Tarsal, but I don't think he wants to openly feud. You would probably know more about Tarsal than me."

"From what I've seen of Tarsal, he enjoys the fight, even the drama. I haven't been around Ned that much, but the couple of encounters I've had have been quite pleasant," answered Edgar.

"I heard that Hubert Patterson told Tarsal that Ned was planting boxes of Marigolds outside the Main Avenue Church. Of course, Tarsal couldn't let Ned outdo him, so built the biggest flower boxes that would fit under the portico of The MAIN CHURCH of the Righteous. Turns out Ned had no such plans to add marigolds in boxes to the front of "his" church," said Chuck. They both laughed and shook their heads.

"Has Tarsal ever asked you if you believe animals have souls?" asked Chuck as he signaled to Cora Jean to bring them more coffee.

"How's it going, gents? Get you anything besides coffee? Butterscotch pie on special today," asked Cora Jean as she filled up their coffee mugs."

"I couldn't force down another bite," said Chuck, patting his stomach.

"Same here," said Edgar. "That's a huge sandwich, but I manage to eat it all every time. No room for pie, even though it does look delicious. Looks like this new item on the menu is keeping you hopping."

"You're not just a kidding. Me and Jenetta have been rushed off our feet. Not complaining, though; the extra money has been good. I'm glad the tenderloin is a regular item, but my dogs have been barkin' up a storm these last few weeks," replied Cora as she walked away, popping her gum loudly.

"Okay, let's get back to our conversation," said Edgar, stirring cream into his coffee. "How do we approach this? Any ideas?"

"The Wilsons had a fire last week and lost nearly everything. What if we, you and I, announce that we're going to do a fundraiser for the family? Tarsal would look like a real jerk if he argued against that idea," said Chuck.

"From what I've seen, I don't think Tarsal cares if he looks like a jerk. But I don't think he'd like to be embarrassed by the whole town being up in arms over him not wanting to cooperate for such a worthy cause. The Wilsons have five children, and they really need help. A few family members are helping, but they still need so much."

"Let's do it! Should we take it to our boards or announce it on Sunday?" asked Chuck.

"Hmm. We could call an emergency meeting of our boards so we can get started sooner. They are in dire straits. I'll go back to the office now and start calling the board. Maybe we could get the Community Building at the fairgrounds. People could donate items, have a bake sale, that sort of thing," said Edgar.

"That sounds good. I can call Sam Chance at the Examiner and ask him to put an announcement in the paper with clothing sizes for the children and the parents. This is exciting."

When Reverend Beagle presented the plan to help the Wilsons at the board meeting that night for the MAIN the Righteous, none of you will be surprised to know that Tarsal kicked up a fuss.

"What do you mean we're working with that idiot Ned Cochran's church? No way. No how. I don't mind helping out the Wilsons, but we can do it ourselves.

"Give it a rest, Tarsal," said Hyoid Henley, Tarsal's cousin. "No one cares about your stupid feud, most of all Ned. It doesn't make sense to do it separately. Like Reverend Beagle said, we can do it at one big location where everyone can show up and not be confused about where to donate. We don't want to take a chance of people not showing up because they don't want to add to the feud." Every jaw dropped at Hyoid's speech. That was the most they had heard him say EVER. He always seemed to defer to his older cousin.

"That makes sense," said Frank Stenner as heads nodded. "Let's not lose sight of our goal: to help the Wilsons."

"Right. Let's take a vote," said Reverend Beagle.

Of course, everyone except Tarsal voted in the affirmative. "I should have known better than to hire a pastor named Beagle," grumbled Tarsal as he got up to storm out of the room. Then Hubert Patterson yelled, "Where are you going, Tarsal? Off to start another church?" Tarsal slammed the meeting room door to the sound of raucous laughter.

All the townspeople were excited when they saw the announcement in the Chanceville Examiner. They were good-hearted folk and loved the chance to help each other, ready to put all differences aside. They prepared to show up the following Saturday with lots to donate. When Eugene and Daisy Wilson, who had been living with his parents since the fire and trying to figure out how to clothe their family, saw the notice in the paper, they both cried tears of joy and relief.

The Main Avenue Church and the MAIN CHURCH of the Righteous are pleased to announce they are combining forces to organize a Day of Giving to the Wilson Family, who recently lost their home and possessions in a fire. They have five children. They are in need of clothing (sizes listed below) and household items. All donations are appreciated.

The event will begin at 10:00 am and end at 3:00 pm. The Loone County Park Board happily waived the fees to use the Community Building. Sid Topp is donating barbeque sandwiches; the Dainty Donut Bakery and Very Dry Cleaners is donating various donuts and pastries and free laundry services to the Wilsons for a month. The A-1 Beverage Company is donating soft drinks. If you have food items you'd like to donate, contact Mayrose and Milton Matthews, as they are coordinating the bake sale. Come early and stay late! Ned Cochran is handling donated items. So check in with him at the Community Building office; he will direct you where to place your items.

Tippy Top is gathering items to be raffled off. The Williams family has offered to pay for the children's school books and supplies for the following year.

It was a fine July morning, not too hot or humid, unusual for summertime in Indiana. The town showed up in full force. Some businesses had donated the following items: a lawn mower, a radio, a typewriter, a toolset, and many other items to be raffled off to raise more money for the Wilsons, who would need to find a home to rent soon. It was wall-to-wall people at Dora Wilsons' house with two extra adults and five young children. She loved her grandchildren, but all that commotion was starting to get on her already fragile nerves, a life-long condition.

With Ned in charge, both churches had members who volunteered to help organize the donated items. They set up areas for several categories of goods to keep things organized. It's a good thing they had been foresighted. The amount of items donated was almost overwhelming. Reverends Peevish and Beagle were happy to see the two congregations working together. Although some items were in the head scratching category.

"Hi Hubert," said Oblivia Young to the old man as he approached the kitchen goods section she was in charge of. "What's that you've got there?"

"It's a butter churn. Haven't you ever seen one of these before?"

"Yes, I have, but I'm not sure what the Wilsons can do with this."

"Churn butter," said Hubert, looking at her as if she were the stupidest person on Earth, possibly the galaxy.

"I KNOW what it's for, Hubert," she said, trying not to shout at him. "But they don't have access to a dairy as far as I know. I appreciate your kindness, but I'm not sure this is the most practical item for the family."

"Beggars can't be choosers," he said and thumped the old wooden churn hard on the concrete floor, where it immediately shattered to pieces. Hubert just walked away.

"Hubert! Come back here, clean this mess up," yelled Oblivia. "You can't just walk away!" Apparently, he could. As usual, Hubert's hearing was selective when he wanted to avoid being bossed around. Oblivia gave up and began cleaning up the mess herself.

He had already forgotten about the churn and was thinking about lunch.

"Can I have two barbeque sandwiches, Sid?" asked Hubert when he finally reached the front of the line at the food tent. "I'm starving. I worked up a real appetite, lugging that butter churn here. Sid decided not to ask why he lugged a butter churn to a charity event. Knowing Hubert, he was sure he wouldn't understand the explanation anyway.

"Sure you can. That'll be $1.50," said Sid, handing him two wrapped sandwiches.

"What do you mean, $1.50? Isn't this for charity? Everything should be free. I'm not paying no $1.50 for two measly sandwiches."

"You get slaw and chips also. It is for charity. But the charity is not for you. It's for the Wilsons. I donated the food, and the money goes to the Wilson family. If you don't trust me, give the money directly to Eugene or Daisy Wilson."

"That's just plain stupid. Not sure I trust them Wilsons either. Maybe they just wanted free stuff." said Hubert, handing the sandwiches back to Sid.

"Right. The Wilsons set their house on fire, risked their lives, and lost everything they owned to get some free stuff. Keep the sandwiches anyway. I can't serve them since you touched them." For once, the old man didn't argue. Sid just shook his head as he usually did with the old coot. He took $1.50 out of his own pocket to pay for Hubert's 'free" sandwiches. Then Sid noticed Tarsal approaching Hubert. He guessed he shouldn't have been surprised to see him there, most likely to cause trouble than to help. He was glad when they walked out of hearing range. Sure, their conversation would annoy him even more than he already was with those two.

"What was that all about, Hubert?" asked Tarsal as he walked beside him.

"That crook Sid Topp tried to charge me for free sandwiches. I'm not falling for it. Wasn't born yesterday."

"No, you weren't. Glad Sid didn't sucker you in. He'll probably keep all the money himself. He should never have banned me from the diner. I've got my eye on him, believe you me," said Tarsal. He walked away from the old man, looking for more places to spy. He headed for the tool section.

"How much for this?" Tarsal asked Hal Hendrix, who was manning that area, as he picked up a hammer.

"These items aren't for sale. This is a collection spot for items donated to the Wilsons," answered Hal. Do you have something you don't use that you'd like to donate? You've got plenty of time to go home and get something."

"Nah, I have just the right amount of everything."

"Don't you have an extra buck or two? You could give money," suggested Hal. He didn't think he had ever heard anyone say they had just the right amount of everything.

"I could spare it, I s'pose. But who knows what the Wilsons would do with it?"

"You're right, Tarsal. They might go crazy and buy groceries."

Tarsal nodded, totally missing the point as he walked away to spread more joy. Unfortunately for Reverend Beagle and Ned Cochran, they were the next people to cross Tarsal's path. Edgar Beagle tried to nod and keep walking, but his strategy didn't work.

"I hope you're happy with yourself, Rev, consorting with the enemy," snarled Tarsal.

"I'm afraid I don't know what you're talking about," said Edgar, looking at Ned, who knew exactly what Tarsal was referring to.

"I don't think of us as enemies, Tarsal," said Ned. "We just don't agree on some things. Besides, it's for a good cause. Shouldn't we all work together?"

"Not so sure about the good cause. I'm beginning to think Hubert might have a point. This could all be a scam."

"How would that work?" asked Edgar. "The Wilsons lost everything. What could they possibly have to gain from this?"

"Might not necessarily be the Wilsons. Maybe some volunteers are keeping cash donations or selling donated items."

"You know what, Tarsal Henley? Enough already. You're the only one who wants to keep this stupid feud going. You've got your two churches and two graveyards. Time to move on," said Ned. And with that, Tarsal walked away, unwittingly doing what Ned wanted.

"That was great, Ned. Maybe the healing can begin. As I told Chuck Peevish when we decided to combine efforts, I never understood the feud anyway," said Edgar.

"Don't feel bad. None of us did. It wasn't all Tarsal. We let it get out of hand. I'm just as much to blame as Tarsal for not putting a stop to it. I got caught up in the heat of the moment," answered Ned. "Tarsal has always had a way of getting under my skin.

"Don't blame yourself. Sometimes, people have a way of doing that, and we aren't our best selves. I think you can be forgiven for that," said Edgar. About that time, they saw Chuck Peevish heading for Sid's sandwich stand and caught up with him.

"Hey, fellas. How's it going?" asked Reverend Peevish. "Looks like a big turn out today." Ned and Edgar filled Chuck in on their conversation with Tarsal. "Wow, it's hard to believe people feel that way, even Tarsal, but it looks like we can begin healing as a community and start planning more community events together." The three men agreed. Then, they decided to buy some lunch from Sid.

"These look great, Sid," said Ned. I'm starving. I'll take two with slaw and chips. I heard Hubert thought you were scamming him."

"Yes, he wanted a free meal, basically," said Sid as he handed the meal to Ned.

"That's Hubert," agreed Ned. Once seated at the picnic tables under Sid's tent, they continued their conversation about today's event.

"I think the Wilsons are going to be okay. I heard that Jonathan Acre of the Really Real Estate Company has a very nice house over on Grove Road for rent that he's willing to give them at a reasonable price and donate the first two months' rent. Steele's Hardware is donating paint and supplies, and the Wilsons will do the painting themselves. They should be able to move in about a week." said Chuck. "Guy Hooks, who owns Snap-Up Tools, is donating a couple of his vans to help move the stuff donated here when the Wilsons are ready. The fair board has agreed to allow us to keep all the donations in the Community Building until the Wilsons are ready. The Chanceville Gutter Snipes Bowling League has volunteered manpower to help move everything."

"Our vet, Doc Leash, told me he has a collie pup for the kids when they get settled in. Those kids will go crazy. I'm so proud of our community," said Ned. "And I'm tickled pink to begin putting that stupid feud to rest.

If you were a pollster taking a survey about the success of the Day of Giving, nearly everyone would say it was a great success, especially the Wilsons. The town folk felt good about how generous they could be when working together. They were also pleased that the two churches worked together in harmony.

Little did they know they would soon have an opportunity to work together again soon. Hubert Patterson would need all the help he could get. Storm clouds were gathering over Chanceville, Indiana.

CAST OF CHARACTERS

Major Characters in Bold

Ned Cochran, Electrician, Husband to Gardenia
Gardenia Cochran, School Art Teacher, Wife of Ned
Ted Cochran, Electrician
Tarsal Henley, Builder, Husband to Scapula
Scapula Henley, Secretary MAIN CHURCH of the Righteous , Wife of Tarsal
Hyoid Henley, Plumber, Tarsal's cousin
Trout Finn, Pastor, Brother to Alpaca Finn
Alpaca Finn, Librarian, Sister to Trout Finn
Mayrose Mayhern, Retired first grade teacher
Michael Mayhern , Father of Mayrose Mayhern
Margaret Mayhern, Mother of Mayrose Mayhern
Milton Matthews, Retired history teacher
James Matthews, Retired accountant, brother to Milton Matthew
Celia Matthews, Housewife, wife of James Matthew
Bertram Benedict Bunntington, Co-owner of Williams Brothers Stationery and
    Haberdashery, Brother to William, Wilman, Uncle to Wally
Wallace Williams, the Elder, Co-owner of Williams Brothers Stationery and
    Haberdashery, Brother to Wallace and Wilma, Uncle to Wally
Wilma Williams, No known employment, Late sister to Wallace and William Williams,
    Mother of Wally
Magnum Paltry, Private Investigator
Wally Williams, Ne'er do well, Son of Wilma Williams, Nephew to Wallace and William
Hubert Patterson, Retired mill workeer
Babette Poodle, Blind, Twin to Annette around 40 years old
Annette Poodle, Blind, Twin to Babbette around 40 years old
Melvin "Muddy" Poodle, Chanceville Businessman, Late father of Annette and Babette
    Poodle
Poppy Smith, housemaid, to the Blind Poodle sisters
Mrs. Little, owner of White Jasmine Tearoom
MerryLynn Tarmack , assistant to Geraldine Nurse Loone County Libratrian
Babs Haylo, Cashier at Woolworths, Psychic Medium
Ben Haylo, Deceased, Husband to Babs
Clara Broom, Housekeeper , Williams Family
Henrietta Sharp, Housekeeper , Mother of Clara Bloom Williams Family Housekeeper
Clarence Broom, Clara's late husband
Clarence Broom, Jr., Clara's son

CAST OF CHARACTERS

Rod Kurten, Handy man, Williams Family
Hank Wheatley , local farmer
Mr. Trinket, Woolworth's manager
Ivy Greenly, hospital volunteer
Sid Topp, owner of Tipp Topp Diner, Husband to Tippy
Tippy Topp, Sid's wife
Sal Topp , Original owner of the Tipp Topp diner, Sid's late dad
Lawrence Steele, owner Steele's Hardware
Gerald Nozay, Food Inspector for the Loone County Health Department
Jonathan Acre , Really Real Estate Company
Doc Ivory, Town dentist
Geraldine Nurse, Town librarian
Fern Oldhat, Owner of Lovely Locks Salon and owner of a boarding house
Misty Mae, hairdresser at the Lovely Locks Salon
Lindy, hairdresser at the Lovely Locks Salon
Doc Trueblood, Town doctor
Trachea Carmichael, Doc Trueblood's nurse
Yesper Orange, Loone County Sheriff
Pearly Ringwald, Loone County Sheriff's Dispatcher, Niece of Sheriff Yesper's wife
Cora Jean Mitchell, Waitress at the Tipp Top Diner
Jenetta Joyner, Waitress at the Tipp Top Diner
Maxine Crabtree, hospital volunteer
Hal Hendrix, owner of Hendrix Funeral Parlor and Wax Museum, Husband to Tammy
Tammy Miller Hendrix, wife of Hal Hendrix, Wife of Hal
Elizabeth (Lisbet) Hendricx
Peggy Hendrix, Wax Figure designer and dresser, Mother of Hal
Vera, Tammy Hendricks' grandmother
Prissy Paulson, owner of Hem and Haul Fabric Store and Trash Removal
Doc Leash, town veternarian
Grandmother Chagrin, Grandmother to Alpaca and Finn
Grandmother Finn, Grandmother to Alpaca and Finn
Darrell Davis, paramour of Alapaca in Saints of the Lakes
Mrs. Burl Tree, Farmer's wife, owner of cabin in the woods
Junebug, Mrs. Tree's beagle pup
High Horse Harry, self-appointed town crier
Porter Pander, inventor of the Quack's formula
Joshua Moot, conman
Bertram Benedict Bunntington, Attonery for Moot and Porter
Theodore (BigTeddy) Munson, Small time crook
P-tess Ptarmigan, Manger of the Grouse Inn Motel
Agent Russell Ruby, FBI
Agent Al Mann, FBI Supervisor
Agent Sigmund Colon, FBI Agent
Maynard "Mole" Burrow, Police Evidence Lockup Manager

Albert Finch, Owner of the Grouse Inn

Aunt Piney, lovelorn advice columnist

Edgar Beagle, pastor of the new MAIN CHURCH of the Righteous

Chuck Peevish, pastor of the new Main Avenue Christian Church

Paula Peevish, store clerk and manager of Williams Brothers Stationery and Haberdashery , wife of Chuck and niece to Peggy Hendricks, cousin of Hal Hendricks

Oblivia Young, church lady, wife and Henry and mother of Chester

Henry Young, husband to Oblivia

Chester Young , Oblivia and Henry Young's son

Sara "Sugarpants" Peterson, hospital volunteer manager of Hendricks Wax Museum

Tim Peterson, husband of Sara "Sugarpants" Peterson

Althea Goodnight, neighbor of Sara and Tim Peterson

Violet , Mr. Trinket's assistant manager at Woolworths'

Kenneth, Sixteen year old stockboy at Woolworths

Charlie Towne , Chanceville Train Stationmaster

Lydia Burger, Wife of Mayor of Saints of the Lakes

Widow Collins, Late Church Member

Foo Foo , Poodle, Widow Collins dog

Joe Collins, Late husband of Widow Collins

Johnny Perkins, Possible love interest for Alpaca/brother-in-law of Sadie Stenner

Doris Perkins, Late sister to Sadie Stenner, wife of Johnny Perkins

Harold Freeman, Possible love interest for Alpaca

Frank Stenner, Civil Engineer

Sadie Stenner, Music Teacher, Wife of Frank Stenner

Nurse Jackson, Nurse at the Loone County Hospital

RaeAnn , Nurses Aid at the Loone County Hospital

Lily Lawson, Loone County Justice of the Peace

Daniel Only, Owner of Only Grocery Store

Sally Forth, Owner of the Sally Forth Home for the Elderly and Infirm

Sharon Martin, Citizen of Chanceville

Marten Martin, Citizen of Chanceville, Husband of Sharon

Sam Chance, Owner and Publisher of the *Chanceville Examiner*

Wilsons, Family who lost everything in a fire

ABOUT THE AUTHOR

Rebekah Spivey studied creative writing and sociology at Indiana University. She has lived and worked on the Isle of Mull in Scotland. She is a lifelong writer and lover of words who has co-created and led a group called Poetry Detectives, an informal group that discusses poetry in a non-academic way in order to make the genre more approachable. She has a seventeen-year association with Women Writing for (a) Change, Bloomington, a group that supports giving every person a voice through writing. Rebekah has been a certified facilitator with Women Writing since 2013 and currently facilitates a semester-long virtual class. She has coordinated a Women Writing for

(a) Change retreat on the Isle of Iona off the west coast of Scotland. And facilitates winter writing retreats and semester core classes for Women Writing.

Rebekah retired in 2012 from the *Indiana Daily Student* newspaper at IU after seventeen years as part of the professional staff.

She has been a part-time senior editor for Holon Publishing, a self-publishing company since 2019. And is an editor for private clients.

Rebekah will be publishing her first novel *Marigolds in Boxes* in June 2024.

Printed in the USA
CPSIA information can be obtained
at www.ICGtesting.com
JSHW020033130924
69596JS00004B/17